TEN DAYS IN JULY

Tom Kerr

Order this book online at www.trafford.com
or email orders@trafford.com

Most Trafford titles are also available at major online book retailers.

Printed in the United States of America.

ISBN: 978-1-4251-6306-8 (sc)
ISBN: 978-1-4251-6307-5 (e)

Trafford rev. 09/30/2011

 www.trafford.com

North America & international
toll-free: 1 888 232 4444 (USA & Canada)
phone: 250 383 6864 ✦ fax: 812 355 4082

DEDICATION

TO THE MEMORY OF MARY

ACKNOWLEDGEMENTS

The author would like to express his appreciation to the following individuals

Phyllis Francis for reading the initial draft of the book, correcting spelling and grammar and suggesting numerous changes in content.

Carolyn Holmes for the illustration of the cover.

John Hulett for suggestions concerning the cartoon in the newspaper on Day Five.

Tim Penning for help with the computer.

Steve Swatsenbarg for his many hours of computer assistance in preparing the document for publication. An extra thanks.

DISCLAIMER

This novel is a work of fiction. The characters, places, and incidents are either the creations of the author's imagination or are used fictitiously. Any resemblance to actual incidents or persons, either living or dead, is coincidental.

PROLOGUE

By 1998 the people of Northern Ireland had been subjected to thirty years to what has been called "The Troubles", an internal war between the Nationalists, who wanted to combine the six counties of Ulster with the Republic of Ireland and the Loyalists, who wanted Northern Ireland to remain part of Great Britain.

In 1968 the minority of the country, mainly the Catholics, started demanding fair and equal treatment from their government. When the Catholics started demanding one vote for one man, equal employment opportunities and equal housing, the Protestant majority, Unionists(Loyalists), staunchly resisted, afraid of losing their absolute control.

October 5, 1968 is the date most historians agree was the start of "The Troubles". On that date a banned Civil Rights march in Derry was attack by the RUC(Royal Ulster Constabulary-the Police force of Northern Ireland). This attack lead to three days of rioting.

On January 4, 1969, civil rights advocates and students from Queen's University in Belfast organized a march from Belfast to Derry. As the marchers reached Burntollet Bridge, they were attacked by a large number of Loyalists using sticks and stones. The attack was observed by the RUC who did not intervene. It was later learned that a large number of the attackers were members of the Auxiliary Police.

As a result of this attack, riots erupted in both Belfast and Derry.

In August of 1969, there was a communal uprising in Derry, now known as "The Battle of Bogside". The rioting commenced when the residents of Bogside confronted the RUC and the Apprentice Boys of Derry, who had been granted permission to march along the city wall past Bogside. The rioting in Derry ignited sectarian riots in other major cites in

Northern Ireland, particularly in Belfast where more than 200 Catholic homes were burned by Loyalist crowds.

When the Catholics looked for help from the IRA(Irish Republican Army) it was discovered that the organization existed in name only. The IRA had less than twenty weapons and was incapable of protecting their people. This situation did not last long.

In January 1970 the IRA was re-organized and split into two separate groups, the OIRA(Official Irish Republican Army) who wanted to obtain civil rights by constitutional means and the PIRA(Provisional Irish Republican Army) or PROVOS, who believed force was the only means of achieving their aim.

The Provos were opposed by a number of Loyalists organizations such as the UDA(Ulster Defense Association), the UFF(Ulster Freedom Fighters) and the UVF(Ulster Volunteer Force).

During the thirty years of "The Troubles" over 2800 people were killed, first based on politics, but later the killings turned to revenge killings, retaliatory killings, sectarian killings and personal killings.

Over the years the initial aims of the Catholics changed from a demand for equal rights to the aims of the Nationalists.

In the mid-1990s, at the instigation of Tony Blair, the British Prime Minister, Bill Clinton, the President of the United States, Bertie Ahern, the Taoiseach of Ireland and a number of both Catholic and Protestant political and religious leaders in Northern Ireland, a step towards a peace settlement was initiated. US Senator George Mitchell was appointed to form an international organization to study and come up with a solution.

On April 10, 1998, Mitchell submitted the group's final draft to be voted on by the population of both the Republic of Ireland and Northern Ireland. On May 22, 1998 a referendum on the Agreement was held and the results were 85.46% Yes and 14.54% No.

The question was, what would occur after the signing of the Agreement?

Day One

July 22, 1998

Garda Headquarters
Dublin, Ireland

At 24 minutes after nine o'clock, Garda(Garda Siochana-the Republic of Ireland's National Police Service)Sergeant Michael McGrath of the Stanorlar Station telephoned the Garda Headquarters in Dublin and asked the operator to connect him with the Special Operations Section. The operator transferred the call to the office of Chief Superintendent Patrick T. Kerrigan. After the third ring, Kerrigan picked up the phone.

"Special Operations."

"Yes, this is Sergeant McGrath in Stanorlar."

"Yes."

"We had a surprise border check this morning and we picked up two very interesting individuals."

"So?"

"I think someone from Special Operations should come up here to transfer them to Dublin."

There was silence for a few moments.

"Can't you send then down…with an escort?" asked Kerrigan.

"I don't think that would be too wise."

Again, a few moments of silence.

"We've very busy here and…."

"Could I speak to your supervisor?" snapped McGrath.

Kerrigan closed his right eye, turned his head to the left and looked at the picture on the wall of his office. He was about to teach the Sergeant in Stanorlar a few choice words in Gaelic as his door opened and his secretary backed into his office carrying a tray containing his morning tea along with a plate of fresh rolls.

"Sorry I couldn't get the phone, but....sorry," said Mrs. Roberts as she turned and saw Kerrigan with the phone in his hand.

"Sergeant McGrath, this is Chief Superintendent Kerrigan, head of Special Operations."

Without changing the tone of his voice, McGrath said,

"Sir, if you knew who we picked up, I'm quite certain you would want them in Dublin and not in Stanorlar."

Kerrigan looked at Mrs. Roberts, then at the fresh rolls, smiled and said,

"You think they're that important."

"Yes sir, I think they're that important."

McGrath's tone of voice had not changed and he was not the least apologetic about his earlier comments.

"Do you think I would be interested in talking to them?"

"Yes sir."

The tone of the Sergeant's voice was enough to convince the Chief Superintendent to travel to Stanorlar.

Kerrigan looked at his watch, swung around and looked at the map on the wall behind his desk. He squinted when he saw the distance to be over three hundred kilometers. He mentally calculated how long it would take him to drive the distance…a good four to five hours, unless he went up through Ulster.

"Someone will be there by three, no, make it four this afternoon."

"I would suggest at least two."

"Right, two people will be there by four."

"Excellent sir, I'll be waiting at the station for them."

"Fine," said Kerrigan.

The Chief Superintendent turned around, replaced the phone in its cradle and looked out the window for a moment. He turned and looked at Mrs. Roberts who was pouring the tea into his oversized cup.

She turned and looked directly at Kerrigan with her "tsh, tsh smile."

"A little tetchy this morning Chief Superintendent?"

Kerrigan couldn't help but shake his head and smile at her. She always had the right words to put him in his place.

"I'll be gone for the rest of the day and maybe tomorrow."

"Wonderful, then maybe the rest of us can catch up with our work. You couldn't make that three days could you?"

"You're full of vinegar this morning young lady. Have a good night?"

"That's none of your business Chief Superintendent Kerrigan," said Mrs. Roberts as she turned and headed for the door. She stopped, turned around and said,

"Enjoy you tea and don't eat all the rolls…save some for Jamie."

Before Kerrigan had a chance to reply, Mrs. Roberts was out the door.

"She knows what I'm going to do before I know," thought Kerrigan as he picked up his cup of tea.

Chief Superintendent Patrick T. Kerrigan was the perfect example of an Irish policeman whether in Dublin, NYC, Boston, Chicago or New Orleans. He was large boned, fair skinned, stood six feet, two inches, weighted just a little bit over two hundred pounds and had a full head of red hair. He celebrated his thirty fourth year in the Garda last year and had no intention of retiring until he hit the golden age of fifty-five, which was just three years away.

Kerrigan joined the Republic of Ireland's police force on his 18th birthday and was one of the youngest Detective Sergeants at the ripe old age of twenty-three. He rose in rank for two specific reasons, his incessant study of criminology and hard work.

From the time he decided to become a police officer at the age of fifteen, he checked out and read every book on criminology at both the public and university library.

At sixteen he convinced Professor Holmes, Professor of Criminology, to allow him to "sit in" on every lecture in the department. There was one condition…he was not allowed to ask any questions during the lectures. The questions were saved for after class in the Professor's office.

With Holmes' assistance, Kerrigan was permitted to visit with various members of the Garda along with the Criminology students.

Once he entered the service of the Garda, he rose rapidly to the rank of Inspector. It was at that point in his career his supervisors and ranking members of the Garda realized Kerrigan was not "politically minded".

In 1978, Kerrigan insisted on continuing an investigation in spite of "the wishes of a politically appointed Assistant Commissioner". The investigation resulted in the demotion of the Assistant Commissioner's brother and three other members of the Garda because they falsified evidence against a member of the UFF(Ulster Freedom Fighters), a known Loyalist terrorists.

Based on Kerrigan's disclosure, the man was set free and returned to Ulster. Once in Northern Ireland, he continued his terrorist activities until his own people assassinated him because of the bad publicity the UDA (Ulster Defense Association) was receiving.

Kerrigan was warned and was well aware his disclosure insured he would never be appointed into the Commissioner ranks as an Assistant, Deputy or Commissioner. When question about the situation later, his only comment was a simple..."So be it."

In the late 80's and early 90's the Special Branch of the Garda continually received unfavorable publicity because a number of their activities were deemed unlawful by the Justice Department.

In January of 1996 the Commissioner of the Garda, at the suggestion of the Minister of Justice, formed a special unit with the title of "Special Operations".

This unit reported directly to the Commissioner and was assigned responsibility for the investigation of specific terrorists organizations. Again, at the suggestion of the Minister of Justice, the Commissioner appointed Kerrigan to head the unit, who at the time was in charge of the Domestic Robbery Section.

Kerrigan picked up the phone, dialed six, and then shifted the phone from his right hand to his left hand. With his right hand he opened his desk drawer. He was looking for the gas credit card.

"Meyers," said the voice on the phone.

"Jamie, could you come into my office for a moment?"

"Yes sir."

"Bring your cup."

"Yes sir."

The phone went dead in Kerrigan's hand. He looked at it for a moment, smiled and replaced it in its cradle. At the same time he spotted the credit card. He picked it up, put it in his shirt pocket and closed the drawer. A split second later, there was a knock on his door.

"Come in Jamie."

Meyers entered and stopped in front of the Chief Superintendents' deck.

"Have a seat," said Kerrigan.

Meyers took the straight back chair directly in front of Kerrigan's desk instead one of the two leather bound easy chairs.

"Tea?"

"Yes sir.'

Kerrigan poured tea into the cup Meyers placed on the tray, then asked,

"How's your load?"

"Far from finished," said Meyers, a phrase he had picked up from Kerrigan.

"Care for a little trip?"

"Where to?"

"Stanorlar."

"Stanorlar, isn't that up in County Donegal?"

"That's right…about a four or five hour drive."

"Will I be staying overnight?"

"It's we and I don't know right now. Is it a problem if we do?"

"No sir, but I need to let Molly know."

"We'd better make plans to stay overnight, just in case."

Meyers nodded.

"What time are we leaving?"

"As soon as we finish our tea, go home and pack a few things for overnight. I'll pick up an official car and met you in say an hour and a half."

"Here?"

"No, I'll pick you up at your house."

"Fine sir," said Meyers as he started to push himself up from the chair.

"Drink your tea and have one of those rolls. We're not in that much of a hurry," said Kerrigan.

Ten minutes later, three of the rolls were gone and both cups were empty.

As Meyers stood up, he said,

"I'll see you in ninety minutes."

"Right," said Kerrigan.

Eighty-five minutes later, Kerrigan pulled up in front of Meyers' house on the outskirts of Finglas. Before he had time to shut off the engine or blow the horn, the front door of the house opened and Meyers came walking out carrying a small overnight bag. He opened the rear door, tossed the bag in the back seat, closed the door and opened the front door on the passenger side and asked,

"Do you want me to drive?"

"No, you can drive back this evening…if we come back. You can get your rest going up."

"Yes sir," said Meyers.

He opened the door all the way and slid into the passenger seat, slipped on his seat belt and nodded to Kerrigan.

"Are you going up through Ulster?"

"Yes, thought I'd take N2 up to Balygawley and A5 over to Straband, then west to Stanorlar."

"That'll be quicker if the UDR(Ulster Defense Regiment) doesn't have the roads blocked."

"We'll just have to take a chance."

Meyers stretched his legs and wiggled in the seat until he was comfortable.

"You haven't told me why we are making this trip."

"A Sergeant McGrath called and said they picked up a couple of individuals whom we would be interested in."

"Did he say who they were?"

"No."

"He didn't give you a clue?"

"No Jamie, he just insisted someone from the Special Operations Section should get their butts up there to take charge of these individuals. From the tone of his voice I decided he was serious.   After you left I called the Constabulary Personnel Section to make certain a Sergeant McGrath was assigned to the Stanorlar Station, then I made another call to Stanorlar to reaffirm with McGrath about the time we would arrive. I also asked him to make reservations for us to spend the night."

For the next five minutes neither man spoke. Both were thinking about whom they would find in Stanorlar.

"Let's hope they are a couple of Loyalists," thought Meyers.

The Loyalists' terrorist groups were Meyers' specialty. They were one of the reasons Meyers became a police officer. The other reason was because both his father and grandfather were police officers. His grandfather was a Superintendent in the Metropolitan Police Force(Scotland Yard) in London and his father was an investigator in the Military Police.

During one of the bloodiest years of "The Troubles" Meyers' father was a member of the Scottish Regiment sent to Northern Ireland.

In December 1971 a bomb placed in the hallway of McGurk's bar in northern Belfast exploded, killing fifteen people, including two children. Sixteen others were seriously injured.

The official reports issued by the RUC and the British Army stated the bombing was committed by members of the IRA even though an eyewitness' report identified the bombers as loyalists and the bombing was claimed by loyalists immediately after the attack.

The only dissenting voice was Captain James T. Meyers. He told his superiors it was irrational to blame the IRA for the bombing, particularly since the target was a bar owned by a Catholic family and occupied solely by Catholics.

In addition, he pointed out to his superiors the recent intelligence reports indicated the bar was targeted by two of the known loyalist terrorist organizations. He also questioned the total absence of Constabulary personnel in the area at the time of the explosion.

In January 1972, Captain Meyers prepared a report on his conclusions, listing the reasons for his disagreement with the official report. The report contained summaries of interviews with over thirty individuals.

The report was to be forwarded to his Commanding General in England.

On the night of the 7th of Febrrary 1972, Captain Meyers and his wife left their apartment in the western district of Belfast on their way to an official party in Lisburn. As the couple started to enter their car, three men walked up to the couple and one asked Captain Meyers,

"Are you Captain Meyers of the Scottish Regiment?"

Meyers turned, looked at the man, smiled and said,

"Yes sir, can I help you?"

The individual nodded, said "yes", drew a gun from his coat pocket and shot Meyers. At the same time, the other two individuals drew their weapons and shot the Captain and his wife to death.

Upon examination of the bodies, it was determined the couple had been shot a total of eight times by their assailants. The same weapon, a 32-caliber weapon, caused all of Mrs. Meyers' wounds. Captain Meyers' wounds were caused by a 38-caliber and 45-caliber weapon.

The assailants were never identified and the killing of the Meyers remained one of the many unsolved crimes. Mysteriously, Captain Meyers' report on the McGurk bombing disappeared from his office and was never forwarded to his Commanding General in England.

The Meyers' young son, Jamie, who was eight years old at the time, was adopted by his maternal grandmother, Molly York, who lived in the Republic.

When Jamie was sixteen years old, his father's assertion were proven correct when a member of the UVF(Ulster Volunteer Force) confessed to his involvement in the bombing of the McGurk bar.

Jamie Meyers' education and police career mimicked that of Kerrigan's with the exception that he graduated from the University with a degree in Criminology and did not join the Garda until he was twenty-eight.

After graduation from the university, Meyers joined the Army and served as a peacekeeper in both Africa and the Middle East for four years. Upon discharge from the Army, he applied and was accepted in the Garda.

Meyers spend his first four years as a "street cop" in downtown Dublin. At the beginning of his fifth year he was assigned to the robbery division. He was promoted to Sergeant in 1995 and to Detective Sergeant in 1996.

During his first six years in the Garda, Meyers read every report on terrorists' organizations available, both official and unofficial. When Kerrigan was appointed to head the Special Operations Section, Jamie Meyers was one of the first to be selected by Kerrigan to become a member of the unit.

Four and a half hours later, after two brief stops at the border, going in and out of Ulster, the two officers arrived in Stanorlar. It took them only minutes to find the police station in downtown Stanorlar and another two minutes to park in the station's parking lot.

The two were about to start walking towards the station when an individual in uniform stepped out of a car parked in one of the official parking spaces and said,

"Chief Superintendent Kerrigan?"

Both Kerrigan and Meyers stopped and turned in the direction of the voice.

"I'm Chief Superintendent Kerrigan," said Kerrigan.

"I'm Sergeant McGrath sir," said the individual as he walked toward the pair.

"Thank you for coming up."

After shaking hands, Kerrigan said,

"This is Detective Sergeant Meyers."

McGrath and Meyers nodded to each other, then shook hands.

"Glad to meet you," said McGrath.

"The same," said Meyers.

A few moments of awkward silence followed the introductions.

"You said it was important for someone from Special Operations to come up," said Kerrigan.

"Yes sir," said McGrath, hesitating, looking both directions, then looking directly at Kerrigan.

"Sir, could I see some identification?"

"Certainly," said Kerrigan.

Both Kerrigan and Meyers removed their black leather cases containing their credentials from their coat pockets and held them up for McGrath to examine.

"Thank you. Now, if you will follow me, I'll take you to the two we picked up this morning."

"Do you know who they are?" asked Kerrigan.

"Yes sir, McCaul and O'Connor."

Kerrigan and Meyers looked at each other in disbelief, then at McGrath.

"Are you certain?" asked Meyers.

"I'm certain," answered McGrath.

"How did you get them?" asked Meyers.

"They just drove right up to the border. One of the lads at the stop recognized O'Connor and that was it."

"No resistance?" asked Kerrigan.

"None. Could be because McCaul is sick. He was in the rear seat. But they came along like a pair of lambs...and so polite. It would frost the devil's you know what."

"And where are they now?"

"I had them put in the station in Convoy."

"Does it..."

Before Meyers could finish his question, McGrath said,

"They have a small jail in the rear of the station. I didn't want to bring them here. I was afraid someone would recognize them and get word across the border. I left two of my men in Convoy to make certain nothing went wrong."

"Very good thinking Sergeant, very good," said Kerrigan.

"Thank you sir for the compliment, but I'd like to get them off my hands. You never know what will happen with those two around."

"I know," said Kerrigan.

"I was in Belfast visiting my sister when they made their escape from Castlereagh. I sure don't want something like that happening here."

"I don't blame you. We'll take them off your hands as soon as possible. Now, would you take us to them?"

"Yes sir."

"Do you want to go in our car?" asked Meyers.

"I prefer not. I'll go in my car and you can follow, if that's all right with you sir."

"Fine," said Kerrigan, nodding to McGrath and motioning to Meyers to head back to their car.

It was less than ten kilometers from Stanorlar to Convoy and the drive took less than twenty minutes.

McGrath pulled into an alley between two stone buildings, drove less than ten meters and turned left into a parking lot, which was nothing more than the concrete floor of a building demolished years ago. The remains of the wall and roof had long ago been used in the construction of other buildings and to stoke fires on cold winter nights.

Sergeant McGrath pulled his car into a line of small cars and indicted to Meyers to park in the second row.

The three men got out of their cars, locked the doors and without an spoken word, Kerrigan and Meyers followed McGrath back up the alley to the main street. After only ten steps to the right, the Sergeant stopped, turned and knocked on the large oak door.

They heard the scrapping of metal against metal. The door opened only a few inches, then swung open wide.

McGrath walked in followed by the two officers from Dublin. Once inside the station, Kerrigan and Meyers turned and saw a young officer holding a service revolver in his left hand.

Before either of the visiting officers could say a word, McGrath said,

"This young man is Constable Arbor, one of my men."

"Kerrigan and Meyers," said Kerrigan as he stuck out his hand and shook hands with the young man.

Meyers shook Arbor's hand, all the time looking at the weapon in the Constable's hand.

"We're not accustomed to having such prisoners. We're small town officers," said McGrath as a heavy set officer walked up to the four.

"This gentleman is Sergeant Fabian, the officer in charge of this station. Sergeant, this is Chief Superintendent Kerrigan and Detective Sergeant Meyers from Special Operations."

"Glad to meet you sir," said Fabian as he shook Kerrigan's hand. He turned to Meyers, shook hands and said,

"You're included in the welcome Detective."

"Thank you," said Meyers as he shook hands and smiled at the sergeant.

"If you will follow me please," said McGrath as he turned and walked to the rear of the building through a door in the center of the brick wall. The rear area contained two cells on the right and an open area on the left which contained a long oak table with six round back chairs, a cupboard, a sink and a two-burner propane stove. In the far left corner was the water closet.

Each of the two cells on the right contained a wash basin, two iron bunks bolted to the wall, a small table, no more than two by three feet and two straight back chairs. In one of the cells the bunks were pulled up against the wall, increasing the open space within the cell. In the other cell, the bunks were occupied by two individuals, both sleeping soundly.

As the four men approached the table, a young man stood up. McGrath stopped, turned to face Kerrigan and Meyers and said,

"This is my other officer, Constable Christian."

Kerrigan and Meyers shook hands with Christian.

"It's awful quiet in here," said Kerrigan, more as a question than a statement of fact.

"It's been that way for awhile," said Christian, "both are asleep."

"How long have they been asleep?" asked Meyers.

"About an hour. The little one was coughing and hacking ever since they were brought in. He tried to sleep, but was restless. The big one took care of him, putting wet towels on his forehead and keeping him covered.

The doctor was here about two hours ago. He gave the little one a shot and some pills to take and within half an hour he was asleep. Once he fell asleep, the big one laid down and fell asleep."

McGrath looked from the guard to Kerrigan and said,

"I arranged for the doctor to come and check..." he hesitated, then added, "the little fellow. He looked pretty sick to me."

Kerrigan nodded.

"What did the doctor say?" asked McGrath.

"Nothing."

"Nothing?"

"That's correct Sergeant. I asked him how the prisoner was and all he did was shrug his shoulders and walk out, with nary a word."

McGrath looked embarrassed and confused.

"I'll give him a call right now," said McGrath.

"Just a moment," said Kerrigan, "were there any other prisoners?"

"We did have a couple, Burke and Keane, who were let out this morning," said Fabian.

"Before or after McGrath arrived with these two?"

"Before. I let them out right after Mike called and asked if he could bring the two here."

"How many others are stationed here?" asked Kerrigan.

"I have three others, but since Sergeant McGrath came up, I gave my men the rest of the day off."

"Good. By the way, who are Burke and Keane?"

"Burke and Keane are the two village drunks. They spend every Wednesday night in here," said Fabian, "Wednesday night is the weekly meeting of the village Gaelic Club. Burke and Keane get into it every Wednesday night. Neither of them can hold their drink nor keep their mouths shut."

Kerrigan nodded. He was satisfied with the answer, but concerned about the situation. After a few moments of silence he turned to face Fabian and McGrath and asked,

"Do the people here know who we have in here?"

"I don't think so. The two who were on duty when Sergeant McGrath phoned were gone by the time he arrived with the two," said Fabian, "the only one who saw them here was the doctor."

"Of course my men in Stanorlar know who they are," said McGrath.

Kerrigan looked away and stared into the distance. He was thinking. Finally he turned to McGrath and said,

"Why don't you call your doctor friend and see what he says about McCaul?"

"Yes sir."

"Will you be needing me any more?" asked Fabian.

"No, I don't think so," said Kerrigan.

"Good. I'll be leaving, it's time to make the afternoon rounds of the village. I'll also make the evening rounds and I'll check with you in the morning. If you need me, I'll be home between half five and half seven, then after nine o'clock."

"Thank you for your assistance Sergeant," said Kerrigan.

Fabian smiled, nodded, walked through the door leading to the front room and departed his station. The door to the outside was shut and locked by Constable Arbor.

"Jamie, I want you to stay here in Convoy. I'm going back to Dublin. I need to get all the information available on these two so we know just what we're facing during the next few days."

"Too bad Sergeant McGrath didn't tell you who he had in the pokey before we left," said Meyers.

"I know, but he didn't and I don't really blame him."

Meyers nodded his head and said,

"I don't either."

McGrath walked up to the two, waited for a lull in the conversation, then said,

"The doctor wasn't in, he's making a house call in St. Johns. I left a message with his nurse."

"Good," said Kerrigan.

During the next hour, Kerrigan questioned McGrath about the capture of McCaul and O'Connor. He wanted the exact location of the border crossing where the two were arrested; the name of the officer who recognized O'Connor and the other officers who assisted in the arrest. He wrote down the names of every individual involved along with their rank and station. He requested McGrath to go over the story twice to make certain nothing was left out. When he concluded asking questions, McGrath asked,

"Now, can I ask a question?"

"Certainly."

"Are these two now your responsibility?"

Kerrigan smiled and said,

"Yes Sergeant, they are now our responsibility, but I would like for you and your men to remained here for a little while longer."

"Yes sir," said McGrath, but the look on his face told Kerrigan he had other questions.

Kerrigan attempted to answer these unasked questions.

"I'm going to head back to Dublin. Detective Meyers will remain here with you and your people, but I would appreciate it if you and your men would stay until I can get my people up from Dublin."

"Yes sir."

Kerrigan looked at his wrist watch. It was four fifty.

"If I can contact them now, they should be here no later than ten this evening. Can you and your people hold out that long?"

"Yes sir."

"Good. Now, if I can use the telephone to call."

"Yes sir, it's on the desk."

As Kerrigan walked up to the desk where Constable Arbor was sitting, the young Constable stood up, moved away and motioned with his head for the Chief Superintendent to take his chair.

"Thank you," said Kerrigan.

Arbor nodded, turned and walked to the rear where McGrath, Christian and Meyers were sitting.

Ten minutes later, Kerrigan walked to the back and took a seat at the oak table. Before Kerrigan was seated, Arbor stood up and returned to the front.

"Jamie, would you drive me up to Letterkenny? I've made arrangements for quick transportation to Dublin. They said they'd be ready a little after six."

"Yes sir," said Meyers as he pushed his chair back and stood up.

"Detective Meyers should be back in an hour or so."

"Yes sir," said McGrath.

"We want to thank you and your men for your assistance. You can make certain it will be noted in the official files," said Kerrigan as he shook McGrath's hand.

"Thank you sir."

Before departing the station, Kerrigan shook hands with Constables Christian and Arbor, thanking them personally for their assistance.

Once in their official car, the two Dublin officers drove in silence for the first ten minutes.

"We're headed for Letterkenny, but where in Letterkenny are we going?" asked Meyers.

"To the military base this side of town. It should be marked on the highway. I contacted an old friend at the base and he's arranged for his people to fly me down to Dublin in one of those new jet helicopters. Said it wouldn't take but about an hour and he would put me down at the Army base in Dublin."

"Who is coming up this evening?"

"Carter and Lewis for the present. They'll fly back in the helicopter."

"You want me to wait for them?"

"No, Kevin, Kevin Kavanaugh, my friend at Letterkenny, said he'd drive them down to Convoy when they arrive. I would prefer you get back to McGrath and his people as soon as possible. I'm afraid Sergeant McGrath is going to have apoplexy if we don't relieve him and his men within a few hours."

"I see," said Meyers as he nodded.

"If Kevin is correct, Carter and Lewis should be here no later than eight or eight thirty, then McGrath and his men can go home."

Dr. Marek arrived at the station a few minutes before six. He was greeted by McGrath and escorted directly to the cell containing McCaul and O'Connor. O'Connor was awake, but McCaul was still sleeping.

Christian unlocked the cell, then backed away so the doctor could enter.

McCaul was covered with two blankets and was facing the wall of the cell. Very gently the doctor rolled McCaul over so he could examine him.

"This man is sick, extremely sick, but I don't know what's wrong with him. The medicine I gave him has knocked him out, which is good, because his body is telling him he needs to sleep. His temperature is high and he's dehydrated. Has he had anything to drink since I was here before?"

"Nothing," said Christian.

"I didn't think so," said the doctor as he picked up his bag.

"Isn't there anything you can do for him?" asked O'Connor.

The doctor turned around and looked at the big man. He studied him for a few moments, shook his head and said,

"No. He needs to be put in the hospital so they can start pumping fluids into him."

Turning to McGrath, the doctor said,

"Is there any chance of taking him to the hospital?"

McGrath answered by shaking his head.

"I don't have the authority doctor. He's no longer my prisoner, he belongs to the Special…"

"Isn't there someone you can call and get authority to move him?"

McGrath looked at his wrist watch and said,

"The people in charge should be here at any time."

"Tell them this man needs to be put in the hospital immediately."

"I'll tell them," said McGrath.

"Tell them to call me if they have any questions. I have one more call to make and I'll be back at the hospital in about an hour."

"Yes sir," said McGrath. He could feel his stomach tightening up.

"Before I go to the hospital, I'll check back with you Mike."

"Thank you."

"I have to leave now," said the doctor as he waited for Christian to unlock the cell door.

As the doctor left the cell, O'Connor said,

"Thank you sir."

"You're welcomed."

Dr. Marek turned and walked to the front where he waited until Arbor unlocked the door.

Once the doctor was out of the building, McGrath asked O'Connor if he was hungry.

"As a bear. I haven't had anything to eat since early this morning and I need to go to the bathroom…like now," said O'Connor.

"Christian, our friend need to go to the bathroom," said McGrath.

Constable Christian walked back to the cell, opened it and escorted O'Connor to the water chamber at the rear of the station. Since the WC was enclosed with no windows, Christian stood outside the closed door.

The toilet was flushed and the water in the basin turned on for a few seconds. The door opened and O'Connor walked back to the cell, the door of which was still open.

Once O'Connor was secured in the cell, McGrath asked Christian,

"What about meals for these people?"

"It will be here in a few minutes. Sergeant Fabian said his wife will bring it at exactly half six, which is just about three minutes from now."

"Good."

At exactly thirty minutes after six, there was a knock on the front door of the station. Arbor had anticipated the arrival of the food and was standing next to the door, ready to unlock it. As he was about to slid the latch, McGrath shouted,

"Arbor, make certain it's Mrs. Fabian."

The Constable jumped back from the door, turned and looked at McGrath. He was at a loss for the moment.

There was another knock on the door.

"Open the damn door," said McGrath, "just make certain it's Mrs. Fabian.

Arbor slipped the iron latch back, placed his left foot a few inches from the door and opened it just enough so he could look out.

"Mrs. Fabian?" asked Arbor.

"And who else would it be bringing a basket of food for you?"

"I don't know."

"Let her in," said McGrath.

"But…"

"Just let her in."

Arbor took a deep breath, moved his foot back and opened the door. In walked a woman he hoped was Mrs. Fabians.

"Good evening," she said as she walked to the rear of the station.

"Good evening," said the men.

"I hope you're hungry, I cooked a big roast with lots of potatoes and carrots, some boiled cabbage, home made soda bread and a cream pie," she said as she set the basket of food on the table.

"We're all hungry," said McGrath.

"Good, I also made some chicken soup for the sick one, but I see he's still asleep."

"Yes ma'am, he's been asleep most of the day," said O'Connor.

"Will you stay and have a bite with us?" asked McGrath.

"No, no. I have to get back and get the kitchen cleaned up. I do need my basket if you want some breakfast."

"Certainly," said McGrath as he opened the basket and removed the bowls of food.

"We certainly thank you for everything Mrs. Fabian," said McGrath.

"You're welcomed Sergeant. It's nice to cook for people who appreciate my cooking. You do know, this is the first time in months I've had to bring dinner over. Usually it's only breakfast for the boys who are picked up in the evening."

"Well, I'll see if I can't get Sergeant Fabian to arrest me sometime so I can have another chance to enjoy your cooking," said McGrath.

"Now you don't have to do that. Any time you're up this way, just drop in and I'll be happy to fix you a meal."

"I'll keep that in mind."

Mrs. Fabian picked up her basket and walked to the front of the station.

"You boys have a good evening."

"Thank you ma'am," said Arbor as he opened the door and held it open until she was out of the station. He closed the door, slipped the latch closed and headed for the rear of the station.

McGrath had already set the table with the dishes and silverware from the cabinet. He put the kettle on for tea and was dishing out a plate for O'Connor as Arbor took his seat.

Once the plate was fixed for O'Connor, McGrath slipped it through the rectangular slot in the bars at the bottom. The slot was just wide enough for the plate. After the plate of food was slipped through the slot, two smaller plates were slipped through, one with a large piece of soda bread and butter, the other with a large piece of pie.

"Tea will be ready in a few minutes," said McGrath as he took a seat and enjoyed Mrs. Fabian's home cooked meal, in spite of the knot in his stomach.

At seven ten, the four men had finished eating and were enjoying their tea when there was a loud knock on the door. The lawmen looked at each other for a moment, then McGrath said,

"You'd better see who it is."

Arbor pushed his chair back and walked to the front of the station. As he passed the desk, he picked up the government issued revolver. He placed his foot within inches of the door and slipped the latch open. As he had done with Mrs. Fabian, he opened the door just wide enough to look out. He stepped back, pulled the door wide open and announced,

"It's the doctor."

The doctor entered, walked past Arbor to the rear of the building. He looked at McGrath and asked,

"Have you heard anything from the people with authority to move this man?"

McGrath shook his head in reply.

"Let me in the cell, I want to check him."

Without being told, Christian was out of his chair and unlocking the cell door.

As the doctor entered, O'Connor stood up, moved the two chairs closer to his up turned bunk in order to give the doctor more room. The station was silent for the next five minutes as the doctor carefully and gently examined the sleeping prisoner. When he was finished, he turned, walked out of the cell, stood in front of McGrath and said,

"Mike, you really need to get him to the hospital."

McGrath was close to panic at the moment. Here he was with two of the most wanted men in Ireland, wanted by the British, the Constabulary and the Garda and they weren't even his responsibility.

"The man is very sick Mike. He's extremely dehydrated and needs fluids pumped into him. He needs to be in the hospital now....right now."

"I don't know what to do Doctor. As I told you, I don't have the authority to have him transferred to the hospital."

"Well, someone had better get the authority to get him there or you're going to have a dead man on your hands."

"Holy hell," was McGrath's only comment.

After a few minutes, the doctor asked,

"Do you want me to call the hospital and tell them to come and get him?"

McGrath was close to that case of apoplexy. His breathing rate increased along with his heart rate.

A loud knock on the front door startled everyone.

"See who it is," said McGrath.

Arbor looked at his superior for a moment, picked up his revolver from the desk and walked to the door.

"I hope he doesn't shoot someone," thought McGrath.

The same thought went through the doctor's mind.

Arbor opened the door just enough to see see who knocked, then he swung the door open and almost shouted,

"It's Detective Meyers."

"Thank God," said McGrath, "thank God."

As Meyers walked into the station, Arbor slammed and locked the door, barely missing Meyers with the edge of the door.

Meyers immediately sensed something was wrong. He stood just a few feet inside the station and looked towards the rear.

"What's wrong?"

McGrath walked up to him and said,

"The doctor just finished examining McCaul and says he needs to be in the hospital…immediately."

Meyers looked from McGrath to the doctor, who had walked up to the pair.

"Is that correct doctor?" asked Meyers.

"That's correct detective. The man is extremely ill and needs to be hospitalized immediately. The one thing I'm worried about is that he is extremely dehydrated and needs to be given fluids now."

"Can't you give him some fluids?

"No. I don't have the equipment. He needs to be in the hospital."

"Where is the closest?" asked Meyers.

"In Letterkenny. Shall I call them?' asked the doctor.

Meyers looked at the doctor for a moment, then at McGrath. He walked back to the cell containing McCaul and O'Connor and looked at the still form of McCaul for less than five seconds, turned and looked at O'Connor. He saw something in the big man's eyes that made him turn to the doctor and say,

"You'd better call the hospital doctor."

Doctor Marek smiled and nodded, turned, walked up to the desk, picked up the telephone and dialed the operator.

Only Meyers heard O'Connor whisper a thank you. Meyers nodded, turned and walked back to where McGrath was standing.

"This does complicate matters a bit."

"Not just a bit," was McGrath's reply.

During the next five minutes, Meyers walked back to the cell and looked at McCaul. All he could see was his face but he was unable to see the beads of sweat on the man's face. He did see the sporadic shaking of the body.

"They'll be on their way in less than five minutes," said Dr. Marek, "they'll have the equipment to start an IV and I asked them to bring extra fluids, the man looks like he's extremely dehydrated."

"Thank you doctor," said Meyers, "did they say when they will be here?"

"They should be here within half an hour or so."

Meyers turned and walked back to the front of the station as the doctor returned to the cell containing McCaul.

"How are you going to…." said McGrath, who was cut off in mid-sentence by Meyers.

"I need to make a telephone call, then I'll tell you."

McGrath's reply was merely a nod of the head.

Meyers walked to the front desk. The telephone call he made was to the Special Operations Section.

Meyers was connected with Supeintendent Ceantt, who was second in command of the Section. All the people in the station heard Meyers tell the individual he was talking to that Chief Superintendent Kerrigan was on his way to Dublin in a helicopter and about the condition of "the little one" and "you will understand when the Chief gets back". He then told the individual what he told the doctor to do about calling an ambulance. From that point on in the conversation, the only words heard were three "yes sirs", two "no sirs", two "I agree", one "I'll take care of it" and "good night sir."

Meyers hung up the phone and sat down at the desk for a few moments before standing up and returning to the rear of the station. He passed between the cell containing McCaul and O'Connor and the two men sitting at the table. Upon reaching the far end of the table he turned and said,

"Would you gentlemen give me a few minutes alone back here?"

"Certainly," said McGrath as he stood up. He looked at Christian and nodded his head towards the front of the station.

Without being asked, the doctor pushed open the cell door and walked to the front of the station, followed by McGrath and Christian.

For the next twenty minutes, Meyers and O'Connor carried on a conversation which could not be heard by the others. The content of their conversation would remain known only to the two.

At ten minutes before eight there was a loud knock on the front door.

Automatically the four in the front of the station turned and looked to the rear.

Meyers stood up and said,

"That's either the ambulance or the men from Dublin. Would someone open the door?"

"Arbor," said McGrath.

The young Constable slipped out of his chair, walked around the desk to the door. He had forgotten his service revolver. He turned and looked at McGrath, who stood up and walked over the desk and picked up the revolver.

"Go ahead and open the door," said McGrath, "but find out who it is before you open the door."

Arbor turned back to the door, looked at the inanimate object and said,

"Who is it?"

"I'm Carter. I work from Chief Superintendent Kerrigan and I have…"

Before he could finish the sentence, Arbor pulled open the door.

Instead of entering the station, Carter remained on the outside, looking into the station. He hesitated for a moment until Meyers said,

"Come on in Carter."

Carter slowly entered the station, followed by a young man in his early twenties and a very distinguished looking individual in the uniform of the Irish Army.

Arbor closed and locked the door.

The three newcomers stood in the middle of the room and looked around, first at Arbor, then at the three men who had occupied the bench, but who were now standing.

"You made it here in record time," said Meyers as he joined the group.

"Gentlemen, this is Colonel Kavanaugh and these two," nodding towards Carter and Lewis, "are Constables Lewis and Carter from Dublin," said Meyers.

The three shook hands with each of the men as they introduced themselves.

"The Colonel was good enough to bring Lewis and Carter down from Letterkenny."

After the introductions, Meyers said,

"Colonel, could I speak with you for a moment...in back?"

Not waiting for an answer, Meyers turned and walked to the rear of the station.

Kavanaugh looked at the other men, then at Meyers' back. He hesitated for only a second, then followed Meyers.

Upon reaching the table, Meyers turned and waited for the Colonel.

"Sir, I have a real problem and I need help. I hate to ask you for another favor, but..."

"What is it Detective?"

Turning and looking at the cell containing McCaul and O'Connor, Meyers said,

"The man in the bunk. The doctor says he needs to be in the hospital now. The doctor has called for an ambulance to take him to the hospital in Letterkenny."

Kavanaugh looked at Meyers, frowned and said,

"So?"

"Superintendent Ceantt, Superintendent Kerrigan's Deputy wants me to bring him to Dublin and...."

"He asked you to ask me if I could arrange it?"

"Yes sir."

Kavanaugh took a deep breath, turned and looked at the men in the cell for a moment, turned and faced Meyers and said,

"I need to make a telephone call."

"There's a phone up front on the desk," said Meyers as he turned and walked toward the front of the building, followed by the Colonel.

Looking at McGrath, Kavanaugh asked,

"Is it all right if I used your phone to call Letterkenny?"

Without hesitating, McGrath said,

"It's not my phone, but please use it."

He wanted to know who owed the phone, but before he could ask, Meyers said,

"It's an official phone of the station and the individual in charge is not here at the present…hell Colonel, go ahead and used the phone."

Kavanaugh laughed and shook his head. Without any further comments he walked over to the desk. Arbor jumped up and said,

"You can sit here sir."

"Thank you," said the Colonel as he took Arbor's seat. He picked up the phone, dialed the operator and asked her to connect him with the Army base in Letterkenny.

None of the others spoke or moved. They stood silently as if frozen in place.

"Yes, connect me with the base hospital please," said Kavanaugh.

He turned and nodded at Meyers. After a few seconds, he said,

"I'd like to speak with the doctor on duty please."

Another few seconds of silence.

"Doctor Edwards, this is Colonel Kavanaugh. Yes, I'm fine, but I have a little mission for both your people and the support company from Dublin. The helicopter group."

Another short period of silence. Kavanaugh looked toward Meyers and shook his head.

"I know you don't Captain, I'll take care of the arrangements. What I want from you is a doctor and two medics to take a man from the base to Dublin."

"I know Captain, but find me one. The patient will be there in…."

Turning to Meyers, Kavanaugh asked,

"When will the ambulance be here?"

Meyers looked at the doctor.

"It should be here any minute."

"Dr. Edwards, the patient will be at the base in less than thirty minutes, so you had better start rounding up your people and…just a minute."

Kavanaugh put his hand over the phone, looked at Doctor Marek and asked,

"Will the patient need anything special?"

"He's very dehydrated, so they better take extra saline and glucose solutions and possibly an oxygen supply."

The Colonel nodded, took his hand off the phone and repeated what the doctor said, word for word, then added,

"The patient will be at the helicopter pad on the parade grounds. Yes I know. Thank you Captain, now connect me with the operator please."

A moment later, he continued.

"Please connect me with base operations at the air field."

The phone at base operations was picked up after the fifth ring.

"Where in the hell have you been Willie?"

Kavanaugh laughed at the answer, then said,

"Call whatever flight crew is on duty and tell them we have a MedEvac going to Dublin in about thirty minutes."

Silence.

"I don't give a damn which one takes it. Just have the MedEvac chopper on the pad in front of headquarters. The pad on the parade field. Have it there in thirty minutes, ready to go, understand?"

Silence.

"One of the three had better be ready when I get there or you know whose ass will be in the fire. That's right."

A very short silence.

"I'll see you in thirty minutes or less Willie and thanks."

Kavanaugh replaced the phone in its cradle, took a deep breath and said,

"They'll be ready by the time we get there."

The doctor walked up to the Colonel and Meyers and said,

"I didn't catch all of the conversation, but from what I heard, I assume you're not transferring the patient to the hospital in Letterkenny. Is that correct?"

Kavanaugh looked from the doctor to Meyers and then back.

"Yes sir. The patient will be transferred from the ambulance to a MedEvac helicopter and flown to Dublin where he will be transferred to a general hospital. Isn't that correct Detective Meyers."

"Yes sir," said Meyers.

"These MedEvac choppers are nothing more than flying ambulances. They're equipped with everything, sometimes more than a regular ambulance."

"I know," said Doctor Marek, "I spent a few years in the British Army as a medic before going to Medical School and becoming a doctor."

At the mention of the British Army, Meyers could feel the hair on the back of his neck stand up. He immediately thought about the identity of the prisoners being compromised, depending on the doctor's political persuasion.

"I informed my superior the condition of the prisoner and he suggested we get him to the general hospital in Dublin. I hope this doesn't offend you," said Meyers.

"No, no, not in the least. In fact I think it is a very good idea. Do you know which hospital he will be admitted to?"

"No sir."

"Then you won't be needing my assistance any longer?"

"No sir, but I would appreciate it if you would remain until the ambulance arrives so you can make certain the medics know exactly what to do for the patient."

The doctor nodded and said,

"I'll be happy to do so. They should be here any time now."

The words weren't out of the doctor's mouth before someone knocked on the door.

McGrath did not have to tell Arbor to answer the door. The young police officer was at the door with his foot in place and his service revolver in his left hand.

"It's the ambulance," said Arbor as he opened the door to admit the two men carrying a folded stretcher between them.

"In the back," said Arbor.

Once they were inside the building, Arbor closed and locked the door, turned and followed the medics to the rear of the building. He was followed by McGrath and the doctor, leaving Meyers, Kavanaugh, Carter and Lewis in the front of the station.

While McCaul was loaded and strapped onto the stretcher, Meyers informed Carter and Lewis of Ceannt's instructions.

Meyers would escort McCaul to Dublin, McGrath and his people were to be relieved and sent home. Carter and Lewis were to remain and guard O'Connor. Prior to leaving, Meyers would contact Sergeant Fabian and inform him of the situation.

The two young officers nodded and Carter turned to Lewis and said,

"I'll take the desk for the first watch, you have the cell. OK?"

"Fine," said Lewis. He turned and started back to the rear.

"Tell Sergeant McGrath I'd like to see him," said Meyers.

"Yes Detective," replied Lewis.

"What's taking them so long?" asked Meyers.

"It looks like the doctor is starting an IV," said Kavanaugh.

McGrath walked up to Meyers and said,

"You wanted to see me?"

"Yes. I know that Chief Superintendent Kerrigan would wants me to thank you again for you assistance. Also, you and your men are free to leave as soon as the little one is loaded in the ambulance and on his way to the hospital. Before you leave, do you have Sergeant Fabian's number?"

"It's on the desk," said McGrath.

Meyers walked up to the desk and dialed the number listed for Sergeant Fabian. After the second ring the phone was answered by Sergeant Fabian.

Meyers explained to the Sergeant what was going on, who was leaving and who was remaining in the station.

"Then there will only be three for breakfast, right?"

"Right," replied Meyers, "one prisoner and two of our people. Constable Lewis and Constable Carter."

"Do you want us on duty tomorrow?" asked Fabian.

"How many?"

"Just two of us," said Fabian.

"Fine, just so you are here in the station with our people."

"No problem. I'll join them for breakfast in the morning, and you have a good trip to Dublin."

"Thank you. Also, I know Chief Superintendent Kerrigan wants me to thank you for your help."

"Tell the Chief Superintendent any time."

"I will. Good by."

"Good by."

Meyers hung up the phone and walked back to where McGrath was standing.

"I want to thank you again," said Meyers as he stuck out his hand.

McGrath's hand was wet with perspiration.

"I'd say any time, but I prefer this to be the last time for something like this."

Meyers smile and nodded.

"Arbor, Christian, get you stuff. We'll be going home as soon as the ambulance leaves," said McGrath.

"Are we coming back?" asked Christian.

"No," said Meyers, "you can go home and get a good night's sleep. Perhaps Sergeant McGrath might even give you a day or two off."

"Maybe a day, but not two," said McGrath.

During the next few minutes, McCaul was carried to the ambulance and secured. Meyers thanked the doctor again for his assistance and climbed into the ambulance.

Once everyone was out of the building, Carter secured the door.

As the ambulance departed Convoy and headed for the Army base in Letterkenny, the doctor entered his car and McGrath and his men entered McGrath's car and within seconds both cars were out of sight.

Colonel Kavanaugh followed the ambulance to the base, but just prior to entering the installation, he pulled ahead of the ambulance. The two vehicles slowed almost to a stop at the guard gate, but were wave on through by the guard who was informed by the Duty Officer of the tentative arrival of the Colonel and the ambulance. The guard saluted Kavanaugh and the two vehicles proceeded to the helicopter pad in front of the Headquarter's building.

On the pad was a Heuy helicopter with the international medical symbol of a red cross on a white background. Within seconds, the military medics removed McCaul from the ambulance and transferred him into the helicopter.

Meyers got out of the ambulance, signed a voucher for the ambulance crew, walked over to the Colonel, shook hands and thanked him for his assistance.

"Tell Kerrigan....no, I'll tell him. You do want me to call him and let him know you're on your way?" asked Kavanaugh.

"Yes sir, if he is there yet. Thanks again."

Kavanaugh nodded.

Meyers turned, stooped over and walked under the rotating blades of the helicopter. One of the crew stuck out his hand and helped him aboard, then showed him where to sit. Once he strapped on his seat belt, the crewman gave the pilot the thumbs up.

Within five minutes the helicopter was on its way to Dublin.

Day Two

July 23, 1998

Garda Headquarters
Dublin, Ireland

A few minutes after eight, Meyers arrived at Headquarters. Ten minutes later, Kerrigan walked passed his secretary, nodding his good morning greeting and continued into his office. He put his briefcase on the desk, slumped into his chair and closed his eyes.

Before he had a chance to fall asleep, Mrs. Roberts knocked on the door and opened it without waiting for an answer. She walked into the office carrying a tray containing a pot of tea, two cups, milk, sugar, napkins, spoons and a plate of homemade cinnamon rolls.

"You look like you need more than a cup of tea this morning," she said as she placed the tray on the coffee table in front of Kerrigan's desk.

Kerrigan forced his eyes open and looked at her for only a second before closing his eyes again.

"Jamie will be here in a minute. He called and said he needed to see you as soon as you arrived."

"How did he know I was here?" asked Kerrigan.

"I called him."

Opening one eye, Kerrigan looked at Roberts and asked,

"Couldn't you have given me a few minutes?"

"No sir. The damn phone has been ringing since seven this morning. You have a stack of phone messages. Plus, the Assistant Commissioner wants to see you, as soon as you arrive."

"You haven't told him I'm here, have you?"

"Not yet," said Mrs. Roberts as she smiled at the sleepy Chief Superintendent, who now had both eyes open.

"When Jamie gets here, lock the door and don't let anyone know I'm here."

Before he could finish his sentence there was a knock on the door.

"If it's anyone but Jamie, send them away."

"Even the Assistant Commissioner or perhaps the Commissioner?"

"Don't be funny this early in the morning."

Mrs. Roberts turned and walked to the door, opened it slightly and when she saw Meyers, she opened it all the way and said,

"You'd better get in here Jamie before our boss decides to go to sleep."

Meyers walked into the room and stood looking at Kerrigan as Mrs. Roberts closed the door. She turned and both stood looking at Kerrigan, not knowing what to do because the Chief Superintendent had both eyes closed.

"Take a seat Jamie," said Kerrigan as he opened his eyes.

"Morning sir," said Meyers, "how'd you sleep?"

"Like a dead man."

"That's exactly what you look like," said Mrs. Roberts, who was the only individual in the building who could say such a thing to the Chief Superintendent without fear of retaliation.

Meyers smiled and nodded his agreement only after checking to make certain Kerrigan's eyes were closed again.

Mrs. Roberts poured two cups of hot tea, handing one to Meyers and placing the other on Kerrigan's desk.

"I'd better get back outside before someone else finds out you're here. What should I tell the Assistant Commissioner the next time he calls?"

"Tell him….tell him…hell, I don't know, think of something to keep him out of our hair for…"

Kerrigan opened his eyes and looked at his watch.

"Until at least eleven o'clock."

"Done," said Mrs. Roberts as she walked out of the room and closed the door.

After almost ten minutes of silence, while Meyers drunk his tea, Kerrigan opened his eyes and asked,

"What time did you get to bed?"

"About four."

"Then how in the hell can you so bushy tailed this morning?"

"I have no idea, but I feel great."

"That's the trouble with young people."

Meyers had no earthly idea what Kerrigan meant by the statement and he didn't ask for an explanation. He remained silent and took another drink of his tea.

"We need to find out how McCaul is doing this morning," said Kerrigan.

"He's still pretty sick."

"How do you know? Did you call Dr. Shaw?"

"No sir, I went by the hospital this morning to check on him."

Kerrigan stood up, stretched his back muscles for about ten seconds and flopped back down in his chair.

"Did you see Dr. Shaw?"

"No sir. Taylor said he went to bed in one of the empty rooms about six this morning and I didn't want to wake him."

"Then how do….?"

"Taylor said they finally got McCaul's fever down, but the doctor told him McCaul was still pretty sick."

Kerrigan nodded, looked at Meyers for a moment, turned and looked at the wall.

"How many people do you have at the hospital?"

"Three, Taylor, Hubbard and Cassidy."

"They've been on all night?"

"Yes sir."

Again the room became silent. Kerrigan looked at the picture on the wall to the right of his desk as if he was talking to the person portrayed in the picture.

"We may have to get men from downstairs to keep a watch on McCaul."

"Superintendent McBride has taken care of it sir."

"Good," said Kerrigan as he looked from the picture to the ceiling.

"I want you here to take care of anything pertaining to McCaul, except the guards."

"Yes sir."

"I'm going to need just about everyone in the Section."

Again, Meyers had no idea what Kerrigan was talking about. He knew the Chief Superintendent was thinking out loud, so he remained silent.

Finally, Kerrigan nodded his head, picked up the pitcher of milk, added some to his tea and without stirring it, he finished the cup.

"Jamie…"

Kerrigan did not finish his sentence. Instead he again looked at his watch, looked over at the picture on the wall and took a deep breath.

Twenty seconds later, he turned to Meyers and said,

"I'm going back to Convoy with Ceantt and some of the others. I'd like for you to stay here and keep in close contact with Dr. Shaw. In addition, I want you to start making arrangements to hide both McCaul and O'Connor. Once the word is out about these two….."

"Yes sir," said Meyers, happy to find out he was not expected to make another trip up North.

"Contact the military and see if there's a possibility of housing the two in one of their stockades, some place outside of the city."

"Yes sir," said Meyers as he finished his tea, placed the empty cup upside down on the paper napkin, stood up and asked,

"Anything else"

"That should do it."

"When are you bringing O'Connor back?"

"Probably Saturday or Sunday. I figure over the weekend would be better than a week day. I'll call you and let you know when to expect us."

"Yes sir, I'll see you this week end."

Meyers turned and walked out of the office.

During the next twenty minutes, Kerrigan called in Longman, Ceantt and McBride and informed them of his plan, which was nothing like what he told Meyers.

Looking directly at McBride he asked,

"How many men have you assigned to watch over McCaul?"

"Eight, three eight shifts a day, plus two on reserve."

"Who are the two on reserve?"

"Horn and Constance."

"Good. Get word to Horn and Constance that they are going up north with the rest of us."

"Yes sir."

"Are you coordinating with Meyers?"

"Yes sir."

"Fine. You'll be in charge of the office until we get back."

"Yes sir."

Turning to Ceantt, Kerrigan said,

"You had better contact all the others and tell them they had better head home, pack a bag, kiss their wives good by and be back here by noon. I want be out of here by one o'clock. Any questions?"

No one had a question.

Day Three

July 24, 1998

Londonderry, Northern Ireland

At twelve minutes before twelve noon, Melvin Harper, the well known reporter and writer for Station INL, one of the principle Radio/Television stations in Londonderry, walked into the office of Joseph Marsh, Chief Engineer of the station.

The two men were almost the same height and weight. This was the extent of the similarity. Harper possessed a shaggy head of wild blond hair that appeared not to have seen a comb or brush in days. His eyes were blue and his complexion was white. Marsh's complexion was that of a surfer. His skin was a golden brown from years of outdoor living. Marsh's hair was dark brown with a military trim and perfectly combed. The part on the left side of his head was like a narrow dirt road between stands of tall pine trees. His neatly trimmed mustache appeared to be the same shade of brown as his eyes and hair.

"How would you like a little trip down to the Republic this afternoon?" asked Harper.

Marsh looked up at Harper, smiled, shook his head and said,

"No thank you Mr. Harper. I don't feel like being crammed up in that mobile hunk of junk you call an automobile."

"As my favorite American television star says.....surprise, surprise, surprise. I have a new car," said Harper.

Marsh continued to smile and shake his head.

"What happened to the old one?"

"It wouldn't start yesterday, so I had it hauled in by Mr. Betts. He said it didn't have a drop of oil in the crankcase, whatever a crankcase is, and the engine froze up. Can you believe that?"

"Very easily," said Marsh.

"You sure you wouldn't like to ride in my new car?"

"Is it bigger than the old one?"

"A great deal larger. It's a red Mercedes. I bought it from a school teacher."

"A Mercedes?"

"Right. A red Mercedes coup."

"Let me check with Mr. Jacobson."

"You've changed you mind about going?"

"Never rode in a red Mercedes coup before," said Marsh, "give me twenty minutes. If Mr. Jacobson says it's alright, I'll be ready to go. I'll be down stairs in the lunch room."

"No big hurry," said Harper.

Thirty minutes later, Marsh and Harper were in the red Mercedes coup, headed south.

Harper told Marsh he had a "tip" concerning the arrest of a couple of Provos in the Republic. Allegedly, the Provos were picked up by the Garda at the border during a routine border check. There hadn't been any official word about such an incident, but late this morning one of Harper's sources telephoned him from Enniskillen. He told Harper he heard a rumor the two Provos were stopped and arrested as they attempted to cross the border into Northern Ireland at a little hamlet called Ballindarlt, right across the border from Straban.

Harper decided the rumor had a ring of truth to it and if true, it would make a good lead story for the evening news. Then, depending on who the two Provos were, the story could possibly be dragged out for at least two and perhaps three or more days.

Harper explained to Marsh that everyone would be interested in the story. The Protestants would be interested in the fact the police in the Republic were doing something to halt the passage of IRA men back and forth across the border. Of course the Loyalists would be overjoyed that a couple of Provos were captured by the Garda. Their interest would continue up to and including the trial of the suspects. They would make wagers on just what kind of sentence they would receive from the judges in the Republic.

On the other hand, the Catholics would be interested in the story because they would want to find out whose father, husband, brother, uncle or cousin was arrested by the police in the Republic. They would have the same interest in the trial and sentencing, but from another stand point.

"As reporters, we can't lose," said Harper, "we just have to make certain when we broadcast our story we give all the facts, plus we must make certain we don't slant it, no matter our personal feelings. If we do it properly, we keep everyone's interest."

Marsh felt a little ting of pride for being included as a reporter.

"A little difficult to do, isn't it Mel?"

"Not after you lived with it for as many years as I have."

"You mean you don't favor one side over the other?"

"Not in the least. You'll find a lot of good on both sides and also a lot of bad."

After taking a deep breath and shaking his head, he continued,

"Whenever someone is hurt or killed, it doesn't matter whether it's a Nationalist or a Loyalist, they are all Irish and it breaks my heart every time it happens."

Marsh looked over at Harper as the car passed the commercial buildings in midtown. He never expected to hear a statement like this from Harper. He thought of him as the typical reporter as portrayed on television, that is a hard hearted, heavy drinking misfit who didn't give a damn about other people. That was before he found out Harper was only days from being ordained a Catholic priest when he packed his bag one night and walked out into the world he had been protected from for so many years. Perhaps all the years in the seminary did have an effect on the man, even though he would deny it.

Before they were completely out of Londonderry, Harper pulled into a parking lot of one of his favorite pubs.

"I'll buy you lunch today.....pay back for riding in my hunk of junk," said Harper.

Marsh laughed and said,

"Great, I thought I would have to do without anything to eat for the rest of the day."

"Oh no, we're having an early lunch in case we don't have time for dinner this evening. No telling when we'll have time to eat after we get finished in Convoy."

"Convoy, never heard of it," said Marsh.

"Well, you have now," said Harper as he opened the door and stepped out of the car.

Once in the pub, Harper ordered fish and chips along with a pint of Harps. Marsh didn't know what to order. It was too early for him to eat fish, which he considered a dinner meal, so he settled on a roast beef sandwich and a pot of tea.

Before their lunch arrived, they were joined by two individuals who were identified as reporters from one of the daily newspapers.

After being introduced to March, the two reporters started asking Harper about the rumor that one of the city councilmen was going to submit his resignation at the next Council meeting.

Harper knew all about the resignation. It was based on the fact the councilman, one Daniel Riley, had been indulging in a little extra curriculum activity with the daughter of the President of one of the financial institutions in Londonderry.

"From what I hear, the rumors are true gentlemen. It seems Mr. Riley has personal problems within his family to which he needs to devote more time and energy."

What the statement meant was Mr. Riley's wife found out about these little forays and raised holy hell, threatening to perform the "Bobbitt technique" on Mr. Riley if he ever looked at another woman.

When the reporters queried Harper further about why Riley was resigning, all he told them was he also heard Mrs. Riley had a lingering illness requiring Mr. Riley to spend more time at home.

The statement was explained to Marsh later as meaning Mrs. Riley was sick and tired of the old man fooling around and she wanted him at home so she could keep and eye on him.

After lunch, the two reentered the red Mercedes coup and continued on their way to the Republic. Once they crossed the border, the drive between Straban and Convoy was made in silence.

Marsh was attempting to correlate the feelings expressed by Harper and Harper's life style. Harper never blinked when using some of the most obscene words or expressions; he could tell the dirtiest jokes; he could out drink most men twice his size and it was well known that he associated with some of the "loosest" women in Londonderry.

Yet he would not elaborate on the difficulties of Riley and when he said his heart broke every time someone was killed, the look on his face and in his eyes told Marsh he was speaking the truth.

The man was a contradiction. Marsh attempted to analyze Harper by taking each of his attributes and placing them in the right-hand column, then listing each of his undesirable traits in the left-hand column.

As Marsh's unscientific analysis of Harper continued, he remembered what others told him about the man. They said Harper was the epitome of a great reporter.

During his brief association with him, Marsh found this to be true. He could find out the "dirt" about anyone. He seemed to enjoy the hunt more than the kill. He would find the dirt, but would never divulge it.

Marsh could not think of one time when Harper reported anything derogatory about an individual during his broadcasts. His main targets were the policies of the various political parties, government policies and government activities. He would criticize the actions of the Army or the police, but he never mentioned individual's name. Marsh could not remember one government official ever questioning a statement made by Harper. This indicated that Harper was broadcasting the truth.

Marsh was still playing his mental game when the red Mercedes passed the sign indicating they were entering Convoy.

Harper took his foot of the accelerator and the car gradually slowed and smoothly glided down the street. The car slowed almost to a creep before Harper pulled in next to the curb and stomped on the brake pedal. The car stopped instantly, not like his previous vehicle.

"This is our destination…the local police station."

Marsh did not see any signs indicating the building was the police station, but he knew if Harper said it was the police station, it was the police station.

Harper was out of the car and walking up the stone steps of the gray stone building as Marsh was shutting the car door. Harper waited to knock on the green door until Marsh reached the top of the stairs.

After twenty seconds they heard steel scrapping steel and a metal bolt scraping across a metal latch. The door was opened only a few inches and the person holding the door asked,

"Yes?"

"It's Melvin Harper, from Londonderry."

The door opened just enough for the young Constable to see the two men standing outside.

Again, the young officer said,

"Yes sir."

Harper didn't know whether the man was speaking to him or answering a superior on the inside.

After another twenty seconds, the door opened all the way and Harper walked into the station, followed by Marsh, but before they could go much further, the police office put out his arm and said,

"Hold it sir!"

He then turned and looked at the individual sitting at the desk behind the railing and said,

"There's another gentleman with him."

Harper looked around the young officer and saw Sergeant Fabian at the desk.

"This is Mr. Marsh, one of my associates," said Harper.

Constable Carter received a silent reply from Fabian. He lowered his arm and nodded to Harper and Marsh.

"Well, well, if it isn't Mr. Harper, our favorite commentator from across the border," said the Sergeant as he pushed up from his chair and walked to the rail.

"Good afternoon Sergeant Fabian. How are you this fine day?"

"As good as could be expected with the damp weather these last few days. Every one of my poor joints hurt."

"Sorry, but I have the same problem. Are you taking anything to relieve the pain?"

"Just aspirin," said Fabian, "but I know you didn't come down here to ask about my health. What can we do for you?"

"What's this I heard about a little excitement around here?"

"Must be a rumor I've not heard about," said Fabian, "who's spreading such stories?"

"Oh, a little bird told me about the luck of the Irish down here."

At that moment, Kerrigan, who was in the rear of the station, stood up and walked to the front.

"Is that right?" asked Kerrigan.

"Well, well now, if it isn't the famous Irish detective, Chief Superintendent Patrick T. Kerrigan. This does verify the rumor, now doesn't it? Just what would the famous Super be doing up here, away from the fair city of Dublin?"

"How are you Mel?" asked Kerrigan, sticking out his hand and ignoring Harper's previous comments.

"Fine Patrick and how are you and the family?"

"The children are growing like weeds and Mary Ellen is still as lovely as the day I met her," answered Kerrigan.

"Patrick, I'd like you to meet Joseph Marsh, our new engineer at the station."

"Happy to meet you Mr. Marsh," said Kerrigan as he extended his hand to Marsh, who took it and felt the almost vise like grip.

Marsh was certain Kerrigan cold have easily crushed every bone in his hand. The handshake was firm and with feeling.

"You can learn a great deal about a man just by the way he shakes your hand," thought Marsh. Something his father told him years ago and over time it proved to be quite true. Many relationships were determined on the initial handshake.

Before Marsh had a chance to say anything, Harper said,

"Now Joseph, here is the embodiment of a real Irishman. He has all the virtues the rest of us only wish for. Of course, you never want to cross his path or you'll regret it. Right Patrick?"

"I'm one of the most gentle creature the good Lord put on this earth."

"And you're going to have to go to confession on Saturday Patrick, for if I've ever heard an untruth, that statement was one. And with such a whopper, the good father will probably give you at least a dozen Hail Marys."

"Mel me boy, you're going to give this gentleman a grave misconception of me," said Kerrigan.

Turning to Marsh he said,

"Is this rogue showing you're the seedy side of Derry. Of course it is the only side he knows."

"He has shown me some of the most interesting spots in Londonderry," said Marsh.

"I bet," said Kerrigan.

Before Harper could add any comments, Sergeant Fabian walked up and said,

"Can we offer you gentlemen some tea?"

"I'd appreciate a good cup of tea sir," said Marsh.

"It'll be ready in a few minutes," said Fabian as he walked to the rear of the station.

"Now Mel darling, just what are you doing here in the Republic?" asked Kerrigan.

"I heard a rumor about a couple of Provos being picked up near the border and being transferred to the Convoy station. We came down to see if the rumor was true or just a rumor. Is it true?"

Looking at Marsh, Kerrigan said,

"I just wish I had the informants this man has working for him. I wouldn't have to leave my desk to solve 99% of my cases."

Marsh didn't know what the say, so he smiled and nodded his head.

"Well?" asked Harper.

"Your informant was partially right, but first, what I'm about to tell you is not for publication at the moment, understand?"

"Come on Patrick, I'm a reporter, remember?"

"That I know Mel and if you don't agree, good day to you and I'm pleased to have met you Mr. Marsh," said Kerrigan as he looked directly at Harper.

The room was silent for a full fifty seconds, then Harper said,

"Understood!"

"Thank you Mel. Now, the lads up here picked up two Provos and guess who they are? McCaul and O'Connor."

The room was again silent for a few moments.

Kerrigan and Marsh both saw the surprised look on Harper's face, which he attempted to conceal.

"They haven't been heard of for years."

"I know," said Kerrigan.

"Have they been in the Republic all this time?" asked Harper.

"No, not according to O'Connor. We heard the group dispersed after the break out, some going to England, some to America, some to the Middle East. It surprised us when they were picked up."

"How did you get them?"

"Luck! The Garda put up a routine border check of cars coming out of Ulster. The people in the Republic do a lot of shopping in the North, so occasionally the tax people checked all the cars coming into the Republic. They had a nice roadblock, so our people thought it might be a good idea to check cars going the other way. That's how the two were caught," said Kerrigan.

Harper looked over at Marsh, then back at Kerrigan. He started to say something, but Kerrigan answered his question before he had a chance to ask it.

"You can see our prize in a few minutes."

Fabian walked up to the three and said,

"The tea is ready."

Looking at Kerrigan, he asked,

"Would you like it here or in the back?"

"How about here Sergeant," answered Kerrigan, looking over at the table in the front area of the station. The table usually contained outdated magazines and newspapers which had been cleared off yesterday.

"I'll get the chairs and..." said Fabian.

"No, you get the tea, we'll get the chairs," said Kerrigan, indicating the chairs which lined the wall of the station.

Fabian nodded, turned and walked to the back. Kerrigan and the other two moved four chairs to the table just as Fabian returned with a tray containing a large pot of tea, cups, milk, sugar, spoons and napkins. He placed the tray on the table, picked up the tea pot and poured one cup and handed it to Marsh. He looked at Kerrigan and Harper. Kerrigan nodded his head to indicate he would also like a cup, but Harper shook his head. If it didn't have something strong in it, he didn't want it.

"Are you going to let the information out?" asked Harper.

"Hell, it's already out. You found out about it, didn't you?"

"Well yes, but..."

"We're going to let it be known we picked up a couple of Provos, but we're not going to tell people who they are, not yet."

"That won't work Patrick and you know it."

"Oh yes it will. We pick up a couple of suspected Provos every couple of months. Most of them are not really IRA, just people who talk like they are. You know the type."

Harper nodded and said,

"I think I will have a cup of tea."

Fabian reached for the pot and started to pour but stopped when Kerrigan held his hand over the cup.

"Just a minute," said Kerrigan as he reached in his coat pocket and removed a quarter liter bottle of Irish whiskey.

"Perhaps we'd better fortify it with this."

Harper smiled, nodded his head and said,

"I'm grateful Patrick."

"You can return the courtesy the next time I'm up in Derry."

"I'll be more than happy to do so."

Harper looked up at Fabian, nodded and watched him pour the hot tea into his cup. When the cup was three quarters full he made a motion with his right hand to indicate enough tea was in his cup.

"Now we don't want to completely ruin the taste of good Irish whiskey, do we?" he asked.

Once the pot was pulled back, Kerrigan unscrewed the top of the whiskey bottle and handed it to Harper, who smiled, took the bottle and filled the cup. He handed the bottle back to Kerrigan, picked up a spoon, stirred the mixture, took a drink, smiled and set the cup on the table.

"You are a true friend Patrick," said Harper.

"Always be nice to the press is my philosophy Mel, always be nice to the press."

"And they will always be nice to you?"

"Exactly."

"Now Patrick, you wouldn't be trying to fill the room with some of that famous Irish Blarney, would you?"

With a hurt look on his face, Kerrigan said,

"Mel Harper, you wound me deeply. You know I've always been right up front with you, in fact…"

"In fact you have, particularly when you wanted something," said Harper as he took another drink of his fortified tea.

"You know this could be a big story in Ulster, a really big story."

"I know."

"You're doing this to punish me, right?" asked Harper.

"Mel, all that whiskey has pickled your brain. You found out something happened down here, but you didn't know what it was or how big it could be, right? All I'm asking is you keep it quiet for a day or two until we have a chance to check out what the lads told us. As soon as we've checked their story, I'll let you know and you can have your headlines. Agreed?"

Harper smiled, finished his tea, wiped his mouth and said,

"Agreed."

"That's better."

Turning to Marsh, Kerrigan said,

"This agreement includes you, you do understand that don't you?"

"I'm not a reporter, I'm just an engineer at the station."

"Just don't say anything to anyone at the station. If someone else finds out, your friend will lose out on a good story."

"I understand," said Marsh.

"Good," said Kerrigan.

"Are you going to let the RUC have them after you're finished talking with them?" asked Harper.

"Probably. It will depend on what the Attorney General decides."

Harper nodded.

"After checking their car, the boys didn't find any weapons, explosives or anything illegal."

"A little different than in the 70's."

"You're right," said Kerrigan.

"Just remembering the old days."

"I remember them," said Kerrigan.

Harper reached for the pot, poured himself a quarter cup of tea, swirled it around, finished it in one swallow and said,

"I'm ready when you are."

Kerrigan nodded, looked over at Marsh, who interpreted the look to mean...."are you finished?"

Marsh had to take two drinks from his cup to finish the tea. The second one caused him to choke.

After fifteen seconds of coughing, two pats on the back from Harper, Marsh stopped coughing. He then used the paper napkin to wipe the tears from his eyes.

"Sorry."

"I'm sorry," said Kerrigan, "I shouldn't have rushed you."

"I should have warned you to dilute the tea with a little Irish whiskey," said Harper with a smile.

"Perhaps you're right."

"Are you alright now?" asked Kerrigan.

"I'm fine."

"Good, let's go see our guest."

"Your guest? I thought you said he had two?" asked Harper.

"You're right, but you will only get to see one," said Kerrigan.

Harper looked directly at Kerrigan, but didn't say a word.

Kerrigan pushed up from his chair and headed towards the rear of the building, followed by Harper and Marsh.

Sergeant Fabian remained in the front.

In the rear, Marsh and Harper saw for the first time the cells, which could not be seen from the front because of the brick partition which provided the right wall of the first cell.

As the trio approached the rear, the individual in the cell, who was sitting at the small table, turned and looked at the three. He stood up and walked as far as he could, being stopped by the iron bars of the cell.

Looking at the man in the cell and without turning towards Harper and Marsh, Kerrigan said,

"You have a couple of visitors from the North."

Nodding towards Harper, Kerrigan said

"This gentleman is the famous journalist, Melvin Harper and his associate Joseph Marsh."

A few moments of uneasy silence followed as the prisoner looked at Harper and Marsh, while Kerrigan stood back, observed O'Connor's facial expression. Kerrigan was looking for some sign of recognition, but O'Connor's face remained expressionless, only a blank stare, interrupted by a nod of the head.

"Can we ask a few questions?" asked Harper.

O'Connor looked at Kerrigan for a split second, then at Harper and again nodded.

"Do you mind if I sit down?" asked O'Connor.

"No," said both Harper and Kerrigan.

O'Connor turned around, picked up one of the two chairs in the cell and moved it so it faced the trio, then took a seat.

"Can I ask you your name?"

O'Connor smiled and said,

"I'm Thomas O'Connor."

Harper smiled and said,

"I know. It's been a long time Mr. O'Connor, you probably don't remember me, do you?"

"No."

"I covered your trial in Belfast and interviewed you right after you and Mr. McCaul were sentenced."

"A lot of people interviewed us, before, during and after the trial," said O'Connor.

"I know," said Harper.

After a silence of approximately twenty seconds, Harper asked,

"Where's McCaul?"

O'Connor looked at Kerrigan, then back at Harper, but before he could answer, Kerrigan said,

"Mr. McCaul is sick with the flu or croup, so we moved him to a hospital in Dublin."

Harper looked over at Kerrigan who was slowly shaking his head, indicating to Harper there should be no more question about McCaul.

Harper nodded, turned to O'Connor and asked,

"Can I ask where you've been for the last few years?"

"Before you start your questioning, perhaps we should try and make it a little more comfortable," said Kerrigan, motioning with his head towards the table and chairs.

"Let's move the table and chairs over here, right in front of the cell," said Kerrigan.

Harper nodded, turned and walked over to the table, followed by Marsh. The two moved to the opposite ends of the table, lifting it up and immediately dropped it.

"Damn, what's this thing made out of, lead?" asked Harper.

Kerrigan laughed and said,

"Good Irish oak. Here, let me get hold of it. You grab the chairs."

Harper moved out of the way so Kerrigan could reach the end of the table he dropped.

"You knew that damn thing weighed a ton, didn't you?" asked Harper.

Kerrigan laughed and said,

"Not really Mel, but I did know it probably weighted more than you."

Kerrigan and Marsh picked the table up and moved it to the front of O'Connor's cell, placing it lengthwise against the bars.

In the meantime, Harper picked up a chair and waited until the table was moved, then placed it so the individual sitting in it would be facing O'Connor. Without waiting for the other two, he occupied the prime space.

Kerrigan and Marsh each picked up a chair and placed them on opposite sides of Harper.

"Can we start asking questions now?" asked Harper.

Kerrigan nodded, folded his arms and leaned back in the chair, making it groan as he put his weight against the back.

"As I asked before...before being interrupted, where have you been for the last few years?" asked Harper.

"In Australia, most of the time."

"Since the break out?"

"No, after the break out, Ron and I stayed in Belfast for about eleven weeks, then to England, Liverpool for three weeks or so, then to Australia."

"You were in Belfast for almost three months after the break out?"

"Right, until the middle of September."

"Where?"

"In an apartment a couple of doors from the Constabulary Station on Donegal Street, right across the street from the UDR(Ulster Defense Regiment) sub-station."

"No?"

"God's truth," said O'Connor.

"You stayed in hiding in an apartment a couple of doors from a RUC station?"

"No, not in hiding. Both of us had jobs. I went to work every morning and some times for a walk in the evening. Got to know some of the lads at the station enough to nod to them in the morning or evening when I came home from work."

"You're kidding me, aren't you?"

"No sir, you can ask Ron."

Harper shook his head, Kerrigan laughed and Marsh didn't know whether to try and look serious or laugh, so he looked up at the ceiling in an attempt to retain a noncommittal look on his face. He failed.

Looking at Kerrigan, Harper said,

"You're sure I can't broadcast this tonight?"

Laughing, Kerrigan said,

"Remember our agreement."

Looking back at O'Connor, Harper asked,

"Do you remember the address on Donegal Street?"

"No, but the apartment was directly across the street from the UDR station. They put their station there so the boys could run across the street and take a pee in the RUC station. On the other side of the street was the boundary for the Security Area."

Kerrigan laughed louder and was joined by Marsh.

"As soon as these two laughing hyenas stop laughing, I'll get on with my questions," said Harper.

Finally Kerrigan stopped laughing, pushed his chair back and stood up.

"Good," said Harper, "now we can continued. No one recognized you?"

"No sir."

"There's an old axiom, it's easier to hide in plain sight," said O'Connor.

"Why did you stay so long in Belfast? You know everyone was looking for you. Your pictures were on the telly and in the newspapers. Didn't anyone asked any questions?"

"No sir."

"What did you do during the eleven weeks?"

"I worked as a stone mason. I worked on the Army barracks in Lilburn."

"You worked at the Army base in Lilburn?"

"Yes sir."

"And McCaul?"

"Ron had an evening position at the library. He worked from four until closing, which was usually around mid-night. When he told them he was leaving, they threw a party for him and invited two of the councilmen, who attended the party."

"You're making this up, right?"

"No sir."

"Where was the party?"

"At the library."

"That's unbelievable."

"God's truth Mr. Harper, God's truth."

All Harper could do was to shake his head.

"The entire country was looking for the two of you and you stayed in the middle of Belfast in plain sight. Unbelievable. After you left Belfast, you said you went to England, right?"

"To Liverpool?"

"Yes."

"Why Liverpool?"

O'Connor looked up at Kerrigan, back at Harper, smiled and said,

"It's a good place to sail out of."

He knew Kerrigan would love for him to tell Harper about his connections in Liverpool. Kerrigan knew Liverpool, with it's large Irish population, was the source of money, arms and personnel for the Provos.

"You stayed there for three weeks….why so long?"

"We were waiting for a ship to Australia. The one we were suppose to get on took off a couple of days early. We didn't know it until we arrived in Liverpool, so we were forced to wait around for the next one."

"OK, you stayed in Liverpool for three weeks."

"Not a full three weeks, we were in Liverpool a little over a fortnight, sixteen days to be exact."

"Fine, sixteen days in Liverpool, then on a ship to Australia?"

"Yes sir."

"Now, you have been out of prison for, let's see, almost six years," said Harper.

"Five years, nine months and sixteen days," said O'Connor.

"Five years, nine months and sixteen days," repeated Harper, "which means you were in Australia for, let's see, for about five years, five months and a few days, is that correct?"

"Not quite."

"No?"

"No, we left Australia the latter part of May and we were on our way here for almost three weeks. We arrived in Dublin on Tuesday, the 17th."

"It didn't take you three weeks to fly from Australia to Ireland. Why so long?"

"We flew from Australia to Taipei. There we boarded a ship, which took us from there to main land China and then to Nicaragua. We stayed in Nicaragua for two days, caught a plane to the states, then to Ireland."

"What ship were you on?"

"The Golden God."

"It wasn't coming to Ireland?"

"It was, but Ron got sick and wanted to get home."

"Why didn't you fly into Belfast or London?"

"We were informed the police still have wanted posters on us at both airports and we'd never made it through customs."

"And Dublin?" asked Harper.

"We came in with an American tour group. Customs didn't bother the Americans or us."

Harper looked over at Kerrigan, who just shrugged his shoulders.

"Where have you been since the seventeenth?"

O'Connor looked at Kerrigan and smiled.

"All right, you have been in the Republic since the seventeenth. Why were you going to Ulster?"

O'Connor looked away for a moment, turned back and looked at Harper.

"Ron said he wanted to go home. He wanted to go back to his home in Wales."

"So why didn't you catch a flight from Dublin to Wales?"

"Ron was too sick. He could hardly sit up for ten minutes at a time. It was impossible for us to fly, so I made arrangements for a boat to take us from Ballycastle to Scotland, where I had a car waiting to take Ron to Wales, but...."

"But your luck ran out," said Kerrigan.

"That it did," said O'Connor.

Harper detected no animosity in either his tone of voice or his expression. One could almost feel sorry for him.

"Just how long has McCaul been sick?" asked Harper."

O'Connor closed his right eye, turned his head to the right and looked at the wall of the cell.

"A little over a week, maybe ten days. He started getting sick a week ago, the day before yesterday. On Friday, the Golden God was leaving Nicaragua, but Ron said he didn't want to take the ship.

"So why didn't you fly from Nicaragua to Ireland?"

"Simple, no flights from Nicaragua go directly to Dublin, besides, we needed to be in a group of tourists. It's simple to get lost in a tour group. The Americans are always coming to Ireland, so we flew to New York and I inquired about when the next tour group was flying to Ireland. It worked."

"So you joined this tour group?"

"Well, I guess you could say that. Half the plane was this special group of Professors who were interested in medieval architecture. They were going to tour some of the famous ruins in Ireland.

One of the gentlemen proposed going to Tara to see if it could be resurrected from the bog. Another was interested in the story about the Ark of the Covenant being buried at Tara. I'll have to say, they were a very interesting group."

"And you joined them?" asked Harper.

"In a matter of speaking."

"We had no trouble mixing in with the group as we departed the plane. Two of them even helped me with Ron. He could hardly stand up straight. That's probably why we got through customs so fast, the Custom officials didn't want to have a sick person on their hands."

"And from Dublin?" asked Harper.

"As I said before, I rented a car and started out for Ballycastle."

Twenty seconds of silence followed during which Harper looked at Kerrigan and asked,

"You've had them since Wednesday?"

Kerrigan nodded.

Turning back to O'Connor, Harper asked,

"What did you do in Australia, for....five years, five months and so many days?"

"I worked as a Master Mason for a firm in Perth, building schools."

"And McCaul?"

"He taught History at the College in Perth."

Harper looked at his notes for a few moments, then asked,

"Why did you come back?"

"O'Connor smiled and shook his head. His smile changed to a smirk and he said,

"We just got home sick."

"Bull shit!!" said Kerrigan.

This made O'Connor smile.

"Patrick, such language," said Harper.

"You've never heard it before?"

"Only from you," answered Harper.

"Bull shit," repeated Kerrigan.

"Now Patrick, let me get on with my interview without crude interruptions."

"Sorry for the interruption, but I'd really like to know the reason for the return," said Kerrigan.

"I told you," said O'Connor, "we got homesick."

Before Kerrigan could utter his mild, but crude comment, Harper asked,

"Really Mr. O'Connor, what was the reason for your return?"

"The truth?"

"Certainly."

"I have no idea. The Army Council sent word for us to return to Ireland as soon as possible. They gave no reason."

"No other orders or instructions?"

"No sir. We were told to pack our bags and stand by. Within a week we received travel orders, with tickets to fly to Taipei and to board the Golden God, whose destiny was Ireland."

"Then you really don't know the reason? Do you have any idea why they ordered you to return to Ireland?"

"I can only make a guess. Two possible reasons. The first is the indiscriminate killing of Catholics. As you probably know, more Catholics who have nothing to do with the Provos, politics or any Nationalist organization are being killed by the Protestants.

Some say there is a conspiracy or collusion between the Constabulary, the Army and some of the Loyalist terrorists groups. The word is the killings are being planned by a group of Loyalist politicians and businessmen. Interesting, wouldn't you say?"

"I've heard the accusations," said Harper.

"The second possible reason, plans are being made now in case the peace talks don't hold. It's possible that if things don't work out the way the Provos want, then..."

"Then you two would be here to raise holy hell!" said Kerrigan.

Again O'Connor smiled, shrugged his shoulders, looked over at Kerrigan and said,

"You know the British...they don't understand anything but force. It's the method they used to build their empire and it's the only method they understand, God help them."

Kerrigan nodded his head in agreement.

"But you were headed for Ballycastle when you were picked up, why?"

"As I told you, to get Ron home."

"After that?"

"I was going to contact the Council."

"And?" said Kerrigan.

"I really don't know. It would be up to the Council."

As Harper and Kerrigan thought about O'Connor's answer, the room became silent. Neither believed his story completely. They believed the Army Council ordered the two to return to Ireland, but not without telling them the reason.

Yet, O'Connor's two possible reasons for their return could be true, particularly the latter one.

"No more questions? Could I offer you gentlemen some tea? I have some in the pot" said O'Connor.

"No thank you," said Harper.

Looking at Kerrigan and Marsh, O'Connor asked,

"Would you gentlemen care for some tea?"

Both shook their heads to indicate a negative reply.

"If you don't mind, I'll get myself a cup."

"Please do," said Harper.

O'Connor stood up, turned and walked back to the table on which a enamel pot sat on a small electric burner. While he poured himself a cup of tea, Harper turned to Kerrigan and asked,

"How much time do I have Patrick?"

Kerrigan looked at his watch, then said,

"How about an hour. That should give you more than enough time."

"Excellent. Thank you."

"You're welcomed, just remember the conditions."

"I'll remember."

Upon his return to his chair, O'Connor asked,

"Do you mind if I put my cup on your table?"

Harper looked over at Kerrigan, who nodded and said,

"Go ahead."

O'Connor placed his cup of tea on the table on the other side of the bars, then leaned back in his chair and said,

"All right Mr. Harper, you have a whole hour to find out as much as possible about the terrible Thomas O'Connor."

"That's not very long, particularly with all the questions I have for you."

"Then I'd only ask the important ones."

"I will," said Harper, "and the first one I would like to ask is do you know some of the men who escaped with you have been arrested?"

"Yes, I know. But four of them are still at large. Isn't that correct Chief Superintendent Kerrigan?"

"That's correct," answered Kerrigan.

"Did any of then go to Australia with you?" asked Harper.

"No."

"Then they're still here in Ireland?"

"I didn't say that. I said none of them went to Australia with Ron and I."

"Do you know where the other four are?"

"I have no idea."

"You haven't been in contact with any of them since the break out?"

"That's correct. Once we were out of that hell hole, we split up. Ron and I stayed in Belfast and I had no idea where the others went. I didn't ask and I didn't want to know."

"Then you and McCaul had nothing to do with the robberies right after the break out?"

"Correct again. We were instructed to stay put until we received orders. We did exactly what we were told to do. Then we received orders to go the Liverpool and catch a ship to Australia."

"That's the reason the boys almost got caught in Tralee. The planning was very bad and the execution of the plan was worse. We almost netted them all," said Kerrigan.

O'Connor looked from Kerrigan to Harper with a questioning look on his face.

"You didn't know about the robbery in Tralee?" asked Harper.

"We heard about the robbery, but we didn't know who was involved. We heard about Phillips and Vickers being picked up in Ulster last month. I have no idea about Chastain and Mayberry?"

"You have no idea where Mayberry and Chastain are at the present time?"

"No."

"OK, let's change the subject. While in Australia...."

"While in Australia I did nothing but honest work. When we arrived in Perth, arrangements were already made for us to go to work."

"How did they arrange work for you as Irish immigrants?"

"We weren't Irish immigrants, we were provided with papers proving we were born and raised in Australia."

"Under what name or names?"

"My name was Thomas Yearwood and Ron's new name was Donald Majors."

"Amazing," said Harper, "amazing."

After a thirty second break, Harper continued,

"When you received orders to return, why aboard ship and not by air, at least to some country in Europe?"

"I really don't know. We were scheduled to fly out in late May, but then word came that we were to go to Taipei and catch a ship which would be going to Ireland. Again, all the arrangements were made for us."

"By whom?" asked Harper.

"I really don't know. Our contact was a man by the name of Jack Newman. We were instructed to met him in an Irish pub in Perth upon our arrival."

"Did he furnish you with your documents?"

"You mean the ones indicating we were Australians?"

"Yes."

"No, that was done in Liverpool. We boarded the ship with Australian passports. Upon arriving in Perth we went to the pub and met Mr. Newman. He made the arrangements for our apartment and for our employment."

"How often did you met with Mr. Newman?"

"Three times."

"Just three times?" asked Harper.

"Yes. Once upon arrival in Australia and twice before we departed. I received a letter in the mail instructing us to met him at the Pub and when we got there, he gave us our orders from the Army Council to return to Ireland. He gave us airline tickets to fly to Paris and instructed us to catch a ship from LaHarve to England and then to Ireland.

Ten days before we were scheduled to leave, I received another letter to met Mr. Newman. When we arrived at the pub, we were informed our schedule had been changed and we were given our new travel schedule and documents which included tickets to fly to Taipei and tickets for the ocean voyage on the Golden God, plus a good amount of travel money."

"Those three times were the only times you had any contact with the organization or Newman?"

"Yes sir."

"No other contact with the Provos or IRA?"

"No sir."

"All right, would you continue about your journey?"

"We flew to Taipei, boarded the ship, the Golden God, which had been loaded with agricultural machinery made in Taipei. On the 4th of June the ship sailed for Fuzhou, China where it picked up some plants and a group of Chinese botanists. We then crossed the Pacific, through the Panama Canal and up the coast to Nicaragua."

"Was it passenger ship?" asked Harper.

"Far from it. It was an old freighter. She must have been forty years old. The Captain was a Swede who was getting ready to retire. This was to be his last voyage. He told us he was taking the ship in for refitting. That was the reason it was headed for Ireland."

"You said it had agricultural machinery, where was it stored?"

"In the hole."

"Then where were the plants stored?"

"On the forward deck. There were two giant containers and a trailer on the deck. The containers were full of tropical plants and the trailer housed the Chinese botanists."

"What kind of plants?"

"I have no idea, just plants."

"Didn't you look at them?"

"No, none of the ship's crew or passengers was allowed near the trailers. The area was roped off and signs all over the place saying the area was Off Limits."

"Were other passengers aboard besides you and McCaul?"

"Yes, an American and his wife."

"Didn't you talk to them?"

"Only at meal time. They stayed to themselves, said they were on their honeymoon."

"Do you remember their names?"

"Their name was Fowler, Andy Fowler and her name was Sarah."

"Did Fowler say what kind of business he was in or anything about himself?"

"No, even at meal time, neither of them talked very much. They were polite, but they never volunteered any information about themselves. Not the typical Americans."

Another short break, then Harper continued.

"You said you left the ship in Nicaragua. Why did the ship stop in Nicaragua?"

"That's where they unloaded the farm machinery."

"Did the Fowlers remain aboard?"

"No, they left the ship right after Ron and I left."

"I see," said Harper.

"When Ron came down sick, we decided to get back to Ireland as soon as possible. It took me a full day to make arrangements to fly out of Nicaragua."

A few moments later, Harper finished writing in his little black notebook.

RUC Headquarters
Belfast, Northern Ireland

After the departure of Harper and Marsh, Kerrigan called his old friend, Chief Superintendent Douglas Rothchild of the Royal Ulster Constabulary, and asked him to join him in Killygordon for dinner.

"I realize it's a far piece for you to travel Douglas, but Mary Ellen made some of her delicious tarts. In fact there are two special one I know you'll especially like.

Immediately two questions entered Rothchild's mind. First, what was Kerrigan doing in Killygordon? That was a great distance from Dublin. The second question was when did Mary Ellen learn to bake?

He had never known Mary Ellen Kerrigan to bake. She was an excellent cook, but as far as he knew, she never in her life baked a cake, pie, loaf of bread or a tart, at least that was what Kerrigan told him at least a dozen times. Her mother, who lived with the family, did all the baking.

He didn't know exactly who Kerrigan was talking about, but he knew "two special ones" were probably two individuals on their wanted list and Kerrigan had them in Killygordon.

After supplying the answers to his two question, he smiled to himself, a sort of *"congratulations you clever one,"* for he understood Kerrigan's request.

"It's almost two o'clock Patrick. I still have a few papers to get out. I won't make it for tea, but I'll be happy for you to buy my dinner, then we can sample Mary Ellen's tarts for dessert."

"That sounds fine Douglas, I'll be at my cousin's house."

Rothchild understood the last message without thinking about it. His cousin's house indicated Kerrigan would be at the police station in Killygordon.

Ten Days in July

As he hung up the phone, Rothchild looked down the hall at the office where Captain Lamb, the exchange Army officer from Australia, was sitting at his desk reading a report. Ever since their return from Rathfriland, where they attended the funeral of one of the officers killed in the explosion of two Constabulary cars, Lamb had been going through reports.

As Rothchild continued to look at Lamb's closet size office, his mind's focal point vaulted from Kerrigan's telephone call to the reports he should finish reviewing and sign, back to Lamb and the reason he was in Northern Ireland.

The three subjects rotated around his brain like a spinning top. Even as he attempted to concentrate on one subject, the three continued to revolve and he was unable to focus on any one of them.

He finally closed his eyes for a few seconds. That was enough to clear out the confusion. His mind made the decision to think about Lamb.

He continued to look down the hall, perhaps that was what primed his thoughts.

"Now, what in the hell was I thinking about Lamb? Oh yes, why would they send him over here?"

He looked up at the ceiling and wondered why he had the fan going, shook his head and refocused on Lamb.

"Certainly, he's an explosive expert and they don't have many bombings in Australia. Well, they sure sent him to the right place. We have more than our share."

He looked over at the small table next to his desk stacked high with reports to be reviewed.

"That was it," he thought.

Watching Lamb read the report on his desk, making notes and picking up another report, made Rothchild feel guilty. He was unable to concentrate on the reports he needed to read. He would start reading one and within seconds his thoughts would stray, usually back to Kerrigan's telephone call. He thought for just a split second of handing Captain Lamb the stack of reports and asking him to review them. The thought made him smile.

He looked away from the table and back down the hall to the small office, just in time to see Lamb stand up and walk out with a file in his hand.

"Captain Lamb," called out Rothchild.

The young man stopped, put both feet together, made a perfect right face and walked towards Rothchild's office. He stopped on the other side of the open door.

"Yes sir?"

"I was just wondering what you're so interested in," asked the Chief Superintendent.

"I've been going through the files of all deaths of RUC personnel caused by explosions during the last five years."

Rothchild's curiosity was satisfied with a very plausible answer. His interest in Lamb vanished as quickly as it entered his thoughts. Now only two subjects were on the spinning wheel. He was trying to make up his mind on which one to concentrate.

"Is that all sir?" asked Lamb.

The question surprised Rothchild, for he had dismissed Lamb from his thoughts seconds ago, which meant Lamb should have physically disappeared.

"Yes, that's all. Keep up the good work."

"Yes sir," said Lamb as he turned and walked back down the hall, trying to determine what the Chief Superintendent's meaning of "keep up the good work" indicated.

Rothchild was thinking the same thing.

"Why in the hell did I tell him to keep up the good work?"

Rothchild smiled, leaned over and picked up one of the folders from the small table. He looked at it, but was unable to focus on the words. He was thinking about Kerrigan.

His thoughts flashed back over the years of his association with Kerrigan. Their friendship was initiated in the latter part of the sixties, before the "Troubles" started.

Both were recently promoted Detective Sergeants investigating a robbery of a train running from Dublin to Belfast. If it had been an ordinary robbery, they would have never met. Instead of being merely a robbery, it was a robbery plus multiple homicides.

The crime became the investigative focal point of both the governments of the Republic of Ireland and of Northern Ireland. In addition to the investigative forces of the two Irelands, the British government sent in a number of people from their SIS and the Metropolitan Police.

The reason so much effort was put into the investigation of the robbery was not the theft of three and a half million pounds, but the murder of the three innocent men.

At the end of six months, no clues were uncovered to lead to an arrest, so the government representatives from the Republic, Northern Ireland and England mutually agreed to reduce the investigative effort.

In one day, the investigative force was reduced from twenty officers to two. The case was given to two young investigators, Rothchild from Northern Ireland and Kerrigan from the Republic.

The two were informed they had six months to work on the case. If it was not solved by the end of the six months, both countries would put it in their "unsolved" files.

Nine months and ten days after the robbery and murders, two of the mailbags from the robbery were discovered by a group of children in a field north of Castlerwallen. In addition to the mailbags, skeletal remains were also discovered at the site.

The day after reporting this information to their superiors, the young officers were informed Chief Inspector North of the Metropolitan Police, who had been in charge of the investigation from the beginning, was to take charge of the investigation.

During the next six weeks, the investigative team headed by North, found nothing more to help solve the robbery and murders.

Only three bank notes were recovered and these were not from the currency shipment, but from a Grandmother to her three Grandchildren in Birmingham.

Rothchild and Kerrigan were informed the skeletal remains was sent to Scotland Yard, but no match was made to any known missing individual in Northern Ireland, the Republic or England, including Wales and Scotland.

On the 7th of October, just one day short of the anniversary of the robbery, North announced the investigation in the area of Castlewallen was concluded and all the investigators were to return to their respective Organizations.

"Does this include Detective Kerrigan and myself?" asked Rothchild.

"If I remember correctly, you two were given six months. According to my calculations, the six months will be up tonight at midnight. Is that correct?"

Rothchild looked at Kerrigan who shook his head and shrugged his shoulders. He turned back to face North and said,

"Yes sir, that's correct."

The next morning Kerrigan and Rothchild bid each other farewell and returned to Dublin and Belfast respectively.

On the 18th of October, Kerrigan received from Chief Inspector North copies of all the interviews conducted by the various officers. In addition he received a list of all the letters, bulletins, notices, bills and announcements found in the site discovered by the children.

Six weeks later, both Kerrigan and Rothchild were informed the case was considered closed by all the investigating agencies. They were instructed to prepare a final report and send it, along with all their records, to North.

Both dutifully followed the instructions, sending their final reports along with their original reports to North, but retaining copies of every piece of paper in their personal files. Neither was satisfied the case was concluded, even though they could see the reason for shelving the investigation. All the leads had come to a dead end.

Within two months after the termination of the investigation, Kerrigan and Rothchild were involved in other investigations.

Gradually the robbery became only a passing thought as the days, weeks and months passed and the history of Ireland made headline news in every newspaper from London, to New York, to Tokyo, to Moscow and Paris. The year was 1970.

Highway A40
Between Convoy and
Londonderry

On the return trip to Londonderry, Harper told Marsh the story of McCaul and O'Connor, explaining that most was probably true, but at least a quarter of it was fiction, embellished by either admirers or enemies of the two.

According to the most popular story about the two, their friendship was formed instantaneously at their first meeting, even though their character, education and background were totally different.

O'Connor was large and muscular with shoulders so broad he found it almost impossible to obtain a shirt or jacket to fit. Although he was large of frame, he was not tall. He was only five feet and nine inches tall. His face was broad and his blond hair was coarse and closely cropped. If he had been born forty years earlier in a country across the English Channel, he could have been the model for Hitler's Aryan race.

Even though he was extremely strong, he was extremely gentle. He was big enough and strong enough that he was never called on to defend himself from any of the boys or men in the neighborhood.

His speech, as well as his knowledge and instincts were the products of the Belfast slums. He survived without help from anyone.

Between the ages of twelve and fourteen, he survived by doing odd jobs in the neighborhood, but mostly by stealing food, snatching cloths from unattended cloths lines and sleeping in abandon buildings.

From the age of fourteen on, he earned his living with bricks and mortar. First as a day laborer, cleaning old bricks for re-use, then as an assistant to an apprentice, and then from an apprentice to a bricklayer and finally to a master mason.

Over the years he continued to be employed while others were forced to go on the dole. One reason for his continued employment was he never made any type of political commitment. Although he was raised in a mixed neighborhood, where both Catholics and Protestants lived in poverty, the only religion he knew was the religion of the street. Even though he was raised Catholic, he was neither Catholic nor Protestant.

The last time he was inside a church was when he was twelve. He remembered the day vividly. That particular Sunday was the same day he last saw his family, his large, alcoholic mother, who was too drunk to attend church, his father, the man from whom O'Connor inherited his gentle nature and his two younger sibling, a brother named Timothy, age nine and a girl named Rose, who was just seven.

The family was packed and ready to depart for America, to live in a place called Chicago. His Uncle Ralph was settled in one of the suburbs of Chicago and according to his last letter, he was the proud owner of a small bakery. He wanted his brother, O'Connor's father, who was an unemployed baker, to come to America to help him in his business.

Uncle Ralph sent the money for the plane tickets and told his brother to sell all their furniture and pack only their cloths. A furnished apartment over the bakery was awaiting them.

Arrangement were made for his mother's sister and her family to move into their apartment upon their departure. For months his aunt and her family had been searching for a 3 bedroom apartment. With the departure of the O'Connor family, their apartment would be available.

A month before the family's departure date, Thomas decided he would not join the family in their migration to America. He did not inform either of his parents of his intent to remain in Ireland, but acted as if he would make the journey with them.

During the week prior to their departure, his mother, between binges of drinking, methodically went through the children's dressers and picked out the cloths to be taken to America.

Since they were leaving on a Sunday afternoon, they would wear their Sunday clothes to church and then wear them on their trip to the United States.

Each of the children was given one small suitcase in which to pack their cloths. During the process of selecting the clothes to go in each suitcase, his mother set aside most of the boys' clothes and a number of his sister's dresses, plus all her toys. These were to be left for his aunt's family.

His sister held back her tears as she watched her mother toss her favorite dress and all of her toys into the corner. She knew better than to complain or even to comment about her mother's selection. It could mean a slap across the mouth or a night without supper. Likewise, Timothy, his younger brother watched in silence.

The Saturday night before the scheduled departure, Thomas unpacked his suitcase and placed his sister's favorite dress, along with two other dresses he knew she liked and as many of her stuffed toys as would fit into his suit case. He put the clothes his mother selected for him, along with most of his clothes she put in the corner for his aunt's family, in a cotton tote bag and placed it in the janitor's closet in the hallway.

Sunday, after church, the family was subjected to the tearful goodbyes and well wishing, spiced with envy, by family and friends. The O'Connor family was then driven to the airport by a neighbor, who dropped them off at the entrance.

Ten minutes before boarding their plane, Thomas said he had to go to the bathroom.

"Why didn't you go a while ago like your brother? " asked his mother, who was 90 percent sober, the results of staying away from the bottle and drinking hot, black coffee while the rest of the family attended church.

"I didn't have to go then."

"Well, hurry up about it."

"Yes, ma'am."

His father followed him to the restroom. When they entered the private sanctuary of the gentlemen's restroom, his father put his hand on his shoulder. Both stopped and Thomas turned and looked up at his father.

"Yes sir?"

"You're not going with us, are you?"

The question caught Thomas by complete surprise. He was close to tears, but held them back with all the will power of a 12 year old.

"No sir."

"I didn't think so. Are you going to be all right? There's no one here except you Aunt Amy and her family."

"I'll be all right."

His father stuck out his hand. Thomas took his father's hand, who shook it for what seemed to him a very long time. His father pulled him towards himself and hugged him tight for a few moments, backed off and took an envelope out of his pocket and handed it to him.

"Take this, it will help."

"Yes sir."

Thomas took the envelope and stuck it in his coat pocket.

"Stay in here for the next half hour, get in one of the stalls and stay there. Understand?"

"Yes sir."

Thomas watched his father turn and walk out of the room.

After he was certain the airplane his family boarded had departed, he took the envelope out of his coat pocket and opened it. It contained two handwritten notes and 23 ten pound notes, his father's meager savings. One note was his Uncle Ralph's address and telephone number in Chicago. The other note was a mere two sentences, which read, "Take care Thomas and remember I love you. God bless you. Your father."

He placed the note and the money in his wallet along with his savings of 13 pounds. Twelve years later, the notes from his father were still in his leather wallet.

Three weeks before his 24th birthday, he called his Uncle Ralph in Chicago. He learned from his Aunt Amy that his mother was dead and his father had remarried. He had married a Jewish lady from Poland who immigrated to America a few years after the O'Connor family.

From his Uncle, he learned his father opened his own bakery in a different part of town and was now the proud owner of one of the best businesses in the neighborhood. He also learned his brother recently graduated from Loyola and had accepted a fellowship to do graduate work at Notre Dame. His sister was a Junior at the University of Chicago, majoring in Sociology.

Thomas asked how his mother died and after a few moments of hesitation, his Uncle asked,

"Do you want the truth?"

"Yes sir."

He could hear his Uncle take a deep breath.

"Your mother was in, in one of her conditions and fell down the stairs and broke her neck. The doctor said she was dead before she reached the bottom of the stairs."

After almost ten seconds of silence, O'Connor asked,

"How long ago?"

"Almost seven years ago Thomas. We, your father and I attempted to locate you. He called Amy, but she said she did not know where you were and…"

"Do you have my father's address and telephone number?"

"Certainly. Just a moment, I have both the business address and their home address and telephone number."

After receiving the addresses and numbers, Thomas thanked his Uncle for the information about the family.

"Are you going to call your father?"

"I don't know."

"Your father would really like to talk to you, you know that don't you?"

"Yes sir. I know. It's just…. Would you do me a favor and tell my father and Timothy and Rose that I'm fine. You can tell them they can expect to hear from me in the near future and thank you again Uncle Ralph and thanks for taking care of the family."

"You're welcomed Thomas. It's been nice talking to you and think about calling your father."

"Yes sir."

O'Connor did not make the call to his father that day, nor did he get in contact with his family "in the near future," as he promised.

At the age of 24, Thomas O'Connor was a master mason, working his way up the ladder with skill and hard work. During working hours and after work at a pub or some social event, when asked about his religion, his answer was,

"I believe in a God who is not solely Catholic or Protestant," then in order to answer the next question before it could be asked, he would add, "neither is He solely Hebrew or Islamic."

O'Connor had absolutely no interest in politics. He told his friends and co-workers he could care less whether Northern Ireland was a part of the Republic or part of England.

He was only sixteen when "Bloody Sunday" occurred in Londonderry. He never gave it another thought because it was only one of a hundred incidents happening in Northern Ireland at the time. Shootings and bombings occurred every week. As long as they never interfered with his work, he remained unconcerned.

Five months before his 23rd birthday, O'Connor met Rosemary Mullens at a neighborhood dance. She was a tall, thin girl with long auburn hair and fair skin. Rosemary's hair reminded him of his mother's hair.

This meeting turned into a friendship, which over a period of a year turned into a romantic relationship. The only problem O'Connor had with the relationship was with Rosemary's family. All the members of her family were Nationalists. Both of her brothers were active members of the Sinn Fein political party, but swore they were not members of the Provos, even though they supported the Provos' activities when it came to the protection of the Catholic area.

Whenever O'Connor visited Rosemary, the father or one of the brothers would invariable bring up the question of politics. O'Connor could not be drawn into either a political argument or even a discussion. He would only smile and shake his head, which both frustrated and infuriated the Mullens men.

After a year of romancing Rosemary, O'Connor asked her father for permission to marry his daughter. Mr. Mullens agreed, with the provision they be married in the Church. To this O'Connor agreed and he even agreed, at Rosemary's request, to talk to the parish priest about renewing his Catholic religion.

The couple decided to marry on O'Connor's 24th birthday, the 7th of November.

O'Connor was as happy as he had ever been during his life. Once he decided to marry and settle down, he used half of his savings to buy one of the small, burned out houses not far from the Mullens' home.

During the next five months, every day after finishing his regular work, instead of spending the next couple of hours in the pub, he would rush to the shell of the house and work four to five hours. By bartering with fellow construction workers and contractors, trading his skill as a master mason for lumber, roofing material, sinks, toilets, a hot water heater and paint, the house was completely refurbished from top to bottom.

By the first of September, the house was his. He had no mortgage payments to make and by working extra hours, he made enough to purchase a used car.

He never expected to be this happy in his life time. He owned a house and a car, he was engaged to a fine young woman and in his pocket he had a contract that would keep him fully employed for the next five years.

His world collapsed two weeks before his wedding, the last week in October. On Thursday evening as the Mullens brothers returned home from a Sinn Fein meeting, they were met at their front door by three men dressed in black. No words were exchanged, only the sound of automatic rifle and pistol fire.

The youngest brother was reaching for the door latch when the first blast caught him in the right shoulder and back, knocking him against the door. This gave the older brother a split second to jump for cover behind a hedge row, which was little or no protection.

As the younger brother slumped against the door, Rosemary opened it just as the man with the automatic rifle pulled the trigger for the second time. He attempted to halt the firing, but already half a dozen rounds had struck Rosemary in the thigh and stomach. As the gunman attempted to aim the rifle up and away from her, the last two rounds hit her in the middle of her chest and head. She never knew what hit her. She was dead before her body slumped to the floor.

The shooting stopped as abruptly as it started. The three assailants stood silently, looking at the two bodies outlined by the light from the hallway.

"My God, you've killed a woman," shouted a trembling voice.

"Let's get the hell out of here," said one of the men.

Two of the men turned and started to run, but the third stood looking at the ghastly scene. His two comrades stopped, turned, ran back, grabbed him and pulled him along, down the dark street that was beginning to light up as porch lights came on.

Rosemary's older brother survived the attack.

Rosemary and her younger brother Michael were buried the following Saturday. The church was filled to overflowing at the funeral Mass. The Constabulary estimated the crowd numbered over fifteen hundred, including O'Connor.

The following Monday O'Connor, with the help of a Catholic friend, contacted a member of the Provisional IRA. Three months later he learned the names of the three gunmen who ambushed the Mullens brothers and killed his Rosemary. Within ten days of learning the names of the men, members of the UFF, along with approximately a thousand mourners, escorted three coffins to one the Loyalists' principle cemeteries.

Ronald McCaul was small and wiry, with a narrow face surrounding a thin mouth, thin nose and sunken dark eyes. The abundant mop of coal black hair surrounding his face, covering his ears and hanging down over his coat collar highlighted all of these features.

McCaul's appearance was a disguise he learned long ago to use to conceal his true personality. On first appearance one would take him for an alcoholic, a drug addict, an out of work musician, a halfwit or a combination of at least two of the proceeding personalities. He enjoyed the masquerade. He preferred giving the wrong first impression. It always gave him the upper hand in any conversation or argument.

With his ruffled hair, unshaven face and drooping eyelids over his sunken dark eyes, people automatically assumed he was not a person they wanted to either listen to and talk with.

Their surprise was always the same when he started to talk. McCaul was not only highly intelligent, but he was articulate to the point he was almost spell binding when he spoke, a trait he inherited from his father.

The voice which emerged form his body was deep and mellow. When he asked a question or made a statement, people would look around to see from where originated the voice, thinking it was impossible for it to come out of the pitiful individual standing in front of them.

McCaul's intelligence was accompanied by a brooding personality. He was an individual who wanted to right every wrong in the world and was frustrated knowing his life was too short to accomplish the mission.

The strangest fact concerning his association with the Provos was he was not even Irish, in spite of his name.

McCaul was born and raised in Newport, Wales, where his mother's family first established residence over three hundred years earlier. He and his two older sisters were raised in his mother's family home, in spite of the fact his father wanted the family to reside in Cardiff, where he was a member of the faculty. His mother triumphed as usual. The family settled in the Random house in Newport immediately after the wedding of Professor Roger McCaul and Miss Helen Random.

McCaul's father was born and raised in the out skirts of London, but migrated to Cardiff as a young history lecturer. Within a year of his arrival at Cardiff, he met and became engaged to Helen Random, the only daughter of Lord and Lady Henry Random.

Before Roger and Helen were married, Lord and Lady Random moved from Newport to their estate outside of London. As a wedding present, Helen received the Random house in Newport.

Over the years Roger worked his way up the ranks of academia to the rank of full Professor. A number of envious faculty rumored his rise in rank was greased by the influence of the Randoms. This was not true. He earned his rank through hard work and through his writings.

When Ronald was ten years old, his father was offered a research Chair in History at Queen's University in Belfast. This offer was based on his brilliant work published two years previous entitled, "The Political Parties of Ireland – Their Effect on World History."

Professor McCaul knew he was at the pinnacle of his career at Cardiff. He would never become Chairman of the Department. The present Head was only two years older than Roger and let it be known he had no intentions of moving from the position. If Roger remained, he and the Head of the Department would retire within a few months of each other.

Since no Research Chair in History was available at his present University, McCaul made the decision to accept the offer from Queen's University. He accepted the position in spite of his wife's objections and her refusal to leave Wales. All of his pleading was in vain.

She argued her obligation was to her family, her friends and her community. She would not leave the quiet civilization of Wales to journey to the strife-ridden country of Northern Ireland. She refrained from stating her real reason for refusing to leave Newport, one Dr. Arthur Morrow.

Helen was certain no one knew about her affair with Morrow. The young doctor started his private practice in Newport a few months before Ronald was born. Their affair started when Morrow substituted for her family doctor during a post birth check up.

Roger became suspicious within a few months and became certain within six months. He blamed himself for the affair. He realized he spent most of his time reading books and articles, doing research for his own writings, writings which were published and which were responsible for his rapid rise in rank. He wanted to face his wife with the facts of her relationship with Morrow a number of times, but could never gather enough courage.

After the first year, Roger never bothered about the affair. It gave him more time to work on his books and not feel guilty about spending less time with his wife. It was advantageous to both parties, or perhaps to all three parties.

One day as he sat in his office overlooking the campus, Roger came to the surprising conclusion the affair of his wife with Dr. Morrow actually made his marriage more stable. Both he and Helen were happier, she had her lover and he had more time to do research and write. One advantage of the affair was his wife never refused his bedroom advances. She was possibly afraid a refusal would bring on suspicion.

After Ronald's first birthday, the periods between the Random's marital relations grew longer and longer. Only seldom did they share the same bed.

When Roger McCaul accepted the Research Chair at Queen's, it was the first time in twenty years he went against his wife's wishes.

Belfast, the home of Queen's University, was not unfamiliar to Professor McCaul. He previously visited the area a number of times during the period he was researching material for his book. During most of his visits to Ulster, he stayed with friends who were on the faculty at the University. Usually his visits were for only a few days and the host knew they would always be welcomed at the Random house when and if they visited Wales.

Upon his permanent move to Belfast, one of his new colleagues suggested McCaul look into the possibility of obtaining a room in a boarding house run by one Mrs. Sarah Toland. McCaul was informed one apartment would soon be available at the Tolands' house. Dr. James Dumn, who presently roomed at the house, was retiring and moving to the West Coast of Ireland to be close to his son. McCaul was also informed the room would not be vacant long because the Toland house was one of the preferred boarding houses for faculty members. The rooms were large and well furnished, the food was excellent and the house was within walking distance of the University.

The Tolands' house was one of the old mansions previously owned by an English family. The previous owners had no desire to live in Ireland after the start of the "Troubles". They placed the house on the market in the early seventies, where it remained unattended and vacant for almost five years, finally selling it cheap just to get a little money out of their inherited vacation home.

The house and yard, without proper care and maintenance, quickly deteriorated to the point no one was interested in the real estates. The lack of proper maintenance was the basic reason for the low price, a price the Tolands could afford.

Mr. Toland was a retired railroad engineer who enjoyed puttering around the yard, repairing furniture, painting and the other chores he did not have time to do while working for the railroad. With his expertise in repairing and painting and his love of flowers, within a few months the house and grounds took on the beauty of former times.

In order to supplement Mr. Toland's retirement check, Mrs. Toland decided to open a boarding house for faculty members.

The Tolands, Frank and Sarah, their daughter Jamie and Mrs. Toland's sister, lived on the first floor of the house. The eight bedrooms on the second and third floors were modified into four efficiency apartments consisting of a bedroom, sitting room and WC.

McCaul obtained the vacated apartment of Dr. Dunm with the assistance of one of his fellow history professors and the unknown help of Jamie Toland.

Jamie Toland was a political science lecturer at the University. She first met Roger McCaul during one of his visits to the University during the time he was researching his book. Their first meeting was during his initial introduction to the head of the Political Science department, three years previously. Contacts during the next two years were during his visits to the University to obtain information for his book. These meetings were limited to brief greetings and hand shakes.

When the announcement was made about McCaul becoming a Research Professor, Jamie, during a casual conversation at the dinner table, stated it would be nice to have McCaul as a member of the little group. She suggested to one of the present boarders, a member of the History Department, that he let Professor McCaul know about the upcoming availability of Dr. Dumn's apartment. Within a fortnight of Dr. Dumn's departure, McCaul's personal baggage arrived at the Tolands' house.

During the first year after McCaul's move to Ireland, he traveled back to Wales each month to visit the family. During the second year, the visits were ever other month and by the third year, it was four times a year. From the fourth year on, the visits to Wales were two weeks at Christmas time and three weeks during the Summer vacation. Helen never visited him in Ireland.

During the Fall of his first year in Ireland, McCaul and Jamie became close associates, in spite of the twenty year difference in their ages. They talked about politics and history.

With the long history of Ireland and the different politics involved, they had a great deal to discuss. They stimulated each other to learn more about their respective fields.

After long walks during which extended discussions took place, each would spend every spare minute of the next few days in the library searching for answers to questions posed by the other. It was an unceasing game. Each meeting produced more questions.

If asked, neither could pinpoint when the physical attraction for the other actually commenced, but both could vividly remember when the spark turned into a flame.

It was a cold January night, two weeks after McCaul's return from his Christmas visit with his family in Wales. After their walk from the Tolands' house to the University, around the campus and back to the house, Jamie followed McCaul to his room. They were in the middle of one of their many discussions which consisted mainly of questions and answers. Jamie continued to ask questions and attempted to explain away some of McCaul's answers with answers of her own. When she was out of questions and answers, she got up and started to leave, but turned and asked,

"Would you like for me to stay?"

McCaul had wanted her for a long time, but being timid and shy with women, he had not made any advances. He knew she cared for him, but thought it was more in a teacher:student relationship. Neither showed any outside signs of affection. When she asked the question, he was caught completely by surprise.

After that January evening, many of their long walks ended with making love. After each liaison, he felt less and less guilty and his feelings for his wife dimmed along with his guilt.

From the age of eleven, Ronald McCaul was never close to either his mother or father. His mother was too interested in her social activities, her garden club, cocktail parties, his sisters and Dr. Morrow. His father was in Ireland and only spent five or six weeks each year with him. He grew up with no close family ties. His closest friend was Michael Leary, the Irish gardener who took care of his mother's flower garden and his grandfather's rose gardens.

Michael Leary had worked for the Randoms for almost forty years, being hired by Ronald's grandfather in the early 1920's. He was hired as a gardener and caretaker, but over the years he became a very close friend of Ronald's grandfather.

When Lord and Lady Random moved to London, they asked Michael to go with them, but Michael wanted to know who would take care of the rose gardens. Lord Random agreed and made it known to his daughter and son-in-law that Michael was to be retained and cared for as before.

Roger McCaul knew more about Michael than he shared with any member of his family. Mrs. McCaul was just happy to have someone care for the gardens.

Lord Random deposited a sizable amount of money in a bank account for Michael, to be used as he saw fit. The old Irishman never touched a shilling of the money. He continued to work as a gardener and caretaker for the McCauls, continued to occupy the small cottage next to the servant quarters and continued to be Ronald's friend.

Over the years Ronald listened to the folk stories of Ireland, about the feats of Cuchulain, the Hound of Ulster and about King Conchobor and the warriors of the Red Branch. In addition to the folk tales, Michael Leary told him about Cromwell's conquest of Ireland and the toll he extracted for rebellion. He told him tales about how the great landowners had the right of life and death over their tenants and how the Irish were forced from their land so it could be handed over to English soldiers, English royalty and new settlers from Scotland. He told Ronald about the great migration of the Scot Irish out of Ireland during the latter part 1700's and of the potato famine of the 1840s when over a million died of starvation and another million migrated to America, Canada, Australia and New Zealand.

He told the young lad of the Irish national heroes, such as Wolfe Tone, Robert Emmett, Daniel O'Connell and Charles Parnell. He told Ronald about the Easter Rising, about Thomas Clarke, Padraic Pearse, James Connolly and James Plunkett and how they were executed by Sir John Maxwell's firing squads.

The old man told young McCaul about the great Irish writers and poets, of Keating, Yeats, Hyde, O'Reilly, Petrie, O'Curry and O'Donovan, of Pearse and Shaw.

Because of the stories told by Michael Leary and the loan of dozens of books by the great Irish writers, young McCaul was determined to major in Irish and English literature.

He was fascinated by what the writers could do with the English language and how so many people who read the stories failed to comprehend their true meaning.

His favorite author was Reverend Jonathan Swift, whom he considered the greatest English satirist. A great many people did not understand the meaning of some of his stories, particularly a story like Gulliver's Travels. The Americans even made a cartoon movie of the story, which was changed from one of the most poignant political satires ever written to a fairly tale of the adventures of a giant in the land of small people.

If he could only learn to write like that!!!

On a Summer evening in 1984 while the McCaul family was on vacation in Spain, Michael Leary passed away. In spite of Mrs. McCaul's objections, but at the insistence of her father and mother, the family returned immediately to Newport in order to make arrangements for the funeral.

When Ronald asked the staff about Michael Leary's death, he was informed it must have been a very peaceful death because when they found him, he was in his overstuffed chair with a book of poetry in his lap. The book was opened to Keating's "Mo Bheannacht leat a Sgribhinn."

He was told the old man died with a smile on his face.

Ronald thought, *"He knew he was returning to the Ireland he loved, the Ireland he exiled himself from for over sixty years."*

Mrs. McCaul was the only one surprised by the number of people at the church. Michael Leary's funeral was attended by at least one member of almost every family in Newport. Over half the people attending the funeral were unknown to the McCauls and the Randoms.

Helen McCaul was unaware so many people knew and cared for Michael Leary.

What was the biggest surprise to the McCauls was the number of University people, along with their families, in attendance. So many people attended the funeral that the little Catholic Church was filled thirty minutes before the service started. Every pew was filled to capacity and the space in the rear and down the aisles on both sides were filled with people who wanted to pay their respects to Michael Leary.

These were the people whom the old man had helped out in different ways over the last sixty years. Some he helped with information about their gardens and flowers. Others he helped by being someone who would listen to them when they were troubled and needed someone to whom they could tell their troubles to in confidence.

The pain some of these people suffered was not the physical pain of a cut or burn, but the psychological pain of being ignored or "put down" by a spouse or parent. The pain or trouble was not so great when one could talk about it and share it with Micheal Leary. By talking to the Irish gardener, their troubles were spread out, diluted to the point where it was not an unbearable burden, diluted to the point the troubled one could handle it.

It was a known fact, only a few people in the population have the capacity of thinning out the hurt. The old man was such an individual. He would listen and agree and nod his head and continue his work, but always keeping his eyes on the person, child or adult, who was sharing their problem with him. Sometimes he would listen for hours without saying a word. His reply could be the nod of his head or shake of his head to indicate and…"is that right," or a smile when the person talking finally decided his or her troubles were not as bad as they thought. They didn't realize they had evenly divided their troubles.

The young people who came to him for advice or help, realized now they would not have anyone to help them or their children. His favorite method of helping the young ones was in telling of a story to explain the actions or feelings of parents.

The children Michael Leary had comforted by wiping tears from their eyes or bandaging busted knees or sharing their troubles returned as adults that day. Here was a person who would be missed by many and yet the McCaul family knew so little about the man.

After the funeral, the McCauls gathered in the garden which for so many years Michael Leary tended. They were awaiting the arrival of guests, a selected few whom Mrs. McCaul invited for tea, the selected few who were the socially acceptable of Newport. Helen McCaul couldn't let a funeral go by without making a social event out of it.

Ronald and his father sat in the swing overlooking the small lake, while the two McCaul girls went into the main house to freshen up and while Mrs. McCaul visited the kitchen to make certain the food was properly prepared and arranged. She did not know who prepared or how the food was prepared, that was the job of the cook. She only wanted to make certain it was properly arranged on the serving trays and served in the proper manner at the appropriate time.

During this particular period was one of the few times Ronald and his father had a few minutes alone while in Newport.

"You know father, I must have talked with Michael almost every day of my life since I can remember, that is every day I was here and yet I know hardly anything about him, except he was from Ireland."

"He never talked much about himself, now did he?" said Professor McCaul.

"No sir, he didn't, but I talked with him every day and…"

"His gift was listening, you talked and he listened. You know men who do the same thing in London and Birmingham, they get payed 25 to 30 pounds an hour for listening to your troubles. Of course they have those all important certificates hanging on the wall which informs the world they are Psychologists. That son, is the difference and, oh yes, the 25 to 30 pounds."

"Did you ever talk with him, I mean did you tell him things you never told anyone else?"

"Yes I did. From the day I married your mother until my last visit. When we were first married, it was a different world here for me and I was confused and angry. I would talk to him for hours and he would listen. Over the years he must have listened to me for at least a few thousand hours.

Why just this last Christmas, we talked for good three or four hours, no, I talked for three or four hours and he listened."

For a few moments each looked out onto the lake and watched the two swans lift up from the water, circle the lake and fly north.

"They must be headed for Scotland," said Ronald.

"Then they're not very smart swans, are they?" laughed Professor McCaul.

"I guess not," agreed Ronald.

The two were silent for a few minutes as Ronald thought about Michael Leary.

"He never went back to Ireland, did he?" asked Ronald.

"No, he never went back to Ireland," answered his father.

"I wonder why not?"

"He never told you?"

"I never asked," said Ronald.

Professor McCaul dug into his coat pocket, removed his pipe and tobacco pouch. While he filled his pipe, he said,

"I did."

"You asked him why he never visited Ireland?"

"Well, not exactly. I asked him why he came to England. He came over in 1922. Do you know your Irish history?"

"Not really," answered Ronald.

"After the war to end all wars was over in 1918, the Irish started pushing to get their independence from England. During the war, they were preparing for a fight, getting organized, hiding arms, things they didn't do prior to the Easter Rising in 1916. They started while the war was still being waged in Europe, hoping England would be too involved in the war to pay much attention to the home front. The armistice came too soon. By 1919, though not completely organized and ready for a fight, they started their fight for independence.

By 1921 the English had their fill of the fighting and offered to talk instead of fight. The Irish signed a peace treaty without obtaining the complete independence they wanted, but obtaining dominion status like Australia and Canada. This did not satisfy all of the Irish, but when voted on by the Dail, it was approved. The anti-treaty group walked out of the government and this was the start of the Irish civil war.

Now Michael Leary was just twenty-two years old. He had served in the British Army from 1917-1919 and returned to Ireland in 1919. He was a member of the IRA from 1919 until 1921 when the peace treaty was signed and was one of the first to join the Irish Free State Army, the official Irish Army after the treaty.

He was one of the junior officers in an army convoy traveling in western Cork in August of 1922 on an inspection tour of various units of the Free State Army by the Army's Commander-in-Chief. In a place called Beal na mBlath, the convoy drove into an ambush by anti-treaty rebels. The only person killed in the ambush was the Commander-in-Chief, General Michael Collins.

Although we talked about the ambush a number of times over the years, once as he was staring at the picture of Collins did he whispered,

"And I spotted the red bonnet with the purplish-pink flowers."

When I questioned him about it, he shook his head and said,

"A slip of the tongue!!"

He never explained the statement. Within a week of Collin's death, he deserted the Army and sailed to England. Your Grandfather hired him as a gardener and he remained here for the next sixty plus years."

"But why wouldn't he go back to Ireland?"

"I really don't know. All he said was he wouldn't go back. Whether it was because he deserted the Army or because he blamed himself for the General's death or because he was disgusted with his own people for killing each other, he never said. He did say if the General had lived, there would only be one Ireland today, not two."

Against his mother's will and without his father's knowledge, Ronald made arrangements to finish his university education in Ireland. With the aid of some of his father's friends at the University, he managed to obtain admittance to Queen's University.

When he informed his father of his decision, he was surprised that his father was delighted with his decision. His father even suggested he could possibly make arrangement for him to stay at the same boarding house.

Ronald's reply was a polite thank you, but he would prefer to find a room where the people were more his age. He reminded his father of the stories he told about the other occupants of the boarding house. They were all middle aged or older, scholarly, eccentric and wanted the house quiet by half nine every evening. Ronald stated he doubted he would have too much in common with them. His father agreed.

In the Fall of 1984, Ronald made his first visit to Ireland, an Ireland he had heard about from old Michael and which he had read about since he was able to read. An Ireland his mother refused to allow him to visit, even after his father was settled into his new position at Queen's. Her excuse was his father was too busy to take care of a visitor. Whenever he asked why the family never visited his father in Ireland, her reply was always the same.

"Your Father will be home in a few weeks, therefore it makes no sense for us to travel over there, besides, with all the trouble in Ireland, I have no desire to subject you or the girls to it."

Professor McCaul returned to Ireland in late August and Ronald arrived the following month.

His father arranged for an extra bed to be placed in his sitting room and for Ronald to take meals with the other boarders. This arrangement lasted for only five days. Ronald arrived in Belfast on a Monday afternoon and by Friday morning he had completed arrangements for his own accommodations.

Upon his arrival at Queen's, he outlined a definite plan, then followed it to the letter. This type of planning was what made him famous or infamous years later.

During the first two days, Ronald located each building where his classes were to be taught, the library and the best place to obtain meals. During the third and fourth days, he scouted the area around these designated points and found a rooming house within a short walking distance to each location. On the fifth day he paid a deposit on a small room and on the sixth day his father helped him move into his new abode. After the initial move, the remainder of the day was spent in rearranging the sparse furniture to give him the maximum amount of living space.

After he moved, he and his father had very little contact. They would meet on campus occasionally and chat for a few minutes or have a cup of tea or lunch together. Other than these infrequent meetings, the two did not socialize. This was due mainly to Ronald's study load. He had very little time for socializing, with his father or with anyone else.

One cold, misty day during mid-winter, Ronald's aspiration of becoming a great English writer came to an abrupt end. Suddenly he was no longer possessed with the burning desire to be another Jonathan Swift and write satirical stories.

His father, Professor McCaul, was the cause for ending his ambition of becoming a great twentieth century satirist.

From his first day at the University, Ronald heard rumors about his father's lectures, yet he never attended one. He finished his history requirement at Cardiff and his study of Irish and English literature required all his time. On this particular day, he was in the library with Mary Elizabeth Boyle, a fellow student, who was also majoring in English literature. They finished lunch, and as usually, were preparing to spend the next three hours in the library reading or looking up references to read.

Ninety minutes into their study period, Mary Elizabeth started packing her books into her backpack.

"Where're you going, it's not even two o'clock?"

"I told you at lunch, I want to hear your father's lecture. Are you coming?"

He looked at her, waiting for her to ask him again.

She shrugged her shoulders, swung the backpack over her shoulder and started out.

"Wait a minute, I'll go with you."

She stopped, turned, then said impatiently,

"Well, hurry up, I want to get a good seat."

"But it's not even a quarter till," said Ron as he threw his books into his satchel and attempted to put on his coat at the same time as he was attempting to lock the satchel.

Mary Elizabeth was halfway out of the library by the time Ronald managed to get his coat on and his satchel locked. He was forced to run in order to catch up with her.

The two didn't talk until they arrived at the lecture hall.

Already, over three quarters of the chairs were filled.

"See what I told you," she said.

They took seats in the next to the last row.

"Will we be able to hear him for here?" asked Ronald.

"Oh yes."

By five minutes before two, the lecture hall was full, not only the seats, but along the walls on both sides. Ronald turned and looked in back.

Between the last row of seats and the back wall was a ten-foot wide area. Ronald calculated at least fifty people were standing in the area.

As he looked around, he saw that not all the people in attendance were students. He recognized a number of faculty and staff, both Irish and English.

At exactly two minutes before two, Professor McCaul walked into the room and up to the podium. He placed his lecture notes and his pocket watch on the podium, looked over the crowd and glanced at his watch. He adjusted the podium, shuffled his notes and looked at his watch for the second time. As the second hand made it way towards the twelve, he looked out at the crowd and back at the watch. Just as the second hand passed between the 12 and the 1, he said,

"Thank you for coming. I hope you will enjoy and learn from this lecture."

Ronald learned later his father started each lecture the same, at the exact time and with the same sentence.

The subject for this particular day was, "Early 20th Century Ireland. The basic reason for the two Irelands of today."

Ronald never heard one of his father's lectures, nor read one of his essays or books. To him Professor McCaul was the mild mannered individual who never raised his voice, who wore steel rimmed glasses, read a great many books, was an excellent fly fisherman, was polite and soft spoken, who cared nothing for his wife's socialite friends or her social ambitions. He was not distinguished in any way. To Ronald, he was the typical college Professor, a very unexciting individual who lived in his own little world.

Ronald did not recognize the man behind the podium. He was not the man he knew as his father. This man was a vibrant speaker, who spoke with eloquence so each and every word could be heard and understood by all.

He was not like the Irish Professors, who would speak so fast three or four of their words could run together in the production of a new word.

Professor McCaul was not only eloquent in his use of words, but dramatic in their delivery, making the statement exciting.

There was no whispering, no movement or no noise in the large lecture hall, except for what the speaker was saying. No one wanted to miss a word.

This particular lecture covered the beginning of the Gaelic League as the Irish continued their crawl from under the oppression of the Penal Laws. Laws which forbid Irish Catholics, the legal inhabitants of the land, from receiving an education or entering a profession, of holding public office or engaging in commerce. The Irish of this period had been under the heel of the oppressors so long they had lost all their national pride.

The Gaelic League was the beginning of the end for this oppression. It started the fire of a national renaissance, which expressed itself in art, literature, social idealism, personal dignity and finally revolution.

McCaul spoke about the personalities of the period. He spoke of Arthur Griffith, W.B. Yeats and Lady Gregory, of the Abbey Theater and of a new political movement. He told the listeners of a weekly newspaper call the "Sinn Fein" in which Griffith told the Irish they were capable of conducting their own affairs.

Professor McCaul spoke about John Redmond, the political leader of the Irish who was afraid of the threats of Sir Edward Carson and his Ulster volunteers. He told of the Nationalists who also raised a volunteer army and the possibility of a civil war.

During the fifty minutes, the one characteristic Professor McCaul displayed more than any other was passion, a passion for history. Not just history itself, but the understanding of history. He would first describe a particular event and its consequence. Once the event and its consequence were explained, he would return to the history prior to the event and explore and explain the basic reasons.

His voice was not the voice Ronald was familiar with, but the passionate voice of a preacher, a preacher attempting to convince people the importance of history and what should be learned from history. He ended his history lesson with the statement,

"For God's sake, learn about the mistakes so they are not repeated!!"

His lecture ended exactly at 2:50 PM, on the minute, with the same statement he used as the end of every lecture, which was,

"Thank you for your attention."

He picked up his lecture notes, which he never used and stuffed them into his brief case.

After his final statement, the hall remained absolutely silent for 50 seconds until Professor McCaul walked out the side door.

The subject of the fifty minute lecture ended on the dawn of the Great War, the war to end all wars. It was the third of fifteen lectures to be covered during the fall term.

Each week the lecture hall filled earlier and earlier, until by the end of the term, no seats were available for the two o'clock lecture after one twenty and no standing room after one thirty.

A number of individuals in the audience did not enjoy listening to the sins of their ancestors; some were ashamed while others felt no shame at all. One particular point all the audience could understand was the similarity of the situation in the Ireland of today with that of yesteryear.

Within the audience were a number of individuals whose outlook on the political situation in Northern Ireland was not only changed, but who were determined to have a hand in the change. One was Ronald McCaul.

At the conclusion of the series of lectures, Ronald McCaul's passion was no longer English and Irish Literature, but Irish political revolution.

Ronald McCaul completed his classes in Irish and English Literature his first term, mainly because to drop a class without a good excuse would result in a failing grade and the possibility of being force to drop out of school. That was the last thing Ronald McCaul wanted.

During the Christmas vacation he and his father had numerous opportunities for long discussions of Irish history, sparked by his father's lectures. Through out the three weeks, Ronald McCaul attempted to learn about the complete political history of Ireland, a history that required this father thirty years to accumulate. He was a young man in a hurry.

Upon his return to Belfast, he changed his major to Political Science, against the advise of his Faculty advisor. During the next two terms, he enrolled in nothing but Political Science and History classes. Because of his interest and analytical mind, he became one of the favorite students of the Political Science Department. His quest for information seemed to be unquenchable.

By the end of his last term at the University, his advisor believed McCaul had read and digested almost every reference book on the political history of Ireland. He even borrowed and read books form the private collection of members of the Department.

It was during his last term that he became acquainted with Jamie Toland. She was the youngest faculty member of the Political Science Department. She told Ronald she was hired by the Department based on three factors:

The first was she was the Department's most outstanding graduate. Second, her specialty was the Nationalist movement, an area that was not covered satisfactorily since the death of Professor Hogan two years before she graduated. The third reason was the most impressive. Her aunt was the Department Chairman's mistress.

Any one of the reasons would have been good enough for at least an Assistant Professor position, but since all the other members of the Department were male, the Chairman did not want to ruffle too many of their peacock type feathers.

Ronald McCaul's association with Jamie Toland was both as an Instructor:Student and socially as a friend of his father's mistress.

Professor McCaul's and Jamie's emotional involvement were never displayed when he was present, but just from their eye contact, it was not difficult for Ronald to understand their relationship. What surprised him the most was the fact he felt no animosity towards Jamie or his father.

He knew about his mother's relationship with Dr. Morrow since his twelfth birthday, the day he climbed the large water oak at the rear of the house and just happened to look into the second floor window of his mother's bedroom. The two lovers had not bothered to pull the shades.

It wasn't until after he attended his father's lectures that Ronald realized Jamie was his father's mistress. These two events, the lectures and Professor McCaul's involvement with Jamie Toland, increased Ronald's respect for his father more than a thousand fold. Up until then, he considered his father somewhat of a jellyfish, with no backbone when it came to dealing with his mother.

Since Jamie's main interest and that of the Department, was the Nationalist movement, she made contact with the both the OIRA and the PIRA organizations for purely research reasons. A number of her students were either members of the organization or had connections with members. Through them, she contacted the officials, explained her interests and arrangements were made with the Army Council for her to talk with various members in order to obtain their personal views of the political situation.

The arrangements were always on the OIRA's and PIRA's terms. The meetings with the Official members were open to anyone who chose to attend, but the meetings with the Provos usually involved a telephone call, two to four taxi rides, interspersed with a walk of three to four blocks and ending up at a designated point. She was then met by a member of the Sinn Fein Political organization, who would escort her to some abandon building, where he would knock on the door, then disappear. When the door opened, she would be escorted into a room where she would sit at a table with four to six individuals who wore black hoods to hide their identity. During these meetings, she would ask questions and the individuals would answer.

Over the last two years she continued her contact with the Provos, asking questions and receiving answers, without ever committing herself to their point of views. She was determined to remain neutral, for once she started taking sides, she knew she would no longer be able to analysis the overall situation without bias.

Jamie respected her contact's wishes concerning security and silence about their activities and opinions. She knew she was given information on a trial basis. If this information turned up in police files, she would lose the valuable contact. The Provos respected her for her integrity and the contact continued.

Ronald McCaul's initial contact with the Provos was arranged by a fellow student and it was the beginning of a career as a hunted man, a career which would not end until a Summer day in 1998.

During the last three terms at Queen's University, Ronald became convinced the northeastern part of Ireland, which was called Northern Ireland, was an illegally occupied section of the Republic of Ireland. What his ancestors did to the Irish would have to be corrected, even if it meant going against his own country. He came to the conclusion that the only way this could be resolved was to force the British out of Ulster and let those still loyal to England, either move to England or become true Irishmen.

Even before his initial meeting with the PIRA, he knew the only way to accomplish this was through the same tactics the IRA used in 1919-1921 to force the British to sue for peace and what the Israelis used to drive the English out of Palestine back in the late 1940's. This was the use of terrorism, a type of warfare almost impossible to combat with regular army tactics. Even for a Welshman, this was an extreme.

Before McCaul graduated from Queen's with honors and a scholarship from the Crown, he was a full-fledged member of the PIRA.

His first act of terrorism was nothing more than detonating a car filled with explosives in front of a police station. No one was killed or injured in the explosion.

For the next four years, he was the Dr. Jekyll and Mr. Hyde of Ulster. During the day he was the ideal British subject, receiving a free education from her majesty's government at her majesty's school. At night he met with ranking members of the PIRA, planning arms procurement, selecting hiding places for arms and ammunition, planning attacks on the British Army and retaliatory strikes.

He gained a position on the planning committee within a year of his first contact. Seven months after he was sworn in, he was given the responsibility for planning an attack on an Army convoy. Three previous attacks met with failure. The first failed because the charges failed to go off; the second failed because the charge exploded after the convoy passed. The third one, no one talked about. It was the one in which the explosives when off in the truck on the way to the target, killing two PIRA members.

Ronald's planned attack on a convoy was more than a success. It was a declared victory. Three trucks filled with radio equipment were hijacked by two carloads of Provos. The equipment was stored, the trucks destroyed and the three drivers stripped of their British uniforms, which would be used later. The three were left unharmed, bound to a tree near the eighth hole in the middle of Greencastle Golf Course, blind folded and bare butt. It was the best planned and executed operation the PIRA had achieved in months.

Based on this one operation, Ronald McCaul was advanced from an untried member to a consultant to the Council. Within a year he would be promoted to the planning council and within another year, he would become the chief strategist for the Provos in the Belfast area.

McCaul was not only a master strategist, but he was also a fearless terrorists. When he planned an operation, he insisted on being part of the cell carrying out the operation, whether it was an attack on a police station or Army unit, the withdrawal of funds from a bank or the stealing of arms and ammunition or equipment needed by the Provo.

He was never identified as the master planner to any member of the "cells" or tactical units. For each operation, the tactical unit consisted of different members of the Provos. These units, formed just prior to an operation, consisted of four to seven unacquainted individuals, who were introduced to each other by fictitious names. They would be briefed on the operation, practice one or two times, carry out the mission, disperse and probably never meet again, unless by accident. Never were any of his planned operations unsuccessful up until the fall of 1992.

A number of times the tactical units suffered causalities, but this was always due to some mistake by a member of the unit. If the unit followed his detailed plan, they would always achieve success, without a casualty.

It was during an armed ambush of a UDR unit outside of Lisburn when McCaul first met Thomas O'Connor. The two became close friends after their first handshake. A certain chemistry existed between the two, each complementing the other.

Only with a great deal of pleading was McCaul allowed to contact O'Connor after their initial meeting. This was against all rules set up by the governing council. After two weeks of pleading, the council relented and allowed the contact to be reestablished. It was then that McCaul learned O'Connor's name was not Darby O'Gill, but Thomas O'Connor.

At this time in O'Connor's life, he was no longer the gentle stonemason. His character was permanently changed years before when his Rosemary was killed.

When McCaul met him, O'Connor was the most wanted man in Northern Ireland. He made no secret of his involvement with the Provos and was identified and blamed for fourteen killings, although he had personally killed only seven.

The operation outside Lisburn was an ambush of a UDR patrol making a sweep of an area where a previous ambush of an army convoy occurred. The operation was to be more of a harassment than a killing operation. The Provos wanted to let the UDR know they could and would be hit on their own territory. The only target was to be the command car trailing behind the foot patrol. It was to be destroyed.

This particular tactical unit was composed of five men, including McCaul and O'Connor. The operation called for the placement of the unit on a ridge above the road the UDR was sweeping. They were to let the patrol pass, then as the command car came by, the unit was to open fire with all their weapons, which included four AR-14s and one ancient 30 caliber BAR sitting on a tripod. One clip from each rifle was to be fired at the command vehicle. The unit was then to abandon their position and escape in two cars, each headed in a different direction.

Initially the ambush was carried off as planned, but as the unit was withdrawing towards the cars, the individual carrying the BAR was slowed down by both the weight and the bulkiness of the weapon. He was detained long enough for a pursuing UDR man to fire a volley at him. One of the bullets caught him in the right leg, shattering a bone and knocking him to the ground.

McCaul and O'Connor were within a few feet of the cars when they heard the shots, turned and saw their comrade fall. Neither said a word, but both turned and ran toward the fallen man. By the time they reached him, other members of the UDR patrol appeared and turned their attention on the fallen PIRA man. Before they could fix him in their sights, he crawled his way to temporary safety behind a boulder. The UDR patrol changed targets….McCaul and O'Connor.

They contributed reaching safety behind the boulder solely to Lady Luck, for close to a hundred rounds were fired at them, with neither being hit.

"How in the hell are we going to get out of this one?" asked O'Connor, more to himself than to McCaul and the wounded man.

"There's only one way out," said McCaul, "you'll have to carry what's his name while I keep their heads down. When you reach the car, it'll be your turn to keep them busy while I get my ass out of here."

"I can't leave you here," said O'Connor.

"You're not going to leave me here, you're going to take what's his name to the car, then make the soldiers keep their heads down while I make a run for the car."

"But what if…"

"Just leave your rifle here. Two spares are in the boot of the car, plus two extra long magazines. Use them, it'll make them think you have a machine gun."

"Are you sure?"

"I'm sure. When I start shooting, grab him and run like hell. OK?"

"OK."

Again Lady Luck was watching over the three. McCaul's quickly thought out plan worked. It worked because the patrol lost their commander in the command car and no one was willing to take over his responsibility.

The operation was a success. One command vehicle destroyed, one officer and two enlisted men wounded. On the Provos side, one BAR and one AR-14 lost, one man wounded.

It was more than a success for the Provos, it permanently united McCaul and O'Connor.

RUC Headquarters
Belfast, Northern Ireland

After receiving Kerrigan's call, Rothchild reviewed and signed off on the eleven files on his desk. He informed his secretary he would be gone for the rest of the day and would be unavailable.

As he walked out of the building, he thought perhaps he should ask the Chief Constable for permission to journey into the Republic. Half a dozen steps out of the building, he decided against it. He smiled as he remembered his boyhood Catholic friend, who was always quoting the Jesuits.

"It's easier to ask forgiveness than permission!"

"How true," thought Rothchild as he made his way out of the Headquarters' building and down to the parking lot.

Once at home, he showered and changed into civilian cloths. The people in the Republic wouldn't appreciate him showing up in his RUC uniform.

He was just about to write a note to his wife, informing her he wouldn't be home for dinner, when he heard the front door open. Rothchild clicked the ballpoint pen to withdraw the point, put the pen in his shirt pocket and waited for his wife as he heard her steps in the hallway.

She opened the door into the kitchen, saw Rothchild, stopped and said, "Douglas…"

"I was just writing you a note."

"Why are you home so early and why the civilian cloths?"

Rothchild hesitated for a mere second. He didn't want to tell his wife he was going to the Republic, but he wasn't going to lie to her.

"I have to go to the Republic for…"

"To meet Patrick?"

Rothchild hesitated another moment, then said,

"Yes Gert, to meet Patrick."

It was Mrs. Rothchild's turn to extend the silence.

"You be careful down there. You know your type is not too popular in the Republic."

"I know."

"What time will you be back?"

"I really don't know Gert. Don't wait up for me."

"I won't. You just be careful, understand?"

"Yes Gert, I will. Good by."

"Good by Douglas."

Rothchild arrived in Killygordon at 5:45 PM, just fifteen minutes before his regular dinnertime. The police station was situated in the middle of a block of stone buildings, quite different from the RUC stations in Ulster. In Northern Ireland, the Constabulary stations were the targets, thus protected by high fences with razor wire at the top and floodlights that stayed on from dusk to dawn. Here, anyone could walk into the station, unchallenged. It was quite a difference.

Rothchild walked through the door over which hung the weathered sign indicating it was the village's police station. The station was nothing more than one long room, divided by a waist high counter, behind which sat a young constable, who immediately looked up as Rothchild entered.

As he walked towards the barrier, Rothchild gazed at the long cork bulletin board on the left wall on which were stapled and pinned various notices, duty assignments, clean-up schedules and a number of wanted posters, some dating back to the mid-eighties.

Rothchild turned his head and looked towards the young officer. Although he hadn't looked at him except when he entered the station, he knew the officer had not taken his eyes off him. He had watched every move, including his survey of the room. When he reached the counter, he saw Kerrigan sitting at a desk behind the young officer. Before the officer could ask if he could help him, Rothchild said,

"I'm here to see Chief Superintendent Kerrigan."

The officer turned to speak to Kerrigan, but the Chief Superintendent was already up and out of his chair, walking towards Rothchild.

"Douglas, I'm glad you could make it, just in time for your dinner, if I remember right?"

Kerrigan extended his hand across the counter and the two old friends shook hands.

"Yes, I'm anxious to taste some of Mary Ellen's famous tarts," said Rothchild with a smile.

"You and me both," said Kerrigan as he turned back towards the desk he confiscated from the duty officer.

"Let me get my papers and let Constable Nickens get back to his desk," said Kerrigan as he gathered the papers spread over the top of the desk.

Although it appeared he was gathering and stuffing the papers into the oversized brief case in a haphazard manner, if one watched closely, as Rothchild was, one would have observed he picked up each stack in a certain order and placed them in the briefcase in the same manner.

Kerrigan had spent the last hour and a half going through the files he brought with him from Dublin. These files contained all the information available to the Garda on McCaul and O'Connor. The information was from the police force in the Republic, from the Constabulary in Northern Ireland, from the Metropolitan Police in London, Interpol, the CIA and the FBI in the United States. Kerrigan made copies of each file prior to leaving Dublin. What he had been doing for the last hours and a half was reviewing the files for the third time, then constructing one file out of the copied reports and arranging them in a chronological order.

He was surprised by the amount of information in each file that overlapped. A number of the reports were contradictory, giving different dates and times for the same event. When Rothchild arrived, Kerrigan was in the process of producing a third file that combined the information from two files.

"Are you buying dinner or am I?" asked Kerrigan.

"Why I thought you invited me for dinner?"

"I said I had the dessert. I didn't say anything about buying you dinner."

This conversation was merely for the benefit of Officer Nickens. The two knew Kerrigan was buying dinner. Over the years it became the custom that the visitor was always treated to dinner. The only question was what and where to eat.

Kerrigan walked over to the end of the counter and lifted the hinged countertop, joined Rothchild and the two walked towards the front of the building. Nickens could hear only parts of the conversation, it was something about fishing and catching a couple of prize winning trophy fish. Since he wasn't a fisherman, the conversation didn't interest him.

Upon reaching the door, Kerrigan turned back and said,

"I won't be returning, so you can have your desk back. Thank you for the use of it."

"Yes sir," said Officer Nickens as he nodded to Chief Superintendent Kerrigan.

He watched the two older men walk out the door and close it almost silently as they left the building.

Nickens remained seated at the counter. He hadn't minded being asked to relinquish the desk. The only reason he was sitting at the desk when Kerrigan came in was that he was using the telephone to talk to his girl friend.

Kerrigan and Rothchild walked down the narrow sidewalk to Rothchild's car.

"I'll let you do the driving tonight Douglas, but before we start, where do you want to eat?"

"It makes no difference to me. You're the one who has the big appetite."

"Good, I was hoping you'd say that. How about some good fish?"

"That sounds fine."

"Good. Let's drive over to Ballybofey, I heard they just made a fresh catch of trout."

"You had it picked out all along, didn't you Patrick?"

Kerrigan didn't answer, he just smiled, then walked to the passenger side of the car to wait for Rothchild to unlock the door.

The two were five minutes out of Killygordon when Kerrigan said,

"You know who we have in the pokey in Convoy?"

He didn't give Rothchild a chance to answer.

"One of your favorite people, Thomas O'Connor."

"You're joking?" asked Rothchild.

"No."

"Didn't you tell me you had two surprises?"

"We have both McCaul and O'Connor, but we had to get McCaul into a hospital. He's in Dublin at St. Francis Hospital."

"What happened to him, shot?"

"No, no, not shot, there was no shooting or anything. I have no idea what's wrong with him, all I know is he was sick when we got there. High fever, chills, the bit. The local doctor insisted we get him to a hospital, so I sent Jamie back to Dublin with him."

After a brief silence, Rothchild asked,

"How?"

"Luck. It was one of these routine checks the tax people do to check on residents of the Republic buying high priced items in the North and bringing them into the Republic without paying taxes. The Garda in Stanorlar decided to check the cars going the other way. They had just put up the barrier when O'Connor and McCaul drove up. They didn't give the lads any resistance at all."

"We've been looking for those two ever since they escaped from the Interrogation Center over five years ago."

"Yes, I know. So have we," said Kerrigan.

"Does anyone else know about this?" asked Rothchild.

"I'm afraid so….."

Before Kerrigan could finish his sentence, Rothchild asked, "Who?"

"Our old friend, Mel Harper."

"He knows you have McCaul and O'Connor?"

"Yes."

"Will he report it?"

"No, not until we release it officially, I have his word on it."

"Are you sure?"

"Yes, but it's possible the word has leaked out."

"Then you had better get them hidden fast. If the Provos find out about them, they'll be down here before you can count ten."

"Yes, I know," said Kerrigan as he flicked the pocket lighter his oldest daughter gave him for Christmas. It was a special lighter for pipes. The only problem was he could never remember to get it filled with butane.

The tobacco in Kerrigan's pipe was aglow and resembled a miniature volcano as the rich brown leaves turned to gray ashes and erupted from the bowl of the pipe. The glow from the pipe was the only illumination inside the automobile since Rothchild always drove with the dashboard lights turned off. This had become habit since the dashboard lights gave off enough illumination to make the driver a target.

The light was just enough to give Kerrigan's face a ghostly aura. If Rothchild had taken a quick glance during one of these moments, he would have seen the big Irishman smiling. It was the type of smile one would see after a joke or a funny incident. It was the type of smile one finds on people who are satisfied with their selves.

"You're expecting them, aren't you Patrick?"

The smile broadened on Kerrigan's face.

"Yes Douglas. That's the reason I got you down here."

After a few moments of silence, Rothchild didn't really know what to say, because as soon as he heard Kerrigan's answer, a dozen questions popped into his head.

"Is he going to get away?"

Again the glow of the pipe illuminated Kerrigan's face and after the short lived volcano, Kerrigan said

"No."

Rothchild wanted to ask if Kerrigan was sure O'Connor would not be rescued. He took his friend's word that he would not escape, yet he was afraid Kerrigan did not have as much experience with the Provos as he had, particularly with a man like O'Connor. Twice he started to ask how the Garda officers was so certain O'Connor would not be rescued and twice he stopped a microsecond before the questions were asked. Instead, he said,

"I wonder how Mel found out about them?"

"I had one of my people call him and within four hours he showed up to interview O'Connor."

"You what?"

Kerrigan didn't answer.

"You've set this whole damn thing up, haven't you?"

"Yes Chief Superintendent Rothchild, I started setting it up as soon as I was positive we had McCaul and O'Connor. And….I thought you would want to be in on the catch."

Rothchild shook his head and said,

"I didn't even bring my service revolver."

"Don't you know it's against the law to transport weapons across the border," said Kerrigan.

"But it's usually the other way," retorted Rothchild.

"Yes, I know. But don't worry, I just happened to have a spare British issue with me, just in case you would like to be in on the excitement that will probably start in about three hours."

"You know when they're coming?"

"We'll know the exact minute they cross into the Republic."

"How?"

Kerrigan didn't answer and Rothchild didn't expect an answer. Instead, Kerrigan said,

"We'll have plenty time to have a delicious meal of fresh trout before we sample one of Mary Ellen's tarts along with a group of other tarts."

He ended his statement with his deep laugh.

"You're sure we're going to have plenty of time to enjoy our meal?"

"Trust me Douglas, my friend, eating is one of the three things I take serious in this life."

"And just what are the others?"

"A man has to have secrets, even from one of his closest friends."

Douglas relaxed his tight muscles against the not too soft back cushion. Kerrigan's last statement somehow made the tension disappear.

Strange, thought Rothchild, how one of his closest friends was from across the border. Either one of them would not hesitate in trusting the other with his life, yet the only three things they had in common were their occupation, their love for fishing and their friendship. Other than these three common dominators, they had absolutely nothing in common. Their background, education, religion, social standing and political ideas were as different as any two individuals could possibly be, yet Rothchild could think of no one else to whom he would trust his life.

The fresh trout was as delicious as Kerrigan had guaranteed and during the meal, if anyone had overheard the conversation, they would have guessed these two men were just two old friends out for the evening enjoying a delicious meal. Their conversation concerned families, fishing and vacations. There was not a word about business.

"If you will excuse me for a minute," said Kerrigan as he pushed up and out of his chair.

"I'll be back in a minute."

Rothchild merely nodded. As he ate, he was thinking about Kerrigan and his plan. He knew his friend would not tell him the complete plan until it was ready to be put into operation, it was just a quid pro quo.

A number of years ago he had called Kerrigan to come up and witness the capture of a group of IRA men from the Republic. The Intelligence Group of the Constabulary, who worked with or for MI5, passed information on to the Constabulary the PIRA planned to attack the West Police Station located on the outskirts of Armagh.

According to the report, the Provos planned to come across the border a little after midnight in two cars and park an explosive laden car next to the station, then detonate it by radio from a safe distance.

Working with the UDR, the Constabulary arranged for a little surprise party for the visitors from the South.

Rothchild informed Kerrigan about the information and invited him to observe the operation. By the time Kerrigan arrived in Ulster, the trap was set. A special unit from a local Ranger unit had set up three land rovers around the front of the station, which was the only open area where a car could be placed to cause damage to the station. One police car was parked directly in front of the station. Each land rover was equipped with floodlights and a mounted 7.69mm air-cooled machine gun.

The special unit was composed of one officer, a young Lieutenant by the name of Sanders, a senior NCO and thirteen specially trained soldiers. Ten RUC Constables supplemented the unit.

The only trouble with the operation was that two carloads of young men from Keady, on their way home from a soccer match in Moy, followed by three hours in the local tavern celebrating their victory, decided it would be great sport to stop and urinate on the lonely police car parked in front of the police station.

When the two cars stopped, Lieutenant Sanders decided his unit was going to receive the sole credit for the capture of the terrorists. As the third man existed the lead car and before the first could relieve himself on the police car, Sanders blew his whistle and the floodlights on the land rovers came on and lit up the front of the station as bright as the noonday sun. This was immediately followed by the Lieutenant's voice over the portable loud speaker.

"Put your hands in the air and don't move."

The young man who had just taken aim at the police car turned abruptly and dampened the legs of his two friends who stood white faced with fear with their hands in the air.

"Everyone out of the cars. NOW!" shouted the Lieutenant.

In less that ten seconds, the other seven soccer players erupted from the cars, falling over one another as they made an attempt to obey the voice from the dark. As the ten half drunk, totally frightened young men stood in the middle of the street, the Lieutenant gave his last command,

"First section, disarm the captives!!"

As soon as the floodlights were turned on, Rothchild realized these were not the expected visitors. During the next three minutes he did nothing but close his eyes and slowly move his head back and forth. This was to hide both his disbelief in what was going on and his pent up anger at the young Lieutenant. The situation wasn't helped by Kerrigan, who was bent over with laughter, which could be heard for at least two blocks in every direction.

The sight of the young man urinating all over his friends and their attempt to escape the warm stream was what started him laughing, but when the others piled out of the cars, falling over each other, not only sustained his laughter, but added to it. By the time Rothchild opened his eyes, the ten "terrorists" were surrounded by the special unit, all fourteen laughing as nine "terrorists" stood with their hands high in the air while the tenth, failing in his attempt to stop the stream of urine, continued to water the pavement. He didn't know which way the Lieutenant wanted him to point his unending stream, making a arch of 180 degrees, then finally shrugging his shoulders and aimed straight ahead. As the stream finally came to a stop, the young perpetrator threw up his hands and shouted,

"I give up," then started laughing.

Rothchild couldn't believe the Lieutenant's next command.

"Search the cars, including the boots."

After five minutes of blanketed silence, interrupted every few seconds by a burst of laughter from one or more of the soldiers, the NCO said,

"Sir, the only things we found are four half empty whiskey bottles, three soccer balls and two bags of smelly soccer uniforms."

Rothchild could barely hear the Lieutenant ask,

"Are you sure?"

The NCO answered in a very loud and clear voice.

"Yes sir, that's all. Four half empty whiskey bottles, three soccer balls and two bags of really stinking soccer uniforms."

"Great show Douglas," Kerrigan said, "this was well worth missing a nights sleep."

As Rothchild thought back about the incident, he had to smile.

"And just what are you smiling about?" asked Kerrigan as he returned to the table.

Rothchild looked up, laughed again, shook his head and said,

"Outside Armagh."

The statement alone was enough to start Kerrigan laughing.

"I just hope your little exercise is not as comical as that one," said Rothchild.

The laughter faded away slowly.

"No Douglas, I don't think it will be as funny as yours, but we're going to try the same thing. We're going to try and take them without any killings."

The smiles faded completely as Kerrigan slipped into his chair.

"Would you like another stout?"

Rothchild shook his head and said,

"I'm not finished with my trout. Don't rush me."

Kerrigan ordered another stout as he looked around the room. He decided it would be hard to call this a café or a restaurant. It was more like the large dining room in a private home with four individual tables and a long bar. Perhaps it would have been better to call it a neighborhood tavern, with the additional convenience of hot food. He decided he would call it a tavern.

He was playing mental gymnastics to keep from thinking about what was going to happen any time now. He was both looking forward to it and dreading it at the same time.

Rothchild finished the last of the trout and was wiping his mouth with his napkin when the man from behind the bar walked over to their table and asked,

"Either one of you gentlemen a Mr. Kerrigan?"

"That's me," said Kerrigan.

"There's a call for you."

"Thank you."

The bartender didn't answer, just nodded, turned and walked back to his station behind the bar. By the time he turned to observe Kerrigan, the Chief Superintendent had already made his way into the hallway where the phone was located between the women's and men's restrooms.

In the mean time, Rothchild was watching the bubbles on the inside of his glass as they escaped the grasp of the glass on their liquid surface and made their way up the side until they reached the surface and exploded into thin air. He watched a group of bubbles make their escape and thought about what could happen when the Provos came across the border to rescue O'Connor. He was hoping they would surrender if they were surrounded and out numbered, hoping there wouldn't be a fire fight which could result in a number of people being hurt or killed, nor did he relish the idea of killing anyone and he didn't want to be one of the ones hurt or killed.

Just as he took a deep breath to force the air into his lungs to supply the oxygen needed for his rapidly beating heart, Kerrigan returned to the table.

"You made a long ride for nothing Douglas. A SAS unit set up an ambush for our guest north of Castlederg. There wasn't much of a fight. According to my man, when the car stopped, the signal for the ambush was given and the boys in their black uniforms opened fire and…."

Kerrigan couldn't finish the sentence. Instead of looking at Rothchild, he looked down at the glass of stout, which had lost all of its foam. He was shaking his head.

"And?" asked Rothchild.

Still shaking his head, Kerrigan raised his head, looked directly at his friend and said,

"and there were no survivors."

"No!"

"Yes, another Gibraltar, another damn legalized assassination by her majesty's personal killers," said Kerrigan with all the sarcasm he could conjure up in his present depressed mood. After the statement, he looked to the right, staring at the bare wall.

Rothchild heard his teeth grind.

"How did the Brits find out?"

"I don't know, I just don't know."

After a moment of silence, he continued,

"Me and my big plans. Five men killed and what for, my ego?"

"Don't be so hard on yourself, the same thing could have happened when they got here, right?"

"No damn it. We would have given them a chance to surrender. We wouldn't have shot then down in cold blood."

Rothchild didn't have a reply.

"Let's get the hell out of here," said Kerrigan, as he pushed on the table away from his chair. Once on his feet, he took his billfold out of his breast pocket, took out two bills large enough to cover the meal and a sizable tip and left them on the table.

The drive back to Killygordon was in silence. Neither of them wanted to talk, mainly because of the chance the other would have a question the other either couldn't or didn't want to answer.

The highway was empty of traffic from Stanorlar to Killygordon. It was only as they pulled into the little hamlet when two cars passed them going towards Stanorlar. Rothchild had to flash on his bright lights to indicate he would appreciate the other cars dimming their lights. They received his message and dutifully dimmed their lights.

Killygordon was almost completely dark when they arrived, the only visible lights were the ones outside the police station and the night light in the pub on the corner.

Rothchild eased his car to a stop in front of the police station, turned off the ignition, but before he switched off the headlamps, he turned to Kerrigan and asked,

"What are you going to do with McCaul and O'Connor?"

The look on Kerrigan's face was one of true surprise.

"Why I'm going to turn them over to your people as soon as the paper work is completed."

Rothchild looked away from his friend, looking at the dashboard for a moment, then snapped off the headlamps. He was still looking at the dash when he said,

"I don't know whether that's a very good idea."

"Why?"

"The paper work. It will go through the Irish Office and the British will demand that the two be turned over to them…MI-5 or MI-6 or the Army. You know what that means?"

The two men stared at each other.

"What else can we do?"

"How long can you hold them without proper notification?"

"We can't now, not with the killings on the border. Everyone is going to know about it and know the reason for it. The Home Office in London is going to want to know why the paper work hasn't already been sent to Belfast," said Kerrigan.

Rothchild turned his stare from Kerrigan to the dim light in front of the police station. He appeared to be studying the light, but Kerrigan knew different. He knew he was thinking of a solution, so he waited.

"Not necessarily."

"Not necessarily what?" asked Kerrigan.

"What if the British didn't know who or what the five men were after, what if…"

"We couldn't be so lucky."

"It's possible. You know how the Provos work. They'll send a "cell" on a mission without telling them all the details or background. They may have been instructed to break someone out of jail, having no idea who it is or how important the individual is to the organization. We'll have to put some pressure on the British for information," said Rothchild, then added, "as soon as I get back, I'll telephone MI-5 and try to find out what they know."

"That might not be too wise," said Kerrigan.

"Why not?"

"The ambush took place just north of Castlederg on one of the back roads near the border by Fern hill and according to my man, no one else was around."

After a moment of silence, Kerrigan said,

"I knew where they were going to cross. That's how I thought I could know when to expect them. You see, I had men on both sides of the border. They were to call me when the Provos crossed over."

Kerrigan looked out of the window of the car and stared off into space, the black space of night.

"The one in Northern Ireland was the one who called to tell me about the ambush."

Again, silence.

"Somebody must have heard the shots, someone must know about it by now."

"Don't bet on it. There's nothing left at the location where the Provos were killed, plus the people in that area are accustomed to gunfire in the middle of the night. It's a favorite area for the Provos to do their practice target shooting."

"Wait a minute, you said the Provos were ambushed and killed. How about the bodies and the car?"

"I didn't finish the story. After the shooting, a Saracen came rolling in, the bodies were loaded into it and taken away. One of the SAS boys drove the car away and now there isn't a trace of what happened on that back road."

"How are we going to find out how the British knew about the Provos?"

"I don't know yet, but you can bet your ass I'm going to find out, one way or the other," said Kerrigan.

"The Provos will know something went wrong, they'll start asking questions."

"You're right about that, but it will be later. They're not going to advertise they sent a raiding party into the Republic. They'll wait a few days and try to figure out what went wrong. They don't know whether your people picked them up or whether they got caught down here in the Republic. It really doesn't make a damn any more. My big scheme backfired on me and nothing was accomplished, except five men were executed, British style."

"You're going to have to live with it Patrick, there isn't a thing you can do to change it. Now, what we have to do is.."

"What I have to do is determine how the British found out about my plan, how they knew exactly where the Provos were going to cross. I didn't tell you, one of my men said the SAS must have been in hiding at the crossing for at least four hours."

"How'd he know that?"

"Because he'd been watching the crossing for the last three hours and there was no activity until the Provos drove up. That meant the British were there a good while before he arrived."

There wasn't anything else to be said. Kerrigan's plan had misfired; there were no captives to interrogate and worst of all, four men knew about the killings, not counting the people who carried it out. That would be a tremendous load for anyone to carry around, particularly Kerrigan's informants on the border. A couple of drinks too many and...

"I'll be leaving you now Douglas, I still have a busy night ahead," said Kerrigan as he opened the car door and slid out, "you drive carefully going back."

"You do the same Patrick. Call me if you have any news and I'll do the same."

Kerrigan nodded, closed the car door and said,

"God bless."

Rothchild acknowledged his friend's blessing with a nod, started the car, switched on the headlamps, eased the car into gear and headed back North.

Kerrigan remained standing on the curb, watching Rothchild leave the little hamlet. He was trying to decide just what to do next. Three items needed to be taken care of this evening or early tomorrow morning before he returned to Dublin.

First, he would need to get all the Special Operations people back to Dublin, as fast as possible.

Second, he had to determine just what to do with O'Connor. He needed to put him some place where he wouldn't attract attention as soon as possible. Jamie will have probably made arrangement for a hiding place some where around Dublin and hopefully without attracting attention.

Third, he needed to tie up all the loose ends in Convoy and Stanorlar.

Before he reached his car, he made the decision to send O'Connor back to Dublin with the majority of the Special Operations people.

Rothchild had over a 150 kilometers to travel. He looked at his watch. It was just a little after nine o'clock. He should be home and in bed before midnight, depending on the weather, in particularly the fog.

"No fog and very little traffic and I'll have no trouble making it home by midnight."

He was not accustomed to driving long distances at night. He never did like to drive at night, even in his younger days when he was a young constable and had to take his share of the night shift duty. He would always attempt to talk his partner for the evening to do the driving.

He wasn't overly tired or sleepy, but as a precaution, he rolled down the window. The night air was cool and he felt the dampness in it, which could indicate fog.

"Just have to be careful in the valleys and by the river," he thought.

His thoughts jumped from the fog and night air to the incident at Fern Hill. Damn the English anyways. They always think they know what is best for Ireland.

Rothchild's thoughts were interrupted by a swinging red light approximately 200 meters ahead. He lifted his foot off the petrol pedal and eased the gearshift into neutral, allowing the automobile to coast up to the individual with the swinging lantern. He automatically stepped on the brake pedal, even though the car had come to a stop. Directly behind the man was a police car parked across the highway, forming a roadblock.

He waited for the officer to stop swinging the light and tell him the reason for the roadblock. Suddenly a second figure stepped out of the darkness, not two meters from the car. Rothchild had been watching the man with the light and did not expect a second person, whose sudden appearance actually scared the hell out of him, causing his body to jerk straight up about three inches.

"Excuse me sir," said the man who suddenly appeared out of the darkness, "could I see your driving permit?"

Even though his heart rate doubled in the last few seconds, Rothchild conjured up his best evil look and stared directly into the man's face.

"You could give a man a heart attack that way," said Rothchild in a not to soft voice.

The man merely smiled, which made Rothchild angrier.

"Your permit sir?"

Rothchild didn't move. Instead he continued to stare at the man, first directly into his face, then he looked him up and down.

The man moved to within approximately a meter of the car. He was standing facing the car, but about a half meter to the rear, forcing Rothchild to look over his shoulder.

Still not moving, Rothchild turned his head to the left and looked at the officer standing in the middle of the road. He was still swinging the lantern.

He turned back to the man who asked for his driving permit.

"Could I see some identification?" asked Rothchild.

The smile was still on the man's face.

"Certainly sir," said the man as he took a full step forward so he was directly in front of Rothchild. He reached into his coat pocket and pulled out a black case. With a flip of his wrist, the leather case opened up and revealed his identification credentials.

"I'm going to turn on the inside light," said Rothchild. He did not want to make any type of movement that could be misinterpreted. He reached down and turned on the light switch. The overhead lamp came on. He then reached out and took the credentials the man was holding, brought it inside the car and looked at it, then looked at the man.

Rothchild had no doubt the individual pictured on the credentials was the same man who was standing in front of him. He was Eamonn Ceantt, Superintendent in the Special Operations Section of the Garda Siochana.

The RUC Chief Superintendent handed the credentials back to the man and very cautiously reached into his coat pocket and removed his identification papers. He handed them to Ceantt. He removed his wallet, took out his driving permit and handed it to the Garda officer.

As Ceantt checked Rothchild's identification papers and driving permit Rothchild observed a change in his facial expression. The smile slowly faded away and was replaced by a stern look.

"So, may I ask what the Royal Ulster Constabulary is doing in this part of the Republic?"

Rothchild looked up at him, smiled and said,

"I was just having dinner with an old friend, Chief Superintendent Kerrigan."

He turned his head and looked straight ahead at the man standing in the middle of the road, turned back, looked up at Ceantt and asked,

"By chance, do you know him?"

The smile returned to Ceantt's face.

"By chance I just might. And may I say, it's a pleasure to met a member of the Constabulary with a sense of humor, Chief Superintendent Rothchild."

There was silence as Ceantt handed Rothchild his identification papers and driving permit.

"May I ask why the road block?"

"Now don't tell me the Chief Superintendent didn't tell you we are expecting some visitors this evening?"

Rothchild wanted to lie to him and tell him Kerrigan hadn't mention it, instead he said,

"How long has it been since you've been in contact with the Chief Superintendent?"

"Since early evening, why?"

"Let's just say it would probably be a good idea to get in touch with him, now."

Ceantt turned and walked towards the patrol car blocking the road. Before reaching the car he said,

"Cassidy, have you heard anything from the Command Center?"

The man with the lantern shook his head and said,

"No, I turned the radio off after the last call. It was running down my battery."

"Damn it man, how do you think we can stay in contact with the Command Center if you turn off the damn radio?" asked Ceantt.

Cassidy just shrugged his shoulders.

"Start the engine and turn the radio back on, now!"

"Yes sir," slurred Cassidy.

The officer started to place the lantern on the ground, changed his mind and handed it to Ceantt. Rothchild saw the Special Operations man was so angry he was tempted to throw the lantern as far as he could, but instead he gently placed it on the ground.

In the mean time, Cassidy entered the patrol car, started the engine and flipped on the parking lights.

"Turn on the damn radio," shouted Ceantt.

"I'm waiting for the generator to go to the plus side, so it…"

"Turn on the damn radio before I…"

"OK, OK," said Cassidy. There was an additional comment, made in a whisper so neither Ceantt nor Rothchild could make out all the words, but it did have something to do with the impatience of people from Dublin.

"It's on, you want me to turn up the volume so you can hear it?" asked Cassidy.

Before Ceantt had a chance to answer, the voice from the radio could be heard by anyone within twenty meters of the patrol car.

"Post six, this is the Command Center. Can you read me?"

"That's us," said Ceantt, "answer them."

"Wait a minute, I have to plug in the microphone."

"You what?"

"I kept hitting it with my leg as I drove up here, so I unplugged it," said Cassidy.

At this point, Rothchild was certain Ceantt was on the verge of shooting Cassidy.

He watched as Cassidy turned on the dashboard lights, bent over and searched the car floor for the microphone. Finally he pulled it out from under the passenger side seat, ran his hand down the cord until he felt the plug and after another ten seconds, he plugged it into the radio. He turned and asked,

"What do you want me to tell them?"

"Just answer them. Push the button and say, this is post six, over, then let up on the button."

Cassidy did what he was told and immediately the individual at the Control Center asked,

"Where've you been, we've been trying to reach you for the last hour and a half."

"Our radio was off," replied Cassidy.

There was dead silence for a few moments.

"Is Ceantt there?"

"Yes."

"Put him on."

Ceannt didn't wait for Cassidy to hand him the microphone. He grabbed it out his hand, pushed the button and said,

"This is Ceantt, go ahead."

"Just a moment please."

In a lower voice Ceantt could hear the man say,

"Here you are sir."

"Ceantt?"

"Yes."

"This is McKay."

Silence.

Ceannt slid into the patrol car and shut the door and motioned to Cassidy to close his door.

Rothchild turned the overhead light off, then turned it back on. He had his notebook in the glove compartment and since he had to wait, he decided to go through his notes. He had the habit of writing down the next day's schedule.

The notes were a mixture of professional duties and personal chores. He knew he was suppose to pick up his uniforms from the cleaners today, but forgot about it after Kerrigan's call. He needed to put that chore in the notebook or he would be looking for a clean uniform on Monday.

"*I better take in the other ones*," he thought. Directly above the notation to pick up uniforms, he made a note to take in his dirty uniforms.

"*Good, that will save me an extra trip.*"

Before he had a chance to write another chore or duty, he saw Ceannt exit the patrol car, slam the door and take the twelve steps that put him right next to his car

"Sir, would you back up so the patrol car can pull out, then you can be on your way."

Rothchild wanted to ask a question, but Ceantt turned, walked a few steps and disappeared into the darkness. Rothchild started his car, put it in reverse, backed up the road approximately ten meters and stopped. The patrol car made a wide semicircle, pulled onto the road and stopped.

Rothchild was wondering why the patrol car stopped when an Army truck pulled out of the woods from where Ceannt disappeared. The rear double wheels skidded across the grass, cutting two deep furrows in the soil as the driver turned the truck onto the road, directly in front of the patrol car, which followed behind it.

Rothchild sat in the darkness for a few moments before putting his car in gear and continuing on his way to Belfast.

He did not hear any of the radio communication, but he knew exactly what was happening.

Kerrigan had instructed the Control Center to call in all their people. What puzzled him was why they were in such a hurry to get back, they'd probably get back in a hurry and then sit around for two or three hours.

Three kilometers up the road and Rothchild's thoughts were no longer on Ceannt, but on which road he would take to get back to Belfast. He thought about taking the road he came down on, but while Kerrigan was on the phone back in Ballybofey, he looked at his map and thought about taking the secondary roads. As he was thinking about which way to return to Belfast, the exit to B165 appeared in his headlights. That made the decision for him. He slowed and pulled off N15, slowed to a stop at the border crossing, showed his identification papers, eased through Clady and was on his way through the darkness. Twenty minutes later he looked at his watch. He was making good time and with any luck he would be home around his target time.

At eleven thirty he arrived at his house in the northern part of Belfast. Being as quiet as possible, he opened the front door, tiptoed into the kitchen and reached for the phone on the shelf next to the refrigerator. He wanted to call Headquarters and tell the duty officer he wouldn't be in till late, probably not until after nine o'clock in the morning.

Before he could dial the number, his wife appeared in the doorway of the kitchen.

"I've been waiting up for you Douglas."

"I told you not to. I told you I would probably be very late coming in."

"I know, but the duty officer called a little after nine and wanted to speak with you. He said it was very important and asked for you to call him as soon as you came in."

She yawned and said,

"I was afraid I wouldn't hear you when you came in, so I've been reading a book since the call."

"I'm sorry, but you didn't have to stay up. I was just getting ready to call Headquarters when you came in, to tell them I won't be in bright and early as usual."

"Well, I'm sorry too," said Mrs. Rothchild as she turned and walked out of the room.

Rothchild just shrugged his shoulders and shook his head. He was always saying the wrong thing, or at least she took what he said to be wrong.

As he stood looking at the doorway through which she disappeared, he was thinking about how she put up with all his late nights, unexplained absences, days of his refusing to talk, his occasional mean disposition and all the rest. If the shoes were reversed, he was sure he would have walked out years ago. He was lucky; he married into a family of police officers. He married a woman who understood better than he did the politics of police life.

During the "bad years" she never appeared unhappy. When he was transferred to the lowly positions because of his failure to go along with the others, she made the best of it. She never complained. In fact, when he was transferred to the "boondocks" she made it appear as an adventure.

He just thanked the good Lord there were no children involved in his humiliation. They both wanted children, but whether it was her incapability to retain a fetus or his weak sperm that produced a series of defective fetuses, was never determined. During the first five years of their marriage, his wife became pregnant three times and each time at the trimester, she suffered a miscarriage. After the third attempt, they gave up and she never conceived again.

"*What the hell,*" he said to himself as he dialed the number for the duty officer.

The duty officer at the Constabulary Headquarters answered Rothchild's call.

"Constable, this is Chief Superintendent Rothchild, I..."

"Sir, we have been trying to reach you since, since before I came on duty at ten."

"Yes," said Rothchild.

"Yes sir. There was a report of a group of Provos hitting a jail in the Republic, in, in...wait a minute sir...in Convoy."

Day Four

July 25, 1998

Ballynure,
Northern Ireland

At exactly 8:34 AM, less than a mile south of Ballynure, a four door Ford sedan traveling south on Highway A8 at approximately sixty miles an hour exploded with such violence the largest remnant, other than the motor, power train and wheels, was a scrap of metal measuring three by thirteen inches. This piece of metal was believed to be part of one of the four doors.

The explosion littered an area two hundred meters wide and close to a half a kilometer long with a thousand plus pieces of scorched metal, rubber fragments from the tires, pieces of cloth and plastic and small pieces of human parts.

Fifty minutes later, Ben Sullivan, the member of the Bomb Squad on weekend duty, arrived on the scene. It was almost an hour later before the other members of the squad arrived at the scene.

Within minutes of the explosion, the local members of the Constabulary closed the road, roped off the area and retained the seven eye witnesses.

The investigators were forced to base their initial conclusions on seven different versions of what occurred at 8:34 AM from the seven.

Initially, the seven could not agree on the number of individuals in the car or the color of the automobile. Two witnesses said the car contained three individuals, two said there were two and two swore only one person was in the car. The seventh witness stated he did not know.

As described by the witnesses, the color ranged from dark grey, to blue to black. All seven did agree the car was a four door sedan.

It was almost two hours after the arrival of the squad before the investigators came to the correct conclusion only two individuals were in the car when the explosion occurred, in spite of what four of the witnesses stated to the investigators.

The investigators knew the identities of the driver and his passenger might never be determined, unless they were reported missing by family or friends and DNA analysis was used for positive identification.

Within four hours, the car was identified by the motor number, which did not match the license plate number. This particular car was reported stolen from a public parking lot in Dublin on the 27th of June and the license plate was stolen from a similar car in Banbridge on the 2nd of July. According to the records, the color of the car was brown.

None of the witnesses reported any erratic movement of the car prior to the explosion. Three of the witnesses, including the only witness injured, were behind the automobile, three were driving towards it and one was on the shoulder of the road changing a flat tire.

The injured man was a 27 year old truck driver who was approximately a hundred meters behind the car when it exploded. Pieces of the metal were blown into the wind shield of the truck, shatter the glass and causing the driver to lose control and veer off the highway into the ditch.

Besides a few pieces of glass embedded in the man's face and hands, the only injuries were a cracked rib and broken nose, which resulted when the truck came to a sudden stop in the ditch.

The explosion was described by four of the witnesses as being a loud, white flash followed instantly by red and yellow flashes. The three other witnesses stated they saw the white flash, but then a blue flash and no red or yellow flashes.

The members of the Bomb Squad had no time to compare notes at the time. After interviewing the witnesses, they attempted to pick up every piece of the car while the medical personnel removed what remained of the two bodies. The human remains were placed in one black body bag and transported to the morgue of the local hospital, where the medical examiner would attempt to separate the hunderds of pieces into two individual lots. Each lot would remain at the hospital until either identified and passed on to their families or buried by the government after a court order was issued by the presiding judicatory authority.

Before the highway was allowed to be cleared and washed down, the members of the squad made three "sweeps" of the area to make certain all the remnants of the car had been gathered and bagged, to be checked later by the laboratory personnel.

The pictures and measurements, taken by the investigators during the six hours they were actually on the scene, would be the only evidence of an explosion on highway A8. The remains of the automobile would be stored for further examination, but there would be no possibility of continually viewing the scattered parts of the car at the site.

Once the squad was satisfied no physical evidence remained in the area, the road was washed down by the crew of one of the two fire engines assigned to the scene. Once the road was clean, the road crew immediately went to work removing the large chunks of payment from the area and filling the hole with a mixture of sand, gravel and clay. The chief of the road crew made the determination the road should remain closed until the filled hole could be paved over, which meant a full road crew would have to be called in on Saturday.

Highway A8 was not opened to traffic until ten minutes after nine o'clock on Saturday evening.

Lamb, along with the other members of the Bomb Squad, spent most of the day attempting to determine the exact cause of the explosion. The one piece of metal he picked up was similar to one he had seen previously, but at the time, he could not recall exactly where or when. It would later be identified by Rhoades as a fragment from the top of a butane tank.

Because of weekend duty, Rhoades granted Lamb and the four other investigators one day off. Wednesday was Lamb's day off.

As soon as he reached his apartment, Lamb called Liz Kelly and asked if there would be a chance of her being free on Wednesday. Mrs. Kelly quickly informed the young Australian Captain that she was not only free on Wednesday, but she expected him to pick her up at her friend's house in Hilltown, drive to Castlewallen to her Aunt Mae's Tea Room by ten o'clock so they could pick up some of her aunt's freshly baked desserts.

"And what will we do after stuffing ourselves with all those calories?" asked Lamb.

"You're not going to eat at Aunt Mae's. We're just going to pick up some of her goodies to go along with the picnic basket I will have prepared by the time you pick me up at Bridget's house.

After Castlewallen, I thought we could take a drive down through New Castle, Annalong and down through Kilkeel to the Mourne Park where we will have a picnic lunch. Then later, maybe we could go to Kilkeel or Rostrevor and watch the fishing ships and yachts."

"Sounds like a great idea. I'll pick you up at Bridget's house at exactly ten o'clock Wednesday morning."

Day Five

July 26, 1998

Dublin, Ireland
LAND DAILY TELEGRAPH
NEWSPAPER
SUNDAY, JULY 26, 1998

GARDA CAPTURES AND LOSES
O'CONNOR
(All in less than 72 hours)

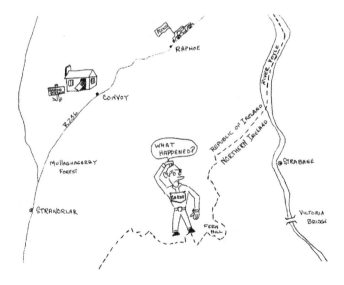

On the morning of the 22nd of July, the Garda captured the most wanted IRA gunman along with the individual believed to be responsible for the strategy of the Provos during the late 80's and early 90's. The two were Thomas O'Connor and Ronald McCaul.

O'Connor and McCaul, along with six others, escaped from the Castlereagh Interrogation Center outside Belfast in 1992, a jail break as famous as that of Bik McFarlane's escape from Long Kesh along with 37 others a decade previous.

O'Connor and McCaul have not been seen or heard of for over five years until last Wednesday when the two were arrested at the border by members of the Garda. McCaul, who was seriously ill, was transferred to Dublin by a military helicopter from the military base in Letterkenny, County Donegal on the evening of the 22nd of July.

According to our source, the head of Special Operations received information from one of his sources that a PIRA unit would be crossing the border in the area of Castlederg on Friday night, the 24th of July, in order to rescue O'Connor. What happened next comes right out of a James Bond movie.

When the Provos reached the Castlederg area, a squad of SAS surrounded them and shot and killed the lot. The bodies of the dead Provos were then loaded into and carried off in an Army Saracen. The difference was that the people who shot(?) the rescue team were members of the Provos dressed in borrowed SAS uniforms and shooting blank bullets.

While the staged assassination of the Provos was taking place near Castlederg in the vicinity of Fern Hill, the real rescue team was on their way to the jail in Convoy where Thomas O'Connor was being held prisoner. Around nine o'clock in the evening the rescue team walked into the jail and walked off with O'Connor, who was then driven up the road into Northern Ireland. Before leaving Convoy, the Provos locked the two Special Operations member, who had been guarding O'Connor in the cell previous occupied by o'Connor.

Great going Garda!!!

Day Six

July 27, 1998

Garda Headquarters
Dublin, Ireland

Monday morning a little after eight and Kerrigan was already in his office. Mrs. Roberts, who always arrived at least thirty minutes before Kerrigan, no matter what time of the morning he arrived, entered his office without knocking thirty seconds after he took off his suit coat. She placed a tray with a pot of hot tea, two cups, cream, sugar, napkins and a plate of pineapple Danish on the small table next to Kerrigan's desk. This was all accomplished without a word being spoken by either. She left the office as silently as she entered.

Kerrigan poured himself a cup of tea, added cream, picked up a Danish and napkin and took a seat in one of the overstuffed, leather chairs in front of his desk.

He slowing ate the Danish and thought about Friday night, then about the Sunday papers. He closed his eyes and visualized the articles and cartoons. Slowly he shook his head back and forth.

There was no mention of any comments by either the Provos or Sinn Fein about the event, yet the newspaper knew exactly what had occurred Friday night. Without mentioning anyone by name, they reported how the Provos outsmarted the Garda and walked off with their prize prisoner.

After Kerrigan was informed the SAS annihilated the rescue unit, he instructed Superintendent McKay, who was in charge of the operation, to send his people back to Dublin. McKay pulled all except two of his men out of Convey, leaving the two to guard O'Connor. He instructed the radio operator to contact Superintendent Eamonn Ceannt and ask him to pull his men off the border and return to Convoy where he was to pick up O'Connor and transport him to Dublin.

It was during the period between when the Special Operation men left Convoy and Creannt's arrival in Convoy that the PIRA unit "liberated" O'Connor, leaving the two Special Operations men in the jail cell previously occupied by O'Connor.

The Chief Superintendent was still feeling the barbs from his loss of O'Connor. The Provos' operation on Friday night was classic. It not only embarrassed Kerrigan, but it embarrassed the whole organization.

The Provos' trick with the "borrowed" British Saracen and uniforms was an escapade which would be added to their journal of achievements… an event which songs will be written about; an episode which no doubt would be the main theme of a whole series of articles and perhaps a book or two.

The English newspapers in particular were having a field day with the story. The written word was bad enough, but the cartoons were worse.

On the editorial page of one English Sunday's paper, a quarter page size cartoon showed a group of buffoons scratching their heads, looking across a stream at a group thumbing their noses at them. Of course, the labels on the Buffoons were the shields of the Garda and the ones thumbing their noses were the Provos.

Kerrigan's thoughts jumped from the events of Friday night to Saturday morning when he received a call to be in the Commissioner's office at nine o'clock. Kerrigan was told he was to meet with not only the Commissioner, but with the Deputy Commissioners, the Attorney General and their staffs.

At the meeting, Kerrigan was told in no uncertain terms by one of the Deputy Commissioners his actions after the arrest of McCaul and O'Connor was reason for dismissal from the force. It was not because his plan failed and subjected the Garda to a great deal of adverse publicity, but because he failed to obtain permission for the operation.

"You knew you did not have the authority to set up this operation without approval from my office," said the Attorney General.

"Yes sir," said Kerrigan, "I knew."

"As the Deputy Commissioner said, failure to obtain authorization is more than sufficient grounds for dismissal from the Garda. Did you realize that at the time?"

"Yes sir," said Kerrigan.

"Then why in the hell didn't you ask approval of the operation?"

"Because I didn't have time to wait five days for approval."

"What in the hell do you mean by that?" asked the Attorney General.

"Last March, when we received word Reynaud and his number one man was due in Dublin for a meeting with Cory, we asked your office to grant permission for a wire tap and the arrests."

"If I remember right, you received the authorization for both the wire tap and the arrests."

"Yes sir, two days after the meeting and one day after Reynaud was back in France and after Cory had disappeared completely."

"But...."

"I made a wrong call on the O'Connor and McCaul incident and I'll take full blame," said Kerrigan.

Turning towards the Commissioner for only a moment, he turned back to face the Attorney General and continued,

"If you gentlemen insist on my resignation, I'll have it on the Commissioner's desk the first thing Monday morning."

The Commissioner could hardly retain a straight face. During the telephone conversation at four o'clock in the morning, the Commissioner suggested Kerrigan bring up the Reynaud case if the Attorney General threatened him.

"No one said anything about a resignation Patrick," said the Commissioner.

"I didn't mean...."

The Commissioner put up his hand to halt the Attorney General.

"You had a good plan Patrick, but the Provos outfoxed you and made the Garda look like a bunch of country bumpkins. Agree?"

"Yes sir, I agree. I was certainly outfoxed, no doubt about it."

"Are you certain it happened the way your informants said it happened?" asked Henry Anderson, one of the Deputy Commissioner.

"Yes sir. I had people on both sides of the border. They reported the same scenario."

"How did they know about the trap?" asked the Attorney General.

"I have no idea how they knew O'Connor was in the jail in Convoy, but that information could have come from any number of sources. The little stage play in the Fern Hill area, that would have been something McCaul would pull, but McCaul was in Dublin and too sick to communicate with anyone."

Looking at the Attorney General, the Commissioner said,

"You have to give them credit Henry, that was one hell of an idea."

"You're correct Commissioner, but it made all of us look like a herd of jack-asses."

"So, we'll get over it, right Patrick?"

"Yes sir, some day."

For the next thirty seconds the room was silent.

"What about McCaul?" asked one of the Attorney General's staff member.

"What do you mean?" asked Kerrigan.

"I mean where is he? How sick is he? Is he being guarded? I'd like to know anything you can tell us."

"We have him in a hospital outside of Dublin. How sick is he? I don't know. The last time I saw him, he looked like he had a good case of the flu and the last question, is he being guarded? Yes, at the present time my men are guarding him, but the special unit which provides protection for visitors and dignitaries has assigned eight men to guard him. Three shifts of two each. One inside the room and one outside the door. The other two are spares, in case one of the others need replacement."

"What hospital?" asked the Attorney General.

Kerrigan looked over at the Commissioner who was shaking his head.

"One of the hospitals outside of Dublin," said Kerrigan.

"Which one?" asked another member of the Attorney General's staff."

"Sorry," said the Commissioner, "I've instructed the Chief Superintendent not to reveal the whereabout of McCaul."

"But…"

"Understandable," said the Attorney General.

"Are there anymore questions?" asked the Commissioner.

The Deputy Commissioners and the Attorney General looked at each other and then at their staff. Every man and woman was shaking their head.

"Good," said the Commissioner, then turning to Kerrigan he said,

"Thank you Patrick. You will keep us informed of any new developments, right?"

"Yes sir," said Kerrigan.

Within two minutes the Commissioner's office was empty except for the Commissioner and Kerrigan.

"Well Patrick, it wasn't as bad as I thought it was going to be. Have you heard anything about McCaul this morning?"

"No sir."

"Keep me informed," said the Commissioner.

"Yes sir."

Kerrigan closed his eyes and shook his head, hoping this would erase the events of the last three days from his mind. It didn't work, but the ringing of the telephone jarred him back to the present.

He put his teacup on the desk, pushed himself up and picked up the phone.

"Kerrigan speaking."

"Patrick, this is Dr. Shaw."

"Yes Henry, is something wrong?"

Kerrigan knew the answer before he asked the question.

"It's about the young man Jamie brought in Wednesday night. The poor fellow is very sick and we don't know what's wrong with him."

"What do you mean you don't know what's wrong with him, I thought he had the flu?"

"Just that Patrick, I don't know what's wrong with him. He has a high fever, with sweats and chills."

"Sounds like the flu to me," said Kerrigan.

"That's what I thought, but the fever is too high. We couldn't get it down with aspirin and we had to give him an alcohol bath."

"Damn," said Kerrigan.

"I thought I'd better let you know because there is a chance we might lose him."

Kerrigan was at a loss for words.

"I'm not sure yet, but his blood pressure has been dropping this morning and the fever is back. We've taken blood samples and sent them to the lab. We hoped they would identify the organism, do the serology and determine which antibiotics we can use. But the reports came back negative. They were unable to identify any specific organism."

"What does that mean?"

"It means we don't know how to treat him. We gave him a broad spectrum antibiotic, but that didn't seem to do any good. We tried an anti-virus mixture and we have to wait to see what happens."

"But it's been five days now, don't you have the results?"

Shaw hesitated for a moment, then said,

"Like you, we thought it was the flu and he would be better in a couple of days. He took a turn for the worse Sunday afternoon. That's when we started the different treatments."

"But Jamie saw him yesterday and said he looked good," said Kerrigan.

"Friday night his fever jumped and he was restless, tossing and turning and trying to get up. After we got his fever down we sedated him so he could get some rest. When Jamie saw him, his fever was down and he was sleeping. This morning the fever returned and we've having a difficult time keeping it below 40 degrees."

"Is there anything I can do?"

"No Patrick, I just thought I'd better let you know. I didn't want you to be completely surprised if the news is bad. I would suggest you contact his next of kin, just in case."

"Thank you for calling Henry. If…"

"I'll call you either way."

"Thank you."

"Good by."

The phone went dead and slowly Kerrigan replaced it in the cradle. He looked at it for a long time as he thought,

"Good Lord, what am I going to do if McCaul dies?"

He walked over to the window and looked out. He stared at the street below, at the people, the cars, the buses, but his eyes did not telegraph the scene to his brain. He closed his eyes and instantly visualized McCaul in the bed in the hospital room.

"I'd better try and contact McCaul's family. I know I would want to be with one of my children if they were dying, no matter what. But what if McCaul is not as sick as Henry thinks and he is up and about in a week? Between that rock and a hard place again."

Kerrigan was worried the Provos would learn where McCaul was a patient. They knew he was taken to Dublin by Meyers, but hopefully they didn't know he was a patient in St. Francis Hospital in Baldoyle.

If McCaul was as sick as Shaw said, perhaps they better start making other arrangements.

Kerrigan picked up the phone and dialed 6.

"Yes."

"Jamie, would you step into my officer of a minute."

"Yes sir."

Almost before Kerrigan replaced the phone there was a knock on the door.

"Come in Jamie."

Detective Sergeant Meyers walked into Kerrigan's office, closed the door and stood facing the Chief Superintendent.

Kerrigan looked at Meyers for almost twenty seconds without saying a word.

Finally, Meyers said, "Yes sir?"

Kerrigan shook his head and said,

"Sorry Jamie, have a seat."

Meyers walked across the room and stood in front of one of the leather chairs that faced Kerrigan's desk.

"Would you like a cup of tea and a Danish?"

Meyers smiled and said,

"Yes sir. Mrs. Roberts told me earlier that she had tea and Danish for me.....in your office."

"How did she know I..."

"I don't know sir."

"Get your cup of tea and Danish and if you will, you can fill up my cup."

"Yes sir," said Meyers as he walked over to the table containing the tea and rolls. He poured two cups of tea, handed one to Kerrigan and proceeded to fix his tea. He picked up one of the Danish and returned to the leather chair.

"Jamie, we have a problem. Dr. Shaw said McCaul is extremely ill and they don't know what is wrong with him. He called to tell me there is a chance he may not make it."

"But Friday night he looked like he was OK."

"I told Shaw that, but he said the fever returned this morning and there is a possibility they could lose him. We should start thinking about what we'll do if he does die."

"Yes sir."

"How secure do you think the hospital is? Any possibility someone might recognize him?"

"We talked about that before, remember?"

"I know, but I'm having second thoughts. We can't afford another Convoy."

"We can supplement the guards with some of our people, the place is not that large."

"That would only draw more attention. They know he's someplace in the area, hopefully they think he's in Dublin. Do you have any suggestions?"

After a few moments, Meyers said,

"They have no idea what's causing his illness?"

"No, they've tried a broad spectrum antibiotic and no results. He still has that high fever, chills, sweats and shakes. They've ruled out the flu but have no idea what's causing him to be so sick."

"His chances of dying?"

"They don't know."

After a few moments of silence, Meyers took a drink of his tea, placed the cup on the arm of the chair and said,

"Sir, there's something I'd better tell you about my talk with O'Connor before I brought McCaul to Dublin."

"Yes."

"O'Connor said he thought, no, he said he was sure McCaul knew he wasn't going to make it, that he was going to die. McCaul made O'Connor promise to get him or his body to Wales if he died."

Kerrigan nodded his head.

"And," continued Meyers, "O'Connor swore to McCaul that if he died, he would see he was returned to Wales."

"All right," said Kerrigan, "if McCaul dies his folks will probably make the arrangements to have his body transported to Wales."

"Yes sir, but what if the government does not allow McCaul's kin to take the body?" asked Meyers.

"That means O'Connor will probably make an attempt to obtain McCaul's body and take it to Wales."

"I'm afraid so sir."

"That could lead to people getting hurt or killed."

"Yes sir."

For a full sixty seconds Kerrigan stared at the tea in his cup. Finally he looked up at Meyers and said,

"Jamie, do you know where McCaul's parents are at this time?"

"Yes sir. His father is a Professor at Queen's and his mother and sisters live in Wales, outside Cardiff."

"We need to contact them and let them know McCaul's condition. I know I would want to be with one of my children if he was…"

"Yes sir."

"Can you contact Professor McCaul and.."

"Would you like for me to take care of it sir?"

Kerrigan frowned for a moment, smiled, let out a little laugh, nodded his head and said,

"Yes Jamie, I would like for you to take care of it."

"Yes sir."

Meyers pushed his way up out of the chair, placed his cup on the table and walked out of the Chief Superintendent's office, crossed the hall and entered his office. He opened the filing cabinet, took out the Garda's file on McCaul and removed the picture of Professor McCaul.

Meyers stopped by Mrs. Roberts' desk and told her he would be gone the rest of the day. She looked up, turned her head slightly, smiled and said,

"See you tomorrow."

Queen's University Belfast, Northern Ireland

The trip to Belfast took just a over an hour once Meyers made it to the outskirts of Dublin. It took another thirty minutes to find a parking space at Queen's University and the building housing the History Department.

Meyers entered the building, checked the directory in the hallway, walked up the stairs to the second floor and checked the schedule posted outside of Dr. McCaul's office. He looked at his watch and determined McCaul would be another twenty minutes in his class. All he had to do was find the correct classroom and the cafeteria. He stopped a young lady who was walking down the hall and obtained directions to the cafeteria.

Twenty-five minutes later, Meyers saw McCaul walk out of the classroom on the first floor and head for his office. He was halfway up the stairs when Meyers caught up with him.

"Dr. McCaul, I'm Detective Meyers from the Garda. I need to talk with you about your son, but not here. In the cafeteria."

McCaul stopped, looked at Meyers and started to ask a question.

"Please continue up the stairs sir, I'll be waiting for you in the cafeteria," said Meyers as he walked passed McCaul.

Ten minutes later Professor McCaul walked out of the History Building and walked to the main cafeteria where Meyers was occupying a table close to back wall. It required almost two minutes for McCaul to see Meyers. He nodded to let the Garda detective know he saw him.

McCaul went through the cafeteria line, picking out a small piece of chicken, two vegetables, a small salad and a cup of tea.

After paying for his meal, he looked around as if searching for a table, then walked directly to the table occupied by Meyers.

Once seated, Meyers explained to him the reason he was in Belfast. McCaul was unable to eat and said he would make arrangements immediately to leave for Dublin.

"I'll be happy to drive you down to the hospital Dr. McCaul," said Meyers.

McCaul took a sip of his tea, pushed the tray of food to the middle of the table and nodded his head. He didn't know what to say.

"What about Mrs. McCaul?" asked Meyers.

"I'll call her as soon as I get to my apartment."

"We can go to your apartment and you can pack a small bag."

"How sick is Ronald?"

"I don't really know sir, the doctor said he is extremely ill and they don't know what is causing the sickness. That's all I know sir."

"I contacted the Constabulary when I read about Ronald being captured and asked them about me visiting him," said McCaul.

"He has been under protective custody sir."

"I realize that, but why couldn't I get permission to visit him?"

"I don't know sir. All I know is that my supervisor asked me to contact you and let you know how sick you son is."

"Did he tell you to drive me to Dublin?"

"No sir."

McCaul nodded his head, pushed back from the table and said,

"I really appreciate your offer to drive me to the hospital. It will only take me a few minutes to pack a bag and call my wife."

"Good," said Meyers.

The few minutes turned out to be a little over thirty minutes. By the time the two arrived at the hospital it was after four o'clock. Meyers escorted McCaul up to his son's room, contacted Dr. Shaw and introduced the two. He then called headquarters, but Chief Superintendent Kerrigan was at a meeting with the District Attorney.

He called Kerrigan's residence, but was informed the Chief Superintendent wouldn't be in until later, in that he was having dinner with the Attorney General.

Meyers bid Professor McCaul and Dr. Shaw good by and headed home.

St. Francis Hospital
Baldoyle, Ireland

The Charge Nurse summoned Dr. Shaw at a few minutes before six thirty. He left the patient he was talking with and walked to the nurses' desk. He looked at her and said,

"Yes?"

"Your patient with the guards. Sister Francis Jane just reported she thinks he has gone into a coma and wanted you to be informed."

"Thank you," said Shaw as he turned and walked down to the end of the hall where McCaul's room was located. He nodded to the guard on duty and entered the room.

Professor McCaul was sitting next to the bed holding his son's right hand and the young nurse was standing on the other side of the bed holding McCaul's other hand. When Shaw entered, both Professor McCaul and the nurse looked up, then Sister Francis Jane said,

"Doctor, I think he's in a coma, but I've really never seen a patient in a coma."

As Shaw nodded, the nurse dropped the patient's hand and backed away from the bed to allow the doctor to get close to the patient.

Shaw walked up to the bed, took his stethoscope from his coat pocket and checked McCaul's heart rate. The beat of the heart was not only faint, it was erratic, skipping a beat every fifth or sixth beat.

Shaw replaced the stethoscope in his coat pocket, removed a small flashlight from the breast pocket of his shirt, gently lifted one of McCaul's eyelids and shined the light into the eye.

Sister Francis Jane was correct, the patient was in a coma.

Checking the monitors above the bed, Shaw saw the patient's temperature was just a little over 38 degrees, his respiration was normal, but his blood pressure was low.

"You're right Sister, our patient is in a coma. Do you have other patients to care for?"

"Yes sir, four others, but I thought I'd…."

"You go take care of the others and then come back here and stay with him. I'll tell the Charge Nurse I've asked you to stand watch."

"Yes sir," said Sister Francis Jane as she adjusted the cover sheet and walked out of the room.

Shaw stood looking at his patient for another five minutes, watching his chest rise and fall. There was nothing he could do for McCaul at the present.

"Professor McCaul, I'm afraid your son might be losing his battle. It doesn't look good now, but it could change, we never know."

McCaul looked up at the doctor, nodded his head and turned back to watch his son.

Turning to the guard sitting next to the window, Dr. Shaw said,

"Would you keep an eye on the monitors until Sister returns? If any of the lights turn red, push the call button. The alarm will sound in the ICU, but that's two floors down."

"Yes sir," said the police officer, happy to have something to do besides looking out the window and re-read the morning paper.

"Thank you," said Shaw as he walked out of the room and down the hall to the Doctors' lounge. Before he took a seat, he called Kerrigan to inform the Chief Superintendent of the patient's condition.

After eating a late dinner in the hospital cafeteria, Shaw returned to the third floor and immediately went to McCaul's room. Sister Francis Jane was seated on one side of the bed opposite Professor McCaul, holding McCaul's hand.

"*God, don't let her fall in love with him!*" thought Shaw. He had seen it happen so many times. Young nurses falling in love with a dying patient and then having their heart broken when he dies.

"Any change in his condition?"

"No doctor, just the same."

Shaw looked at his watch. It was almost a quarter till eight.

"I'm going to try and get a little rest Sister. If there is any change, I'll be in the Doctors' lounge."

"Yes sir."

"Professor McCaul, have you had anything to eat?"

McCaul shook his head, then said,

"I don't want to leave Ronald."

Shaw understood, nodded, turned to the nurse and said,

"I'll be back in about an hour."

"Yes sir," said the nurse.

Shaw smiled at the young nurse. They were so polite and caring when they first started working, but after a few years they lose the sentimentality and become not hard hearted, but accustomed to sickness and death.

Shaw walked out of the room, walked up the hall to the Nurses' station and asked the Charge Nurse to have a dinner tray sent to McCaul's room for the Professor.

From the Nurses' station Shaw walked to the Doctors' lounge. Once inside he slumped down in one of the oversized chairs and within seconds the old doctor was sound asleep.

Shaw's internal alarm clock woke him from a sound sleep at a few minutes before nine. He stretched his weary muscles while remaining in a seated position.

After another few minutes Shaw stood up and walked into the water chamber, turned on the cold water and doused his face with the refreshing liquid. Once fully awake, he walked out of the lounge and directly to McCaul's room.

As Shaw was about to enter the room, the Charge Nurse opened the door. He caught it and held it open.

"I was just on my way to get you doctor," she said in an almost monotone voice.

He looked at her for only a second, looked into the room at the man in the bed. He knew immediately the reason she was on her way to get him.

He let the door go and entered the room followed by the nurse. He walked pass the police officer who was standing with his back to the wall looking at McCaul. Sister Francis Jane stood up, letting go of the young McCaul's hand and backed away from the bed.

As Shaw looked down at Ronald McCaul, he realized the young man was breathing his last few breaths. Shaw had heard the death rattles hundred of time. It was an unmistakable sound. When he was a child, his mother told him it was the call for the banshees.

There was nothing Shaw could do except stand by the bed and watch the life's breath slowly depart. He took hold of McCaul's wrist and felt for a pulse. He could feel a faint one.

"You'd better call the priest Sister."

"Yes doctor," said the Charge nurse. She was watching the doctor's expression. She had worked on this ward since she first came to work sixteen years ago and had known Dr. Shaw from her first day at the hospital. Every time he lost a patient the pain would show in his face, as if he was losing one of his kin. She didn't understand how he could continue to feel so much hurt. She knew that over the years, she and others who worked as nurses, developed both a coldness and a hardness towards death. Not so with poor old Dr. Shaw. He took every death personally and it showed on his face.

"He is only sixty years old and at the moment he looked eighty," she thought as she walked down the hall to the chaplain's office.

"Doctor, Ronald is not Catholic. He was raised a Presbyterian, but I don't know whether he has practiced his religion in the last few years."

"The Priest will give him the last rites of the church and I don't believe it will make any difference to God what religion he practiced or didn't practice. Unless you would rather not have him receive any last blessing?"

"No, no, I think Ronald would be more than willing to receive the blessing."

"Good," said Shaw.

Shaw and Professor McCaul were still holding young McCaul's hands as the priest entered the room.

"You'd better hurry Father or you'll be giving the Last Rites to a dead man."

"How about his kin, have.."

"This is the boy's father," said Shaw as he nodded towards Professor McCaul.

"I'm sorry sir to meet you under these circumstances, but…"

"I understand."

Looking down at Ronald McCaul, the priest asked,

"Is your son Catholic?"

"No, he was raised Presbyterian."

The priest smiled faintly and said,

"Close enough."

He leaned down and opened his sick call case, removed the oil, candle, holy water and a purple scapular. Being from the old school, he said all the prayers in Latin, most of it understood by both Shaw and McCaul.

It appeared to all in the room that young McCaul's last breath and final pulse were timed exactly with Father McClan's

"May your soul rest in eternal peace, amen."

Shaw turned to Sister Francis, smiled and said,

"It's over Sister, you'd better go take care of your other patients."

As she turned, Shaw handed her his handkerchief to wipe the tears from her face. He then gently placed Ronald McCaul's arms across his chest and checked for a pulse on the side of his neck. He could find none. He then checked the eyes, which were already beginning to glaze over.

Death won out one more time.

"Don't take it so hard Henry," said Father McClan, as he folded up his scapular, "there's no fighting God's will."

"I know Father, but God gave us ways to cheat death. The problem is, we're not wise enough to use the methods God gave us."

"I know," said the priest as he shook hands with Professor McCaul, nodded to Shaw and walked out of the room.

Father McClan's words..."it is God's will" were of little satisfaction to Dr. Henry Shaw. He had lost another patient and it hurt. He had acknowledged the Priest's statement that death of this young man was God's will, but he continued to shake his head at what he considered his own incompetence.

"Professor, have you made any arrangements to return to Belfast tonight?"

"No, I was going to try and find a room close to the hospital, hoping I would have more time with Ronald."

"What are your plans now?"

"I'm till going to try and find a room so I can come back tomorrow and make arrangements to take Ronald home."

"Why don't you come with me to the lounge, perhaps a good drink of Irish whiskey will help."

Professor McCaul nodded and said,

"Thank you."

As the two walked pass the nurses' station, Shaw leaned over to the Charge Nurse and said,

"Sister, you can get the young man ready for the morgue."

Even though she answered,

"Yes doctor, right away," she had already started the paper work.

"Do you have the number of the little hotel down the street, the one on Baylor Street?"

"Yes sir, just a moment."

She reached down and picked up a card from her desk, one of the many the manager of the hotel had left on each floor.

"Here it is doctor."

"Thank you," said Shaw as he took the card, then motion to Professor McCaul to follow him.

Shaw walked down the hall to the Doctors' lounge, opened the door and held it until McCaul entered. He then lead the way to his "hospital office" which consisted of two rooms off the lounge. The first room had a desk and chair, two sofa type chairs, a whiskey cabinet, a small refrigerator and a coffee table. The second room was a bedroom with an Army type spring bed, a desk and chair and a stack of medical magazines on a small, square table lifted from the cafeteria.

As the two entered Dr. Shaw's hospital office, Shaw pointed to one of the sofa type chairs and said,

"Have a seat Professor."

"Thank you."

"What can I get you Professor, I have Scotch, Bourbon, Jameson and some soft drinks."

"I'd like a glass of your good Irish whiskey and please call me Roger."

"OK Roger, how would you like your whiskey? With soda water, water or plain?"

"Plain."

"Sounds like a good Irishman," said Shaw.

McCaul mustered a smile. It was hard to smile when one's heart was broken.

Shaw removed two glasses and a bottle of Jameson from the cabinet, then retrieved a bowl of ice cubes from the refrigerator. He placed them on the table and poured a hefty drink in each glass.

After the glasses were half empty and before Shaw poured a second glass, he said,

"Excuse me for a moment Roger, I'm going to call the hotel and see if they have a vacancy."

McCaul nodded and continued to sip the whiskey and stare off into space. He saw, but didn't hear the doctor call the hotel and speak with the desk clerk.

"You're lucky Roger, they have a couple of vacancies and I told them you would be there within the hour," said Shaw.

"Thank you Henry."

"Do you have a toilet kit?"

"Yes, I packed a few things in my bag," said McCaul as he looked around the room, "but I must have left it in Ronald's room."

"Don't worry, I'll call the desk and have them pick it up and you can get it when you leave."

"Thank you again."

"You're welcome."

After a few moments of silence, Shaw said,

"Roger, you said you were going to make arrangements to take your son home."

"Yes."

"You know, he was a prisoner of the Garda and they may not allow him to be transferred to your home."

"Why, he can't do any harm, not now."

"I know, I'm just warning you, the Garda may claim his body."

Shaw expected a violent reply, instead Professor McCaul said,

"We'll see."

Twenty minutes later, Professor McCaul departed the hospital and walked the three blocks to the hotel. After he left, Shaw placed a call to Chief Superintendent Kerrigan in order to inform him of Ronald McCaul's death.

Kerrigan's Residence
Dublin, Ireland

It was after seven when Chief Superintendent Kerrigan arrived home. After greeting his family, his wife prepared him a cup of hot tea and he retired to the parlor to read the evening paper. He was wondering if Jamie had been successful in contacting Professor McCaul.

This was the question Kerrigan was asking himself as he sit in the parlor looking at the evening paper. His eyes were reading the words, but they never made it to his brain, they were lost in the transmission process over that short distance from the eyes to the brain.

What started the loss of transmission was the picture of the dead man on the streets in front of a Constabulary station in Dungannon. Kerrigan read the caption and started to read the details, but the picture of the body quickly shifted his thought processes from the story of the man shot dead in Dungannon to the thought that perhaps this was one of the men who had outfoxed him and pulled off the rescue of O'Connor. The thought of O'Connor automatically lead to his companion, Ronald McCaul and from there to the condition of McCaul. He too might have a dead man on his hands.

He lowered the paper and started to put it down, but a quick survey of the room indicated both his wife and his mother-in-law were watching him, even though one was supposedly watching the telly and the other doing her eternal sewing. He shook the paper as if to straighten out the creases, but before he could turn the page his wife asked,

"What's wrong Patrick? You're a million miles away."

"Nothing darling, just thinking about Jamie. I put a heap on his shoulders today."

"That's not all, is it Patrick?"

"You should have been the detective in the family."

"You're just easy to read, you have something heavy on your mind right now, don't you?"

His mother-in-law hadn't said a word, but the look on her face indicated she agreed with her daughter's analysis of the situation.

Patrick smiled, not at the women, but to himself. He could hide his thoughts from everyone except these two women and Mrs. Roberts. They could almost enter his mind and weed out his very thoughts.

"It's nothing that important," he said.

After only a moment of silence, his mother-in-law spoke for the first time.

"This is the first time in over three years you let your tea go cold and your pipe go out, so don't lie to your wife Patrick Kerrigan. If it's something you don't want me to hear, I'll go to my room right now."

She started folding up her sewing, but Kerrigan stopped her with a wave of his hand as he let go of one side of the newspaper.

"It's McCaul, the one we picked up at the border. He's deathly ill and we're trying to contact his kin in Ulster. That's what I put on Jamie," he said.

The short explanation satisfied the two women. Both nodded, then one went back to watching the television and the other picked up her sewing.

Kerrigan returned to the newspaper and read the short commentary under the picture of the dead man.

"An unidentified terrorist was killed by an alert constable before he could hurl a bomb into the constabulary barracks. Two accomplices escaped in a stolen vehicle, which was later found parked on St. George Street. Details under TERRORIST on page A3"

Kerrigan turned to page A3 in order to read the complete story. The two columns on page A3 merely elaborated on the story. The crux of the episode was at seven fifteen yesterday morning a black car with its license plate covered with mud, sped up to constabulary barracks and squealed to a halt. A man jumped out and attempted to throw a bomb over the fence of the police compound. At that moment a young constable stepped out of the door of the station, realized what was happening, drew his revolver and opened fire. At the first shot, the car started pulling away, leaving the bomb thrower stranded in the middle of the street. The bomb didn't make it over the high fence and exploded in the street, killing the terrorist.

"When will they learn?" thought Kerrigan.

He started to put the paper down, but stopped in the middle of the move. He knew if he put the paper down, both women would eye him again and start delving into the McCaul business. Kerrigan was thinking about what Dr. Shaw told him, particularly the part about there being a good possibility McCaul would not survive.

Kerrigan was again staring into the paper, no longer reading any of the print. He was thinking about what would happen if McCaul did die. There was no doubt in Kerrigan's mind that hell would be raised by the New IRA, the Provos and the radical Nationalists in the North, but also by a good number of politicians in the Republic, particularly those who had little love for the police.

The ringing of the telephone interrupted Kerrigan's thoughts.

"Shall I get it Patrick?" asked his wife.

"No, I'll take it in the other room."

He was already out of the chair and on his way to his "home office" in the rear of the house.

The phone sounded the third time before he reached it. It started its fourth ring as he lifted the receiver.

"Kerrigan here."

"Patrick?"

"Yes."

"This is Dr. Shaw."

"Yes, I know. What is it Henry?"

"Patrick, McCaul is in a coma and I don't think there is much chance of…."

"Damn, damn, damn."

"I'm sorry Patrick, we've done all we could do. We tried every thing."

"I know Henry. I know you've done everything humanly possible and I thank you for that."

"Patrick, there is still a very slim chance he might survive, but…."

"But you wouldn't bet on it, right?"

"Right."

"Thanks for calling Henry, if he.,.."

"I'll keep you informed."

"Thank you Henry."

"Good night Patrick," said Shaw.

The phone went dead in Kerrigan's hand. Instead of replacing it, he stood listening to the buzz. He was attempting to remember Jamie's number, but it escaped him. He called it five dozen times in the last three months and normally he would remember it, but tonight it was lost to him. Finally he replaced the phone and walked back into the parlor.

"Is everything alright?" asked Mrs. Kerrigan.

He looked at her for a good ten seconds before he said,

"No darling, it's not all right. McCaul has just lapsed into a coma and Henry doesn't know just how long, but he's afraid we're going to loose him."

"Oh no. What about his parents?"

Kerrigan didn't reply to his wife's question, he just shook his head, turned and went back to the telephone. Jamie's number had just popped back into his mind as quickly as it had disappeared.

He picked up the phone and slowly dialed the number, wanting to give himself time to think of just what he was going to ask Jamie to do for him. He didn't have a plan worked out at the moment. As he dialed the last number he thought of replacing the phone, but after the first ring, Molly, Jamie's grandmother answered the phone.

"Molly?"

"Yes."

"This is Kerrigan, is Jamie there?"

"Yes."

"May I speak with him please?"

"Just a moment."

Kerrigan heard the woman lay the phone down on the wooden table. Next he heard her footsteps, which faded off as she walked out of the room. After almost thirty seconds of silence, Kerrigan heard heavier footsteps approach,

"Yes sir."

"Jamie, I just received a call from Dr. Shaw."

"Is McCaul dead?" asked Meyers.

"No but Henry doesn't think he'll last much longer."

"I see."

"Did you get in touch with Professor McCaul?"

"Yes sir. I also drove him down to the hospital."

"Good. Now, what about O'Connor, do you think we'd better try and let him know about McCaul?"

"Yes sir, I believe so."

"Do you think you could get word to him about McCaul."

"Maybe, I don't know."

"If possible, let him know McCaul's condition and there is a chance he might die. Let him know that if McCaul dies, we'll keep him informed of any arrangements pertaining to the disposition of the body. Let him know we want no blood shed."

"Yes sir."

The conversation ended on the last two words.

The phone went dead.

Kerrigan walked back into the parlor, stopped for just a moment, then said,

"I'm going for a walk. I'll be back in a little while."

His wife nodded and his mother-in-law didn't take her eyes off her sewing.

In the hallway closet he removed his light rain coat and his hat, which his wife had threatened to throw away at least a hundred times during the last twenty five years.

After walking ten blocks, he walked into a bar he infrequently patronized, bought a pint at the bar, asked for change for a ten pound note, walked to an empty table and placed his beer glass on the table. He then moved to the back of the room. The telephone was located at the end of a short hallway. He picked up the phone, dialed the operator, gave her Rothchild's home telephone number, dropped the exact number of coins requested by the operator in the pay slot. After the third ring, when he was about to hang up, Rothchild answered.

"Douglas, this is Patrick."

"Yes Patrick."

Without any hesitation, Kerrigan said,

"Douglas, I have a little bad news. Our little friend is extremely ill."

After almost ten seconds of silence, Kerrigan said,

"Douglas?"

"I'm still here Patrick."

Again there were a few moments of silence.

"Do you know what is wrong with him?"

"I'm afraid not. The doctor said nothing they have tried has worked and he has no idea just what is causing his sickness."

"Are they going to check further?"

"Yes."

Again there was a short period of silence.

"You do know your people have contacted our people about transferring him?"

"Yes, the Commissioner told me."

"Did he tell you what was to be done if your little friend dies?"

"No. Do you know?" asked Kerrigan.

"Yes. They want him cremated immediately and his ashes scattered so the people up here won't have a reason for a big show."

"The Commissioner didn't tell me."

"The Chief Constable told us today."

"What if he dies here and not up there?"

"I'd guess your people would take care of it, after verification by our people."

"Do you have any idea who would do the verifying?"

"No, but I'd guess everyone will want a representative there, the Constabulary, the Army, the Home Office and a representative of the SIS. They will all want to make certain McCaul is dead. The ones who insisted on the cremation were from the NIO."

"Thanks for telling me."

"Is there anything I can do?"

"No," said Kerrigan.

"You will keep me informed?"

"Certainly Douglas. Good night."

"Good night Patrick."

The line went dead and the buzzing stared to indicate no one was on the other end and the telephone company would appreciate it if he would either hang up or dial another number.

Kerrigan took it personally and slammed the phone on the hook. With just a few more foot-pounds of pressure he would have broken the hook off. He looked at the phone, smiled to himself and walked back to the table where he had placed his beer glass.

Instead of pulling out a chair and taking a seat, he stood looking at the crowd to determine if he might know any of the customers. As he surveyed the crowd, he took small sips of his beer.

He saw no one he recognized. He knew this didn't mean there wasn't someone in the room who recognized him.

He looked at his wristwatch and saw it was twenty minutes to nine. He finished his beer, walked up to the bar, handed the bartender the glass and walked out into the night air.

The walk back to his house took just over thirty minutes because of the various detours he took around the neighborhood. As he opened the door to his house, he saw his wife jump up out of her chair and come towards him. He knew something was wrong.

"Dr. Shaw called. He said it was very important and ask that you call him as soon as possible."

Kerrigan took off his raincoat and hat, hung them on the coat rack in the hallway and walked towards his "home office."

He turned and asked his wife,

"Is he still in the hospital?"

"He's in the Doctors' lounge. You'll have to ask the hospital operator to ring it."

"Thank you."

Mary Ellen nodded, turned and returned to the parlor.

The call to the hospital went through quickly.

"Dr. Shaw please, I think he's in the Doctors' lounge."

The phone rang only once. It was Dr. Shaw.

"Yes Henry, what is it?"

"Patrick, McCaul died about forty minutes ago."

"Oh hell. Do you have any idea what killed him?"

"Not exactly, but we're guessing he died of a viral infection."

Kerrigan looked at the picture on his desk for almost a minute.

"Patrick?"

"Yes Henry, I'm still here. I was thinking, was McCaul's mother there?"

"No, only his father was here. Jamie got him here around four this afternoon."

"Is Professor McCaul still there?"

"No, we managed to get him a room at that little hotel on Baylor Street."

"Has he said what he wants to do with the body?"

"Yes, he wants to take it to his home in Wales. I told him he would have to wait until the morning to get permission from the Garda."

"And?"

"He said he would be back here early in the morning."

"Where's the body now?"

"In the hospital morgue."

"The men who were guarding him. Are they still there?"

"They are in the morgue with the body."

After another long silence, Kerrigan asked,

"Are you going to go home now?"

"No, I have other patients I need to check on. I'll be here for at least a couple of more hours, why?"

"I may want to get in contact with you. I just heard that the NIO wants McCaul's body cremated and I'm about to call the Commissioner and find out what he wants to do. You know, I'm walking on real thin ice right now after Convoy."

"I know."

"I may want to talk with you after I talk with the Commissioner."

"As I said, I'll be here at the hospital for a couple of more hours. If you want me, call the operator. She'll know where I'm located."

"Thank you Henry. If I don't call within an hour, I won't be calling. Understand?"

"Yes. Good by Patrick."

The phone went dead before Kerrigan had a chance to hang it up. For almost three minutes Kerrigan looked at the phone in his right hand while his left hand held down the switch in the cradle, keeping the phone dead. Finally he lifted his left hand and dialed the Commissioner's home phone. He closed his eyes and rehearsed for the third time what he was going to say to the Commissioner.

"Hello."

"Commissioner?"

"Yes."

"This is Patrick Kerrigan."

"I know Patrick, what can I do for you?"

"Commissioner, McCaul is dead. He died about half an hour ago."

"Do the doctors know what he died of?"

"No sir."

"Were his parents notified?"

"Professor McCaul was with his son when he died."

"How?"

"I asked Jamie, Detective Meyers, to go up to Belfast and tell him about his son and he brought him back."

"I see," said the Commissioner.

Kerrigan did not feel any coldness in the Commissioner's voice.

"Anything else Patrick?"

"Yes sir. I was informed the NIO wants McCaul cremated and his ashes scattered so the Provos can't have another show."

"I know," said the Commissioner.

"Sir," said Kerrigan, "there is something else you should know."

"What is it?"

"McCaul had a premonition he was going to die and he asked O'Connor to take his body to Wales if he died."

"Yes."

"He made O'Connor swear he would take him home and we think O'Connor might try and…."

"Get his body?"

"Yes sir."

"What about McCaul's family. Do you know whether they have requested his body?"

"Yes sir, no sir."

"Which is it Patrick, yes or no?"

"No, not yet, but Professor McCaul is going to request the body be sent to Wales tomorrow. Dr. Shaw informed him the Garda might have a say in the decision."

After a full minute of silence, the Commissioner said,

"Patrick, do you think O'Connor would actually try and steal McCaul's body."

"I'm afraid so sir. They were like brothers and you know O'Connor's reputation."

"Well, he'll not get it from us. I want you to…no, I'll make all the arrangements. Where are the men who were guarding McCaul?"

"They are guarding the body, which is in the hospital morgue."

"Fine, where is Meyers?"

"I don't know", said Kerrigan, which was the truth, he had no idea where Jamie Meyers was at the moment."

"I see, is there anything else I should know?"

"No sir."

"You do understand that I'm taking control of the situation, complete control."

"Yes sir."

"I'll talk to you tomorrow. Good night."

"Good night sir."

Instead of replacing the phone in its cradle, Kerrigan reached down and cut the connection by pushing the bar in the cradle down. He held it for only a few seconds, released it and dialed Meyers' number. After the sixth ring he replaced the phone in its cradle and stood looking at it for almost a minute.

He nodded his head at the phone as if he had told the inanimate object what he was going to do next. He walked into the parlor, stopped and said,

"Mary Ellen, I'm going to the hospital in Baldoyle and I have no idea when I'll be back. Be sure to lock up and I'll wake you when I get home."

"Yes Patrick. Is there anything I can do….you know, the boy's parents or anything?"

"No. McCaul's father has a room in a small hotel close to the hospital. Henry took care of the arrangements."

"Alright Patrick, I'll see you when you get home."

"Good night, both of you," said Kerrigan as he turned and walked out of the parlor and into the hallway. Automatically he picked up his raincoat and hat from the coat rack and was out of the door.

The Cross and Shield Pub
Dublin, Ireland

Thirty minutes after receiving the call from Kerrigan, Meyers was sitting in a pub a few blocks for the gate of Mountjoy prison. He slowly sipped the dark brown brew, rehearsing for the tenth time what he was going to say to his friend, a man he had known most of his life or at least as far back as he could remember. A man he grew up with in the south of Dublin, with whom he was in almost daily contact, except for the time he spent in the Army, until he broke the law by belonging to and indulging in the activities of the IRA.

When Kerrigan asked him to try and make contact with O'Connor, Meyers instantly thought of his friend, whom he had not talked to for the last three years, by mutual agreement.

It took Meyers almost twenty minutes of painful soul searching to come to the conclusion that this was the only sure means available to him for carrying out Kerrigan's request.

After convincing himself he made the right decision, Meyers placed the empty glass on the bar, nodded to the bartender to fill it up, slipped down from his stool and walked to the rear of the room. He walked down the hall leading to the bathrooms, but stopped halfway to use the telephone.

He slipped the required coinage into the black box, dialed the telephone number of Timothy Foley, which he still remembered after all these years. He waited for someone to answer the phone on the other end of the line.

"Hello," said a female voice on the other end.

"Rose?" asked Meyers.

"No, this is Kathleen."

Meyers was surprised by the girl's voice. She sounded exactly like her mother.

"Kathleen, is your Da home?"

"No, he and Momma are at the SF meeting in Milltown."

"Do you know what time they'll be home?'

"No. Usually after the meeting they go to the pub for a few."

Silence.

"May I ask who's calling?"

"Yes Kathleen, it's Jamie, Jamie Meyers."

"Uncle Jamie, I haven't seen you in years. Are you back in town for awhile?"

The question left Meyers speechless for a moment. He then realized the meaning of the question. To cover his absence, Foley had told his family he was transferred out of town.

"Yes Kathleen, just for a while."

"Are you coming to the house. Da and Momma will be tickled pink to see you. It's been so long."

"I know it's been a long time."

"Are you coming over?"

Meyers so much wanted to visit Foley and his family, particularly Kathleen and her two younger siblings, yet he knew it wouldn't be practical, not at this time.

"Sorry darling, but I'm just passing through town. Tell your folks I called. OK?"

"OK Uncle Jamie, but I sure wish I could see you."

Meyers could feel the lump in his throat as Kathleen's voice choked up.

"You will, very soon. I promise."

"When?"

"Soon. I have to run now darling. God bless."

"Good by."

Meyers slid the phone back on its hook, gritted his teeth for a moment, turned and said, "*Sonofabitch, sonofabitch, sonofabitch!!!*"

An older gentleman coming out of the bathroom, stopped, looked at Meyers for a second and asked,

"Are you all right?"

Meyers looked up at him, smiled a sad smile and said,

"Yes sir. Just lost my girl friend."

The man smiled, nodded and said,

"You'll get over it. By the time you reach my age, you'll have lost a coupled of dozen girl friends."

Meyers nodded and said,

"I guess you're right."

Meyers headed for the bathroom as the older gentleman walked into the bar. Once in the bathroom, he went directly to the sink and using the coldest water available, he splashed it on his face then dried it with three of the paper towels he extracted from the metal box.

Detective Sergeant Meyers walked back into the bar, reclaimed his stool, picked up his beer and sipped the foam off the top.

During the next fifteen minutes, he finished his drink and decided on his next move.

He knew where the Sinn Fein meeting was being held and he knew how he was going to contact Foley. During the years, even though Meyers and Foley never visited or talked with each other, Meyers kept tabs on Foley by reading the reports from the political section. In addition, on numerous occasions, Meyers drove pass the Foley residence or parked down the street and watched Timothy and Rose and the children as they went to church or played in the yard. He missed his friend's companionship a great deal, but knew it was best for the both of them to break connections.

Meyers left the pub and drove pass the parking lot of the hall where the Sinn Fein meeting was being held. He parked his car on one of the side streets across from the lot, locked his car and walked towards the parking lot.

The meeting in the hall came to an end at twenty minutes after nine at just the moment the Irish sky opened up and let go with a hard rain. The speakers and audience slowly emerged from the building, some hesitating to go out into the down pour, others waiting for their husbands or boy friends to drive the car around to the main entrance.

Timothy and Rose Foley made a dash for their car, which was parked relatively close to the entrance. As Timothy fumbled with his keys, Rose attempted to hold the wind-blown umbrella over both of them. Her attempt to keep them dry blocked the light, which in turned interfered with Timothy's ability to distinguish which key fit the door.

"Hurry, I'm getting wet!"

"Move that damn umbrella so I can see the lock."

Obediently, Rose moved the umbrella and held it directly over her head. This allowed both the light and the rain to fall on both the door and her husband.

"Here we go," said Timothy as he clicked the lock and opened the car door in one swift move.

"Hand me the umbrella and get in."

Rose handed her husband the umbrella, slipped into the car, closed the door, reached over and unlocked the driver's side door just as Timothy reached for the outside handle.

Sliding into the car, Foley said,

"Jezus, my feet are soaked. I stepped into a damn pothole by the curb and the water went over my shoes."

"We'd better not go to the pub, you'll catch your death of cold if you sit around the rest of the night in wet feet."

"But we told the Sullivans we would meet them there in fifteen minutes."

"Go home first Tim and change shoes, then we can come back."

"Tell you what. I'll drop you off at the pub, then I'll go home and put on some dry cloths and shoes."

"You don't want me to go with you?"

"No, by the time I change and everything, the Sullivans will think we're not going to show up and might leave. I need to talk with Carl about the campaign next month."

"Alright, you need to give me some money, I left my purse at home."

Foley reached in his back pocket, pulled out his wallet and handed it to his wife.

"Take what you need," said Timothy Foley as he started the sedan.

The trip from the meeting hall to the pub required only seven minutes.

"Here's your wallet," said Rose Foley, "don't lose it."

The car door opened and Mrs. Foley slipped out and closed the door. Foley rolled the window down and said,

"I'll see you in about twenty minutes. Don't get a table too close to the stage, particularly if Rooney is playing."

Rose answered with a nod, turned and walked into the The Cross and Shield Pub.

Foley rolled up his window and took his foot off the brake pedal. The car slowly moved out onto the road and headed north towards the Foley residence. The car eased to a stop at the stop sign at the end of the block. Foley was about to take his foot off the brake pedal again when Meyers said,

"Evening Timothy."

The car shot halfway across the busy street at full speed, then screeched to a halt in the middle of the street as Foley slammed on the brake.

"What...who...what in the hell," stammered Foley.

"Easy Timothy. Either pull over to the curb and turn around or keep driving and keep your eyes on the road."

"Jamie, Jamie, is that you?"

"Pull over Timothy, please, before you get us killed. You've stopped in the middle of the road."

Foley took his foot off the brake pedal and gently applied pressure to the gas pedal. The car slowly moved across the street and down the road half a block before Foley let up on the gas pedal and applied pressure to the break. At the same time Foley turned the steering wheel to the left and eased the car over to the empty curb. He stopped completely, turned the ignition off and turned around.

"Jamie?" he asked again.

"Yes," said Meyers.

"Jamie, you scared the living shit out of me. I could have had a damn heart attack."

Meyers' smile could not be seen in the dark.

"Your heart is as strong as your breath after a night of drinking."

"You could still scare a person to death, you dumb ass Mick."

"Perhaps."

"How'd you get in the car?"

"Very easily. The same trick we used as kids."

For a full minute the two men remained silent. Finally, Meyers opened the rear door, climbed out and got in next to Foley.

"It's been a long time Timothy."

Again silence.

Suddenly, Foley reached over and hugged Meyers. As he released his friend and backed off, he said,

"God Jamie, it's good to see you."

"The same Timothy, the same. I've missed you and Rose and the children."

"We've missed you too."

Meyers took a deep breath.

"What is it Jamie. Whenever you take that deep breath..."

"You know me too good, even after all these years."

"What is it Jamie. Are you in trouble? Do you need money? Some place to hide?"

"Easy Timothy. I'm not on the run, but I do need help."

"Anything," said Foley.

The one word…"anything"…made that damn lump in Meyers' throat reappear. He knew Foley would do anything for him, just as he would do anything for him. They would do anything for each other except change political views and political loyalties."

"You know about O'Connor and McCaul?"

Foley looked at him, frowned and said,

"I know about O'Connor. Your people lost him up north."

"Correct, the Provos pulled a slick one on us."

Foley smiled, nodded and said,

"So I've heard."

Meyers nodded.

"So what about McCaul?"

Again, Meyers took a deep breath.

"Oh crap. Here it comes," said Foley.

"O'Connor got away, but we got McCaul."

"I know."

"He was sick when he was picked up. That was the reason O'Connor was taking him north. He, McCaul, wanted to go home, and…"

"And?"

"The doctors don't think he is going to make it."

"He's dying?"

"I'm afraid so," said Meyers.

"What of? Was he shot trying to escape?"

"No, no. Like I said, when they picked him up at the border, he was sick. He had a high fever and chills. He's been in the hospital since his capture, but the doctors don't know what's causing the illness."

Silence.

"They've tried everything. My superior received a call from the doctor this evening and they don't expect him to make it."

"Oh hell," said Foley.

"I know. I'm sorry."

"Really?" said Foley.

"Really," said Meyers.

"Sorry," said Foley, "I didn't mean the sarcasm."

"It's all right."

Silence.

"What do you want from me?" asked Foley.

"We don't want O'Connor to try and rescue him. O'Connor promised to take him home if he died and I'm afraid he is going to die. My superior doesn't want any blood shed, and if O'Connor tries to get him, there will be blood shed, a lot of it."

"Just what do you want me to do?"

"Contact O'Connor and tell him not to attempt a rescue. Superintendent Kerrigan, my superior wants him to know that if McCaul dies, we will try and get his body sent to Wales."

"Damn."

"McCaul's father is with him now and he will probably request his son's body if he dies."

"How do you know his father is with him?"

"Simple. I drove up to Belfast this morning and picked him up and brought him back to Dublin. I delivered him to the hospital where McCaul is a patient."

"You did that, why?"

"Because Superintendent Kerrigan asked me to go up and tell him about his son and I volunteered to take him back to Dublin."

"Oh."

"Can you get in contact with O'Connor and deliver the message?"

"How?"

"You can do it and I know you can," said Meyers, "you're in contact with your people up north and they can get the message to O'Connor."

After a few moments of silence, Foley said,

"You're right, but I don't know whether I can get the message to O'Connor."

"Try Timothy, that's all we want you to do. try."

After a ten second silence, Foley said,

"I'll contact the people up north this evening and relay your message. When will I hear from you?"

"I'm going back to the hospital as soon as you drop me off at the next intersection. I let you know as soon as possible."

The conversation ended.

Foley started the car, put it in gear and drove to the intersection of Stillorgan and Mount Merrion Avenue where he pulled over to the curb. Meyers opened the door, turned towards Foley and said,

"Thanks."

Foley nodded as Meyers shut the car door. Foley then eased back into traffic.

Thirty minutes later, Timothy Foley was back at the Cross and Shield Pub. He spotted Rose at one of the tables with four others, the Sullivans and the Raffertys. She saw him and waved. Foley shook his head and pointed to the telephone booth in the corner of the pub.

Once in the phone booth, Foley opened his wallet and took a card out from in between two pictures. The card had eleven telephone numbers on it, with seven of numbers crossed out. The last number was crossed out a week ago.

Slowly Foley dialed the eighth number.

After three rings, a male voice answered.

"Hello."

"This is Timothy Foley, from Dublin."

"Yes Timothy."

"I have information about McCaul."

"Yes."

"The doctors don't believe he is going to last too much longer and if he dies the Garda sent word for O'Connor not to try and snatch the body. They will attempt to make arrangements for his body to be sent home to Wales."

"And who told you this?"

"An old friend who works for the Garda."

"I need a name Timothy."

After a long pause, Foley said,

"Jamie Meyers. He's with the Special Operations Section."

"Just exactly what did this Jamie Meyers tell you?"

"He said the doctors don't expect McCaul to live much longer and if he dies, the Garda does not want O'Connor to attempt to get the body. If he does, there will be a blood bath."

After a short pause, the individual in Northern Ireland said,

"Your message will be relayed to O'Connor. Call back as soon as you have any addition information."

"OK."

"Good night."

"Good night."

Foley hung up the phone, turned and walked to the table where his wife and the four others were enjoying their beer, their snacks and their conversation.

"I see you changed your pants also," said Rose.

"I was wet up to my knees."

"Where did you put your shoes and pants?"

Foley smiled at his wife, shook his head and said,

"I hung my pants and socks on a chair in the kitchen and put my shoes in the oven to dry."

"You didn't, you know they'll…"

"No Rose," said Foley as he laughed at his wife,

"I put them on the rug in the kitchen where you put the kids' shoes when they're wet."

"There went your entertainment for the evening," said Sullivan.

"Maybe not," said Foley as he winked as his wife, who jabbed him in the ribs.

"Let me get you a glass," said Mrs. Sullivan.

"No need," said Foley, "it looks like the pitcher is almost empty. I'll get another pitcher and some snacks, maybe that will put Rose in a good mood."

"Dream on lover boy," said Rose.

Foley needed the few minutes away from is wife and friends to settle his nerves.

In spite of his attempt to enjoy the remainder of the evening by joking with Rose and the others, he was unable to get the thought of his short conversation with Meyers out of his mind.

St. Francis Hospital
Baldoyle, Ireland

Detective Sergeant Jamie Meyers arrived at the hospital a few minutes before eleven and went directly to the third floor. Halfway down the semi-dark hallway he realized something was wrong. There was no guard in front of the door to the room at the end of the hall. He started to turn and walk back up the hall to the nurses' desk, changed his mind and continued to McCaul's room.

The door was partially open. Meyers pushed it with his right foot and it opened wide, revealing a dark, empty room, a room McCaul had occupied earlier.

"Oh no, no, no," thought Meyers.

He turned and walked back up the hall to the nurses' station. He stopped and waited for the nurse to look up at him.   Finally   the charge nurse looked up and said,

"Yes?"

"The patient in the room at the end of the hall?"

"About an hour ago."

Meyers nodded, started to turn, stopped and asked,

"Dr. Shaw?"

"He's in his office off the Doctors' lounge."

"Thank you."

Meyers turned and went directly to the Doctors' lounge, stopped at the door and started to knock, changed his mind and walked into the lounge. He looked around and was about to turn and leave when Dr. Shaw walked out of his two room private office.

"Jamie, did Patrick send you over?"

"No sir, I've been in town and came by to check on McCaul, but the nurse said...."

"He passed away a little over an hour ago and I called Patrick, Superintendent Kerrigan, not thirty minutes ago to tell him McCaul died."

"Where is McCaul now?"

"In the morgue", said Shaw.

"Did Superintendent Kerrigan tell you anything about O'Connor and McCaul?"

Shaw wrinkled his brow and said,

"No, what about O'Connor and McCaul?"

"I'll answer that," said Kerrigan as he walked into the lounge.

The room was silent for the next ten seconds.

"Evening sir," said Meyers.

"Evening Jamie, did you have any luck?"

Meyers looked from Kerrigan to Shaw and back to Kerrigan.

"You can tell me in front of Henry. He's on our side."

"Yes sir."

"Yes sir what?" asked Kerrigan.

"Yes sir, I made contact and my contact is waiting for me to contact him again to tell him whether McCaul is dead."

"Let's hold off," said Kerrigan, "I called my friend up north and he informed me the NIO has requested that McCaul be cremated if he died."

"What's this about McCaul and O'Connor?" asked Shaw.

"Tell him Jamie," said Kerrigan.

Meyers took that famous deep breath.

"McCaul had a premonition he was going to die and he made O'Connor promise to take his body to Wales if he died."

"And?" asked Shaw.

"And O'Connor promised McCaul he would take his body to Wales if he died."

After a slight hesitation, Meyers continued,

"And he will, come hell or high water."

Shaw looked at Kerrigan, smiled and said,

"Well Patrick, like my American friends says, seems you're up to your ass in angry, agitated alligators."

Kerrigan looked at Shaw, shook his head and said,

"No Henry, I called the Commissioner after I heard from my contact. I told him about O'Connor's promise and he informed me that he was taking over the operation immediately, period."

Before Shaw had a chance to say a word, there was a knock on the door. The three men turned and looked at the door and Shaw said,

"Come in."

The door opened and in walked three men, all as large or larger than Kerrigan.

"Yes," asked Shaw.

"We're looked for a Dr. Henry Shaw," said one of the men.

"I'm Dr. Shaw, what can I do for you?"

"The body of Ronald McCaul, we're here to take charge of it," said the man.

Shaw looked a Meyers and Kerrigan, turned and looked at the three men and said,

"The body is in the morgue, three floors down. Just what do you intend to do with the corpse?"

"Guard it to make sure it doesn't disappear."

"I see. Two men from the Garda are guarding it at the present time."

"We're here to relieve them."

"You'll find the corpse in the basement. Go back up the hall to the elevator and go down four floors. When you get out of the elevator, turn to the right and go about twenty meters. The morgue is on the left. You'll see a sign on the door."

"Thank you doctor. Do you have any questions?"

"No, I've been informed the Commissioner has taken command of the situation."

"That's true. Thank you again."

Turning to his two comrades, he said,

"Let's get down to the morgue."

After the three left, Kerrigan said,

"Well, that's that. Jamie, I guess we can go home and get a good night's sleep."

"Not so fast Chief Superintendent Patrick T. Kerrigan, I have a few questions that need to be answered," said Shaw.

Kerrigan smiled at Shaw, looked over at Jamie, back at Shaw and said,

"You know Henry, that bottle in the bottom drawer of your desk would probably loosen my tongue a wee bit."

Shaw shook his head, smiled and said,

"Have a seat and I'll see if I can find some of that magic portion."

Shaw walked into his office, leaving the two police officers in the lounge.

"What did the Commissioner say?" asked Meyers.

"Well, first he said he was happy you arranged for Professor McCaul to see his son," said Kerrigan, "then when I told him about O'Connor and his promise, and the Commissioner said something like, "he'll not get it from us." That was when he said he would take command of the situation and that's the reason the three gentlemen who just left are here, to make certain O'Connor doesn't get McCaul's body."

"You know sir, if O'Connor decides to get McCaul's body, he'll get it or he'll die trying," said Meyers.

"I know Jamie and that's what worrying me. This could mean a lot of blood shed and we need to do something to prevent it."

"What? You just said the Commissioner is in command of the situation."

"I know, but good God man, I don't want to see anyone hurt or killed over a dead body," said Kerrigan.

"Here we are gentlemen, the magic portion," said Shaw as he re-entered the lounge carrying a tray with three glasses and a bottle of Jack Daniels 12 year old bourbon whiskey.

Shaw filled two glasses half full of the dark brew, looked at Jamie and asked,

"How much?"

"About half of what's in the other two glasses," said Meyers.

"Good, I was afraid you were going to refuse and I've heard that you can't trust a man who refuses a drink of Jack Daniels."

Meyers merely smiled at the doctor.

After pouring what Meyers requested, he held the tray in front of him. Meyers took the glass and waited. Shaw held the tray in front of Kerrigan, who took one of the two glasses and waited until Shaw placed the tray on a table and took the remaining glass.

"What do we drink to?" asked Shaw.

Kerrigan and Meyers looked at each other for a moment, then Kerrigan said,

"To a fallen enemy, God rest his soul."

"God rest his soul," said both Shaw and Meyers.

The three tipped their glasses and took a taste of the bourbon.

"Now, tell me more about O'Connor's promise," said Shaw.

"Up in Convoy, O'Connor and I had a chance to talk," said Meyers, "and he told me about McCaul's premonition. O'Connor said he was pretty sure McCaul knew he was going to die and he wanted O'Connor to promise to take him home to Wales."

"And you think O'Connor will try and get the body?"

"Yes sir."

"What about what you were telling Patrick about contacting people in the North?"

Meyers turned to Kerrigan, who nodded.

"I have a contact here in the Republic who is connected with the people in the North. I asked him to contact them and inform O'Connor that we didn't want any bloodshed. That was before I knew McCaul was dead."

"And?" asked Shaw as he looked from Meyers to Kerrigan.

"And we hoped to get McCaul's body up to O'Connor. That was before I found out about the NIO's request," said Kerrigan.

After a few seconds of silence, Shaw said,

"You're tail is really in a crack, isn't it Patrick?"

"No Henry, the Commissioner relieved me. He's in command now."

"That's not what I was talking about," said Shaw.

Kerrigan didn't answer.

"Just how do you intend to get McCaul's body up North now?" asked Shaw, "And don't tell me that's not what is going through that scheming Irish mind of yours right now."

Kerrigan smiled at his old friend and said,

"Henry, I just told you that the Commissioner is in control of the situation now."

"I know what you said, what I want to know is how do you intend to get McCaul's body up north?"

Kerrigan took a sip of the bourbon, shook his head and said,

"I don't know Henry, I haven't figured it out yet."

"But you are going to attempt to do it, right?" asked Shaw.

"Yes Henry, if I can figure out a way of doing it without getting anyone killed and without losing my pension."

"I wasn't sure, but I had a hunch you were going to try."

"Let's just say I've been thinking about it, but it just might not be possible, particularly if the NIO insists of the body being cremated and our people agree," said Kerrigan.

Meyers turned his head and smiled. He knew Kerrigan was doing more than just thinking about it.

After Kerrigan's last comment, the room became silent. Each of the three men had their own thought, not necessarily with McCaul's death.

"Just exactly what did Professor McCaul tell you about taking his son home?" asked Kerrigan.

"He said he would make arrangements to take his son home, that was when I told him the Garda may not release the body to him."

"And what did he say?" asked Kerrigan.

All he said was, "we'll *see.*"

"And?"

"And that was all, he said, "we'll see.""

Kerrigan looked towards Shaw, but didn't see him.

"What do you think he will do?" asked Meyers.

Shaw shook his head and said,

"I don't know for certain, but I'll bet you a bottle of Jameson that he intends to contact his lawyer or some high official and have them put pressure on the Garda and the NIO, particularly if the NIO insists on having the body cremated."

"Do you think the Garda will go along with cremating the body?" asked Meyers.

"The Garda won't have any say, it will be up to the Attorney General and the Justice Department," said Shaw, "and you know how our people are trying to do everything not to upset the politicians up north. It could happen before Professor McCaul can get a court order to halt it."

"Oh Lord, I hope not," said Meyers.

"We'll just have to wait and see Jamie," said Kerrigan, "let's just wait and see."

Twenty minutes later, Kerrigan and Meyers said good night to Dr. Shaw and departed the doctor's private office. As they walked out of the front door of the hospital they passed four individuals guarding the entrance. Kerrigan recognized one. He was a member of the Commissioner's protection unit.

Outside the hospital they saw seven official cars parked fifteen to twenty meters apart, each occupied by two individuals.

"The Commissioner is taking no chances of losing McCaul's body, is he Jamie?"

"He must have half the Garda guarding the hospital," said Meyers, "there's no chance of O'Connor getting McCaul, that's for sure."

Kerrigan's Residence
Dublin, Ireland

Chief Superintendent Kerrigan unlocked the front door, walked into his house, locked the door and walked into the parlor where his wife and mother-in-law were seated. Mrs. Kerrigan was still watching the television and her mother was still sewing.

"Have I…."

Mary Ellen Kerrigan held up her hand to signal her husband to remain silent until the scene on the television came to some type of conclusion.

Kerrigan nodded, smiled and walked over to his chair and sat down. He started to pick up the paper he left on the floor when he departed earlier, but decided against it

Three minutes later, Mrs. Kerrigan hit the mute button on the remote, turned to her husband and said,

"The Commissioner called about half an hour ago. He wanted me to tell you a group from up north would be down on the 30th and you and Jamie are to meet with them."

"Is that all he said, nothing else?"

"That's all Patrick. He said he'll talk to you tomorrow."

Mary Ellen pushed the mute button again and turned to continue watching her program.

Kerrigan pushed himself up from the chair and walked to his home office. He started to call Meyers but changed his mind. He would see him early in the morning and let him know about the visitors from the north.

Day Seven

July 28, 1998

Garda Headquarters
Dublin, Ireland

Chief Superintendent Kerrigan could not concentrate on his work this July day. He had been in his office since a quarter to eight, had been served his tea and Danish and was attempting to read the reports in the two folders containing all the information available on the two cases marked "High Priority".

His mind was not on the two cases, but on what the Commissioner said when he called at exactly eight o'clock this morning.

Kerrigan was informed the NIO was still insisting McCaul be cremated and the cremation was to be conducted at St. Francis Hospital and witnessed by selected representatives from various branches in Northern Ireland, including the British Army, the NIO, the Constabulary and the SIS.

The delegation from Ulster would be met by a delegation from the Republic, which would include members of the Commissioner's office, the Garda, the Attorney General's office and the Irish Army. The Commissioner informed Kerrigan that he and Detective Sergeant Meyers were to represent the Garda. The two delegations were to have lunch together on the 30th and afterwards travel to the hospital to witness the cremation of McCaul.

Kerrigan did not ask the Commissioner if consideration had been given to Professor McCaul's request for his son's body.

In the office down the hall, Meyers was having a similar problem. He was setting in his straight back chair attempting to concentrate on four of the twelve cases assigned to him.

Prior to McGrath's call and his trip north, he had reviewed the information concerning the four cases and made two pages of notes along with a list of thirteen people he wanted to interview.

Meyers closed his eyes and the question that repeatedly entered in his mind since he left the hospital reappeared:

"How in the hell is the Superintendent going to get McCaul's body if they cremate him the day after tomorrow?"

He opened his eyes and looked around to see if any of the others in the room heard him ask himself the question. No one was looking at him, but he still had no answer to his question.

He rocked back in his chair and looked up at the ceiling just as the phone on his desk rang. He picked it up and before he could say a word, Chief Superintendent Kerrigan said,

"Jamie, would you come into my office please?"

"Yes sir," said Meyers as he dropped the phone in it cradle. He stood up, picked his jacket off the rack and put it on as he walked out of the Detectives' room and into the hall. Twelve steps from the door of his office he turned and entered Mrs. Robert's office. He walked pass her desk, winked at her and knocked on Kerrigan's door.

"Come in," said Kerrigan.

Meyers opened the door, walked into the office and moved to the middle of the room and stood in front of Kerrigan's desk. Kerrigan stood up and said,

"I just received a call from Dr. Shaw. He said to make arrangements to move McCaul Thursday night after nine o'clock."

Meyers shook his head, raised both hands as if begging for a gift and asked a one word question,

"How?"

Kerrigan walked around the desk, pointing to one of the two easy chairs, indicating that Meyers take a seat and lowered himself into the other chair.

"I don't know Jamie, all I know is what Henry said and that was for you to be ready to move McCaul's body after nine o'clock Thursday night."

"Do I make the arrangements sir?"

For what seemed like five minutes to Meyers, but was really only five seconds, Kerrigan said,

"Yes."

Meyers nodded his head and asked,

"Anything else sir?"

"Yes. I want you to take either Carter or Longman or one of the others with you when you take McCaul's body north. Understand?"

"Yes sir," said Meyers.

"One other item. I received a call from the Deputy Commissioner. He informed me the delegation from up north will arrive at the Commissioner's office on Thursday around ten thirty. At a few minutes before twelve the Deputy Commissioner and the Attorney General and some of their people will host our Northern friends at Rafter's. Since we will be representing the Garda, we'd better wear our Sunday cloths."

"Then?"

"Then all of us will travel to Baldoyle."

Meyers nodded, indicating he understood.

"Anything else?"

"No," said Kerrigan.

Meyers pushed himself up from the chair, turned and walked to the door. He stopped, turned around and said,

"I'll be gone most of the day sir, I have a long list of people I need to interview."

"Fine," said Kerrigan, "I'll see you in the morning."

"Yes sir," said Meyers as he turned and walked out of the office. As he walked pass Mrs. Robert's desk, he again winked at the woman who returned his wink, a ritual started almost five years ago.

Meyers returned to his office, picked up the three sheets of paper containing his notes, placed them on top of the four case files and placed the bundle in his file cabinet. He turned and returned to his desk where he picked up the paper with the list of individuals he wanted to interview. Before leaving he picked up the phone and dialed Mrs. Roberts and told her he would not be back in the office today.

During the day he contacted and interviewed eleven of the thirteen individuals on his list. As he left the office of the last person he interviewed, he looked at his watch. It was ten minutes after six. He was in Donnybrook, a block off Sandford Road. He looked down the street, located a telephone booth in the middle of the block and took the first parking space available. He reached the phone and dialed his home number.

"Hello."

"Molly?"

"Who else," said his grandmother.

"No one. I just wanted to let you know I'll be home by a little after seven, if the traffic's not too bad. What's for supper?"

"Cold cuts, tonight's my night out with the girls, remember?"

"Nope, I forgot about it."

"I'm leaving at a quarter till, so I'll leave everything in the frig."

"Thanks, have a good time."

"I intend to."

"I'll see you when you get home, don't stay out too late."

"Good by," said Molly.

"Good by."

Meyers hung up the phone and smiled to himself for only a few seconds. He picked up the phone and dialed the Foley's number. After the third ring it was answered.

"Hello," said the female voice.

"Rose?"

"Yes."

"May I talk with Timothy?"

"Jamie?"

"Yes."

For twenty seconds neither said a word, neither could think of just what to say to the other.

Finally Rose said,

"Just a minute."

"Hello."

"Timothy?"

"Yes. I've been waiting for your call."

"I know."

"I figured McCaul was dead when you talked with me last evening. Am I correct?"

"No Timothy. McCaul died while I was waiting for you to get out of the meeting. He died a little before nine o'clock and I didn't know until I arrived at the hospital."

After a few seconds, Meyers continued,

"Did you contact your friends up north?"

"Yes."

"And?"

"Arrangements are being made now. I was instructed to call back when and if I received word McCaul was dead."

"And?"

"They said they would let me know where they would meet you after you told me when you would meet them."

"Good. I'm sorry about McCaul, I really am."

Foley didn't reply.

"Timothy, I'll be leaving with McCaul's body Thursday night after nine o'clock."

"From Dublin?"

"No."

Silence.

"Did your friends say when the arrangements would be….."

"No," said Foley, "they simply said to call back when I received word McCaul was dead."

"You'd better call them, now."

"I will."

"How will I know where to….."

"Call me back in an hour Jamie and I'll let you know where they will meet you."

"All right Timothy and ……"

Before Meyers could finish his sentence, the phone went dead.

As the conversation ended, Foley's facial expression was a mixture of sadness and confusion. His eyes had that faraway look one sees in the eyes of soldiers who have seen too much combat.

Foley hung up the phone, turned to his wife and said,

"I'll be back in a while."

Rose looked at him and asked,

"Are you going to meet Jamie?"

Without changing the expression on his face, he slowly shook his head and replied,

"No, I have to make a telephone call."

"Why can't you….." said Rose, but before she completed the question, she knew the answer. She nodded, turned and continued washing the dinner dishes and waited for the door to shut.

Foley drove almost six kilometers on Stillorgan road before turning onto Anglesea Road where he crossed over Merrion onto Shellbourne road. Once in Ballsbridge, he slowed and looked for a public phone, which he spotted in front of a restaurant. He scanned both sides of the street for an empty parking space. Not one space was empty on Shellbourne, so he drove to the next intersection, made three left turns and found a spot less than a hundred feet from Shellbourne.

After parking, Foley remained seated for a full minute before he looked at his watch.

"Holy hell," he said out loud as he realized he had only thirty-two minutes to make the call and return home before Meyers called back. He knew Meyers would call exactly one hour from the time their conversation ended.

Within two minutes Foley exited his car, locked the door, half walked and half ran up the street to Shellbourne, turned left and walked half a block to the telephone.

"Why in the hell did I come all the way here to make the call? And with my luck the phone will be out of order."

He gave thanks as he reached the phone and saw it was in working order.

He removed a paper with numbers from his wallet, dialed the number below the last number crossed out, put in the exact change and waited for it to start ringing. At the same time, his heart rate increased by at least ten beats per minute.

On the third ring a male voice said,

"Hello."

"This is Tim Foley."

"Yes Timothy?"

Foley paused for a few seconds, trying to remember the exact wording he rehearsed on the twenty-minute drive.

"Timothy, where are you calling from?"

"Dublin, a payphone on Shellbourne, why?"

"Do you have your list with you?"

"Yes."

"Call the next number on the list in exactly three minutes. Understand?"

"Yes."

"Good by."

"Good by."

The phone went dead, but he continued to hold it in his hand. He looked at his watch and exactly three minutes later he dialed the next number on his list.

"Hello."

"This is Foley."

"Yes Timothy, sorry, we needed to change phones. Now, what was it you were going to tell me?"

"McCaul died last night about nine o'clock."

"We know. When will your friend bring the body north?"

"He'll be leaving sometime after nine on Thursday night. He needs to know where you want to meet him and what time."

"We understand. Tell him he'll be met at the rest area two kilometers west of The Bush on R173 at twelve o'clock, midnight, and he must be alone. Once at the rest area, he's to back his van into the area."

Foley merely nodded.

"Timothy?"

"Yes."

"Do you understand?"

"Yes."

"Anything else?"

Foley hesitated a moment, then asked,

"Will O'Connor be there?"

"Yes, along with a few of the boys."

"Will Jamie be alright?"

"If he comes alone and…"

"If he says he'll be alone, he'll be alone. He's as good as his word."

"Then there's nothing to worry about."

"I hope everything works out."

"It will. Anything else?"

"No."

"Good. Thank you for your assistance."

"You're welcomed."

"Good by."

"Good by."

Foley slowly replaced the instrument, turned and walked back to his car. He was thinking about Jamie and whether or not he would go alone to the proposed meeting.

After Foley hung up, Meyers continued to hold the phone to his ear. He smiled and shook his head. Here he was, standing on the sidewalk looking at a dead phone. After a few seconds, he replaced the phone and looked at his watch. It was a few minutes before six thirty.

Meyers walked back to his car, got in and drove aimlessly for almost twenty minutes, thinking about that baloney in the frig. He stopped at a traffic light on North Circular Road, just three blocks from one of his favorite pubs. Within minutes he was in the parking lot in the rear of the establishment and in another five minutes he was seated in a booth eating fish and chips and washing the food down with a pint of Harps.

"Lots better than cold cuts," thought Meyers, *"particularly that German baloney Molly buys."*

At seven twenty-nine he finished the last chip and at seven thirty he wiggled out of the booth and at the same time finished the last of his beer.

After paying his bill, he walked to the rear of the pub where the public phone was located.

He deposited the correct amount of coins and dialed Foley's number.

As the phone rang in the Foley's kitchen, Timothy Foley came through the kitchen door. Before he could reach the phone, Rose picked it up and said,

"Hello."

There was silence on the other end.

"I'll take it Rose," said Foley as he held out his hand. His wife looked at him for a long moment before handing him the phone.

She walked to the towel rack by the sink where she neatly folded the tea towel she was holding and placed it on the rack. She turned, walked into the dining room and pulled the door close.

"Timothy?"

"Sorry Jamie, I just got back home."

"Are you all right?"

"Yes. Rose and I just needed to transfer the phone."

"Did you get the directions?"

"Yes."

"Well?"

"They will meet you at a road side rest area on R173 two kilometers west of The Bush at twelve o'clock Thursday night. You are to back your van into the area.

"Alright, will O'Connor be there?"

"Yes, and you will be alone, right?"

"No, another officer will be with me."

"No Jamie, you have to go alone. That was the condition."

Meyers closed his eyes for a moment. He knew the Chief Superintendent wanted someone to go with him.

"All right Timothy, I'll be alone."

Silence.

"Tell Rose and the children hello."

"I will."

"Good by Timothy."

"Good by Jamie."

MI-5 Headquarters
Belfast, Northern Ireland

Samuel H. Irwin, the Deputy Director of the MI-5 Station in Belfast, was in his office reading the morning edition of the Belfast Telegram News.

Although his office was smaller than the Director's office, which was furnished with government issued furniture, Irwin's office appeared more like a combination of parlor, library and dining room than an office. The reason was that Irwin furnished his office with his own furniture.

When questioned about the luxury of his office, he immediately informed the inquisitor that his office was furnished at no cost to the government.

An antique cherry desk and high back chair were located in front of a large bay type window. Along the bottom of the window was a shelf containing a variety of indoor plants.

Facing the desk was a large, Italian leather sofa. In front of the sofa was a cherry coffee table half the length of the sofa. On each side of the sofa were matching leather easy chairs. Between the chairs and sofa were cherry end tables containing brass lamps and an array of current magazines. The floor beneath the sofa and chairs and running up to the desk was covered by an Oriental rug obtained by Irwin during one of his visits to Turkey.

On the far side of the desk and sofa was an extra large dining table flanked by nine straight back chairs and one captain's chair, all in cherry. Under the table and chairs was another Oriental rug from Turkey.

Around the table, the three walls were lined with bookcases, six feet in height filled with hundreds of books, most leather bound.

On the walls of the office were four, large oil paintings of equal size. The paintings were of different English troop units which participated in the Crimean war. The first painting a person saw when entering Irwin's office was a painting of the famous charge of the Light Brigade.

Irwin was a small, wiry individual in his early sixties. The small amount of gray hair remaining on his head was carefully arranged in a thin layer in an unsuccessful attempt to cover his head.

The half moon glasses he wore when reading were perched on the end of his nose, requiring him to hold his head back with his nose sticking straight up in the air.

Irwin arrived at his office at exactly at 7:10 each morning, fifty minutes before the day shift was due to arrive and an hour and twenty minutes before Dean Norwood, the Director, arrived for work.

Following his routine, he picked up the morning paper on his way to work and upon arriving he prepared a pot of tea. Once the tea was started, he would take a seat in the easy chair to the left of the sofa, unfold the paper and read the entire first and third pages.

This morning, just as the buzzer went off, indicating his tea had brewed exactly eight minutes, the telephone on his desk rang. He looked at the phone, turned and looked at the teapot, then looked down at his watch. He placed the newspaper on the coffee table in front of him, pushed himself up and walked over to the desk where he picked up the phone.

"Yes."

"Mr. Irwin?"

"Yes."

"This is Kapp in communications."

"Yes."

"Sir, we received a message from NSA this morning indicating a telephone number in the Shankill district received a call from the Republic in which the name O'Connor was mentioned."

"Excellent, did they send a transcript?"

"No sir, they only sent the time, the caller's number and location."

"What about the transcript?"

"They didn't mention a transcript."

"Contact them and ask if a recording was made of the conversation and if the answer is positive, ask for a transcript."

"Yes sir. If a recording was made, we'll have to make an official request for the transcript," said Kapp.

Irwin looked at his watch.

"What time is it in the States?"

Without any hesitation, Kapp said,

"2:25 AM."

"Send an official request over my name. Request they send the transcript electronically and tell them we appreciate their assistance."

"Yes sir. I'll bring the transcript up as soon as we receive it."

"Excellent, thank you."

"Yes sir."

Irwin replaced the phone in its cradle and thought,

"They'll probably monitor both numbers for the next year. Too bad we don't have the computer equipment the Americas have, we wouldn't have to depend on them. With all their technology, they know more about what is going on here than we do, technically. But all their technology is useless without agents in place. Something they will have to learn."

After replacing the phone, Irwin moved to the table in the corner where the teapot was located. He poured himself three quarters of a cup of tea, opened the small refrigerator, removed a cardboard carton of half and half and filled his cup. He returned to the middle of the room, placed the cup on the coffee table, picked up the paper, took a seat in his easy chair and continued to read the article on page three about the attack on the Police station in Dungannon.

He took his first drink of tea of this morning and smiled, the taste was to his approval.

He returned to the paper and searched to see if there were any articles about the escape of O'Connor. He found only one short article on page ten stating no official announcement from either Sinn Fein or the Provos about the escape being received by either the police or the newspapers.

"I could add a few details to the story," thought Irwin.

From MI-6 reports he knew McCaul was transported from Convoy to Letterkenny and from there to Dublin where he was transported to St. Francis Hospital in Baldoyle. From the latest reports he knew McCaul was seriously ill and the physicians treating him were still unclear about what was causing his illness.

"God, I'd like to get my hands on that little bastard," said Irwin to himself.

Thoughts about McCaul vanished as he heard the knock on his door. He refolded the paper, stood up and walked to the door.

"Yes."

"It's Kapp sir."

As quietly as possible Irwin turned the latch until he felt it slide out of the locked position. He opened the door and saw Kapp holding a brown folder marked "Secret" and a white paper.

Handing the folder to Irwin, Kapp said,

"Here's the transcript from the NSA of last night's telephone conversation and authorization for me to request the transcript in your name."

Irwin took both from Kapp, took his pen from his shirt pocket and using the folder as a writing board, signed the authorization paper. He handed the paper to Kapp and said,

"Thank you Lester."

"Certainly sir."

Irwin closed the door, locked it, turned and walked to his desk. He placed the folder on the desk and stood looking at it for a moment. He was thinking about finishing both his cup of tea and his review of the morning paper before looking at the information in the folder.

His thoughts jumped to the telephone intercept. He smiled as he congratulated himself for asking the NSA to monitor telephone calls from the Republic when certain names were mentioned during a conversation. *"That computer must be as big as a building to monitor and pick up such information,"* he thought.

If the call had anything to do with O'Connor's activities, he would have to make arrangements to have the number continually monitored by his people.

He looked at the cup and folded paper on the coffee table and then at the folder on his desk. His curiosity won out. He walked to the coffee table, picked up his teacup and returned to his desk. He picked up the folder and took the transcript out. Slowly he read the contents.

"....bath.

(Pause)

"Your message will be relayed to O'Connor. Call back as soon as you have any additional information."

"Anything else?"

"No. Good night."

"Good night."

Irwin knew immediately the NSA failed to record the majority of the conversation. The recorder didn't click on until a few seconds after O'Connor's name was mentioned.

"Well now, we'll just have to make arrangements to put a tap on this telephone."

Picking up the phone, Irwin punched in four numbers and waited.

"Section three, Hardman speaking."

Irwin looked at his watch. It was ten minutes before eight.

"This is the Deputy Director. Which shift are you on?"

"The day shift sir. I came in early."

"Excellent. I'd like for you to find out the locations of two telephone numbers."

"Yes sir."

"You have a pencil?"

"Yes sir."

Looking at the monitoring report, Irwin gave him the two telephone numbers.

"How long will it take?" asked Irwin.

"About three minutes. If you would like to hold sir."

"No, call me when you have the locations."

"Yes sir."

Three minutes later Hardman called and gave Irwin the requested information. One telephone number was in an apartment on Mayo Street in the Shankill district of Belfast. It was a smart move by the Provos to have a telephone in the heart of Loyalists' territory. The other number was a pay phone located in a Pub by the name of the Green Harp, which was located in the Milltown district of Dublin.

"I wonder if the Garda has the telephone in the Cross and Shield Pub taped? Probably not, too many legal hoops down there."

During the next twenty minutes, Irwin filled out the necessary form to have the telephone number on Mayo Street continually monitored for the next thirty days, a restriction put on MI-5 by the political appointees in London.

Day Eight

July 29, 1998

MI-5 Headquarters
Belfast, Northern Ireland

After his morning routine of reading the paper and having his cup of tea, Deputy Director Irwin opened his file cabinet and removed the green folder marked "O'CONNOR". The only documents in the folder were a surveillance report indicating the apartment on Mayo Street was not rented nor occupied and four telephone intercepts to and from the telephone listed to the apartment.

Since yesterday morning, three additional intercepts were added to the initial partial communication supplied by the NSA. MI-5 was furnished one additional intercept by the NSA, but the other two were from the communication section based on his request to monitor the phone.

Irwin dropped the folder on his desk, walked over to the table holding the teapot and poured himself three quarters of a cup of tea and repeated his routine of adding milk to his tea.

He walked back to his desk, but instead of taking a seat, he stood behind his chair and looked at the folder. For the next six minutes he would look at the folder for fifteen to twenty seconds, turn and look up at one of the paintings on the wall for five to ten seconds, take a drink of tea and repeat the stratagem.

He finally placed his cup on the desk, pulled out the chair and slipped into it. Slowly he opened the folder, removed the four intercepts and read them.

(Telephone call from the Green Harp Pub in Dublin to the apartment on May Street, Belfast at 2340 hours, 27 July 1998)

"...bath."

(Pause)

"Your message will be relayed to O'Connor. Call back as soon as you have any additional information."

"Anything else?"

"No, good night."

"Good night."

(Telephone call from Mayo apartment to public telephone on the wharf on Alexandra Road, Dublin, 28 July 1998, 1419 hours)

"Dodson, Kelly here, I have a message for you from O'Connor."

"I've been waiting for a call from him.

Anything wrong?"

"No, no, everything's fine."

"Good."

(Pause)

"Have you picked up the mortar yet?"

"No. I can't get it until tomorrow afternoon. Something about the bill of laden and customs."

"What about the bill of laden?"

"They want to know why one of these wooden containers is so heavy."

"Two crates?"

"Yes, two, one about a tenth the size of the other."

(Pause)

"Why two?"

"The smaller one has the hardware in it. The special items O'Connor ordered. Remember?"

(Pause)

"Are the crates on the dock?"

"No, they haven't been unloaded yet."

"Then how do they know the weights?"

"The weights are on the bill of laden."

"Could this...."

"Appears this ship load is receiving special attention. Every container is being checked by customs against the cargo manifest."

"Are we in trouble?"

"I don't know yet, but I don't think so. Talked with a couple of our boys at lunchtime. They said the people in customs have been called on the carpet for letting too many high priced items get through without paying the import duty. Every now and then Customs picks a ship out of Boston or New York or New Orleans to do a thorough check. Looks like ours will be the one."

(Pause)

"Any chance they might open the crates?"

"I don't know. But once we get the shipment, the big one will have to be opened. It's too big to fit in the van."

(Pause)

"Not on the dock?"

"No. The crates that are not picked up as they unload the ship will be moved into the warehouse on the wharf. That's where we'll open the crate and…."

"Alright. Did they tell you what time the ship will be unloaded?"

"Wednesday morning between seven and twelve."

"Do you know what time you can pick up the…."

"Between noon and three, tomorrow afternoon."

(Pause)

"That's good."

(Pause)

"Donal, after you have the van loaded, O'Connor wants you to take it to Jerry's Uncle's garage and stay there until Thursday evening. After dark, drive up N1 towards Newry, go through Dundalk and three or four kilometers north of Dundalk you'll run into R173 before you reach the border. Get on R173 and about two kilometers before you reach a little place called The Bush there's a rest area. He wants you to arrive at the rest area by twelve o'clock, plus or minus a few minutes."

"But I thought I was suppose to take…."

"Donal!"

(Pause)

"Yes."

"Please listen. Thomas wants you at the rest area at twelve o'clock Friday morning. At midnight. Do you understand?"

"Yes."

"That's where we'll make the transfer."

"The trans….."

"DONAL!"

(Pause)

"Yes."

"Just do as I ask. These are orders from O'Connor. Conditions have changed. Meet us at the rest area at twelve Friday night. Understand?"

"Yes."

When you arrive, back your van in and park next to the table. Understand?"

"Yes."

"If you have any problems with Customs or anyone else, you know who to contact."

"Yes."

"Good. Now, O'Connor wants you to stay out of trouble. Understand?"

"Yes."

"Good, we'll see you Friday night around twelve."

"OK."

"Good by."

"Good by."

(Telephone call from a public telephone on High Street, Belfast to the apartment on Mayo Street, Belfast at 1550 hours, 28 July 1998)

"Hello."

"Who is this?"

"Who is this?"

"O'Connor."

"Sorry. This is Kelsy. What can I do for you Mr. O'Connor?"

"Is McNutt there?"

"Yes…no."

"Which is it Kelsy, yes or no?"

"He's here, but he's in the bathroom right now."

"Then go get him."

"OK."

(One minute and forty-two seconds of silence)

"Neil here Thomas. What can I do for you?"

"Neil, the mortar is here."

"In Belfast?"

"No you…in Dublin. It will be unloaded from the ship this morning."

"Yes?"

"I want you to pick it up."

"In Dublin?"

"Hell no, not in Dublin. Dodson will be picking it up in Dublin, but we don't want him to take it across the border."

"Then how are…."

"Damn it, listen instead of talking, will you?"

"OK Thomas, don't get your…"

"Shut up and listen."

"OK…sorry."

(Pause)

"Dodson will be at a rest area on Route 173 west of a little place called The Bush around midnight Thursday night. I want you to take the white van and meet him there at half past twelve. Understand?"

"But that's in the Republic."

"Damn it, I know that. I just told you, we don't want Dodson to come into Ulster, so we are going to have to make the transfer in the Republic."

"But…"

"But what?"

(Pause)

"Nothing, I just thought that…."

"I'll do the thinking McNutt, understand?"

(Pause)

"Do you understand?"

"Yes Thomas, I understand."

"Good. Now listen. Get the van checked out by Davy's father. Get it filled with petrol, not the cheap stuff you've been buying, the good stuff?"

"Yes."

"Good. I want you to be at the rest stop at exactly twelve thirty Friday morning. Do you understand?"

"Yes, I'm not stupid you know."

"I know Neil, I'm sorry for my temper, but we need that mortar for the job next week."

"I understand Thomas and I'll be there exactly at twelve thirty Friday morning."

"Excellent."

"Will you be there?"

"Yes. A couple of the boys and I will be there around midnight in case Dodson happens to show up early."

"Then I'll see you at twelve thirty, Friday morning."

"Yes Neil. I'll see you Friday morning. Just do exactly what I told you. Make sure the van is in A-1 condition and is full of petrol. OK?"

"Yes."

"Thank you Neil, good by."

"Good by Thomas.

(Telephone call from a public phone in the Ballbridge section of Dublin to the apartment on Mayo Street on 28 July 1998 at 1833 hours.)

".........(lei or lay)."

"Yes Timothy?"

(Long Pause)

"Timothy, where are you calling from?"

"Dublin, a payphone on Shellbourne, why?"

"Do you have your list with you?"

"Yes."

"Call back using the next number, understand?"

"Yes."

"Call back in exactly three minutes, understand?"

"Yes."

"Good by."

"Good by."

(Telephone call mentioning the name O'Connor, from a public phone on Shellbourne Street in Dublin to a payphone on Mayo Street, Belfast on 28 July 1998 at 1840 hours. Intercept supplied by NSA.)

".......Jamie be alright."

"If he comes alone and..."

"If he says he'll be alone, he'll be alone. He's as good as his word."

"Then there's nothing to worry about."

"I hope everything works out."

"It will. Anything else?"

"No."

"Good. Thank you for your assistance."

"You're welcomed."

"Good by."

"Good by."

"Damnit" said Irwin, *"they missed the first part of the conversation."*

Irwin replaced the documents in the folder, closed his eyes and leaned back in his chair. He attempted to decipher their meaning. Exactly what were they talking about?

He opened the folder, took out the intercepts and read them in chronological order, switched them around and read them starting with the last one first. He was certain the message had some hidden meanings, but after thirty minutes, he was still stymied. He closed his eyes again, leaned back in his chair and for the next twenty minutes he had the following conversation with his alter ego.

"Is O'Connor actually going across the border to meet someone? Who? Who is Jamie? Who is Donal Dodson? Who is Neil McNutt? The registry people couldn't come up with any information on any of these people, therefore, these names are not their real names or they are new additions to their little group.

Let's see…this Jamie individual was told to be alone and he's be all right. I have no idea what that meant. Dodson was told to be at the rest area at twelve o'clock and McNutt was told to be at the rest area at twelve thirty. Why?

Jamie could be the representative of the ones supplying the mortar and Dodson is picking it up in Dublin. McNutt is picking it up from Dodson at the rest area west of The Bush. McNutt is the one we will be picking up when he crosses into the North….along with O'Connor."

Irwin opened his eyes, took a deep breath and asked himself the following questions:

"Are the Provos actually smuggling a heavy mortar into Northern Ireland? Apparently yes. Why is it necessary for O'Connor to be at the transfer point? He will probably make payment to Dodson. Right. One thing I can't understand is after they load it in Dublin, why transfer it to another van or truck? Why did Jamie have to be alone? Is the transfer area really at the rest area or is that merely a code name for someplace else? I've never heard of a place called The Bush. It must be a code word for something or someplace. Why not transfer it closer to Dublin? Could it be because O'Connor doesn't want to get that far into the Republic? Could this be a trick by the Garda or the Intelligence people in the Republic to recapture O'Connor? No, we would have heard about it from MI-6….maybe!

The names…used in the communications, Jamie, Donal Dodson, Neil McNutt. Not one of these names are on our list of known members of the

Provos. Perhaps that's exactly what they want. Are they pulling a trick like the UAD with their bombing hoaxes?"

Irwin rocked back and forth in his chair, opened his eyes and attempted to think like the Irish. He was certain he had that special gift, but he was totally mistaken in his conclusion. Only an Irishman could think like an Irishman.

"Are they really planning a transfer of a heavy mortar or is this just one of their shenanigans to get us to chase our tails? If they know we've tapped their phone they could be leading us on another wild goose chase. Yes or No? Damn good question."

Irwin put the intercepts back in the folder, closed it, stood up and looked at the map of Ireland on the wall to his right. He walked over to the map and to his surprise located the small town of The Bush.

"They really know how to work it. The rest area is just a little too far for us to rush over and grab them, unless we could go across the Lough. No, we'd have to involve the Coast Guard or Navy."

Irwin returned to his desk, took a seat and picked up the phone.

"Yes sir?"

"Would you contact Captain Taggart-Holmes and ask him to call me?"

"Yes sir."

Irwin replaced the phone, leaned back in his chair and again closed his eyes. Before he had a chance to contemplate what he was going to ask Taggart-Holmes, he realized he would need a map of the area. He opened his eyes, picked up the phone and dialed the Map Section.

"Yes sir?"

"This is the Deputy Director."

"Yes sir."

"I need a map of the northeast section of the Republic, sections fifteen and sixteen."

"Yes sir."

"What is your most detailed map?"

"We have the military maps with contours at 1:25,000 and.."

"Is that the most detail?"

"It's the most detail of the military maps, but we have aerial photomaps of the area at 1:10,000 and 1:1,000. These are in black and white."

"Good. Would you have someone bring the aerial photomaps of the area covering sections fifteen and sixteen to my office as soon as possible."

"Yes sir."

"Thank you."

Irwin rocked back and forth in his chair and thought about O'Connor.

"If only we can grab him. If I could mastermind the capture of O'Connor perhaps I could get the grade promotion without waiting three years after becoming Director."

The thought made him smile.

A knock on his door brought him back to reality.

"Yes."

"Throckmorton from the map section sir."

"Just a moment," said Irwin as he scooted out his chair, walked over to the door and opened the latch.

"Come in."

The large door slowly opened and a short, dark haired individual backed into the Deputy Director's office. Under both arms he had a number of rolled up maps.

"Put them on the table," said Irwin.

"Yes sir," said Throckmorton as he turned and walked across the room to the large table. Carefully he raised his left arm and at the same time attempted to control the movement of the three rolled up maps that fell on the table.

Once the three maps were under control, he used his left hand to take the three maps under his right arm and place them on the table. He turned and started to say something, but the Deputy Director asked,

"Sections fifteen and sixteen?"

"Yes sir, three of the maps cover each section."

"Good, thank you."

"Anything else?"

"No. I'll call the section when I'm finished with the maps."

"Yes sir," said Throckmorton as he turned and walked across the room and out the door.

As the door closed, Irwin quietly slipped the latch back in place, turned and walked to the table. He picked up the rolled up map on the right, unrolled it, but instead of remaining flat, it rolled back.

Irwin moved to the bookcase, reached in and removed eight books. He spread the maps on the table and using the books as weights, placed them on the corners of the three maps marked A, B and C of section sixteen.

He quickly surveyed the maps and on the one marked "B" he saw in bold letters, "Carlingford." An arrow at the bottom of the map pointing southwest with the notation, "to Dundalk".

This was the only map he needed at the moment.

He walked back to his desk, opened the middle drawer and removed a large magnifying glass. He rubbed both sides of the glass with his linen handkerchief, looked through it, turned it around and looked through it again.

With the aid of the magnifying glass, Irwin studied the area southwest of Carlingford.

"Excellent."

His telephone rang as he placed the magnifying glass on the map.

He walked over to his desk, picked up the phone and said,

"Irwin speaking."

"Yes sir, this is Captain Taggart-Holmes. I have a message you wanted me to contact you."

"That's correct Captain. I'd like to see you in my office, now."

"Yes sir. I'll be there in five minutes."

"Good," said Irwin as he hung up the phone. He stood by his desk for a moment trying to make up his mind whether to take a seat at the desk or walk back to the table. He decided to take a seat and await the arrival of Captain Taggart-Holmes.

While waiting, he closed his eyes and visualized the Captain. He prided himself in knowing in detail the background of every individual who worked in the Belfast Department.

Taggart-Holmes was from the town of Poole, which was located west of Boursmouth in the south of England. He was raised on the estate of his ancestors who made a fortune in South Africa. He was the only child of Lord and Lady James Arthur Taggart-Holmes. His great, great grandfather fought in the Boar war, his great grandfather in WWI, his grandfather in WWII and his father fought in Korea. All were highly decorated for their services. The only war the young Captain was in was the Falklands. He arrived on the field of battle just as the fighting ceased, thus missing the chance to win any distinction as his ancestors. Based on the missed chance for distinctive service in the Falklands, the young Captain volunteered for a second tour of duty in Northern Ireland.

It was his error to request an assignment to Northern Ireland just at the time the personnel section decided he needed experience with the Intelligence Service. Since Northern Ireland was considered part of the British Empire, instead of being assigned to MI-6, he was assigned to MI-5 and instead of being assigned to an infantry regiment, he was assigned to a section directly under the control of the Deputy Director. His particular assignment was to keep tabs on individuals or groups within the British Army suspected of being in alliance with terrorists organizations, either Nationalists or Loyalists.

With the approval of the Deputy Director, his mode of operation was to be assigned for short periods of time to units to which suspected individuals were members.

After escaping without serious injury when a bomb exploded under his vehicle outside Rathfriland, Irwin decided Taggart-Holmes could achieve his mission by remaining at headquarters. He was to read reports of individuals within the units recruited by MI-5 to report on suspected individuals.

Irwin's thoughts were disturbed by a loud knock on his door.

"Yes?"

"Captain Taggart-Holmes here sir."

Again Irwin slipped out of his chair, walked to the door and turned the knob that slipped the latch into the door.

The Deputy Director then walked back to his desk, took a seat and said,

"Come in Captain."

Taggart-Holmes opened the door, walked to the front of Irwin's desk and stood at attention.

"Relax Captain, this is MI-5, not the Queen's Royal Fusilier Regiment."

"Yes sir," said the Captain, who remained at attention.

Irwin stood up and walked over to the table. He looked down at the maps, turned and looked at Taggart-Holmes and said,

"You do know about Thomas O'Connor, right?"

"Yes sir, the gentleman who escaped from the Garda with the aid of a few Provos."

"Correct. Well, the gentleman has plans to smuggle a large caliber mortar into Northern Ireland."

Taggart-Holmes turned, looked at Irwin, frowned and said,

"I thought he was here in Ulster."

"He is Captain, but we have good information he is planning on going down into the Republic tomorrow night to supervise the transfer of the mortar from his contacts in the Republic to a van from Northern Ireland. The mortar will then be transported into Northern Ireland."

"Where?

"Where what?" asked Irwin.

"Where in Northern Ireland?"

"We have no idea."

"How did…."

"Come over here please," said Irwin.

Taggart-Holmes nodded, made a military right face and marched over to the table.

Irwin shook his head and said,

"For God's sake Captain, relax will you?"

"Yes sir."

"According to the information we have, the mortar was shipped out of Boston and was loaded into a van in Dublin yesterday. Tomorrow evening it will be transported to a rest area the other side of Carlingford, two clicks from a little town by the name of The Bush. It will arrive at the rest area around midnight. At approximately twelve thirty a white van will arrive at the area and the mortar will be transferred into it. Where it will cross the border and its final destination is not known."

"I see."

"What I would like for you to do is determine where the van crosses the border."

"And?"

"And once we know where the van crosses, we'll stop it, arrest the driver and confiscate their little toy."

The Captain looked at Irwin and started to ask a question, but before he could speak, Irwin said,

"I've alerted the Army and the Constabulary. The Operations Section in Lisburn is in the process of issuing orders to various units which will cover the various entrances into Northern Ireland."

"But how can the Army cover…."

"Let me explain," said Irwin as he leaned over and placed his index finger on the map.

"This is where the transfer will be made."

Taggart-Holmes looked down at the map and saw Irwin's finger was located on a peninsula north of Dundalk Bay.

"The rest area is approximately two kilometers west of The Bush, which is three clicks south of Carlingford on R173."

Irwin removed his finger, allowing the Captain to get a good look at the map.

When Taggart-Holmes looked up, Irwin said,

"The Army units will be stationed in seven strategically located areas. Locations from which they can quickly cover any road in their particular area.

What I would like for you to do as soon as possible is go into the Republic, locate the rest area and select two locations from which the area can be observed."

"And?"

"And report back to me this afternoon by sixteen hundred hours."

"Yes sir."

Irwin walked towards his desk, stopped, turned and asked,

"Do you need the map?"

"No sir."

"Good. I'll see you at sixteen hundred hours."

"Yes sir," said the Captain as he turned and walked out of the Deputy Director's office.

Ten minutes before ten, Irwin stood up, picked up the folder and walked out of his office. After locking the door he walked down the hall to the Director's conference room.

For the next hour and twenty minutes he listened to the reports from the different sections, but his mind was not on the activities of the sections, his thoughts were on O'Connor and the intercepts.

After the regular ten o'clock briefings, Irwin asked Director Norwood if he would remain for a few minutes so he could talk with him privately.

While the other staff members were headed to the canteen for their mid-morning tea, Irwin opened his brief case and placed the five transcripts in front of the Director.

"These are the five transcripts I believe are tied to O'Connor. It appears the Provos are moving a heavy mortar into Northern Ireland from the Republic."

Norwood took his glasses out of a brown case, slowly put them on and picked up the transcripts. Before reading them he looked at Irwin and asked,

"You did get the message about McCaul?"

"Yes sir."

Norwood nodded, adjusted his glasses and read the transcripts.

Like Irwin, he read them in chronological order, shifted them around and read them again. He took off his glasses, placed them on the table and looked up at Irwin.

"Interesting Samuel. Are there any more?"

"No sir."

"Are you certain it was O'Connor?"

"Fairly certain. Of course we can't be positive."

Norwood turned from looking at Irwin and returned to the transcripts. Slowly he reread each.

"A wild goose chase?"

"Possible."

The Director turned and looked out the window for almost a minute, turned back and asked,

"Who will be going to Dublin?"

"Major Brown, Hooker and myself."

Again Norwood turned and looked out the window for a few seconds, then turned back, looked directly at the Deputy Director and asked,

"What do you suggest we do?"

Irwin suppressed his smile.

"If O'Connor shows up in the Republic and heads back into Northern Ireland, we have an excellent chance of grabbing him. This is also true of the mortar, unless they are trying to hoodwink us.

If they transfer it at the rest area, we will have a good chance of picking it up when it enters Northern Ireland."

Norwood nodded, but asked,

"What about the people in the Republic? Their Intelligence and the Garda?"

"We don't have time sir. You know how long it takes them to do anything, particularly a combined operation."

Again Norwood nodded.

"What do you propose?"

Irwin again suppressed his smile. He knew the Director would drop the operation in his lap. Norwood was only five months from retiring and didn't want to be bothered making any decisions, particularly a wrong one.

"Alert the Army and the Constabulary and have them standing by. When O'Connor crosses the border either the Army or the Constabulary will be waiting for him."

"Where? There must be at least twenty five roads leading into Northern Ireland from the Republic."

"True, but if they make the exchange in the Carlingford area then the best bet is they will use one of the main highways, A2, A3, A4, A5 or A32. With units in Newry, Armagh, Dungannon, Newtown, Enniskillen and Omagh we can cover all the main roads, plus the secondary roads."

Again Norwood nodded, but did not comment, so Irwin continued.

"If we can follow O'Connor and the mortar up to the border, we'll be able to alert the particular unit to stop them when they are inside Northern Ireland."

"Do you think they will come together?"

Irwin frowned.

"What I mean, do you think O'Connor will be with the mortar?"

"I don't know, but if you OK the operation, I'll make sure there are enough of our people to follow both O'Connor and the mortar if they don't travel together."

"What do you think O'Connor will do with the mortar?"

"I think this will be his big exordium onto the scene, his first official appearance in Northern Ireland. He's probably going to do something spectacular with the mortar and personally I don't think he will let it out of his sight."

"Really?"

"Yes sir. I think he has some grand plan for it. Something he and McCaul hatched up before McCaul got sick. I believe O'Connor is going to carry out the plan, perhaps as a tribute to McCaul."

Norwood stared at Irwin for a few seconds, turned and looked out the window. Thirty seconds later he turned and looked at Irwin and changed the subject completely when he asked Irwin,

"Why do you think he and McCaul showed up in Ireland now?"

Irwin was still thinking about the mortar. He hesitated for a moment, then quickly said,

"I really don't know, but my guess is the Provos are preparing an awe-inspiring demonstration of their strength and ability, conceivably to impress the government. Who could get more publicity than Thomas O'Connor with a large caliber mortar attack?"

"On what?"

"Maybe someplace highly visible, perhaps some government building," said Irwin, grabbing an answer out of the air.

"You think that is possible?"

"Anything is possible with those people Mr.Norwood, anything, particularly if the Nationalists feel they are on the losing end."

After a few moments, Norwood asked,

"Do you really think they would attack a Government building?"

"I don't know sir, but if the Provos don't achieve their goals, what better way to destroy the peace process for a long time, maybe forever."

Norwood nodded and said,

"Yes it would Samuel, possibly it would be the end of any peace effort."

"Yes sir."

Again, to Irwin's annoyance, Norwood turned and looked out the window, but this time it was for only a few seconds. He turned, looked at Irwin and asked,

"Did we have any indications McCaul and O'Connor were headed back to Irelancd?"

Irwin gave an almost inaudible combination of a grunt and a laubh.

"Sir, the spooks in MI-6 lost O'Connor and McCaul the day they escaped from the Interrogation Cener. They have no ideaa where they have been for the last five years."

Irwin knew exactly what the Director was going to say next. He was going to change the subject and ask him what he was going to do about O'Connor.

"You have a plan Samuel?"

Irwin could not keep from smiling as he said,

"Yes sir."

"Well?"

"You know the gentlemen at NIO have insisted that McCaul's body be cremated instead of being turned over to his family. The Justice Department, Commissioner of the Garda and the Republic's Attorney General agreed to the cremation."

"I know. So?"

"As you know, Major Brown, Hooker and I are driving to Dublin on Thursday morning to have lunch with the Commissioner and Attorney General and some of their people. After lunch the entire group is scheduled to go to the hospital to view McCaul's body and those who wish to observe the cremation."

"Yes."

"Instead of returning to Belfast Thursday afternoon, I thought Major Brown and I would have a little lay over outside of Carlingford."

"Yes."

"First I'll make arrangements with the Army and the Constabulary to station their people in strategic areas so they can cover the main roads coming into the North from the Republic.

"I sent….I'll send Taggart-Holmes down there to survey the area and locate a couple of good observation points. Thursday evening I'll send him to one of the observation points and Major Brown and I will occupy the other. When the mortar and O'Connor show up, we can follow them until they enter Northern Ireland."

"If and when this occurs, what if the mortar goes one way and O'Connor goes another way?" asked Norwood.

"Brown and I will follow O'Connor and Taggart-Holmes will follow the mortar."

Norwood looked at Irwin, smiled, shook his head and said,

"You've already initiated the plan, haven't you Mr. Irwin?"

Irwin attempted to look surprised by the question, but failed in his effort.

"That's alright Samuel. Just be careful and keep me informed."

"Yes sir."

Belfast, Northern Ireland

As Captain Lamb drove out of Belfast towards Hilltown Wednesday morning, the explosion on highway A8 was buried in the deep recesses of his mind. He was thinking of two entities at the moment. The first was his assignment in Northern Ireland. It was the latter part of July and according to his orders, his year assignment would be up the tenth of February. The other was Elizabeth Kelly.

Just south of Lisburn, Lamb took the number seven exit and pulled onto A1. He looked about at the Irish countryside and thought about the last few months of his assignment here in Northern Ireland. He thought about his work with the Bomb Squad, the death of Constable Kelly in the explosion in Rathfriland, his attendance of Constable Kelly's funeral with Chief Superintendent Rothchild and his meeting with Elizabeth Kelly. Lamb smiled as he thought about Elizabeth Kelly and his purpose for this trip. It was to ask her a very important question.

Today was going to be a day to enjoy the cool, clean air of Ireland. The good Lord was cooperating by providing not only sunshine, but a few cotton white clouds floating around in His blue sky.

At exactly ten o'clock, Captain Lamb pulled up in front of the brick duplex located on the edge of Hilltown. After turning off the engine, he smiled and thought about how Liz was forced to leave her little house in Rathfriland and drive to Hilltown so her family and neighbors would not know she was going on an outing with the young Australian Captain.

The first couple of times they made arrangements to meet in Hilltown, Lamb felt a bit guilty, but this was erased by the thought of the one time in May when he made the mistake of "dropping in" on the widow Kelly. He learned later the waging tongues started waging before he reached her front door.

The woman across the street from the Kelly house was on the telephone with her friend on the other side of town and as Lamb approached the Kelly house the neighbor was narrating his every move to her friend.

By the time he departed an hour later, the rumor about the widow Kelly and the foreign officer had spread like a wildfire.

Lamb only found out about the gossip a week later when he called Elizabeth and asked if she would like to go for a short drive to Castlewallen to visit her Aunt's tearoom.

Elizabeth said she would love to see him, but instead of him picking her up, she would meet him in Castlewaller. It was during their "hot date" at her aunt's tea room, where they had tea, coffee and fresh baked rolls, that Mrs. Kelly told him some of the stories circulating in her neighborhood. It was at that moment when the decision was made that he would no longer pick her up at her house, but at her friend, Bridget Casey's duplex in Hilltown.

Before Lamb reached the door of Bridget's duplex, the door opened and Elizabeth came out carrying a large picnic basket. She stopped, placed the basket on the porch, turned and locked the door. Before she could turn back around, Lamb picked up the basket with his right hand an extended his left hand, which she took.

"Maybe we shouldn't hold hand. Your reputation will be ruined here in Hilltown," said Lamb as he smiled and winked at Mrs. Kelly.

"Perhaps we shouldn't," said Elizabeth as she attempted to pull her hand away.

"To hell with all of them," said Lamb as he tugged on her hand and walked towards the car.

"I agree, to hell with them," said Elizabeth as both laughed and smiled at each other.

The stop at the tea room was short, only time enough for the two to walk in, select two sweet rolls and leave. As usual, Elizabeth's Aunt Mae refused to take any money for the rolls, but as the two walked to the door, Lamb placed two one pound notes on top of the show case.

The drive from Castlewallen through New Castle and Kilkeel to the park in the Mourne Mountains was in almost total silence. The only conversation was when one or the other saw something they wanted the other to see. The total conversations consisted of seven:

"Look there!"

Neither wanted to start a conversation that would require them to look at the other. It was not because they were afraid of missing something on this beautiful summer day, but because each was contemplating asking the other a question.

Physically they were enjoying the scenery, yet their minds were not on the panorama of the Irish landscape, but on how they would ask their particular question without upsetting the other.

Lamb eased the car off the main road onto a gravel road leading to a picnic area deep in the mountains. Thankfully the area was void of any other humans. The absence of others seemed to supply each with the courage to ask their question. Both had worked out the correct wording and were merely waiting for the right moment.

Once out of the car, Elizabeth covered the concrete table with a white tablecloth and Lamb placed the picnic basket on the table along with the sweet rolls.

Elizabeth opened the basket, removed a plate of sandwiches and a bag of chips and handed Lamb the thermos.

"Do you want your hot chocolate now or later?"

"Later," said Lamb.

"Me too. Shall we eat?"

The two slid onto the cool concrete benches and for a few seconds they simply looked at each other. The moment had arrived for both.

Just as Lamb said,

"I have…."

Elizabeth said, "I have…."

Both stopped instantly, looked at each other and laughed.

"Go ahead," said Lamb, losing his courage momentarily.

"No, you started to say something."

Lamb looked away for no more than a second, turned back, looked into Elizabeth's face and shouted,

"Liz, will you marry me?"

Elizabeth could not retain her serious look. She broke out laughing.

Lamb's face turned bright red. The look on his face was that of a badly beaten schoolboy. He shook his head and started to push himself up from the bench when she reached over the table and grabbed his hand.

He settled back on the bench and dropped his head, too embarrassed to look her in the face.

"No," said Elizabeth, "not for another six months."

Lamb looked up, frowned and started to ask her why she laughed at him. Before he could ask the question, she said,

"You didn't have to announce to the world you wanted to marry me."

"But there's no one around," said Lamb in his defense.

"I know, but you nearly scared me to death when you shouted your proposal. It's the first time I've ever heard you raise your voice," said Elizabeth as she laughed again.

The frown disappeared from the young Australian's face and was replaced by a wide smile.

For the next five minutes the two held hands, looked at each other, then turned away, embarrassed by their feelings. After regaining his composure, Captain Lamb said,

"What was your question?"

"You answered it already."

The frown returned to Lamb's face and he said,

"I don't understand."

"Simple Captain Ralph F. Lamb of the Australian Army. I was going to ask you when were you going to ask me to marry you."

The smile returned to Lamb's face.

"In six months, do I have to ask you again?"

"Sorry, you have already committed yourself Captain Lamb. But as Aunt Mae said, I need to wait at least a year. It would be showing disrespect for Harold, yet I know he would be happy to know I found someone to love."

Lamb's face again turned beet red.

"Does that embarrass you?"

Lamb laughed and said,

"No, but you do sound like my mother when she told Dad that in front of Liz and I. Dad would turn red."

"Well, get use to it. I'm not the typical Irish lass who has nothing to say. Someday I just might stand up in the middle of church and declare to all the parishioners that I love you. Now that would really embarrass you, right?"

"You're crazy as a coot Elizabeth Kelly, do you know that?"

"Yes, so does that change your mind?"

"Hell no, please excuse the English."

"Good, now, how about eating this delicious lunch I packed for us."

When Lamb returned to his apartment in Belfast, he was unable to recall what happened after he asked Elizabeth Kelly to marry him. All he could remember was she said yes, but they would have to wait six months.

In addition, she asked him not to mention his proposal to anyone yet. It would only give the wagging tongues more material to talk about.

As he thought about the events of the day, he wondered if Elizabeth would want to be married in Ireland or Australia. It was at that moment he realized she didn't know his assignment was for only a year and in just a little over five months his assignment here in Ireland would be finished and he would be on his way home.

"I'll tell her this weekend," he thought as he dozed off to sleep.

Day Nine

July 30, 1998

Garda Headquarters
Dublin, Ireland

Meyers arrived at Headquarters a few minutes before eight and went directly to his office instead of stopping on the first floor to visit the canteen.

After hanging up his suit coat, he walked over to the file cabinet, unlocked it and removed a green notebook and a legal size table. As he placed both on his desk, he saw the note.

"No meeting at the Commissioner's office. We're to met the delegation at Rafter's at noon."

"Good," he thought as he took a seat and started working. Meyers opened the green notebook to the page marked 28th of July and looked at the single words, symbols, drawings and short phrases, his personal short hand from his interviews. As he deciphered his notes, he transcribed the major parts of each interview into longhand.

Once all the notes were transcribed onto the table, Meyers reworked each partial sentence into complete sentences.

MI-5 Headquarters
Belfast, Northern Ireland

Without the Deputy Director's permission, Captain Taggart-Holmes called his friend, Captain Ralph Lamb at Constabulary Headquarters.

The two had instantly become friends after a rather touchy exchange after the funeral of RUC officer Kelly in Rathfriland. It wasn't until later that Taggart-Holmes learned Lamb had fallen in love with the widow of Constable Kelly, who just happened to be the sister of his current girl friend.

During the weeks after their first meeting, they stayed in almost daily contact by phone and at least once a week had dinner together at the British Officer's club or one of the good restaurants in Belfast.

RUC Headquarters
Belfast, Northern Ireland

A few minutes after ten o'clock, Lamb, together with the other members of the Bomb Squad gathered in the conference room. The meeting was to discuss the final review of the Squad's report of the explosion on highway A8 on the morning of the 25th of July before it was forwarded to the Chief Constable.

After Chief Inspector Rhoades summarized the report, he projected pictures of the results of the explosion on the screen in the front of the room and asked the members if there were any discrepancies with the written report.

"Did the lab send up any additional information about the explosion?" asked Sullivan.

Rhoades shook his head and said,

"I haven't seen anything new. Dexter said they found traces of Semtex, diesel fuel and Ammonium Nitrate and pieces of 24 gage wire, which could be part of the detonator cap. The Semtex was probably used as the detonator.

"Then what caused the explosion?" asked Lamb.

Everyone in the room turned and looked at the Australian Officer. After a few moments of silence, Rhoades asked,

"What do you mean? The Semtex and fertilizer caused the explosion."

Lamb laughed and said,

"I know that sir, but what caused the explosion? What set it off? Semtex is like Comp C, it has to be detonated by a cap and the fertilizer bomb is stable and has to be detonated by an explosion. The question I'm asking is what detonated the Semtex?"

The members of the Bomb Squad looked at one another and shrugged their shoulders or shook their heads in reply.

Rhoades frowned and said,

"Ralph, like the others, I have no damn idea?"

"Sorry sir. Some of the witnesses said the explosion produced a red color, a yellow color, a blue color and a bright white. I'm not certain, but I don't think Semtex or a fertilizer bomb would produce all those colors, unless some other chemical was mixed with the fertilizer. You know something like the chemicals they use to make fire works, sky rockets and Roman candles. Different chemicals produce different colors. I was wondering if anyone has any information about the bomb makers mixing some other chemicals with their fertilizer explosive."

"Anyone have an answer?" asked Rhoades.

"No," said Sullivan.

Williams, Elliot and Jones followed Sullivan with either a "no" or by shaking their heads to indicate a negative answer.

"Do you think some additional chemical caused the Semtex to explode?" asked Rhoades.

"I don't think so sir, I think something beside the blasting cap set off the Semtex, which in turn set off the fertilizer."

"Did the lab people say anything about other chemicals, any metals?" asked Rhoades.

"No sir," said Sullivan, "all they found were traces of the Semtex, diesel fuel and Ammonium Nitrate."

"Chief, the report only lists the three chemical components. If the wire was part of a detonation cap, this indicates they intended to use a detonator to set off the bomb," said Elliot.

"I think what Ralph is asking is could the bomb have been set off accidentally?" asked Williams.

"That's what happened," said Sullivan.

After a full minute of silence, Rhoades said,

"We'll probably never know what caused the explosives to go off. Of course, this won't be the first time we have to send in a report with a number of unanswered questions.

Does anyone have any additions or modifications they want to add to the report?"

The four members of the Bomb Squad shook their heads.

Rhodes looked at Lamb and said,

"Ralph?"

"I agree with the report sir, but I didn't think I was included in the question because I'm merely an observer. So thank you for including me."

Rhoades smiled and nodded. He pushed his chair back and said,

"I'll get the secretary to type the cover letter and the report will be forwarded to the Chief Constable.

He looked at his watch and continued,

"It's a quarter till twelve. I'm buying lunch at Sean's at twelve thirty and who is the lucky person who has duty tonight?"

"I'm the luck person," said Williams.

"Sorry Kurt, but at lunch you're limited to ninety minutes for lunch. The rest of us can stay and partake of a couple of more pints because we are taking the rest of the day off."

"Damn," said Williams, "if you remember, this happened to me the last time."

"So it did," said Rhoades as he headed for the door, "probably because you don't have as much Irish blood as the rest. I'll see everyone at Sean's at half past."

The members of the squad picked up their papers from the table, pushed their chairs back and headed for their office.

As Lamb walked down the hall pass Mrs. Pyle's office, he saw Rhoades standing next to her desk. She looked at him and motioned to him to come into her office.

He stopped in the hall and waited until Rhoades handed her a folder full of papers and walked into his office. Once in the secretary's office, Lamb said,

"Yes ma'am."

"You have a message from your friend, that English Captain," she said as she handed him a folded piece of paper.

"Thank you," he said as he turned and reentered the hall. As he walked down the hall he read the note from Taggart-Holmes.

"How about a late night visit to the Republic. Call me ASAP."

Lamb was smiling as he entered his office and took a seat at his desk. He was wondering what the wild Englishman had in mind this time. It couldn't be another drinking party with the officers from his unit like a few weeks ago, unless they decided to celebrate in the Republic.

Without looking in his address book, he dialed Captain Taggart-Holmes office number.

"Taggart-Holmes speaking."

"Good for Taggart-Holmes," said Lamb, "this is the handsome Australian Army Officer returning his summons by the Queen's own military representative."

"No wonder they shipped your ancestors out of England," said Taggart-Holmes.

"No comment this early in the day. What in hell do you want? You know some of us have to work."

"Sure, sure. What are you doing this evening?"

"Nothing, yet?"

"Great. Want to go on a little venture into the Republic?"

"Can I ask what kind of venture?"

"You can ask, but I won't tell you until this evening."

"Are you buying dinner?"

"No."

"As the Queen's personal representative, you must have a supplementary allowance for entertaining foreign visitors."

"I bought the last time," said the English Captain.

"What do you do, keep tabs on when you buy?"

"Yes you cheap foreigner. You can buy this evening."

After only a few seconds, Lamb laughed and said,

"I guess I can afford it since my boss is buying lunch. Where do you want to meet?"

"Let me pick you up at your apartment at say eighteen hundred hours, that's six o'clock, just in case you've forgotten how to tell military time."

"Six o'clock. Is that AM or PM?"

"Wear some old cloths and I'll see you at six o'clock, PM. Have to go. Bye."

Lamb looked at the phone, smiled and replaced it in its cradle. He was thinking about spending the afternoon helping out his friend Bishop, but after his brief conversation with Taggart-Holmes, he changed his mind. He had a feeling tonight would be a long night, so he decided after lunch he would go directly to his apartment, take a long afternoon nap, get up around seventeen hundred hours, take a shower, put on a pair of jeans and a sweatshirt and wait for Captain Taggart-Holmes to pick him up.

Garda Headquarters
Dublin, Ireland

By eleven thirty, Meyers had finished transcribing three quarters of the notes from his interviews on the 28th of July. He picked up his notebook and tablet, placed them in the filing cabinet and locked it.

He went to the WC and as he returned to the office, his telephone started ringing.

"Meyers here."

"Jamie, are you ready to leave?" asked Kerrigan.

"Yes sir."

"Good, I'll meet you in the hallway."

"Yes sir."

Meyers replaced the phone, checked his desk to make certain he hadn't left any papers or notes out. He walked to the coat rack, removed his suit coat and walked out into the hallway where Kerrigan was standing.

"Ready to meet some of our counterparts from the north?" asked Kerrigan as the two walked down the hall.

"Yes sir. Do you know who they're sending down?"

"Kerrigan shook his head and said,

"I have no idea. It could be anyone from the Chief Constable down. I could never outguess the Constabulary."

"Do you have any idea why I'm invited to eat lunch with the Deputy Commissioners and the rest?"

"Yes, because the Commissioner told the Deputy Commissioner that you and I would meet with him, the Attorney General and the visitors from the north."

"Reckon that's good enough reason," said Meyers as the two reached the stairs and started down. When they reached the ground floor, Meyers asked,

"Do you want to wait here while I get the car?"

"No, I'll walk with you to the garage."

Kerrigan's last sentence concluded their conversational exchange for the next twenty minutes. Once they reached the garage, they entered the car and Meyers drove out into the busy Dublin traffic and drove through the late morning traffic to Rafter's restaurant. He swung into the restaurant's parking lot, found a parking space and parked.

For the next two minutes the two men remained seated in the car, each thinking of what was going to take place during the next four or five hours

"Well Jamie, I guess it's time to meet the people from the north, ready?"

Meyers nodded, turned and opened his door. He waited for the Chief Superintendent and the two fell in step and appeared to be marching in cadence. Upon reaching the front door, Meyers stopped, opened the door and held it for his superior.

Kerrigan looked at him, smiled, nodded and said,

"Thank you."

As they entered the restaurant, they were greeted by the hostess.

"Two?" she asked.

"No, we're here for a party of probably eight or ten from…"

"The Garda?" asked the young lady.

"Yes," said Kerrigan.

"They arrived about ten minutes ago. You'll find them in the Shamrock room, halfway down the hall on the left."

"Thank you," said Kerrigan, "could you tell me how many were in the group?"

"Eleven, the reservation is for fourteen, so it seems we still have one to go."

"Thank you," said Kerrigan as he started down the hallway with Meyers at his side.

"A sizable gathering Jamie, I hope the Commissioner doesn't take it out of our budget."

"He wouldn't, would he?"

"No", laughed Kerrigan.

When they reached the door of the Shamrock room, both stopped, looked at each other for a moment, then Kerrigan nodded and Meyers opened the door and stepped back, allowing the Chief Superintendent to enter the dining room. Meyers wanted to turn and run. He was not comfortable in crowds, but instead, he followed just three steps behind Kerrigan.

Once inside the room the two walked towards a gathering on the other side of the tables and at the same time both counted heads.

There were eleven individuals in the room, just as the hostess told them.

Before they reached the group, the assistant Attorney General stopped talking and said,

"Chief Superintendent Kerrigan and Detective Sergeant Meyers, thank you for coming."

Kerrigan and Meyers walked up to Jerome Nelson, the Assistant Attorney General, who stuck out his hand and shook hands with both. He then said,

"Of course you know Deputy Commissioner Murphy, Inspector Randy Floyd of the Commissioner's staff and Major Ray Blackburn of the Irish Army."

With each introduction, the two new arrivals shook hands with the mentioned individuals.

Nelson then turned to the others and said,

"And these gentlemen are from up North. May I present our guests from the Constabulary, Chief Superintendent Dennis Moore, Superintendent Stewart Crockett and Detectives Dale Burns and Charles Brandt, Major Morris Brown of the British Army and Mr. Samuel Irwin and Mr. Lance Hooker of the SIS."

It required almost a full minutes for Meyers and Kerrigan to shake hands with the visitors.

As Kerrigan shook Irwin's hand, Irwin asked,

"I think I know you Chief Superintendent. Didn't you work on the train robbery back in 1968 and 69?"

"That's correct Mr. Irwin," said Kerrigan.

Irwin smiled and said,

"If I remember right, you gave Chief Inspector North a pretty hard time."

"I was thinking it was the other way around," said Kerrigan.

"Reckon it depends on..."

"Excuse me gentlemen, we're waiting for Henry Anderson, the Deputy Commissioner. He said he would be late. He had a meeting with some American police official from Boston."

Ten minutes later the door opened and in walked the Deputy Commissioner. Again Nelson went through the ritual of introducing the six visitors.

"I'm sorry I'm late gentlemen, but the Americans had a thousand questions and I finally had to cut them off. I told them I'd see them later this afternoon."

Turning to the Assistant Attorney General, Deputy Commissioner Murphy said,

"Well Jerry, how about getting the party on the road since Henry needs to get back to his American friends."

The Assistant Attorney General, as did all the others, caught the sarcasm in Murphy's tone.

He knew Murphy was jealous of Anderson's connection with the Americans, not only the police from Boston, but those from New York, New Orleans, Chicago and San Francisco, cities where a large percentage of the police were of Irish descent.

"Certainly. Please excuse me a minute while I contact the manager. In the meantime, please take a seat at the table. I'll be right back," said Nelson as he turned and walked across the room and out the door into the hall. As soon as the door closed, Murphy said,

"Gentlemen, shall we?"

No one answered, but the thirteen men moved to the long table. Some started to take a seat when they noticed name cards on the table. They then searched for their assigned seat.

The seating was arranged so the two Deputy Commissioners were at each end of the table, while the seven visitors were seated directly across from the seven individuals from the Republic.

Deputy Commissioner Murphy was seated across from the representative from the SIS, Samuel Irwin. Deputy Commissioner Anderson was seated across from Chief Superintendent Moore, Nelson was seated across from Agent Hooker of the SIS, Major Blackburn was seated across from his counterpart, Major Brown, Floyd was seated across from Brandt and Kerrigan and Meyers were seated across from Crockett and Burns. The seating was according to the exacting rules of etiquette, in which Nelson was a firm believer.

Once seated, the men started casual conversations about the weather, travel, sports, fishing and every subject except for the reason for the gathering. Ten minutes into the casual conversation, Chief Superintendent Moore looked from Anderson to Kerrigan and said,

"I hate to break in but would it be possible for you to tell us exactly what happened in Convoy or up on the border. The only information we received was what was on television or what the newspapers published about the event."

All conversation ceased the moment Moore finished his question. Kerrigan looked at Moore and asked,

"You didn't see the report the Commissioner sent to the Chief Constable?"

Moore shook his head and said,

"No sir, I've seen nothing from the Garda about the incident. As I said, the only information I received was what was in the newspaper and on the television."

"Well, it's no big secret Chief Superintendent. What happened was very simple. I made the mistake of thinking I could catch a few Provos by using O'Connor as bait. I figured on luring them across the border and springing a trap as soon as they were in the Republic."

Kerrigan looked across the table at Irwin and Hooker, smiled, looked back at Moore and said,

"Instead, the Provos performed classical theater and fooled me into believing the raiding party was assassinated by the British Army."

"I see," said Moore, but..."

"We had a fairly good idea of just where the Provos would be crossing the border, so I had men watching the area. Sure enough, just as I figured, a car load of Provos appeared in the area and as they were getting out of the car they were ambushed by what was thought to be previously positioned soldiers, believed to be SAS. Instead of the SAS, they were Provos in borrowed British uniforms.

It appeared to my observers that the members of the raiding party were all killed by the soldiers. The bodies were dragged along the ground and dumped into an armored vehicle, which was driven out of the area and headed in the direction of Belfast.

As a result of what my observers reported, I called my people in and while they were regrouping and preparing to head back to Dublin, the real raiding party hit the jail in Convoy and liberated Mr. O'Connor. End of story."

The room was as silent as a church on Monday morning.

Crockett broke the silence when he said,

"But you did get McCaul."

"Yes, we got McCaul, but only because he was too sick to remain in Convoy. He was transported to the hospital in Dublin where he died the day before yesterday."

"Do you know what caused his death?"

Kerrigan looked across the table at Murphy, who nodded his head.

"Again, a report was sent to the Chief Constable about McCaul. What Dr. Shaw, the doctor who was in charge of McCaul's care, told us was that McCaul died from the results of a virus infection, a virus similar to Japanese Encephalitis. The symptoms are the same as the flu, but one out of a hundred or so who contact the disease die and McCaul was unlucky enough to be the one out of a hundred."

"How did he get it?" asked Moore.

"According to Dr. Shaw the virus, that is the Japanese Encephalitis, is transmitted from human to human or animal to human by the mosquito. It is assumed the virus that killed McCaul is transmitted the same way, probably by a mosquito bite during his voyage from Australia to South America via China. All this information is in the report sent to the Chief Constable."

Moore nodded.

The room remained silent until a individual walked up to Nelson and whispered something to him.

"Gentlemen," said the Assistant Attorney General, "I've just been informed they are ready to serve the meal. Could I ask one of our visitors to say grace. Major Brown?"

"I'd be honored," said Brown, who stood up. All the others pushed their chairs back, stood up and bowed their heads.

Brown then bowed and said a short Episcopalian prayer, asking the good Lord to bless the food and those who partake of it.

Once the prayer was completed and the fourteen took their seats, a parade of waiters came out of the kitchen door like a line of ants, each carrying either a platter of food or a pitcher. Within two minutes, all fourteen men were served their meal and the line of waiter disappeared back into the kitchen.

The only sound in the room for the next twenty-five minutes was an occasional request for someone to pass the salt, pepper, bread or butter.

As the last individual finished his meal, Nelson stood up and walked into the kitchen. He reentered the dining room, nodded and returned to his seat and waited for the gathering to be served their dessert and coffee or tea.

A few minutes after one, after the dessert had been consumed and most were finishing their second cup of coffee or tea, Nelson said,

"Gentleman, we need to leave for the hospital in ten minutes. If any of you would like to use the rest room before we depart, it's located down the hall. Just go out the door and turn left. We will meet in the lobby and I would like to leave at no later than twenty after one."

Eleven of the fourteen men stood up and headed for the door. Ten minutes later the fourteen were gathered in the lobby.

"Gentlemen, I'm sorry I won't be going with you," said Deputy Commissioner Anderson. Turning to the seven men from Northern Ireland, he said,

"On behalf of the Commissioner, Michael and myself, I would like to take this opportunity to thank you for coming to Dublin. We realize this trip is strictly official and necessary for all concerned, but let's hope in the future we can meet again and again without having an excuse except to get to know each other and exchange ideas."

Anderson shook hand with the seven, Kerrigan, Meyers, Major Blackburn, Nelson and his assistant. He looked at Murphy and said,

"See you at the office Michael."

Anderson turned and departed. Nelson waited until he was out the door, then said,

"We can all take separate cars or we can double up."

"We have our own transportation," said Chief Superintendent Moore, and I think Mr. Irwin, Major Brown and Mr. Hooker are traveling together."

"That's correct," said Irwin.

"Well then, how about Major Blackburn and Inspector Floyd riding with me. That leaves Chief Superintendent Kerrigan and Detective Meyers."

"Works out just right Mr. Nelson," said Kerrigan, "after the cremation we need to get back to headquarters."

Nelson laughed and said,

"Great, it'll work out perfect."

"Good," said Murphy, "I'll see you in Baldoyle in thirty minutes."

Crockett walked over to Chief Superintendent Moore and asked,

"Sir, would it be alright with you if I rode to the hospital with Superintendent Kerrigan?"

"Fine with me. How about Burns?"

"If it's alright with you sir, I'd like to go with Superintendent Crockett," said Burns.

"No problem. I'll see you when we arrive at the hospital."

"Yes sir."

Ten minutes later the four cars were in convoy headed to St. Francis Hospital in Baldoyle.

As Meyers drove north through the streets of Dundrum towards Baldoyle, Crockett and Burns appeared to be enjoying the scenery.

"This is my first trip to Dublin," said Burns to no one in particular, merely as a comment.

"You've never been in the Republic?" asked Kerrigan.

"Many times, but not in the south, in Donegal. My family has a vacation home outside of Ballyliefin. Only one time as far south as Dundalk."

"You should visit the south, a great deal to see," said Kerrigan.

After a few moments, Burns said,

"I was never comfortable down here. About a year ago I had to pick up a prisoner in Dundalk and I was…"

"Uneasy?" asked Crockett.

"Yes sir, very uneasy."

"The people in the south are not as bad as they're made out to be, isn't that right Detective Meyers?" asked Crockett.

"Just like the Constabulary, we hide out horns under our hats."

All four laughed, then Crockett said,

"Chief Superintendent Rothchild asked me to say hello to you Mr. Kerrigan."

"Thank you."

"Yes sir and may I ask how long you have known Chief Superintendent Rothchild?" asked Crockett.

"Certainly. I've know Douglas a long, long time. We've known each other for thirty years, since 1968, back when both of us were young officers."

Crockett smiled and nodded his head. Kerrigan was wondering what the Superintendent was thinking at the moment.

"Have you known Douglas long?" asked Kerrigan.

"Personally only about twelve years, but I have known of him since the seventies or early eighties. During the time when…."

Crockett stopped, looked at Meyers and Burns, then back at Kerrigan and continued, "when the Army and the Constabulary came under international scrutiny."

It was Kerrigan's time to smile.

"I remember."

The Garda Chief Superintendent wanted so bad to add "when the Constabulary buried Rothchild so deep the postman couldn't find him!!" but decided it would not be politically correct to add the comment. Instead he said,

"Tell the Chief Superintendent "hello" and "thanks."

Crockett frowned and said,

"Thanks?"

"Yes, thanks, Douglas will understand."

Crockett and the other two officers knew Kerrigan would not explain what the "thanks" indicated when he said Rothchild would understand.

"And you are acquainted with a young Australian Army officer by the name of Lamb."

"Yes, he visited my family this Spring, but the visit was cut short when he had to return north because of the explosion in Rathfriland. He did get to spend a nice weekend with us before he went back to Belfast."

"That's what he said," said Crockett, "and he wanted me to tell you he is still looking forward to your son's visit whenever he can make it."

"I'll tell young Patrick. Do you see Captain Lamb often?"

"Often enough, you do know he's an explosive expert?"

"Yes, I know. When Douglas asked me if it would be all right for Lamb to stay with the family when he visited Dublin, he forgot to tell me anything about the young Captain. I didn't know what he did in the Army until I asked him why in the world would an Army Officer be assigned to the Constabulary. He told me it was for training in handling explosives."

"I think we are the ones receiving the training. Captain Lamb seems to know more about explosives than anyone in the Constabulary. Of course, he has been handling them since he was barely able to walk," said Crockett.

"Do what?" asked Meyers.

"Blow up things," said Crockett.

"Why?" asked Meyers, who had been looking at the scenery and not paying attention to the conversation in the front seat.

Crockett and Kerrigan laughed at Meyers' question.

"He was sent over by the Australian Army to learn about explosives from the Constabulary and Superintendent Crockett said he knew more about explosives than anyone in the Constabulary."

"Oh," said Meyers, then with a smirk on his face he said,

"Maybe they should let him get in contact with the Provos or the IFF if he wants to learn about explosives."

"That's not too funny, Detective Meyers," said Crockett.

"Sorry," said Meyers.

Crockett looked from Meyers to Kerrigan, smiled and said,

"Like I was tell Superintendent Kerrigan, this young fellow knows more about explosives than anyone I've met and before you interrupted our conversation, I was going to say the reason was because he calls himself a "blaster". He said he's the second best "blaster" in Australia."

"And who's the best "blaster" in Australia?"

"According to Captain Lamb, his father is the best."

"And they sent him over to learn from the Constabulary?" asked Meyers.

Crockett again looked from Meyers to Kerrigan and said,

"Are all your Detectives the same as this one?"

Kerrigan laughed and said,

"No, Jamie is one of a kind, thank the good Lord."

"I see," said Crockett.

"Well, if Captain Lamb is not learning about explosives from the Constabulary, just what is he doing up there? I thought he would be too busy with all the bombings in the north, first the one in Rathfriland, then the one outside the Army base in Lisburn," said Meyers.

"He has been busy," said Crockett, "with the explosion in Lisburn, he knew exactly what type of explosive was used and just how much. He wrote his report the day after the incident and gave it to the head of the Bomb Squad, who passed it to the Chief Constable. Ten days later the bomb experts from the Army, the Met and the Constabulary verified his report."

"How about the explosion the other day south of Ballynure?" asked Meyers.

"I haven't had a chance to talk to him about that one," lied Crocket.

"Sounds like he knows his business," said Kerrigan.

"That he does, but the other day, he told me the one in Rathfriland has him stumped for the present."

"Did he say why it stumped him?" asked Meyers.

"Not really, all he told me was he didn't agree with the official findings. Of course the findings from six different agencies didn't agree, particularly the secondary explosion."

"Six?" asked Kerrigan.

"Six. The Met, the Army, the Constabulary, the experts from SIS, the American CIA and a team of Japanese bomb experts."

"They can't figure out what caused the secondary explosion?" asked Meyers.

"They all agree the main charge was Semtex, but none agree about the secondary explosion. Some think it was dynamite, some TNT, some Nitroglycerin, while others think it was a fertilizer type mix, but the Japanese think it was a new explosive."

"So what does your Australian expert say caused the secondary explosion?" asked Burns.

"He just said he doesn't know, but he doesn't think the other reports are correct."

After a few moments of silence, Kerrigan asked,

"What was so different about that particular bombing?"

"Nothing other than no one can agree about what caused the secondary explosion, plus it killed two members of the class called the unlucky 72. You've heard about our unlucky 72?" asked Crockett.

"No, can't say I have," said Kerrigan.

Turning to Meyers, Kerrigan asked,

"Jamie, have you heard of them?"

"Are you talking about the young officers from the same class?"

"That's right," said Crockett, "we now have three killed in the line of duty, one by a car accident and one by drowning."

"Good Lord," said Kerrigan, "five out of one class. The odds for that happening have to be one in a couple of million."

"Closer to a few hundred million," said Crockett.

"That's terrible," said Kerrigan, "the class is indeed unlucky."

"These deaths are affecting the morale of the Constabulary. Since the death of the five, ten members of the class have resigned and I don't really blame them," said Crockett.

Neither Kerrigan nor Meyers knew what to say, so they remained silent. Ten minutes later the convoy arrived at St. Francis Hospital.

Dr. Shaw greeted the group in the lobby of the hospital and after the introductions they were escorted to the anti-room of the morgue in the basement of the hospital.

A few minutes after their arrival in the anti-room, a casket escorted by three of the Commissioner's Unit, was wheeled into the room.

"Gentlemen, the casket contains the remains of Ronald McCaul. I'll open it so you may personally review the remains," said Shaw as he released the spring loaded latches on the upper part of the casket and gently lifted the cover.

Once the cover was open and held by the pneumatic lid cylinder, the doctor backed away in order to allow the others to view the corpse.

No one moved for the next thirty seconds until Irwin looked at Brown and Hooker, nodded and walked up to the casket. His two subordinates quickly followed his example.

Once the cork was popped out of the bottle, the others walked pass the casket, some hesitating for a few moments, others merely glancing at the remains.

Once everyone had viewed the body, Irwin said,

"If you will excuse me gentlemen, I would liked to take a few photographs and I must warn you, the flash is extremely bright. I would suggest you cover your eyes or turn away."

Irwin positioned himself at the foot of the casket, held the camera at arms length and snapped the first of three pictures. The next two were photographed from each side of the casket.

"Thank you," said Irwin as he backed away.

Shaw, who had moved to the back of the room, walked up to the casket and asked,

"Would anyone else like to photograph the body?"

No one answered his question. He started to reach over the casket when Chief Superintendent Moore said,

"We would like to take finger prints of the corpse, Burns!"

Sergeant Burns, who was standing next to Meyers, reached down and picked up the box type brief case and walked towards Moore.

"Fingerprints have already been taken of the corpse Chief Superintendent. You will find them in the packet on the table, the one marked Royal Ulster Constabulary is yours. In addition, you'll find photographs of the body and an autopsy report. A copy of the medical report along with a copy of the death certificate for the Chief Constable was forwarded to the Garda."

Moore picked up the envelope marked "CONSTABULARY", opened it and removed eight typewritten pages backed by two cardboard fingerprint documents. He removed the fingerprint cards, looked up at Shaw and nodded.

Looking at Deputy Commissioner Murphy, Shaw said,

"Mr. Murphy?"

"The complete record of what occurred on the border and the information on McCaul, including photographs, fingerprints, autopsy report and Medical report was sent to the Chief Constable by the Commissioner the day before yesterday."

"I presumed as much," said Shaw.

The anti-room was silent for the next twenty seconds.

"Any other requests before...."

Again Shaw was met with silence. After a few moments he slipped the catch on the bar holding the lid and gently closed the casket.

"If you will excuse me, I'll call the gentleman in charge of the crematory, but before I call him, may I asked how many would like to witness the cremation?"

For a moment no one spoke, then Nelson said,

"Those who wish to witness the cremation, would you please raise your hands?"

Ten hands were raised. Nelson looked at the group and called off of the names of the individuals,

"Mr. Irwin, Mr. Hooker, Inspector Floyd, Major Blackburn, Detectives Brandt and Burns and Mr. Murphy, and you three gentlemen from the Commissioner's Unit, I'm sorry but I don't know your names."

"Sergeant MacVoy, Sergeant Addison and Sergeant Austin," said one of the men standing next to the casket.

"And Sergeants MacAvoy, Addison and Austin," repeated Nelson. He scanned the room, stopping when he looked directly at Kerrigan.

"Chief Superintendent Kerrigan?"

Kerrigan shook his head and said,

"No thanks."

Shaw opened the door, looked out and nodded his head at the individual awaiting his signal. The man entered the room, looked at the crowd, walked to the casket and said,

"Doctor, would you hold the door open please?"

"Certainly."

The man started to push the casket towards the door, stopped and asked,

"How many witnesses?"

"There will be ten witnesses," said Nelson.

"If you will follow me," said the man as he started pushing the casket. The ten observers followed the casket, leaving the remaining seven in the anti-room. As the door closed, Dr. Shaw said,

"Gentlemen, if you will follow me, we'll go up to the Doctors' lounge where you can wait for the others."

Once the group reached the lounge, Shaw offered them refreshments, but from the hospital supply, not his private stock. After receiving a drink from an orderly, who had been collared by Shaw to act as bartender, the men gathered into two groups.

One group consisted of Assistant District Attorney Nelson, Deputy Commissioner Murphy, Major Brown and Chief Superintendent Moore. The other groups consisted of Kerrigan, Meyers, Crockett and Dr. Shaw.

The subjects of conversation in the room was the same as at the dinner, with the additional subject of the reason for the insistence of the NIO for the cremation of McCaul.

At a few minutes before four, seven of the ten observers of the cremation entered the Doctors' lounge. The room became deathly silent for almost thirty seconds. Kerrigan broke the silence when he said,

"Detective Meyers and I need to get back to headquarters, so we should be on our way."

Kerrigan and Meyers shook hands with those remaining in the lounge. As they walked towards the door, Kerrigan stopped and talked with Crockett for a few moments, shook hands with him and he and Meyers departed.

Belfast, Northern Ireland

At exactly eighteen hundred hours, Captain Taggart-Holmes pulled up in front of Lamb's apartment in his Ford coupe.

Lamb stepped out of his apartment door, walked to the car, opened the door, entered and said,

"As usual, a few minutes late."

"You're crazy as hell, it's exactly 1800 hours."

Lamb looked at he English Captain, smiled and said,

"Your watch is slow."

"You….."

"Watch that English temper. Remember the Queen's instructions. No rash behavior."

Taggart-Holmes shook his head, pressed the gas pedal hard and let out the clutch, rocketing the little car down the street and bouncing Lamb against the seat.

"Temper, Temper. Remember what the Queen said."

"Go to the devil."

"Good evening Captain Taggart-Holmes, how are you this fine Irish evening?"

Taggart-Holmes didn't verbally answer the question. He merely looked over at Lamb and shook his head.

"Can I ask where we are going this evening?"

"To a fine little restaurant in Newry called the Night's Out. It's suppose to serve the best and most expensive lamb in County Down and since you're buying, I thought we'd try it out."

"Excellent. I took out a bank loan this afternoon just so I could buy your dinner this evening."

"Good. One question before we head south. Did you dress for the woods?"

"Sure did, can't you tell. Good Australian jeans, sweatshirt and tennis shoes."

"Fine, then it's on to Newry."

The conversation ended at that point as the little Ford coupe made its way south on Highway A1. The lack of any verbal exchange was due to one of Lamb's previous comments about Taggart-Holmes' inability to talk and drive safely at the same time.

"OK, we're out of immediate danger. You want to tell me why we're going into the Republic this evening?" asked Lamb.

"Are you sure I can talk and drive?"

"Just keep your eyes on the road. You don't have to look at me when you talk."

"I'll try. The reason for the trip into the Republic is a little bird informed us the Provos are bringing in a mortar supplied by their American friends from Boston. It's so important they insisted on delivering it to no one else but O'Connor.

They set up the meeting in the Republic, right below the border so they would be out of our jurisdiction. But they have to get it into Ulster and that's where you and I come into the picture."

"Who is O'Conner?" asked Lamb, although he knew about him from the articles in the paper and the news reports on television.

"You're kidding me. You don't know who O'Connor is?"

"I've heard the name, but I don't know anything about him," said Lamb.

"Well, let me see. O'Connor was one of the Provos' most famous gunman. Allegedly he killed twelve or more men, most members of the Loyalists' terrorists group, the UVF and the Red Hand Commandos. He also allegedly wounded a number of RUC and Army personnel."

"So? They must have a number of gunmen, right?"

"Yes, but none as famous as O'Connor, particularly since he was missing for over five years and all at once he shows up again in Ulster, thanks to the great work of the Garda."

"OK, he's a famous IRA gunman and he's suppose to pick up a mortar in the South. Why didn't you contact the police in the Republic and let them take care of him?"

"What would they do? They would arrest the people making the delivery and confiscate the mortar."

"Isn't that what the British Army is going to do?"

"No, we want to catch the Provos with the mortar in Ulster. Then a few of the boys who wear black jackets, black berets and sun glasses will end up spending a few years in prison. And, if our friend O'Connor is caught with the mortar…."

"You'll get a medal?"

"Hell no, not unless they force it on me."

"Really, what are we going to do?"

"All we're going to do is inform the lads on this side of the border when and where they cross into Northern Ireland."

"And how are we going to do that?"

Taggart-Holmes looked over at Lamb, smiled and said

"We know when and where the meeting is to take place this evening. After the exchange is made, we'll follow them and radio our lads when and where they cross the border."

"Watch the road," shouted Lamb.

The car swerved back into the correct lane and Taggart-Holmes laughed and said,

"Don't have a coronary, no one else is on the road."

"Thank God."

After a few moments of silence, Taggart-Holmes said,

"Are you still game?"

Lamb looked over at him and said,

"I can't wait."

"You make me proud Captain Lamb."

"I'm happy to know that, but I have one question."

"What?"

"What about the people making the delivery in the Republic?"

The English Captain shook his head and said,

"Afraid they will get away with it, this time."

"Too bad."

"If we can arrange for the capture of the mortar, I can just see the Queen pinning the medals on my broad chest, at least two and maybe three."

Lamb laughed, shook his head and the conversation ended.

A few minutes after they reached Newry, Taggart-Holmes swung the car into one of the city's public parking lots that was less than half filled this evening.

From the parking lot, the two walked a block and a half to the restaurant where Lamb partook of some of the best lamb he had tasted during his short stay in Ireland.

The conversation during dinner was a continuation of their ongoing exchange of information concerning their lives prior to their meeting at Constable Kelly's funeral. Taggart-Holmes had a hundred questions about Australia and Lamb matched him question for question about England.

St. Francis Hospital
Baldoyle, Ireland

Meyers and Kerrigan arrived at the hospital at eight thirty and went directly to Dr. Shaw's hospital suite off the Doctors' lounge. Kerrigan knocked on the door and waited thirty seconds before he opened it. He looked inside, didn't see the doctor, so he closed the door and was about to head to see the Charge Nurse. Dr. Shaw met them in the hall and Kerrigan and Meyers turned and followed Shaw to his office.

"Come on in."

Shaw waited until the two were inside before he entered and closed the door behind him.

"Have a seat for a minute, I need to make a call."

Kerrigan took a seat in one of the chairs, but Meyers picked up an outdated magazine and leaned against the wall. Two minutes later Shaw replaced the phone, walked back into the lounge and took a seat next to Kerrigan. He looked at Meyers and smiled. The look on Meyers face told him the young police officer was confused about the events of the afternoon.

"Can I get you something to drink?" asked Shaw.

Meyers shook his head, but Kerrigan said,

"Your private stock?"

"Of course. Nothing but the very best for the overpaid government employee."

"Right!" said Kerrigan.

"Jamie, you sure you don't want something to drink?"

"I'm certain, I just want to...."

Shaw stood up, held up his hand and said,

"I'll tell you in a minute, after Patrick and I have something to drink."

Shaw walked back into his office, opened the bottom drawer of his desk and removed a bottle of ten year old Jameson Irish whiskey and two glasses. As he walked back into the waiting area, Kerrigan was stacking the out dated magazines on the coffee table to make room for the bottle and glasses.

The doctor handed Kerrigan the bottle, placed the glasses on the table and took a seat.

"Pour your own, but leave a little for me," said Shaw.

Kerrigan looked at the bottle, which was 95% full. He removed the cap, poured his glass a quarter full and poured the same amount in Shaw's glass. He replaced the cap, picked up has glass and held it in the air. Shaw picked up his glass and the two old friends touched their glasses, took a healthy drink and placed their glasses on the table.

Shaw leaned back in his chair, looked at Meyers, smiled and said,

"Alright Jamie, you have some questions?"

"I don't understand Dr. Shaw, how am I suppose to take McCaul's body up north when it was cremated this afternoon?"

Shaw picked up his glass, took a small drink and asked,

"Are you sure that was McCaul who was cremated this afternoon?"

Meyers frowned, looked at Kerrigan for a split second, turned, looked at Shaw and said,

"We all saw him."

"Sorry, you're wrong. You didn't see McCaul, you saw someone who looked like McCaul."

"How?"

"The body that was cremated was that of a derelict. I was saving it for the medical school," said Shaw.

"How did you do it?" asked Kerrigan.

"Simple Patrick, it was a family affair."

Kerrigan and Meyers looked at each other as if the other might understand what Shaw was talking about.

"Henry, what in the hell are you talking about?" asked Kerrigan.

"The story started as soon as McCaul died and his father said he wanted to take him home. It got better when the people up north, particularly the ones from the NIO insisted he be cremated and the Commissioner and the Attorney General agreed. I made up my mind right then that he wouldn't be cremated and have his ashes scattered."

Looking at Kerrigan, Shaw continued,

"Then when you told me Jamie was planning to take him north so O'Connor could keep his promise, I made a decision that might cost me my job and get you two a few years behind bars.

I started making arrangements two minutes after I called you and told you McCaul died. As I just said, the whole episode was a little family affair."

"What do you mean?" asked Kerrigan.

"Give me time to tell you Patrick," said Shaw as he picked up his glass and took another drink. While still holding his glass, he said,

"I called my cousin, Paul Barrett and his wife Susan. Paul is a mortician and Susan is a make-up artist with RTE.

I took a few pictures of McCaul, then, after a little arm twisting, they worked on the derelict for about four hours. When they were finished, I couldn't tell the difference, the derelict looked exactly like McCaul.

You now owe me big time Chief Superintendent Patrick Kerrigan and I intend to collect one of these days."

All Kerrigan could do was nod his head.

Shaw smiled and said,

"The only time I started sweating blood was when that Chief Superintendent from the Constabulary wanted to take the corpse's finger prints. If they would have looked at him close, my derelict didn't have a little finger on his left hand."

"What made you take McCaul's finger prints," asked Meyers.

Shaw smiled and said,

"Jamie, I've been working with the police too many years not to know how they think. I made three copies of McCaul's prints, just in case."

For a few moments, Kerrigan and Meyers waited for Shaw to continue. When he didn't, Meyers asked,

"How did you switch the bodies with the three guards making certain no one stole McCaul's body?"

"Our morgue, which holds twelve bodies, wasn't full when McCaul died. After Paul and Susan finished with my derelict, they put him in the hospital morgue. An hour later the morgue caught on fire, seems some idiot spilled a bottle of ethyl alcohol on a pile of dirty sheets they used to cover the corpses and some how it caught fire.

The procedure for such an accident is for the people working in the morgue area to removed all the corpses out of the area," said Shaw, "and that is exactly what happened yesterday. The eight corpses were wheeled out into the corridor until the fire marshal declared the morgue safe to re-enter. The bodies were wheeled back into the morgue and while I questioned the three guards about what they would do if O'Connor and his people showed up, my assistant merely switched the derelict for McCaul.

At two o'clock we had fourteen visitors, including you two, who positively identified McCaul. Then seven, plus the three guards, who witnessed his cremation.

Tain't no more, as my American friend says, tain't no more."

Meyers looked over at Kerrigan and back at Shaw.

"Like I told you Patrick, the body has to be out of here between nine and ten. The afternoon kitchen crew leaves at nine and the morning crew shows up at ten to start making breakfast."

"The kitchen crew?" asked Kerrigan.

"That's right Patrick, the kitchen crew. That's where the casket is located."

"But I thought it would be in the morgue."

"Wouldn't fit," said Shaw, "there's not room in the morgue. Let me explain. The slabs in the morgue are just big enough to hold bodies and since the body is in a casket, which is in a wooden crate, it wouldn't fit in the morgue, so I had it put in the walk-in refrigerator in the kitchen."

"And the kitchen help didn't say anything?"

"They didn't know it was placed in the refrigerator. It's in with the frozen meats, which were placed in the refrigerator to thaw. The meats for today were removed from the freezer late last night or early this morning. That's what the ten o'clock kitchen crew will do. They'll remove all the thawing meats to be used tomorrow from the refrigerator, so we need to remove the casket as soon as the last afternoon crew leaves and pray none of the morning crew shows up before we have it out. Understand?"

Both police officers nodded their heads.

"Good."

After a few moments of silence, Kerrigan said,

"Jamie?"

"I told Carter to check out a van from the motor pool and be here at nine o'clock. I didn't know where to tell him to go, so I just told him I'd meet him in front."

Kerrigan looked at his watch and said,

"It's five minutes to nine. Do you want to check and see if Carter is here?"

"Yes sir," said Meyers as he turned and walked to the door.

"Tell your friend to drive around back to the loading area," said Shaw.

"Yes sir," said Meyers as he walked out of the room.

Shaw poured himself another drink, looked at Kerrigan and said, "Patrick?"

"No thank you Henry. I have to drive home."

"The advantage of being a doctor," said Shaw, "is after I get rid of you two, I'll crawl in bed in my luxury apartment here and tell the head sister not to wake me until six o'clock in the morning."

"It must be nice," said Kerrigan.

"It is," said Shaw as he took a sip of his drink.

As Meyers entered the hall, he looked out the window at the darkness that was dressed with miniature specks of lights reflected by the minute droplets of water. He was thinking about the trip north and about Timothy Foley. He was wondering if it would ever be possible for them to be close again or had the politics of Ireland destroyed their friendship, the way it had destroyed so many lives.

Ten minutes later Meyers was back on the third floor. He stopped at Shaw's door and knocked once and Shaw immediately opened the door. Shaw turned to Kerrigan and said,

"Let's get this show on the road."

The three men walked to the end of the hall where they boarded the lift and rode it to the basement. Shaw led the way into the kitchen and to the refrigerator.

On a large stainless steel cart was a long, wooden crate.

"We have to take it down to the sub-basement," said Shaw.

"Carry it?" asked Kerrigan.

"No Patrick, we'll use the lift."

With Shaw leading the way, Kerrigan and Meyers pushed the cart out of the kitchen and down the hall to the elevator. Once inside, Shaw pushed the button for the sub-basement. The lift gave a jerk and slowly descended to the bottom, hitting the giant springs on the concrete floor, causing the lift to bounce twice before settling to a complete stop.

Shaw pushed another button that caused the doors to slide open. He walked out into the sub-basement and directed the two officers to push the cart to the right, which led to the loading ramp. The police van was waiting in the loading zone and when Carter spotted Kerrigan and Meyers, he slowly backed up to the ramp.

Meyers hopped down, walked over to the side of the van and said,

"You'll need to pull up, you're too close to the ramp for the doors to open."

Carter let his foot off the brake and the van rolled forward a few feet, far enough from the ramp for Meyers to open the doors.

Once the doors were opened, Meyers said,

"OK, ease it up to the ramp."

When the back of the van was less than a foot from the ramp, Meyers said,

"Hold it, close enough. Put on the brakes and come back here and help us load."

Carter turned off the engine and pushed in the emergency brake. He hopped out and walked up next to Meyers.

"What are we loading, a body?" he said jokingly.

"That's right, the body of a dead sailor," said Meyers.

The smile on the young officer's face disappeared. His eyes widened and he swallowed hard. The other three could hear the sound of the saliva going down.

"I was only kidding," said Carter.

"I wasn't," said Meyers, "now let's get up on the ramp and load the body."

It required all four of the men to lift the wooden crate, roll the cart back, then lower and slide the crate into the interior of the van.

"I would suggest you block it Jamie," said Dr. Shaw as he turned and pointed to the row of empty plastic buckets which once held laundry soap.

"Good idea," said Meyers, but before we do that, would you show me how to open the casket."

"Certainly," said Shaw as he moved into the van, knelt down, reached over and moved the latch locking the cover of the wooden crate in place. He then pushed the lid up and over and indicted to Meyers to hold it. Shaw reached down and flipped two spring loaded catches, took hold of the edge of the casket and pulled it up halfway. He looked at Meyers and said,

"Got it?"

"Yes sir, thank you."

"You're welcomed, now, let's get it blocked."

Shaw moved out of the van and out of the way of Meyers who motioned to Carter to pass him two of the plastic buckets. He placed the buckets on one side of the casket, turned and was handed two more.

The supply of plastic buckets continued until eleven were placed on each side and three each in front and in back of the wooden crate. They fit tight enough to prevent the crate from moving in any direction.

"That should do it," said Meyers as he walked up to the driver's side of the van, got in and released the brakes, allowing the van to roll approximately ten feet from the ramp. Before he could get out, Carter was at the back closing the rear doors.

Meyers was tempted to start the engine and drive off. He did not yield to the temptation. He slipped out of the van, walked along the ramp to the stairs and walked back to where Dr. Shaw and Kerrigan were standing.

During the short walk, he was thinking just how he was going to tell the Chief Superintendent he had to go alone. He decided a direct approach was the best.

Stopping in front of Kerrigan he said,

"Sir, I have to go alone."

"You what?" asked Kerrigan, thinking he misunderstood him.

"I have to go alone," Meyers repeated.

"No Jamie, that's too dangerous."

"It was the only way our friend would promise to show up."

Kerrigan was shaking his head. He wanted to get McCaul's body up north, but he didn't want to lose Meyers.

"We can get some of the boys to follow you and...."

"No sir," said Meyers, readying himself for a blast from the Chief Superintendent.

"I gave my word I'd be alone."

The blast didn't come.

"Where are you going to meet him? No, I don't want to know."

"This side of the border."

Kerrigan looked away into the darkness and the thought of Meyers meeting O'Connor and the Lord only knew how many others. The thought caused a cold chill to run down his spine.

Even though it was only a few seconds, Meyers felt like it was at least an hour before Kerrigan said,

"You be careful Jamie and the good Lord be with you."

"Yes sir, He always has been."

Meyers turned and walked back down the ramp to the stairs, walked down the stairs and over to the van where Carter was standing.

"The Chief wants to talk to you," said Meyers.

Carter walked down the drive to the stairs, up the stairs and walked to where Kerrigan and Shaw were standing. In the meantime Meyers climbed into the van, started the engine, released the brakes and drove off into the darkness.

Carter turned and yelled,

"Wait for me, wait."

"Come here son," said Kerrigan, "we'll go back through the hospital and I'll take you home. I need to tell you something about tonight."

Carter looked at the Chief Superintendent, turned and looked out into the darkness in which the van disappeared and mumbled some mildly profane words.

Newry
Northern Ireland

As Lamb and Taggart-Holmes walked out of the restaurant, Lamb asked,

"What time is this delivery suppose to take place?"

"Some time around midnight, so we have a little over three hours. I would like to be in position no later than 2130 hours, just in case they arrive early."

"Do you know the exact spot?"

"Yes, a rest area west of a village called The Bush on R173. I reconnoitered it yesterday afternoon."

"And we're going to sit out in the woods for two plus hours, correct?" asked Meyers.

"Correct."

"And what if no one shows up?"

"We'll wait until 0100 hours and if no one shows, we'll drive back to Belfast and I'll buy you an early breakfast."

"Then you're not absolutely certain that there is going to be a delivery, are you?"

"99% certain."

"How long to get to the area where they are going to make the transfer?"

"About forty minutes."

"Think you can find it in the dark?" asked Lamb.

"I know so. I drove and walked around the area for about an hour. We'll go down A1 which turns into N1 in the Republic and turn off on to R174 which runs into R173 about nine or ten kilometers. We could go further down N1 and pick up R173, which makes a horseshoe, down one side of the peninsula and up the other side, but I'd rather cut off onto R174."

"Sounds good to me. How about our observation spot?"

"The area I picked out is directly across from the rest area, in the woods with a clearing between the woods and the rest area. Our observation position is off a side road that runs parallel to R173. It's in the middle of a clump of small trees.

Yesterday after parking the car in the trees I walked across the clearing to the rest area. The car was not visible from either the rest area or the road parallel to R173."

"Excellent."

"We can take cover in the bushes which are about 500 meters from the meeting place. According to the information we have, the transfer will take place around 0030 hours. A white van is scheduled to pick up the mortar and transport it into Northern Ireland. Once the transfer is made, we'll follow the van to where it goes across the border."

"And?" Lamb asked.

"And we remain behind them until they are stopped and arrested by our lads."

Lamb smiled and looked over at the English Captain and said,

"That's going to break you heart, right?"

Taggart-Holmes looked at Lamb, smiled, shook his head and said,

"I knew you would like the last part. I have been ordered to stay out of the way until our lads have the situation under control."

"Excellent, I have no desire to be in the middle of a gun battle."

"Worried about getting shot?" asked Taggart-Holmes.

"Nope, worried about getting killed. I have too much to live for right now and I have no intention of getting killed by a wild shot from some Englishman or Irishman over a stupid four hundred year dispute. Sorry."

Taggart-Holmes' temper came close to exploding, but with a great deal of self-control he held his tongue.

As the two reached the car, the English Captain looked at Lamb and said,

"I can't get you back to Belfast, but I'll be happy to leave you here."

It was Lamb's turn to become angry, but as his friend had done a few moments previously, he held his tongue.

The two stood on opposite sides of the car staring at each other. Finally Lamb said,

"Let's go see how good of an observation site her majesty's favorite Captain selected in which to spend a beautiful Irish Summer night."

Lamb attempted to open the door, but it was locked. He started to make another comment, but decided against it.

Taggart-Holmes inserted the key in his door, opened it and pushed the button which released the lock on Lamb's side.

From the parking lot, Taggart-Holmes drove south on A1, which took them into the Republic. Two kilometers later they turned left onto R174, passed Ravendale and finally merged with R173. Six kilometers later Taggart-Holmes turned right onto a secondary road, shifted into neutral and let the car coast to a stop after approximately 500 meters. He turned off the headlamps and the two could clearly see a large thicket of bushes and small trees no more than a hundred meters in front of the car.

Lamb looked over at his friend and said,

"Good show."

Taggart-Holmes slipped the gears into drive and gently pressed the petrol pedal. The car slowly moved forward until it was in the middle of the thicket of trees and ten foot high shrubs. He switched off the headlamps and engine and asked,

"Are you ready?"

"No, not until I tell you I'm sorry for my comment, it was uncalled for and I'm sorry."

The English Captain looked at Lamb and said,

"It's forgotten. Shall we?"

"Let's."

The two opened their doors and attempted to close them with a minimal of noise.

Once outside, Lamb reached in his coat pocket, took out his baseball hat and slipped it on. While Lamb was putting on his hat, Taggart-Holmes walked around to the boot and opened it. He reached in and removed two backpacks and a large torch.

"Here," he said as he motioned to Lamb to take one of the backpacks.

As silently as possible, he closed the lid of the boot and pushed on it until he heard the latch catch.

"This way," he said as he started walking toward the northeast until they reached a small clearing in the middle of the thicket.

"Here," said Taggart-Holmes as he stopped next to a large log which had fallen years ago.

"There's a blanket and night glasses in you pack."

Taggart-Holmes then slipped his backpack off and with the same motion opened it and removed a wool army blanket. He lowered the pack to the ground, unfolded the blanket, doubled it and placed it on the ground. Once on the ground, he removed a pair of night glasses and a large thermos from the pack. After placing them on the ground, he twisted and sat down on the blanket. He looked up at Lamb and asked,

"You going to stand there all night?"

Lamb didn't answer his question. Instead, he opened the backpack, removed a blanket and placed the pack on the ground. He opened the blanket up, doubled it and doubled it again before placing it on the ground. He looked at his friend, winked and said,

"I don't want to catch cold in my arse."

Slowly he lowered himself onto the blanket. He reached into the pack, removed a thermos and night glasses and placed them on the blanket

"I hope that thermos is full of good Irish whiskey."

"Don't you wish. It's full of good English black tea, guaranteed to keep you awake.

"And having to pee twenty times before midnight," said Lamb.

"Only if you have weak kidneys."

Lamb looked at his watch, which appeared only as a black blob on his wrist. He felt with his index finger for the button at the right bottom, found it and pushed it in. Instantly the face of the watch was illuminated.

"We're early, it's only twelve minutes after nine."

"Better early than late. You want to take the first watch?"

"First watch?" asked Lamb.

"Certainly. No sense in both of us staring into the night. One can catch a little nap for say an hour, then the other."

"Okay, point to the meeting place and I'll take the first watch, just an hour, right?"

"Right," said Taggart-Holmes, "come over here and I'll point it out."

Lamb leaned forward and ended up on his hands and knees. He worked his way up to the dead log next to the English Captain.

"Use your glasses and follow my arm," said Taggart-Holmes as he pointed straight ahead and slowly moved his arm to the right approximately fifteen degrees.

Lamb placed the night vision glasses to his eyes and within seven seconds a green field appeared. He moved the glasses to where Taggart-

Holmes arm was pointing and saw the outline of a table and bench and a garbage can.

"What is the distance?" asked Lamb.

"Four hundred and ninety four meters."

Lamb lowered the glasses and said,

"What I could have done with a pair of these back home."

"They don't issue them?"

"Not to me."

"Wonderful invention."

"You going to sat there? I said I'd take the first watch," Lamb said.

Taggart-Holmes nodded, pushed himself up from the ground, picked up his blanket, folded it and placed it on the ground behind the log.

"I'll be back in a moment," he said as he turned and walked towards the car.

Within a few minutes he returned with a bag containing a rolled up sleeping bag which he spread on the ground. He then picked up the blanket and made a pillow out of it. He placed it at the top of the bag and in one motion was down and stretched out on the sleeping bag.

"Call me in about an hour. Good night."

Lamb reached back, picked up his blanket, placed it next to the log and took a seat. Within five minutes his friend was sound asleep.

The drive between the hospital in Baldoyle and the airport north of town took more time than it required Meyers to drive from the airport to Dundalk. The reason was the thick fog that shrouded the city during the late night hours. He was extremely careful about taking corners too fast or hitting potholes left by last year's winter snows.

Upon reaching the airport, he increased his speed, but upon arriving in Dundalk, he realized he was ahead of schedule. It was only twenty minutes after ten. He had a little over an hour to get to the rendezvous point south of Carlingford.

Instead of stopping in Dundalk to rest, Meyers decided he would continue north on N1 and cut back on the southeast road to Gyles Quay.

After reach Gyles Quay, Meyers was again tempted to stop and rest for a few minutes. Since he slept very little last night thinking about his meeting with O'Connor, he was a little weary. He was afraid to stop, afraid he would sleep past the time for the meeting.

"*To hell with it?*" he thought.

The comment was for his own sake after making the decision to drive on to the meeting place where Foley said O'Connor would meet him. If he was early, he could catch a few winks of sleep.

Two kilometers south of Carlingford on road R176, he spotted the rest area.

Meyers backed the van into the rest area, turned off the engine and before cutting off the headlamps, he looked at his watch. It was fourteen minutes till eleven o'clock. He could now catch that forty winks Molly was always talking about.

He rolled the windows all the way down in order to allow as much air as possible into the cab. He slipped down in the seat until his head rested on the back of the seat, rolled his head back and forth until he was comfortable and within seconds he was sound asleep.

- -

During the next hour and a half, Lamb noted each vehicle passing the rest area. In between observing the traffic, he thought about Elizabeth Kelly and contemplated what their life would be like in Australia.

Lamb's thought of the future were interrupted as a black van approached the rest area, stopped, continued forward very slowly, stopped again and backed up left of the table and stopped. By the time Lamb was able to focus in on the driver of the van, the headlights were turned off.

He continued to watch the van for ten minutes, but saw no activity. He looked at his watch, pushed the light button and saw it was eleven o'clock.

During the next twenty-five minutes Lamb periodically scanned the rest area with his night glasses, but observed no visible activity.

Without moving his upper body, he swung his right leg around and gently pushed the toe of his shoe into Taggart-Holmes' back. It required three such motions before the sleeping Captain turned over and opened his eyes.

"Wake up," said Lamb, "we have company."

Instantly Taggart-Holmes sat up and took a position next to Lamb.

"What time is it"

"About a eleven thirty or as you would say 2330 hours, plus or minus a couple of minutes," answered Lamb.

Fumbling with his night glasses, Taggart-Holmes asked,

"How many?"

"I don't know for sure, but I only saw the outline of the driver."

The two officers continued to observe the black van. At ten minutes till twelve a black sedan slowed as it approached the area. The car came to a stop momentarily, then slowly turned into the area on the gravel road and disappeared into the wooded area twenty meters or so in the rear of the rest area.

After approximately five minutes, an individual appeared a few feet from the van. He looked into the van, but instead of opening the van door, he backed away and walked around to the table and took a seat.

Out of the darkness, two other shadows appeared on the opposite side of the table.

Day Ten

July 31, 1998

Rest Area on R173, SW of The Bush County Louth, Ireland

"Detective Meyers?"

Meyers struggled to open his eyes. He didn't know whether the question was part of his restless sleep or came from outside the vehicle.

"Jamie Meyers?" asked the same voice.

Suddenly Meyers was awake. He worked his way upright in the seat and looked around for a moment. He was awake, but he was still unsure whether the voice was real or part of an unfinished dream.

Suddenly a large individual stepped up to the open window, shined a light through the window, but not into Meyers' face. Meyers knew the voice was real.

"Jamie," said the voice.

"O'Connor?" asked Meyers.

"In person," said the individual standing outside the van.

Not knowing whether O'Connor's party had guns pointed at him, Meyers decided it would be unwise to open the door without asking permission.

"Can I get out?"

"Certainly," said O'Connor.

Meyers slowly pushed the handle of the door until he heard the click indicating the door was unlocked. Very slowly he opened the door, got out and stepped on the gravel.

O'Connor stepped forward and asked,

"How long have you been here?"

"Since about a quarter till eleven," said Meyers as he stretched his shoulders and back.

"How about you?"

"About fifteen minutes. We've been watching you sleep."

The two men stood looking at one another for what O'Connor's companions thought to be a very long time, so long, one asked him,

"Are you alright Thomas?"

O'Connor's gaze went from Meyers to the man standing on the other side of the table.

"Fine Davy, fine. Just thinking about our friend here."

Davy frowned. He had no idea what O'Connor was thinking when he called Meyers "our friend."

"Can I talk to you privately Mr. O'Connor?" asked Meyers.

O'Connor looked at Davy, who shrugged his shoulders.

"Certainly. Would you like to have a seat at the table?"

"Fine."

"Davy, why don't you and Neil get the food? We can offer Mr. Meyers a bite, don't you think?"

Davy nodded, turned and walked over to the road where the other man was standing. The two exchanged a few words and walked down the road.

Meyers watched the two men until they disappeared into the darkness. He walked over to the table, turned towards O'Connor and said,

"Mr. O'Connor, I…."

"I thought we passed the formal stage at Convoy. What happened to Thomas?"

The wheels in Meyers' head spun for a microsecond. His first thought was *"who is he talking about?"*, but he realized O'Connor was talking about the two of them.

"Sorry Thomas."

"That's better. Now, what was it you were going to say?"

Meyers took a deep breath, he was about to tell him about what happened this afternoon at the hospital, but changed his mind.

"McCaul was sicker than any of us thought. As soon as we arrived in Dublin, the doctor put him in the hospital."

"I know," said O'Connor.

"Then you know what killed him?"

"No, that I don't know," said O'Connor as he sat down.

Meyers took a seat opposite O'Connor.

"He died of a virus. Something the doctor said was similar to Japanese encephalitis, whatever that is. They weren't able to identify what killed him, even though they did everything humanly possible to save him."

"Was it, is it contagious?" asked O'Connor.

"The doctor said he didn't think so. Since it's similar to Japanese encephalitis it is probably spread by the bite of a mosquito."

After a long silence, O'Connor asked,

"You do have Ron's body in the van?"

Meyers could not remember what he was going to say at the moment, even though he had worked it out after hours of thinking about it.

"Jamie?"

"Yes?"

"You do have Ron's body?"

Meyers looked over at the police van, turned back and looked directly at O'Connor and said,

"I sure hope so!"

Meyers was expecting an explosion of words immediately. Instead O'Connor looked at him for a very long thirty seconds, then said,

"What do you mean, you hope so?"

"Just what I said, I sure hope so."

After a period of silence for another thirty seconds, O'Connor said,

"Would you like to explain?"

Without taking his eyes off O'Connor, Meyers said,

"As you well know, before McCaul died I made tentative arrangements to bring his body here, if he died."

"Yes," said O'Connor.

"Well this morning, no.."

Meyers looked down at his watch, pushed the bottom button and saw it was after midnight.

"As I was about to say, yesterday morning, Thursday morning, a delegation from Northern Ireland arrived in the Republic with the sole purpose of witnessing the cremation of McCaul, which was insisted on by the NIO. This delegation included people from the NIO, the Constabulary, the British Army and the British SIS.

The above delegation was met by a delegation from the Republic that consisted of two Deputy Commissioners who represented the Commissioner of the Garda, representative of the Attorney General, the military and the Garda. The last two were Chief Superintendent Kerrigan and myself.

Both delegations viewed McCaul's body and after viewing the body, some took pictures. The body was then taken to the crematorium and cremated in front of witnesses from both delegations."

"So Ron's body was cremated, is that right?" asked O'Connor.

Meyers looked away from O'Connor and gazed into the darkness for a few seconds. He turned back, looking directly at O'Connor and said,

"Well, I sure hope not. I'm hoping the body I have in the van is McCaul."

"Tell me Jamie, how in the hell is that possible?"

"Because that is what I was told by Dr. Shaw, McCaul's doctor. He said he arranged for McCaul's body to be switched with the body of a derelict and….and with the help of a mortician and make-up artist, the body of the derelict was made to look like McCaul and that was the body cremated."

After the long sentence, Meyers was out of breath.

"And you believed the doctor?"

"Yes."

"Well Jamie, we'll just have to wait and see, won't we?"

Meyers frowned and thought, *"sounds just like Professor McCaul!"*

He looked directly at O'Connor and said,

"I reckon so."

"And the body is in the van?"

"Yes, in a wooden crate along with twenty eight plastic soap cans."

"A wooden crate?"

"Yes, a wooden crate."

"Not in a casket?"

"The casket is in the wooden crate."

"And just how are we going to know you have McCaul's body?"

"Well Thomas, I reckon the best advise I can give you is that you will just have to take the top off the crate, reach down, open the casket and look in, that is unless you know of another way," said Meyers as he smiled weakly at O'Connor.

O'Connor glared at Meyers, but when he saw the smile on his face, he started to laugh.

"Thank you Mr. Meyers, I'd never thought to do it that way."

Meyers looked toward the noise of gravel being walked on and saw O'Connor's two companions approach, each carrying a wicker basket.

O'Connor turned, saw the two men, turned back to Meyers and asked,

"How about a little something to eat?"

"Great, I'm starved," said Meyers as he thought about the butterflies in his stomach.

When Davy and Neil reached the table, Meyers was formally introduced to them, using only first names.

For the next twenty minutes, the four men ate beef sandwiches supplemented with loose lettuce, sliced tomatoes and pickles. The two large thermos contained hot tea, which was poured into foam cups by Davy and passed around.

Between bites of food, the four talked about the nasty weather the country was enduring at the moment, the qualities of their favorite soccer teams and the chances of regional and national championships.

The only political conversation concerned the election in England and the chances of Conservatives winning back the majority.

When the four had eaten their fill, Davy refilled the foam cups with hot tea and the discussion of British politics continued for the next ten minutes. At the first break in the discussion, Meyers asked,

"Is your van here?"

"Not yet," said O'Connor.

Davy and Neil started picking up the remaining food and placing it in one of the wicker baskets.

"We'll take this back to the car," said Neil.

"You'd better wait for Donal, he'll probably be hungry," said O'Connor.

"You're right," said Davy.

At exactly 12:30 a white van slowly came to a stop as it reached the rest area, turned and slowly backed into the area.

"Davy, would you tell him to back it up next to Jamie's van?"

Davy stood up and walked over to the newly arrived van.

Neil said, "I'll help direct him in.",

Within less than sixty seconds, the white van was parked next to the police van. The driver turned off the engine, switched off the lights, opened the door and slipped out.

"Exactly on time," said O'Connor.

The driver of the white van smiled and winked at O'Connor, then threw his arms around Davy and said,

"Good to see you cousin."

Davy patted the man on the back and said something not audible to the others. He then pushed back, turned Donal towards the table and said,

"Donal, this gentleman's name is Jamie."

Meyers stood up and shook hands with the man named Donal.

"Any trouble?" asked O'Connor.

Donal looked at O'Connor, smiled and said,

"Not yet, but I sure as hell would like to know what's going on. You told me to take the material directly to the shop, then yesterday…"

"I'll explain later," said O'Connor.

"Are you hungry? asked Davy, "Da furnished the makings and Mother fixed the sandwiches and cookies."

"Starved. I haven't had anything to eat since lunch."

"There's still plenty to eat on the table. Help yourself," said Davy.

As Donal took a seat at the table, O'Connor looked at the others and said,

"Shall we?"

"Me too?" asked Meyers.

"Yes," said O'Connor.

Meyers slipped off the bench, stood up and followed the three men.

When they reached the rear of the two vans, Meyers said,

"If one of you will open the door of the other van, I'll…."

"No Jamie," said O'Connor.

"But I thought that was what you wanted to do?"

O'Connor shook his head, looked off into the darkness for a moment, turned and said,

"We're not transferring the casket to the van."

"But that…"

"No Jamie."

"But why…"

O'Connor held up his right hand and said,

"I'll explain it to you later Jamie. A little patience?"

The Irish policeman looked at O'Connor for a full ten seconds, turned slowly and looked at Davy and Neil.

It was too dark for him to see their faces clearly and he doubted he would be able to read anything even in the light of day.

"Jamie, I'd like for us to remain right here for a little while. OK?"

"OK," said Meyers.

Twelve minutes later O'Connor said,

"I think that's long enough."

"Shall we?" asked O'Connor.

The four men walked around the vans and back to the table.

"Are you about finished Donal?" asked Davy.

"Almost," said Donal, "tell Aunt Beth and Uncle Claude thanks."

"I'll tell them."

"Are you ready to leave?" asked O'Connor.

Donal looked up at O'Connor, frowned, turned and looked at his cousin and then back at O'Connor.

"You mean I just stopped by to have an early morning snack?"

"That's about it Donal," said O'Connor, "but it was a very important stop. I'll tell you the reason one of these days. All right?"

Before Donal took the last bite of the sandwich, he said,

"Let me finish my sandwich and I'll be on my way."

O'Connor walked to the table, took a seat next to Donal and spread out a map between the two lanterns.

"I'd like for you to take this route back," said O'Connor as he ran his index finger along the route marked with a yellow magic marker.

Donal looked at the map for almost a minute, turned and looked at O'Connor, frowned and said,

"That's a long way around Thomas."

"I know."

"OK, you're the boss."

"You know the route now?" asked O'Connor.

"Yes Thomas, I know the route, I think I have it memorized, plus I'll take your map, just in case."

"No. Look at it again and memorize it. If you're stop, I don't want them finding the map."

"OK," said Donal as he looked at the map.

"Now drive careful, particularly here in the Republic. We don't want you picked up before you get into Ulster."

"You think they'll pick me up?"

"Yes."

"But why?"

"You're the bait."

"For what?"

"I'll tell you...."

"I know," said Donal, "you'll tell me one of these days."

"That's correct. Just remember Donal, what you don't know won't hurt your."

Donal looked over at his cousin, who smiled and nodded. He turned and looked at O'Connor and asked,

"Any chance of me getting my lovely head shot off?"

"Not unless you do something stupid. If the Constabulary or Military signal you to stop, for God's sake, stop. Don't give them any smart talk. Just do exactly as they tell you."

"But why should…."

"Donal," said O'Connor, "trust me. You'll be all right if you just follow the route I outlined for you. If anyone stops you, stop and if they question you, answer all their questions, truthfully. Understand?"

Donal shook his head and said,

"No, I don't understand, but I'm sure you'll explain it to me one of these days. Right?"

"Right," said O'Connor as he smiled at Donal, "now, how about being on your way and thanks for your help."

"I guess so," said Donal as he picked up the map, folded it and handed it to O'Connor. He scooted off the bench, stood up and shook hands with the four men. He reached over and picked up a handful of cookies and walked to the van.

Within a minute he drove out of the rest area and onto R173.

- -

"What do you think they did behind the vans," asked Irwin.

"I have no idea sir."

"Do you think they transferred the mortar to the white van?"

"Probably," said Brown, "according to the intercepts."

"That's right, according to the intercepts. But I wonder about O'Connor, he's still there."

"Are we going to follow the van?" asked Brown.

"No. I'm waiting to see what O'Connor is going to do."

"But, what about the van?"

Irwin looked over at the Major, smiled and said,

"I have it covered. You remember that young captain who was assigned to the various units, the one who had his vehicle blown into the air?"

"You mean Captain Taggart-Holmes?"

"Yes. He's on the tail of that white van right now. When it goes across the border it'll be stopped by either the Constabulary or the military and we'll have the Provos' heavy artillery."

Brown turned and looked at Irwin, who was still looking through his binoculars at the individuals remaining at the rest area.

"You didn't tell me," said Brown.

"They're probably transferring the mortar to the white van," said Taggart-Holmes.

"I can't see anything except the guy stuffing his face at the table," said Lamb.

"We'd better get ready. I don't want to lose that van when it heads north."

Lamb rolled off the blanket, reached down, picked it up and stuffed it into the backpack. He squatted behind the log, picked up the night vision glasses and watched the man at the table.

"Anything?"

"No, the driver is still eating."

"Good," said Taggart-Holmes as he prepared to leave.

"Here they come," said Lamb.

The two watched as the four who disappeared behind the vans reappeared at the table. Three stood by the table while one took a seat next to the driver of the white van. He removed a paper from his back pocket, spread it on the table and appeared to have a conversation with the driver.

Finally, both men stood up. The driver picked up the paper from the table, folded it and handed it to the other man. He shook hands with the four men, reached down and removed something from the table and walked to the white van.

The headlights of the van came on and it slowly moved onto the road where it stopped momentarily, then turned onto the road.

Once the van was out of sight, Davy and Neil walked over to the table where Davy started putting the uneaten food in one of the wicker baskets while Neil gathered the paper plates, napkins and foam cups and placed them in the trash container.

Meyers looked over at O'Connor and asked,

"Just curious Thomas, but did you know about what happened this morning, I mean yesterday morning, the delegation from up north and the cremation?"

O'Connor smiled and said,

"Yes Jamie, we knew about the gathering at St. Francis Hospital and about the cremation."

"Then why did you show up tonight if you thought McCaul was cremated?"

"I didn't say that."

"What do you mean?"

"I didn't say I thought McCaul was cremated."

Meyers looked directly at O'Connor, shook his head and said,

"Then you knew about the switch?"

"Yes."

"How?"

O'Connor shook his head and said,

"Can't tell you that, but I can tell you we knew about the NIO demanding the cremation of McCaul and we knew about the switch and the cosmetic make over. What we don't know for certain is whether or not McCaul is in the casket in the back of your van."

"You didn't think this was a trap?"

"I didn't think so, but it was a little difficult convincing some of the others."

"Why didn't you think it was a trap?"

O'Connor looked at Meyers for a moment, looked away and said,

"Because of you."

After almost half a minute, Meyers said,

"Thanks."

O'Connor nodded and said,

"But I'm quite sure our British friends are all set to spring their own little trap."

"How do you know?"

"Speculation," was O'Connor's reply.

"How do you really know?"

"Let's just say we know. How we know, I can't tell you. What we know is the British Army and the SIS have a system of monitoring every telephone conversation in Ulster. We think they heard Foley's initial conversation with our people."

"And?"

Neil and Davy walked up to where Meyers and O'Connor were standing and both looked at Meyers, then at O'Connor.

"We do know the telephone that was used to contact Foley was being monitored, so they know exactly where we are and what time all of us arrived."

Meyers frowned and asked,

"They know we're here?"

"Yes."

"Do they know who I am?"

"I don't think so."

"But you're not sure, right?"

"That's right."

"I may be looking for job after tonight."

"Sorry Jamie, but we could always use a good man," said O'Connor as he smiled at Meyers.

"Right!!"

"*One more thing to worry about,*" thought Meyers.

"As I was saying, I'll bet you a bottle of good Irish whiskey they are watching us at this very minute."

"But how..."

"We gave them something to think about this morning, didn't we Neil?" said O'Connor, referring to their telephone conversation.

"That we did Thomas, that we did," said Neil.

Meyers just shook his head.

"Don't worry about it Jamie, we always attempt to keep a couple of steps ahead of them. We know which phones are monitored and we....you don't really need to know our little secret."

"Let's hope your little secret worked in this particular case."

"I think it did," said O'Connor, then turning to Davy and Neil, he said "you two had better be on your way."

Davy looked at his watch and said,

"We're right on schedule Thomas, almost to the minute."

"I know," said O'Connor.

Turning to Meyers, he said,

"Jamie, I would like for you to remain right here by the van for the next few minutes. You could be checking the engine, the tires, walk over to the trees and take a pee, but remain here in plain sight for at least ten minutes. All right?"

Meyers shrugged his shoulders and said,

"All right, but I need a torch."

O'Connor reached in his pocket and produced the flashlight he used to wake Meyers almost an hour ago.

"Here, you can have this one."

"Thanks."

"Good," said O'Connor, "now I'll shake your hand, but I'll be back in about ten or fifteen minutes."

Neil shook hands with Meyers without saying a word. He merely nodded. As Davy shook hands with Meyers, he said,

"Good meeting you Jamie."

"The same," said Meyers.

The three men from Northern Ireland walked back into the woods.

Three minutes later the black sedan came out of the woods on the gravel drive and slowed to a momentary stop before turning onto the highway. Davy was in the driver seat and Neil was seated behind him in the rear seat. Both stuck their arms out the windows and waved to Meyers, then the car slowly drove onto the highway and turned left, towards the little village of The Bush. Meyers squinted and focused his eyes on the car. He thought he saw someone in the front seat with Davy.

- -

"Let's move," said Taggart-Holmes.

The two men grabbed their backpacks, thermoses, night glasses and sprinted towards the Ford coupe. Instead of placing the material in the boot of the car, they threw it in behind the seat and within seconds the car came out of its hiding place and was on the dirt road headed towards highway R173.

"Turn on you headlamps," shouted Lamb as the car's rear wheels spun on the black top road attempting to spin off the water from the mud and grass.

The car's tires suddenly grabbed hold of the pavement and for a split second Lamb felt like he had just been shot out of a cannon. The car careened towards the opposite side of the road and only by the quick action of Taggart-Holmes was the car steered into the middle of the road.

Two hundred meters before the intersection with R173 they saw the van pass heading west. Within seconds they were at the intersection.

Taggart-Holmes slowed, but did not stop. He turned left and both could see the taillights of the white van.

"He's head towards N1, just like we thought," said the English Captain.

"Where will that lead him?"

"Depends. He can turn off to the right up ahead about five kilometers and take R174, the road we came down on or he can stay on 173 and head towards Dundalk."

"And?" asked Lamb.

"God only knows, he can head due west and stay in the Republic all the way over to Sligo, which is on the west coast of Ireland. And if you know your Irish geography, he can then turn north and stay in the Republic until he's north of Northern Ireland."

"Then you think I'm going to get an early morning tour of Ireland?"

"No, any place along the route he can turn north on one of the secondary roads and drive right into Northern Ireland."

"Well, I think I'll lean back and enjoy the ride," said Lamb, "but I was thinking about what you said concerning how you would inform your people."

Without taking his eyes off the road, the English Captain turned on a switch with his left hand.

"A handy dandy radio borrowed from the Ranger Unit. According to the Sergeant who installed it this afternoon, all I have to do is turn it on and I'll be in contact with someone at the Control Center, who in turn is in contact with all the units on the border."

"Interesting, but does it work?" asked Lamb.

Suddenly a loud voice came over the radio.

"Wild Hare, are you there?"

Both Taggart-Holmes and Lamb came a few inches out of their seats. After a moment, both started laughing.

"That scared the crap out of me," said Lamb.

"Hell, I'm checking to see if my seat is wet."

"Wild Hare, Rabbit Hole here. Please reply."

Taggart-Holmes reached down and removed a microphone from a hook below the radio. He pressed the button on the side of the microphone and said,

"Wild Hare here. We are following a white van that is headed west-north-west on R173."

"Any other vehicles?"

"Negative."

"Keep the van in sight."

"Roger."

- -

"How many in the sedan?" asked Irwin.

"I see three, two in the front and one in the back."

"Good, that's exactly what I see. You better start the engine Major, we don't want to lose them."

Major Brown started the engine, put the car in gear and made a tight one hundred and eighty degree turn. They were only four hundred meters from the intersection and within less than two minutes were on R173 following the black sedan, which drove through The Bush and Carlingford.

"It looks like they are headed right up through Omeath and across the border," said Brown.

"Get on the radio and contact the Control Center," said Irwin.

Brown lifted the microphone from its hook on the dashboard, pushed the button to activate the radio and said,

"Welsh Rabbit calling Rabbit Hole."

"Rabbit Hole here."

"The main subject is in a black, four door sedan. At the present time it is south of Omeath on R173. Appears to be headed for the border south of Newry."

"Roger. We'll alert the Newry detachment. Stand by."

Four minutes later, the black sedan turned left onto a secondary road that ran east and west.

"Hurry and contact the Control Center," said Irwin.

"Rabbit Hole, this is Welsh Rabbit. Come in."

"Rabbit Hole here."

"Rabbit Hole, the main subject has turned off R173 and is headed west. Copy?"

"Roger."

"They are turning south now," said Irwin.

"Rabbit Hole. Subject is turning south."

"Do you see any road signs?"

"Negative," said Brown.

"Just a moment," said the voice over the radio.

Half a minute later the radio crackled and the voice from the Control Center said,

"It appears they are going around the mountain."

Brown looked over at Irwin and saw the Deputy Director nod his head.

"Tell them to forget about the Newry detachment. The bastards are going deeper into the Republic."

"Yes sir," said Brown as he pushed the microphone button and said,

"Welsh Rabbit here. Appears main subject is heading deeper into the Republic and there is no need for the Newry detachment to be alerted."

"Thank you Welsh Rabbit, but we figured that out five minutes ago."

"Find out who the wise ass is on the radio," said Irwin.

"Sir, would you handle the radio, this back road is too dangerous for me to try to drive and use the radio at the same time," said Brown.

"Hand me the microphone."

"Yes sir," said Brown as he handed the Deputy Director the microphone.

Irwin took the instrument, pushed the button and shouted,

"This is Deputy Director Irwin. Who made that last comment?"

There was no answer.

"Sir, you have to release the button before they can answer," said Brown.

Irwin looked at Brown, released the button and waited thirty seconds. He was about to push the button when the voice from the command center said,

"You have a question?"

Irwin pushed the button and shouted,

"Yes, I have a question. Who was the smart ass who made the last comment?"

"That was my comment Mr. Irwin."

"And just who in the hell are you?"

"Colonel J.P.R. Towers, Commanding Officer of the 17th Military Police Detachment."

Brown looked over at Irwin, who had his famous scowl on his face as he attempted to think of a reply.

Brown turned his head to the right and relaxed his facial muscles. The expression on his face turned into a very wide smile. It required all of his will power to keep from laughing out loud.

"Sorry Colonel Towers, a slip of the lip."

After a moment of silence, the Colonel replied,

"An extremely good lesson Mr. Irwin, you never know who you are talking to on the radio."

"Please accept my apology Colonel."

"Apology accepted Mr. Irwin. Is the sedan still in view?"

"Yes," said Irwin, "about three hundred meters ahead of us."

"Thank you. Keep us informed."

Irwin placed the microphone on the double hook attached to the dashboard, crossed his arms and stared out the front window. It was time to sulk.

Major Brown kept the double tail lights of the black sedan in view as it traveled around the mountainous area of the peninsula, turning southwest until it intersected with R173.

Meyers frowned as the car disappeared into the early morning darkness. He was certain all three men were in the sedan.

"A few minutes," he said to himself.

As he was about to turn on his flashlight, he saw a flash of light in the field across the road. It disappeared as quickly as it appeared, but reappeared four more times for less than a second, each time a little farther to the right.

He continued to look in the direction of the light, but nothing further appeared in the area. He turned on his flashlight, shined it on the rear tires of the police van and slowly walked around the vehicle, shining the light on each of the tires. He opened the hood and shined the light from side to side.

After closing the hood, he decided to take O'Connor's advice. He walked into the wooded area on the side of the rest area and relieved himself. While in the woods, he shined the light on his watch and saw it was twenty minutes after one in the morning.

Meyers walked back to the table, took a seat and stared out into the darkness across the road. His thoughts once again returned to Convoy and his conversation with O'Connor. A great deal of the conversation made more sense now than it did at the time.

Suddenly he heard footsteps on the gravel. He turned around and saw a figure coming towards him from out of the woods. He was about to turn on the flashlight and shine it at the dark form when O'Connor said,

"Thought I went off and left you?"

Meyers didn't answer, he merely watched O'Connor come closer and closer. When he reached the table, Meyers said,

"I thought I saw you in the sedan."

"That was Oscar," said O'Connor.

"But…."

O'Connor raised his right hand and shook his head.

"When are you going to tell me what is going on?"

"Could you wait, say half an hour?"

"And then?"

"Ask and you shall receive," said O'Connor.

"Agreed. Half an hour."

"Thank you. Now, we need to get moving."

"It's your show," said Meyers, "I'll ask no more questions until your half hour is up."

"Splendid. I'm going to ask you to drive down to Greenore. Do you know where it is?"

"Across from Cranfield Point?"

"Right," said O'Connor.

"Down the road about ten kilometers?"

"Right again."

Meyers started to ask the reason, but stopped before he uttered a word.

O'Connor smiled and said,

"You'll understand when we get there."

Meyers nodded and said,

"Do you want to see McCaul now or when we get to Greenore?"

"Let me look at the lad now."

Meyers got up from the table and walked to the rear of the police van. O'Connor followed close behind him.

When Meyers opened the van doors. one of the plastic buckets rolled out. O'Connor jumped back as the can hits the ground, then looked up and saw the other plastic buckets in the rear of the van.

"What the hell?"

"I used them to keep the crate from bumping into the sides."

"Oh," said O'Connor as he reached down and picked up the bucket. He handed it to Meyers, who carefully squeezed it in next to the crate.

"Perhaps we'd better wait," said O'Connor.

"It's up to you," said Meyers.

"Let's wait."

"Fine."

O'Connor stepped back allowing room for Meyers to close the doors. Once the doors were closed and locked, Meyers stood for a moment looking at O'Connor, asking him a question without saying a word.

Meyers answered his own question by turning and walking to the driver's side of the van. He opened the door and entered, followed by O'Connor on the other side.

"Just pull back on the road and…." Said O'Connor.

"I know, but how about fastening your seat belt first," said Meyers as he started the engine. He waited for O'Connor to fasten his seat belt before slipping the van in gear and slowly moving out onto the road.

Within twenty minutes of departing from the rest area, the black police van was on the far side of Greenore.

"See that shack down on the left, where the light is," said O'Connor.

"They're leading us on a wild goose chase," said Irwin.

"That's what it looks like," said Brown.

"They could have turned right out of the rest area and been exactly where they are twenty minutes ago," added Irwin.

Major Brown merely nodded in agreement.

Brown and Irwin followed the black sedan as it made its way onto N1, where it turned left towards Dundalk.

"They're leading us right back to Dublin," said Irwin.

"Looks that way sir. Shouldn't we inform the Control Center?"

Irwin answered Brown's question by picking up the microphone, pushing the button and saying,

"Rabbit Hole, this is Welsh Rabbit. Subject vehicle has headed south on N1 towards Dundalk."

"Message received."

Irwin replaced the microphone and looked out the side window, then said,

"If they go through Drogheda I'll have Control contact the Garda and inform them O'Connor is back in the Republic."

Brown looked over at Irwin and slowly shook his head.

"You don't think that's a good idea Major?" snapped Irwin.

"No sir."

"And why not?"

"Because O'Connor is not going to the Republic if the mortar is going to Northern Ireland."

"Then why are they headed south?"

"I have no idea."

The answer came in less than twenty minutes. After the black sedan passed through Dundalk it continued for nine kilometers and entered the outskirts of Castlebellingham where it slowed and turned into a petrol station.

Brown had enough distance to slow down and stop a good hundred meters from the station. The two watched as the driver pulled into an empty parking space between two cars. He got out, walked into the station for a few minutes and returned to the car. As the sedan backed out and left the station, instead of continuing south, it turned and headed north.

"A wild goose chase," said Brown.

"Son of a bitch," was the only comment Irwin could think of saying at the moment.

The black sedan passed through Dundalk and continued north on N1.

"Sir, shouldn't you inform the Control Center?" said Brown.

"Not yet. They could turn off to the left any time and we'd look like real idiots if we caused the Newry detachment to scramble again."

Major Brown didn't question the Deputy Director.

Once north of Dundalk, the black sedan slowed to fifty kilometers an hour.

"Why are they slowing down?" asked Irwin.

"I have no idea sir."

- -

"For the next hour and twenty-five minutes Taggart-Holmes and Lamb followed the white van through Dundalk, west to Carrickmacross, north to Castleblayney, northwest to Monaghanm and southwest to Clones. Outside of Clones the van crossed the border.

Taggart-Holmes reached down, unhooked the microphone, pushed the button and said,

"Rabbit Hole, this is Wild Hare, over."

"Rabbit Hole here, go ahead."

"The van just crossed the border on A74, headed towards Newtownbutler."

"What is your location?"

"Approximately one and a half kilometers due west of Clones."

"Do you still have the van in sight?"

"Yes."

"How far behind the van?"

Taggart-Holmes looked at Lamb and asked,

"How far would you guess?"

"A quarter of a mile. Tell him about three hundred meters."

"Approximately three hundred meters," said Taggart-Holmes.

"Drop back another two hundred meters, but don't lose site of the van. Do you read?"

"Roger."

Lamb looked at his watch. It was three minutes after two o'clock in the morning.

"There's a drive way on the other side of the shack. Turn in, back up and turn around," said O'Connor.

Meyers followed O'Connor's directions, driving the van pass the shack and turning into the driveway. He applied his brakes until the van stopped, slipped the gear into reverse, backed up and pulled in front of the building. As the van came to a stop in front of the wooden structure, two men seemed to appear out of nowhere. Both were dressed from head to toe in black and both were carrying handguns which they kept at their side.

"It's me, O'Connor," said O'Connor.

The two men nodded and walked to the back of the van. Looking into his side view mirror, Meyers watched both men place their weapons in shoulder holsters. One of the men disappeared into the darkness while the other was barely visible in the rear view mirror until he turned on his torch. The illumination highlighted only his face.

"Jamie, can you see the man on your side?" asked O'Connor.

"Yes."

For the next thirty-five minutes Taggart-Holmes and Lamb followed the van as it passed through Newtownbutler, Denagh and Lisnaskea.

Approximately two kilometers outside of Lisnaskea the van stopped momentarily, turned off A34 onto B514.

Taggart-Holmes immediately reported this to "Rabbit Hole." Ten seconds later, the voice on the radio said,

"Appears they're headed for Enniskillen. If they don't stop or turn off when they turn onto A4 outside of Tamlaght, they'll be stopped. Copy?"

"Roger," replied Taggart-Holmes.

Twenty-three minutes later the white van stopped at the intersection of B514 and A4. Before the driver had a chance to pull onto A4, two armored cars pulled up in front and back of the van and ten soldiers instantly surrounded it.

By the time Taggart-Holmes and Lamb stopped a hundred meters behind the halted van, the driver was standing on the shoulder of the road with his hands pointed skyward.

"We need you to back the van down to the dock," said O'Connor, "the man you see in the mirror will direct you to the dock and I'll watch this side. The road is extremely narrow, so drive slowly. I'd hate to see you end up in the water."

Meyers eased the gearshift into reverse, took his foot off the brake and allowed the van to slowly move backwards.

The individual in back continued to move his torch back and forth until the van's rear wheels left the gravel road and bumped over and onto a wooden dock.

"Slow," said O'Connor, "you have only about twenty meters to the end."

Meyers slipped the van out of gear and softly applied his foot to the brake pedal, allowing the van to coast what he judged to be about ten meters.

At that point, he pressed hard on the brake pedal. The van's wheels locked, but the van continued to move, the rubber tires sliding over the wet wooden dock.

He pulled the gear lever down into forward, took his foot off the brake and pushed the gas pedal. The rear wheels started spinning, but the van continued to move backwards.

Just as Meyers thought of opening his door and jumping to safety, the van stopped momentarily and started going forward.

Meyers pushed on the brake pedal for a second time, locking all four wheels, but the van continued to go forward about two meters before coming to a complete stop.

O'Connor was laughing. Meyers looked at him and asked,

"What in the hell is so funny?"

"You, you should have seen the look on your face. It appeared like you were getting ready to desert the ship."

Meyers' eyes narrowed for a moment, then he smiled and said,

"You don't know how close I was to bailing out. If we hadn't stopped, I'd be half way to Greenore."

"I should have told you, the dock has a large wooden barrier close to the end. Reckon they've had a few go over, so they've block it."

"Thanks for telling me."

Taggart-Holmes set the brake, turned off the ignition and the lights and hopped out of the car. Just as Lamb opened his door, one of the soldiers, a Sergeant, shined his flashlight at the stopped car and shouted,

"You gentlemen please remain where you are. This is a military operation."

Lamb closed the door and settled back in his seat. Taggart-Holmes started to ask who was in charge of the operation but changed his mind, nodded and reentered the car.

"We'll see what happens now."

"I'd suggest you turn on your ignition, your radio isn't on without the juice," said Lamb.

Taggart-Holmes looked at Lamb for a moment, reached down, turned on the ignition and started the motor.

"Wild Hare, this is Rabbit Hole. Has the van been stopped?"

Taggart-Holmes picked up the microphone, pushed the button and said, "Roger. The van was stopped before it turned onto A4 and at present the driver is standing outside the van with his hands in the air."

"Good. Just a moment."

"Can you see what's going on?" asked Lamb.

"Looks like they are just holding the driver, waiting for someone or for instructions."

"Wild Hare, this is Rabbit Hole. We're in contact with the Ranger's Command in Enniskellin. They are in contact with the patrol that stopped the van and will be relaying the information to us. Please stand by."

"Roger."

Taggart-Holmes released the button, replaced the microphone, turned to Lamb and said,

"The next order will probably be for us to return to Belfast. They might say "thank you"."

"Looks like the boss man just arrived and they're getting ready to open the doors of the van," said Lamb.

The two watched as the driver was escorted to the rear of the van where he said something to the new arrival, a Lieutenant.

The driver reached in his pocket, removed a key and opened the two doors. He stepped back as the Sergeant stepped up and entered the van. A minute later the Sergeant reappeared at the rear of the van, shook his head and jumped down. He handed his flashlight to the Lieutenant, who entered the van.

Within a minute the lieutenant stepped down from the van and said something to the Sergeant, who passed on the Lieutenant's order.

Four of the soldiers leaned their weapons against the side of the vehicle and two entered the van. Within seconds the two commenced handing out bags to the two others, who stacked them on the side of the road.

Lamb counted the bags as they were stacked on the ground.

"Twenty-four," said Lamb.

After the bags were removed, the soldiers in the van passed out a wooden box, which had handles on both ends.

The box, which measured approximately 2/3rds of a meter by 2/3rds by ½ meter, was placed next to the stack of bags.

The lieutenant reentered the van. Twenty seconds later, he stepped down form the van, handed the flashlight to the Sergeant, shook his head and walked back to one of the armored cars.

- -

"They appear to be headed into Northern Ireland," said Brown.

"I see that Major," said Irwin, "but I'm not going to alert that wise ass Colonel until they cross the border."

Major Brown wanted to say something, but again held his tongue and continued to follow the black sedan. Two minutes later the sedan crossed the border into Northern Ireland.

Brown turned to Irwin and said,

"Sir, you…"

"I know, I know," said Irwin as he jerked the microphone off the hook, pressed the button and said,

"Rabbit Hole, this is Welsh Rabbit. The black sedan just crossed into Northern Ireland."

"WHERE?" came a shout over the radio.

"On N1 or A1."

"I thought you were headed south?"

"We were, but they turned around and headed north."

"Why didn't you inform us they turned around?" shouted Colonel Towers, a question to which Mr. Irwin did not have an answer.

He looked at Brown, smiled and gently placed the microphone on its hook, took a deep breath and said,

"Major, I want you to stop the sedan. Speed up, pass it, then block the road."

"But sir…yes sir."

- -

"You're welcome," said O'Connor as he opened his door and stepped out. Before he shut the door, he said,

"Be careful getting out, the dock is slippery as goose grease."

Meyers put the van into park, put on the emergency brake, turned off the engine and lights, opened the glove box, removed the flashlight, opened his door and gingerly stepped out onto the dock. As he walked to the rear of the van, he almost stumbled over the barrier.

"Easy," said the man who had been directing him, "the water's cold."

"Besides," said O'Connor, "we don't want anything happening to you or we'll catch bloody hell."

Meyers had no idea what he was talking about, but he appreciated the two men's concern for his safe being.

"Where's Shamus?" asked O'Connor.

Right behind you," said a voice in the dark, a voice that made both O'Connor and Meyers jump. The voice came from the edge of the dock, not three meters in back of O'Connor.

"Don't do that!!" shouted O'Connor.

"Sorry Thomas, I thought you saw me when you got out of the van."

"If I had seen you, I wouldn't be asking where the hell you were, would I?"

The man didn't answer.

Changing the tone of his voice, O'Connor said,

"You'd better signal the boat."

"I've already signaled it. It's on its way in," said the man called Shamus.

Turning to Meyers, O'Connor said,

"I'd like to take a look at Ron now."

"Can I ask questions now?" asked Meyers.

"Not yet, but I have a sneaking suspicion you've figured out what's going on."

Meyers nodded, turned, walked to the rear of the van and opened the doors. Using his flashlight, he illuminated the interior.

"We need to move all these buckets first."

"Hand them out and we'll stack them on the dock. The fishermen can use the buckets," said O'Connor.

Meyers crawled into the van and for the next five minutes, a process resembling a bucket brigade took place on the small wooden dock outside Greenore as the white plastic buckets were passed out and neatly stacked on the dock.

"You want to come in now Thomas?" asked Meyers as he took his flashlight, turned it on and shined it on the floor of the van.

O'Connor climbed into the van and worked his way forward, next to Meyers.

"I have a question," said O'Connor.

"Yes."

"Why did you take such a chance?"

Meyers looked into O'Connor's eyes and said,

"I thought you meant what you said in Convoy about taking McCaul home and I knew I'd be safe with you."

Not breaking the visual connection, O'Connor nodded and said,

"I meant what I said and thank you."

"And you can thank Chief Superintendent Kerrigan and Dr. Shaw," said Meyers as he turned and inched his way to the front of the crate.

"And Chief Superintendent Kerrigan and Dr. Henry Shaw," said O'Connor, "you do know we were aware of what occurred at St. Francis Hospital yesterday and today?"

"I figured you did."

After a long silence, O'Connor asked,

"Is McCaul in the casket?"

Meyers laughed softly, winked and said,

"I certainly hope so, but we'll just have to take a look, won't we Thomas?"

O'Connor did not have an immediate answer to Meyers' question. He was almost certain McCaul was in the casket, but he wasn't 100 percent certain.

- -

Two kilometers south of Newry on Highway A1, Major Brown sped pass the black sedan, pulled in front of it and turned on his left blinker as a signal to the driver of the sedan to pull over.

Brown slowly pulled over onto the shoulder of the road and was followed closely by the black sedan. Both came to a stop at the same time.

Suddenly two armored vehicles appeared out of the dark. The lead vehicle passed the black sedan, came to a stop and backed up until its rear bumper was only a few inches from the front bumper of the government car.

The second armored vehicle slowed and stopped a few inches from the rear bumper of the black sedan.

Armed soldiers immediately surrounded both vehicles. Irwin rolled down his window and looked up at the individual who had his weapon pointed at his head.

Attempting to speak in a commanding voice, Irwin asked,

"Who's in command?"

In spite of his attempt, the word "command" was at least two or perhaps three octaves higher than the rest of the sentence.

The young soldier's face lost its stern look, which was replaced by a large smile. He had a difficult time saying the name of his commander because he was attempting to speak and laugh at the same time. Finally he said,

"Captain Taylor."

"What in the hell is so funny?" shouted Irwin.

The soldier continued to laugh, turned his head and yelled,

"Captain Taylor sir, there's a gentleman here who wants to know who's in command."

Irwin glared at the soldier and asked,

"What's your name?"

A large individual stepped around the soldier and said,

"Captain Raymond Taylor of the 17th Military Police Unit. May I have your name sir?"

"I'm, I'm Deputy Director Irwin of the…"

"Yes, I know who you are sir. Colonel Towers informed me."

"Then why are your men pointing their weapons at us?"

"Military procedure. When we intercept a vehicle or vehicles, military protocol is to keep the occupants covered."

"Well, you know who I am, would you be so kind as to order your people to lower their weapons?"

The Captain's head turned and as his eyes made contact with the four soldiers guarding Irwin's vehicle. He smiled and nodded.

Instantly all the weapons were lowered.

"Thank you. Now, may I ask why you boxed us in?"

"Colonel Towers' orders," said the Captain, "he informed us you were trailing a vehicle and both vehicles were to be stopped."

"How did you know you stopped the correct vehicles?"

The Captain smiled, shook his head and said,

"Sir, you may not know it, but your car and the other vehicle are the only ones on the road at this time of the morning according our lookouts."

He raised his left arm, looked at his watch and said,

"It's a quarter after two in the morning."

Without further words, Meyers reached over and slid the latch locking the cover of the wooden create in place, pushed the lid up and over until it hit the side of the van. He then reached down and flipped the two spring-loaded catches, took hold of the edge of the lid and opened the upper half.

Holding the lid of the casket with his left hand, he held the flashlight in his right hand and shined the light on the corpse.

McCaul was dressed in a black shroud with his hands folded on his chest. The right hand was over the left hand. For a long moment the two men looked at the corpse, then suddenly O'Connor reached down and took hold of the right hand, lifted it and held it between his two massive hands.

"Oh God, what if the left hand is missing a little finger," thought Meyers as he watched O'Connor hold the hand. He almost dropped both the lid of the casket and the flashlight as he felt his heart rate increase. He could feel his pulse in his temples, his ears and his neck. He closed his eyes and prayed.

When he opened his eyes, he leaned to the right as far as possible. He looked at O'Connor and saw he was still holding McCaul's cold hand, but his eyes were closed and his chin was on his chest. Meyers couldn't hear a sound, but he knew the big man was praying.

He lowered his head and looked beneath O'Connor's hand. The left hand of the corpse was not missing any fingers.

- -

The radio in Taggart-Holmes car came alive.

"Wild Hare, this is Rabbit Hole. Identify yourself to the patrol and check the van. Copy?"

"Roger. What about the bags? Do I have authority to open them?"

"Yes!"

The English Captain opened his door, stepped out of the car and walked towards the van. The Sergeant turned, shined his flashlight on Taggart-Holmes and started to say something.

"Sergeant, I'm Captain Taggart-Holmes of the Tenth Royal Fusiliers, temporarily assigned to MI-5 in Belfast. We have been following the van since around midnight. I have orders to inspect the van."

The Sergeant looked at the Captain for a moment before saying,

"Could I see some identification sir?"

Taggart-Holmes looked at the Sergeant and the nine soldiers holding weapons, held his hands out in front of him and said,

"I'm going to reach in my back pocket and remove my ID card."

Slowly he reached into his rear pocket and removed his wallet. He removed his ID and handed it to the Sergeant, who shined the light on the card. The Sergeant compared the picture on the ID card with the man standing in front of him, handed the ID back to the Captain and said,

"Thank you sir. I'm Sergeant Duggan of the 7th."

Taggart-Holmes nodded his head and said,

"My privilege Sergeant Duggan."

The Lieutenant in charge reappeared next to Sergeant Duggan, looked at Taggart-Holmes and then at the Sergeant.

"Sir, this gentleman is Captain Taggart-Holmes of the Tenth Royal Fusiliers, presently assigned to MI-5 in Belfast," said Sergeant Duggan.

"I'm Lieutenant Ronald Mucin of the 7th sir," said Mucin as he stuck out his hand.

"Pleasure to met you Lieutenant," said Taggart-Holmes. Turning to Sergeant Duggan he said,

"Could I borrow you torch?"

"Certainly sir," said Duggan as he handed the Captain his flashlight.

"Sergeant, the gentleman in the car is also an officer. I would like for him to join us."

"Yes sir," said Duggan. He turned to the man next to him and said,

"Andrews, you heard the Captain."

"Yes Sergeant," said Andrews as he started running towards the coupe.

Lamb opened his door and as the overhead light came on, he looked at his watch. It was twenty five minutes after two o'clock in the morning.

"Sir, your presence has been requested by the Captain," said Andrews.

"Thank you," said Lamb as he stepped out of the car and walked up to the van.

After Lamb was introduced to the Sergeant and the Lieutenant, Taggart-Holmes and Lamb entered the van and within sixty seconds were back on the road. Taggart-Holmes handed Duggan his flashlight, looked down at the box and bags stacked on the side of the road and said,

"Sergeant, do you have something to open the box?"

"Sir," said the soldier standing next to the box, "the box has a lock on it."

"I see that," said Taggart-Holmes.

"Well sir, I think I can open the lock."

"How?"

"Something I learned from my uncle."

"Go ahead then and show me something you learned from your uncle," said the English Captain.

The young soldier handed his weapon to the soldier next to him and drew his issued knife. He knelt down by the box and turned the knife so he was holding the blade. He took hold of the lock with his left hand, holding it in the palm of his hand, then hit it with the metal knob on the end of the knife handle and the lock popped open.

He looked up at Taggart-Holmes, smiled and said,

"There you are sir."

Taggart-Holmes looked at Lamb, Mucin and the Sergeant, looked down at the soldier and said,

"Thank you."

"Yes sir," said the young soldier as he stood up, replaced his knife in its scabbard and retrieved his weapon from his companion.

"Amazing talent."

"I agree," said Lamb.

"Shall we take a look?" said Taggart-Holmes, more as a comment than a question.

- -

After what seemed to Meyers to be at least ten minutes, O'Connor gently replaced McCaul's hand and leaned back.

"Shall I close it?" asked Meyers.

"Yes," said O'Connor, "close it and lock it please."

Meyers gently closed the lid of the casket, allowing the spring loaded catches to reset. He reached over and lowered the cover of the wooden crate and slipped the latch in place.

O'Connor leaned against the side of the van, looked at Meyers and said,

"I don't know how it was all accomplished without being discovered, but there's no doubt the body is that of Ron."

"You'll have to thank Dr. Shaw, he orchestrated the whole thing after he found out McCaul was to be cremated and his ashes scattered."

"I know, but you're the one who transported it up here."

"With the help of Chief Superintendent Kerrigan," said Meyers.

"Right, with the help of Chief Superintendent Kerrigan."

After a silence of almost half a minute, O'Connor asked,

"Aren't you going to ask me how I know for sure it is McCaul?"

"No, I'm not going to ask, but I'd really like to know."

"On his right arm, just above the hand, there are three souvenirs from his British interrogator. He used an expensive Cuban cigar."

Meyers nodded.

Suddenly O'Connor leaned back and said,

"Ah, hell…."

Meyers watched as the blood drained from the man's face. He didn't know what to do or say.

"Are you alright?"

"No," said O'Connor, "I'm sick to my stomach."

"Get out and get some fresh air, that'll help," said Meyers, hoping O'Connor would hold on to the contents of his stomach until he made it out of the van.

O'Connor made it outside the van, took a couple of deep breaths and nodded to Meyers. The two stood together on the wet dock for close to four minutes without saying a word.

Shamus and the other man were nowhere to be seen. Meyers knew they could be standing within three or four meters and not be seen.

He was correct.

"Here comes the boat," said a Shamus, who was no more than four meters from O'Connor.

"Damn it man, don't do that," said O'Connor.

"Sorry Thomas," said Shamus.

O'Connor turned and looked out at the lough and then looked across at Cranfield Point.

"Not there Thomas, out to the right. They're still out at sea," said Shamus.

Both O'Connor and Meyers looked out towards the open sea and saw only a thin white line. After a few seconds the faint outline of the vessel was visible.

"That man has the eyes of an eagle," said Meyers.

"That's the reason he's our lookout," said O'Connor, "he can see a mile in the dark, but you can't see him half of the time."

Meyers nodded and asked,

"Can I ask questions now?"

"All you want," said O'Connor.

"I'm assuming you're taking McCaul on the boat."

"That's correct."

"To Wales?"

"Yes, to Wales."

"Do you know who is in the other car?" asked Irwin.

"No sir, but according to the information we received from Belfast, it is suppose to be an individual by the name of Thomas O'Connor."

"Correct and do you know who O'Connor is?"

"Not really."

"For your information, a few years ago he was the Provos' top gunman."

"In that case, we've made quite a coup."

"You mean I've made quite a coup."

"Mr. Irwin!" said Major Brown.

Irwin looked over at the Major, turned back to the Captain and said,

"That's right Captain, we have made quite a coup. Now, can we get out and take a look at OUR coup?"

"Yes sir," said the Captain as he nodded, stepped back and added,

"Please be my guests."

Irwin and Brown slowly exited their vehicle and for a moment stood looking at Captain Taylor.

Irwin looked towards the black sedan and said,

"Shall we take a look at our trophy catch?"

"After you sir," replied Taylor.

As the three men moved up to the sedan on the driver's side, Davy rolled down the side window and looked out. He started to ask what the hell was going on, but following O'Connor's instructions, he looked up and asked,

"Can I help you?"

Taylor looked at Irwin.

"Mr. Irwin?"

"It's your coup also Captain."

Taylor smiled, looked down at Davy and said,

"Would you gentlemen please exit the vehicle?"

"Certainly. Is something wrong?"

"Please exit the vehicle," said Taylor.

Slowly Davy opened the door as Neil opened the rear door and both moved out of the car and stood looking at Irwin, Brown and Taylor.

"Tell O'Connor to get out," said Irwin.

"Who?"

"O'Connor," snapped Irwin.

Davy and Neil looked at each other. Davy shrugged his shoulders and said,

"I don't know what you're talking about mister."

Irwin stepped forward, pushed Davy aside and looked in the vehicle. He stood up straight and looked at Neil and Davy.

"Where's O'Connor?"

"Mister, I have no idea what you're talking about."

"We saw the three of you in the car not thirty minutes ago when you stopped in Castlebellingham, turned around and headed back North," said Irwin.

Again Davy looked at Neil, turned, looked directly at Irwin and said,

"Sir, we were in Dublin for a wedding and left the party a little after one."

"Don't give me that crap. We followed you from outside The Bush up and around the mountain and down through Dundalk. We saw you pull into the station in Castlebellingham. You got out of the car, went into the station, got back in the car and headed north."

"Not us," said Neil, "we've been in Dublin since noon. Went to my cousin's wedding at five o'clock this afternoon and have been at the wedding party until we left. Just like Davy told you."

"You lying bastards, we saw you outside The Bush and..."

"Mr. Irwin," said Major Brown.

Irwin looked at Brown who was slowly shaking his head.

"We must have been following the wrong car sir."

Irwin's eyelids narrowed until they were only slits. He knew they had followed the right car. He turned to Taylor and said,

"Would you have your men search the car and the boot. He could be hiding there."

Taylor looked from Irwin to Brown to Davy, who smiled, handed the Captain the keys and said,

"That key will open the boot."

"Thank you," said Taylor.

Turning to Irwin he said,

"I'll inspect the car. Would you like to...."

"Yes I would," snapped Irwin.

Taylor walked to the rear of the car, inserted the key and opened the boot. He removed a flashlight from his belt, turned it on and shined in on the interior. He looked at Irwin.

"Check the car and leave the boot open," said Irwin.

"Major, would you stand here and make sure no one magically appears?"

"Yes sir," answered an embarrassed Major as he walked to the rear of the vehicle.

"OK Captain, let's check the car."

Taylor looked from Irwin to Brown, who was nodding his head.

Irwin and Captain Taylor walked to the left side of the car, opened both doors and inspected the interior of the vehicle, finding nothing except a pile of newspapers on the front seat.

"Sir, there's nothing or no one in the car," said Taylor.

"I see that," said Irwin.

Looking back at Brown, Irwin said,

"Major?"

"Nothing sir."

Irwin walked around to where Davy and Neil were standing, stopped, looked at them, one at a time and said,

"I have no idea how you pulled it off, but I know O'Connor was in this car."

Again Davy shrugged his shoulders and looked at Neil.

Irwin continued to stare at the two men, first one and then the other. After thirty seconds he realized his staring was not going to produce results. He turned to Brown and said,

"Major, are you ready to get back to Belfast?"

"Yes sir."

Turning to Captain Taylor, Irwin said,

"Would you have your men move your vehicles so we can leave?"

"What about these two?"

"What about them?"

"Do you want them held?"

As Irwin walked pass the Captain, he said,

"Ask Colonel Towers."

Taggart-Holmes walked over to the box, pulled the lock out of the hasp and using the hasp as a handle, opened it.

"Sergeant, your torch please," said the Captain.

"Here sir," said Duggan as he handed Taggart-Holmes his flashlight. "Thank you."

Holding the light in his left hand, he shined the light on the interior of the box and slowly removed its contents, which consisted of two bricklayer's trowels, three plasterer's trowels, two cement edgers, two cement trough makers, two mason hammers, two wooden sticks, a spool of heavy twine and a semi sphere of blue chalk.

Taggart-Holmes stood up, handed the flashlight back to Duggan, looked down at the bags and asked,

"Sergeant, would you have one of your men open one of the bags?"

"I'll do that sir," said Duggan as he switched the flashlight from his right hand to his left, reached into his hip pocket and removed a long blade knife. He opened it with one quick flick of his wrist then walked over to the stack of bags, picked up one, placed it on the roadway and with three quick motions he sliced the cloth once lengthwise and twice crosswise. He stepped back and looked at Taggart-Holmes.

"Thank you," said the Captain as he walked up to the bag, knelt down and with his right hand sifted the contents of the bag, which was nothing but white powder.

He stood up, looked at Duggan and said,

"Let's try another."

During the next thirty-two minutes, the Sergeant from the 7th cut open the remaining twenty-three bags and Captain Taggart-Holmes examined each to find nothing but white powder. When the exercise was completed, the front of Taggart-Holmes clothing and face were covered by a thin layer of white powder.

As Taggart-Holmes stood up, Lamb could not keep from smiling as he looked at his English friend. The two officers looked at each other and Lamb said,

"Damnedest looking weapon I've ever seen."

"Don't say another word you damn foreigner," said Taggart-Holmes.

After thanking Sergeant Duggan and Lieutenant Mucin for their assistance, Lamb and Taggart-Holmes returned to Belfast in almost total silence, each with their own thoughts.

Lamb was daydreaming of Elizabeth Kelly, while Taggart-Holmes' thoughts were about returning to England for the Summer holidays.

Eight weeks later, the owner of Forger's Home Remodeling Company of Enniskillen, County Fermanagh, Northern Ireland, received a check from Her Majesty's government for 2250 pounds for the twenty-four bags of special mortar mix containing very expensive Virginia marble and Vermont granite.

- -

Captain Taylor contacted Colonel Towers and informed him of the situation and asked for instructions.

Seven minutes after the departure of Irwin and Brown, Captain Taylor apologized for stopping Davy and Neil and told them they were free to be on their way.

"Thank you," said Davy as he entered the black sedan.

"Thanks," said Neil as he walked around to the passenger side of the sedan, opened the door and picked up a stack of newspapers that covered a deflated rubber dummy and pitched them in the rear seat.

"Be careful of Oscar, we might need him again," said Davy.

"Always," said Neil as he picked up the rubber dummy, slipped into the front seat and placed Oscar on his lap.

The armored vehicle pulled away from the front of their vehicle and as they passed Captain Taylor and his unit, Davy waved to them and said,

"Have a nice morning."

- -

"The craft coming in is an old Coast Guard patrol boat. They're carrying five full drums of fuel aboard, plus two fuel tanks about three quarters full. Enough fuel to take us to Wales," said O'Connor.

"What about the Coast Guard and the Navy?" asked Meyers.

"We have their schedules," was O'Connor's only answer.

Meyers nodded and said,

"And they said McCaul was the planner. You've done yourself proud."

"Thank you," said O'Connor and before Meyers had a chance to ask another question, O'Connor said,

"When the boat docks, would you ease the van back to the block so we can transfer the crate?"

"Certainly."

The skipper of the craft cut the boat's engine and was coasting, if that is the word to use for a boat moving across the water without the use of its prop. As it neared the dock, the engine came to life and its propeller reversed and stirred the water. The thrust of the props remained on for only a few seconds, enough to slow the craft to the point where it was barely moving. Even at such a slow speed, when the hull hit the bumpers on the end of the dock, it was enough to cause all four men to partially lose their balance. No one went down, but each to had to grab hold of some part of the van to keep from falling.

"Thomas!!!" shouted Meyers, "the crate!"

The contact of the boat with the dock was enough to tilt the dock downwards almost a foot, causing the wooden crate to start sliding out of the van.

Meyers grabbed one side of the crate, but it was still moving. Out of nowhere, Shamus and the other man jumped over the barrier and were pushing against the moving crate, pushing hard enough to stop its movement.

"That was close," said Meyers as he let go of the crate and backed away.

"Too close for comfort," said O'Connor.

Meyers thought, "*Way too close for comfort.*"

If the crate had hit the dock, there was an excellent chance it would have slipped into the cold, black water of the lake.

Meyers walked up to the front of the van, got in, started the engine and waited for O'Connor or one of the others to signal him to moved the van.

"Back up real slow," said O'Connor.

"Stand where I can see you," said Meyers.

O'Connor moved up the dock to the right side of the van and was standing perpendicular to Meyers. Using his hand as a signaling device, he directed Meyers to move the van to within a few inches of the barrier.

"Good, hold it."

Meyers applied the brakes, set the emergency brake and cut off the engine. He climbed out and stood next to O'Connor.

"Well Thomas, can I ask what's going to happen after you deliver McCaul to his family in Wales."

"I really don't know. Let's hope things improve, let's pray for no more killing."

"If that happens, will you stay?"

O'Connor looked at Meyers for a long moment, shook his head and said,

"I don't know Jamie. My desire for retribution faded over the years and Ron lost his enthusiasm for the cause. Neither of us had any desire to return, but the organization said they needed us."

O'Connor looked at the two men standing behind the van, waiting for him. He turned back to face Meyers and said,

"With Ron gone, I'll take him home and I really don't know what I will do, a lot depends on what happens with the peace treaty."

Meyers wanted to ask him more question, but O'Connor said,

"Sorry Jamie, I have to go. Will you help us load the crate?"

Meyers nodded, turned and walked to the end of the dock, carefully stepping over the barrier. O'Connor followed him.

Very gently the men eased the wooden crate out of the van and the two men holding the front passed it to the two men on the boat. As the men on the boat backed up, Shamus and the other man stepped over the railing and took the crate from Meyers and O'Connor.

"Where are you putting it?" asked O'Connor.

"Behind the wheel house. We'll lash it down and cover it with canvas. The skipper said he didn't think it was wise to try and put it below," said a member of the boat crew.

"All right," said O'Connor.

For the next five minutes, the boat crew, with the help of Shamus and his companion, tied the wooden crate to the deck and covered it with a double layer of canvas. O'Connor and Meyers stood on the dock in silence. Meyers still wanted to ask questions, but he didn't really want to know all the answers, so both remained silent.

Shamus walked up to the railing and said,

"We're ready Thomas."

"OK", said O'Connor. He turned to Meyers and stuck out his hand. Meyers extended his and the two shook hands for the last time.

"Thank you Jamie, and thank the Chief Superintendent and Dr. Shaw for me."

"I will Thomas. Good luck."

"Thank you," said O'Connor as he turned and stepped over the railing of the boat, being aided by Shamus, who looked at Meyers and said,

"Thank you Irishman."

Meyers smiled and said,

"You're welcomed Shamus."

While O'Connor, Shamus and Meyers were saying their farewells, the two crewmen untied the lines holding the craft to the dock, pushed the boat away from the dock and jumped aboard the vessel.

Meyers backed away and took a seat on the barrier, watching the boat silently slip out into the main body of the lake. When it was a little over a hundred meters from shore, he saw the fantail go down and the bow of the boat go up as the throttle was pushed forward.

The wake from the craft left a white line in the dark water, a line which became thinner and thinner as the boat slowly reached the sea and disappeared from sight.

Meyers looked at his watch, pushed the button so the face would light up and saw that it was ten minutes after three, the latest he had been up in a long time.

For the next thirty minutes, the Irish police officer remained seated, looking out into the darkness of the lake. He could see the light from the lighthouse on Cranfield Point, but the wake of the boat was long gone.

He would have remained seated if the weather had remained the same, but the clouds decided to deposit some of the water they were holding, first as a light sprinkle. He knew the sprinkle would soon turn to heavy drops.

Meyers closed the rear doors of the van before the first heavy drop fell. He was inside the cab when the first gust of wind smeared the raindrops across the windshield.

He cranked the engine, turned on the lights and slipped the van into forward gear. As he came off the dock onto the road, he thought about O'Connor and Shamus and the others.

He was wondering if the retired patrol boat would make it to Wales and allow O'Connor to keep his promise and deliver his friend to his final resting place.

His thoughts jumped from O'Connor and McCaul to Davy and Neil and Oscar. He had forgotten to ask O'Connor about Oscar and the white van. He did have questions to which he wished he had the answers. Questions like: Who supplied O'Connor with all the information at the hospital; why did the white van stop at the rest area; who was Oscar and what about Carter, would he tell about the incident at the hospital?

Epilogue

In early 1999, it was learned that O'Connor and McCaul had been ordered home from Australia by the Army Council for the sole purpose of making certain none of he Nationalists splinter groups did anything to upset the peace process. The threat of retaliation by O'Connor and McCaul was nullified when McCaul died and O'Conner disappeared, resulting in a number of horrific incidents attributed to the splinter groups.

In a little over two weeks after O'Connor disappeared, one of the most horrifying incidents of the Troubles occurred in Omagh, County Tyrone, Northern Ireland. At approximately ten minutes after three on the afternoon of the 15th of August, 1998, a car bomb exploded in a busy street in Omagh, killing 29 men, women and children and injuring 220. It was described as "Northern Ireland's worst single terrorist atrocity" by the BBC.

The bomb was the work of the Real Irish Republican Army(RIRA), a splinter group of the Provisional Irish Republican Army(PIRA).